FINDING HOME

Kevin Mullin

Written Words Publishing LLC
14189 E Dickinson Drive, Unit F
Aurora, CO 80014
www.writtenwordspublishing.com

Published by Written Words Publishing LLC March 1, 2022

ISBN: 978-1-7356856-4-9 (paperback)
ISBN: 978-1-7356856-5-6 (eBook)

Library of Congress Control Number: 2022902791

Cover designed by Written Words Publishing LLC

Manufactured and printed in the United States of America

PROLOGUE

We all think we live ordinary lives, but every one of us is different and unique, with different families, friends, and experiences. We make choices that lead us to adventure or boredom, adversity or harmony, hate or love, or maybe emptiness or fulfillment. Each of us has a story to tell and if we're lucky, an audience who wants to hear it. My great-grandmother, Amy, thought she lived an ordinary life but as I got to know her, I discovered that she was a truly exceptional woman. She lived a life that, in today's world, would be considered heroic and extraordinary.

Throughout my school days, when I had to do written assignments on subjects such as what living person do I admire, my paper would always focus in on Gramma Amy. Interviews of people who lived through World War II or Vietnam, or monumental events like the assassination of Kennedy were all adventures with her. She was born in 1920, so not only did she live through most of the 20th century, she was able to capture her memories and bring them to life for me. I could almost see the worlds she remembered. Her love of life simply emanated from her recollections into my pen, earning me an 'A' on every paper.

By the time I entered my senior year, the English teachers in my school had all read my papers and sometimes shared them with the rest of the faculty. There were some teachers who I never met, that occasionally stopped me in the halls to encourage me to keep writing. The papers starring Amy Collins Webb, Super-Gramma, were all show-stoppers. My senior year creative writing teacher, Mr. Hill, suggested I expand a bit and write an entire biography about her.

"If done right, Jenny," he said, "You could capture how an earlier generation lived. It would be such a shame to let all those stories be forgotten."

"But Mr. Hill, there's so much I don't know."

"Most likely the boring stuff. Ninety percent of a human's life is spent being bored. We look at things to occupy our time, whether we watch television, read books or whatever. You can fill those missing gaps with educated guesses. Just enough to keep the story flowing."

"But it wouldn't be a true biography."

"No, it would be creative writing." He pointed to the header on the classroom door that reiterated: *Creative Writing.*

It made sense. I remembered her reminiscences. I had her old letters and diaries. She broke her leg when she was 90 and moved in with us and we spent a lot of time reading and rereading them and she would tease out old details.

"From that energetic young girl to this bedridden old woman," I heard her say once, "How did that happen so fast?"

But when I was with her, she had no time for melancholy. There was still life for her as long as someone else wanted to be with her. And that someone was me.

Her story had it all—the uprooted child, the fight for acceptance, her discovery of who she was, and her place in the world. As an adult, she was an army nurse during World War II and a Hollywood actress. She never let us call her a movie star. She called herself a 'with' or an extra who spoke. But she considered her highest calling to be a mother of five.

Mr. Hill reasoned that a well written volume about such a woman could generate real interest. It might also inspire people to try to make life better for themselves and others.

The following pages are my attempt to do just that. I will admit to taking some liberties with her remembrances. As she told her stories in the first person, I chose to write the book that way. I don't try to imitate the New York or Southern accents, since I think such attempts ultimately make the story more difficult to read and understand. Gramma Amy rephrased most of her conversations because in those days, a lot of people swore or called people derogatory names based on race or creed. What she did repeat by accident, I leave out by choice. Please remember that when we deal with people, we do not deal with perfection.

CHAPTER 1

MY FIRST FAMILY

In the early days, both my parents worked. It was unusual to have a working mother during the Roaring Twenties, but our situation required it. And although my mother may have preferred to be with her children, she never made that preference known to others. We needed the income, so it had to be done. She worked in a doctor's office and that's what kept us afloat the first few years of their marriage. She told me that she worked through her pregnancy with me and then my younger sister, Julia.

My father was as wonderful a man as you could ask for. Whenever he met someone, he introduced himself as, 'Michael Collins, but not *that* Michael Collins.' The adults always laughed or smiled. It took me a few years to understand that there was a famous Michael Collins in the Old Country, who fought for Ireland's independence.

He always had time, attention, and love for me. He treated us all fairly and equally, but I felt there was a special attachment to me. It made sense. After all, I was the oldest. He knew me longer than my siblings.

During this time, Papa had no troubles *getting* a job. It was *keeping* a job that proved to be the challenge with his fiery temper. He worked on the docks and was fired for fighting. He got a job in construction but hit his foreman for some reason and lost that job. He worked as a day laborer most of the time but rarely at the same place twice. And a man with his reputation was never any employer's first choice.

He would get an occasional call for a temporary position and leave us to shovel coal, trim hedges or anything he could do when opportunity knocked. Sadly, opportunity usually slunk quietly past our door more often than not.

Not long after Julia's birth, my father met some new people he called his "Italian friends." They found him occasional work in one of the speakeasys, which was a natural fit for him, even though he gave up drinking. More accurately, *especially* because he gave up drinking.

This was during the Prohibition era when alcohol was illegal. Nobody could make, drink or sell it. A speakeasy was a place where you could buy liquor even though it was against the law. If you spoke about it in public, you were expected to use a soft voice so no one else could hear. Thus, the term 'speakeasy.'

The speakeasy work was inconsistent, but he liked that sort of thing. Sometimes, he would drive a truck and make deliveries to various underworld establishments. Other times, he would stand around and look tough, which was easy for him. They needed him often because of his work ethic but seemed to forget about him a lot more because of his temper. He could be working from early morning to late at night every day one week and then be searching for a day laborer job the next. Usually with no success.

It was nice to have him home on those weeks. We always had time together, just the two of us. We called it our 'alone time' and I never witnessed any of his temperamental outbursts. Julia got the same amount of time, but he found me easier to talk to. I think that was because when he spoke to me, the conversation was about him. When he was with Julia, it was about her.

He spent hours with me and my sister, making us feel important and loved. We cuddled, played games and walked around; the things fathers and daughters do. He loved telling me his battle stories from The Great War. It was an exciting time in his life. He was quite the hero. He took out a machine gun nest towards the end of the war and saved the lives of four fellow soldiers. He also received the Bronze Star for bravery.

"You were so successful in the army," I said one day, "Why didn't you stay? I bet you could have been a General."

He laughed, but it was a forced, sad sound. "I had a difficult time figuring out who the enemy was," he finally replied. And that was as true a statement as was ever spoken.

"You see, the war was over, but we were still in France. Just sitting there drinking wine. I prefer beer but I can develop an appreciation for wine when it's the only thing available."

"I didn't know you ever drank. Isn't it illegal?"

"It was legal then and it was legal there. But I had this cocky little Major who decided the base was going to be dry from now on because where he came from was dry."

"Dry?"

"No booze allowed," he explained, "And he told me to pour out a freshly bought bottle of red wine with some Frenchy sounding name. It was France, after all, so the name would sound Frenchy."

He paused to sip his seltzer water.

"'No, sir,' I said to the Major all respectful and polite.

'You don't have that authority to turn a base dry or a man into a teetotaler.' 'That's insubordination,' he yelled. Then he called the MPs on me. So, what could I do? I obviously lost the wine now because of him, so I said, 'That's not insubordination. This is.'" He swooshed his fist through the air like he was hitting an invisible enemy.

"And I broke his nose."

He was dishonorably discharged from the army after that. Because he was such a hero, they didn't put him in jail, but that dishonorable discharge followed him. He blamed it for his inability to get a job, though my mother blamed his temper. He was sent to Fort Anderson, near Faucette, Louisiana, where he was formally discharged in the summer of 1918.

In Faucette, he met Mary, my mother, and fell hopelessly in love with her. Sadly, the Major he hit was married to my grandfather's sister. If that wasn't bad enough, my grandfather was also an army Major. How embarrassing. It certainly didn't endear him to my mother's family.

From what little I was told, Papa found out about the family connection *after* he met, fell in love with, and started calling on my mother. Of course, everyone in her family disapproved of him. He was bellicose and belligerent. He was highly impressed with his own limited intellect and opinionated with the wrong opinions. The family viewed him as an aggressively stupid Irishman with no prospects.

"It's one thing to be stupid," my grandmother told my mother, "But it's not good enough for him to just be stupid. He has to be aggressive about it and make sure everybody around him knows he's stupid."

And that was quite a bit kinder than anything my grandfather had to say about him. Of course, being of genteel southern society, they were polite and kept their opinions to themselves when he called to visit my mother. Whether that politeness was born out of noble upbringing or self-preservation was a point my Mama and Papa discussed upon occasion with no agreement ever forthcoming.

My Papa tried to make amends. He did little chores around their house without being asked. He helped at her grandmother's restaurant but wasn't allowed anywhere near the kitchen. Gramma Morris, the matriarch of the business, told him anyone who dated her granddaughter couldn't know anything about food and therefore was not welcome in her kitchen. He socialized and tried to make friends around the town to no avail. He even quit drinking to make my mother happy.

Regardless, my grandparents saw no benefit and much disgrace for their daughter if they allowed her to fall any further under the spell of his charisma. For her own good, my mother was forbidden from seeing him. So, the lovers did what all young people do in the face of such intolerance: they eloped.

They moved back to New York in the early spring of 1919. The only one in the family who kept in touch with them was her sister, Cassie, who would become my second mother. In fact, Aunt Cassie was there to help after I was born in January 1920. She did not come to help when Julia was born in December 1920. Those two sisters loved each other very much, but they loved each other more with 1,300 miles between them.

Papa made Aunt Cassie uncomfortable, I learned later. I never saw it, but Papa was an intense and angry man. That was a mystery to me because, in my eyes, he was such a blessed young man. He had a pretty, young wife, a nice family, and a good job. And at six foot three, he was very good looking with reddish brown hair, laughing blue eyes, and he had the gift of Irish blarney. He was such a smooth talker, all the charm in the world, he had. He would have gone far if only he could have controlled his temper.

Everybody loved him when they met him, but as they got to know him, not so much. Most people agreed with his in-laws regarding his aggressive stupidity and narrow opinions. He yelled and screamed at and pushed and shoved anybody who dared disagree with him. Towering over most other men, he was strong and knew how to win a fight. When he couldn't win an argument with thoughts and ideas, which was often, he won with his fists. He embarrassed my mother a great many times, but he didn't care because winning a fight proved he was right. And being right meant a lot to him.

Even so, he was wonderful to me. I never saw his rage. I saw a father who loved and provided for me, and who more than protected me. He taught me how to protect myself. As I was a bit smallish as a child (and as an adult), he was afraid that when I went to school, I'd run into bullies. So, he taught me how to fight when I needed to. He showed me how to make a proper fist and he'd hold out his palms for me to hit.

"If it comes to punching some boy, don't pull back. Follow through. End it as fast as you can. Always aim for the nose. Nothing ends a fight faster than a broken nose."

Actually, walking away might work better, but he never thought about that.

By late 1921, Mrs. Carnahan moved in upstairs from us. She was a retired governess who worked for Teddy Roosevelt's cousin. She'd been pensioned off and, to my great benefit, she wound up being our neighbor. Mrs.

Carnahan, having nothing to do with herself, volunteered to take me to her apartment while my mother dealt with Baby Julia. She said it would be good for her soul. This led to my special relationship with her.

She was so good with children, especially me. It was nice to have my own adult, no sharing her with my sister. I wished she was my real mother. I sometimes thought my mother wished Mrs. Carnahan was my real mother too.

She made learning fun by singing alphabet songs to me and playing little math games. Her favorite was a story about a sparrow that sneezed so hard, he blew off all his feathers. Now he was unhappy because he couldn't fly. A wise old owl flew down and told him he needed to gather up 1,000 feathers and attach them back. His friend crow found three and his other friend rabbit found four. I had to figure out he now had seven. Every day another friend came in with some feathers, and I was adding numbers together until I became quite good at it.

If I had problems, she used pencils. Two pencils on the table. Two more equals four. That three-dimensional way of learning until I was used to adding, subtracting, multiplying, and dividing, all of which I learned before starting school.

She taught me how to multiply in my head. Double digits and triple digits. Easy if you know how. First multiply by tens then ones. I was soon able to do it all the time, like it was second nature.

And I was reading before I started school. I could read *The Wizard of Oz, Anne of Green Gables* and other books for youngsters. My mother and Mrs. Carnahan both thought I'd be the head of the class as soon as I was in school. Mrs. Carnahan was quite proud of me, while my mother was more neutral.

My mother was always a bit indifferent to me. Almost always critical. She favored Julia. I always thought that was because she was younger, much prettier and needed more attention, but it was more than that. I learned that with any disagreements with Julia, I was always at fault and she could do no wrong. She took advantage of that until I started school and she began to miss me. Once she realized that she loved me and I was important to her, we were more than sisters. We were friends. She even defended me when my mother was overly harsh about some small little crime I may or may not have committed.

By 1923, my little brother, Patrick, was born. His crib was a dresser drawer for the first few weeks, until he was too big for it and my old crib was repaired and set up for him. When he was walking, he was by my side every minute of the day, unless I was at school or Mrs. Carnahan's apartment. So, even with a father who was gone a lot of the time and a mother who always seemed overwhelmed by keeping house, we were a close and happy little family. My early childhood may not have been perfect, but I was thankful. I had a wonderful neighbor, a sister and brother I loved, and a father who treated me like gold.

Most of my school days are long forgotten, but the first incident I can remember clearly was from second grade. We had a field trip to the art museum. They were having a retrospective of the pre-war modern art of Europe. We were honored to view some of the works of the great modern artists of the day—Picasso, Braque, Matisse, and Cezanne.

Most of the exhibit was Cubist art. Squares and rectangles, circles and triangles slapped together to almost seem like something. A host of art greeted us, but as children used to picture book illustrations, our appreciation of the great works in front of us was limited.

"What is that supposed to be?" Timmy Harper, one of my more aggressive classmates, asked while observing a colorful work. A long rectangle that appeared to be supported by two cylinders with triangular bases with rectangle posts shooting straight up and ovals leaking sting-like lines to the original rectangle.

"It's a painting of a bridge," our tour guide, a young art student with unruly orange hair and crooked teeth replied.

"Did the artist ever see a bridge?"

The next painting fared no better.

"That doesn't really look like anything," a girl said. It was a huge canvass with three humanoid figures with flat arms and grotesque faces with painful expressions and anguished eyes.

"It's a portrait of three young women," came the answer, "We have the camera now. The great men here decided it was no longer important to paint what they *see*. They painted what they *feel*."

"If they felt like that, shouldn't they have gone to a doctor?" I asked.

The tour guide closed his eyes for a couple of seconds, then looked at my teacher, who had her face buried in her hand while glancing at the floor. I thought it was a practical question and I had the support of my classmates. It received no answer.

I was content to be silent during class discussions after that. My grades in school were stellar, due to Mrs. Carnahan's tutoring. The other students all liked me, possibly because although I almost always knew the answers, I only raised my hand when no one else did. After all, nobody likes a know-it-all, especially children. Mrs. Carnahan made sure I knew that and I took it to heart.

But if anyone asked me for help, I would always work with them to understand the lessons. A couple of the boys wanted me to *do* their work for them, but I said 'no' and had nothing more to do with them. Timmy pushed me against the wall one day because I wouldn't do his math homework. My father's lessons were not in vain, and although I didn't break his nose, he certainly had a fat lip.

I got a punishment at school, and later at home by my mother. Timmy's mother so very kindly spoke to my mother about it without including those boring details about me refusing to do his homework and him pushing me first. Some women have an overabundance of maternal instinct and an underabundance of impartiality.

My father told me I did just fine. I could hit hard; therefore, there were better victims for Timmy to find. My mother harrumphed about it, even though she did admit that she was annoyed with the demand for free homework and the push against the wall. She was especially irritated that these minor little details were omitted by Mrs. Harper.

"It's different here than where your mother comes from," my father explained to me. "There, people have manners and class. In New York, we have assertiveness and passion. Here, manners and class get you nowhere. You have to be aggressive to succeed. Some guys do whatever it takes to get to the top. They will use and abuse you if you let them. You have to nip it in the bud or it becomes a real problem."

"Girls shouldn't fight," my exasperated mother exclaimed. "What will people think of us? And what about Julia?"

"What about her?" My father was confused, "She's got a real fine left hook."

"I don't care about her left hook."

"I do. Her right cross is kind of weak and she leaves herself wide open."

My mother sighed in frustration. "What will the neighbors think?"

"They'll think, 'Wow, those girls can punch. We better play nice.' What do you want them to think?"

"I don't want them to think our children are going around hitting people all the time."

All the time? It was once. And it was self-defense.

"If either of them *start* the fight, I'll make them regret it," he said simply, the implicit threat striking fear into both of us. "But it was a life lesson for the lad. We have to teach children life lessons all the time, that's our job. We use words with our children and they work. Some people's kids need something a bit more…memorable."

And his words worked with me and Julia. Patrick would need a bit more physical encouragement to behave, but that was natural with boys, my father said. With me, he just handed over advice and lessons to help me through life. Sometimes *very* loudly.

My mother's life lessons were more into the whacking part of parenthood. When I said or did something not to her liking, she used to whap me on the top of my head with a serving spoon. Julia never got the spoon treatment because she would start crying at the sound of a harsh word. When she misbehaved, she was consoled, hugged and comforted.

But such soft treatment was not for people outside of the family. My father occasionally stopped at the cafes and was quick to argue and never hesitated to get in a fight, which he always won, as far as I know. Sometimes he came home with injuries, usually bleeding knuckles or a blackened eye. His opponents were usually carried home.

He was not a man to take lightly.

So much of my life changed in 1927. Prohibition was in full force for over seven years by then and the people rejected it completely. The citizens wanted their alcohol and weren't going to stop drinking. The bootleggers couldn't furnish enough booze. The police couldn't destroy it fast enough. The gangs and mobsters fought over territory and couldn't meet demand. Men were gunned down in the streets as the bosses fought for control. And there was lots of money for everyone in the supply chain.

Papa was soon to be in that supply chain.

CHAPTER 2

A NEW JOB

My father's big break came one day right after he was paid for cleaning fish for a restaurant supplier. It was one of his less desirable jobs. No matter how much he washed, the smell of fish followed him. But the man gave him a fair day's wage for his efforts and told him he could come back the next day. Papa smiled a thanks, pocketed the cash and made his way home.

He always walked home to save the subway fare. His path traveled through a corner of Little Italy, where some of his Italian friends lived. He was familiar and comfortable with the area. After he walked a few blocks, he felt a pull on his jacket. When he looked down, a little Italian boy started running away from him. Papa quickly realized the boy had his wallet and chased him down. He caught up to him in an alleyway between two sooty brownstones where the boy was shielded by two young toughs carrying lead pipes.

The older boy was obviously well used by the streets with several nasty scars running down his face. To his right, the younger one couldn't have been older than sixteen, with a determined, fearful expression on his face which told my father he was desperate and capable of anything.

My father gave them a disarming smile. "Now boys," he soothed with his lilting, almost singing voice, "Just to let you know, I'm a war veteran, and you can give me what's mine and we can forget this ever happened."

The younger boy said something in Italian. Whatever it was, his voice was more than a little disrespectful. My father's smile was replaced by a warning scowl. It was his signal that he was ready for a fight, though those two didn't know that. They also didn't know my father was not the man they wanted to fight with.

"You go home, Mick," the older one said in bad English. "This is America. Finders keepers, losers weepers."

'Mick' was a name people used to call the Irish in those days and it was not meant to be a particularly friendly or respectful term. Most Irishmen had last names that started with 'Mc.' It was the Gaelic way if saying 'son of.' If Papa's name was McCollins, that would mean 'son of Collins.'

"Really?" my father's voice switched into warning mode. "You know what I just found? Two lead pipes, two broken punks, my wallet, and a pickpocket stuffed headfirst in a garbage can."

"Tough talk, Mick."

My father feinted to the left, towards the younger one who lunged forward, swinging the pipe like a baseball bat. Papa wheeled out of its path and grabbed his arm, twisting it behind his back so high his shoulder dislocated. He screamed in pain while his friend swung his club at my father, who pulled back, holding the young thug as a shield. The pipe smashed into the victim's other arm, breaking it near the shoulder. He was crying in pain and completely out of the fight, unable to do anything with his ruined limbs.

My father quickly dropped his prey and grabbed the other punk's wrist, twisting it until he dropped his weapon. Then he smashed his fist against the bone side of his elbow, enjoying the crunching sound of the bone and cartilage. The punk just howled in pain and defeat. Papa grabbed him by his collar and threw him up against the dirty brick wall headfirst to shut him up. He stared at the little pickpocket next, who threw his wallet at him and started to run but stopped when he looked behind my father.

My father heard a click behind him and saw two big Italian men strolling towards him. One had a .38 pointing at him while the other had his hands in his pocket as he surveyed the scene. The latter one seemed to be in charge. He had smooth swarthy skin with even features and twinkling eyes. The other had an acne scarred face that appeared to be the aftermath of a cannon battle. His brown eyes slightly drooped and his eyebrows had grown together but he took everything in at first glance.

"I can't believe I'm seeing this," the first man said to Droopy Eyes. "Can you?"

"I'm just stunned, boss."

Boss yelled something in Italian and the two conscious thieves stepped forward, while Droopy Eyes kicked at the third. He whimpered at first but stopped when he saw who he was looking at and simply stood up. The child stood just a bit behind the two beaten thugs who were in no shape to do anything else but obey. Boss yelled out some more Italian, and then they all walked by them, heads hung in shame or fear, while nursing their wounded arms.

Boss told my father, "Pick up your wallet. Make sure it's all there. Then I want to talk some business with you."

Boss nodded to Droopy Eyes who holstered his revolver. They walked a bit further into Little Italy. My father told me afterwards that the smell of pasta, sauteed garlic and roasting tomato made him hungry at the first whiff. And the smells seemed to change a bit with every footstep.

"You're Irish, right?" Boss continued, "I bet you come in here and it's all the same to you. But Italians are all different. Just take a sniff. Someone from Naples is cooking. Smell the tomatoes and beans? A few steps down and you'll have sausages and artichokes, lots of zucchini. Sicily. A bit further, there'll be rice and cheeses with shellfish. Rome. All different. All good. All better than boiled potatoes."

Papa gave the man a withering eye. "We Irish eat more than potatoes."

"Cabbage ain't no better," Droopy Eyes said, laughing at his own lame joke.

Boss threw him a withering look and continued, "Do you now? With no regular job? Just a day laborer and taking whatever comes along? You don't got no steady dough coming in, do you? I can tell. You dress like a worker. Clothes don't matter to you or other things matter more, right? You got a family to provide for, right? Wedding ring gives that away. I bet your wife works, right?

"So, you do whatever comes along. Grunt work. Honest day's pay for honest day's work, right? Just a guy taking care of himself. But you can be more than that. You got brains, guts. Granted, taking on a couple of punks like that may not be that great, but you dispatched them so quickly, it impressed me. We can use a man like you, right Jimmy?"

"That's right, Boss."

Now that wasn't an idle question. Jimmy was agreeable because he was seeking approval. The boss was young but obviously an important man. Jimmy was younger and just wanted to be important. A goal he would never reach.

My father was impressed with the boss. His grammar was atrocious, but the diction he used was sound and his vocabulary implied more education than his speaking indicated. Boss also had a holster bulging under his jacket, which automatically commanded respect.

"Well now," Papa replied, "I'm glad to be meeting your approval, friend. But I must say, I think you could have said all this back there. We must be walking down here for some other reason. And I'm hoping it to be beneficial to a poor man like me."

"Very perceptive of you Mister…"

"Michael Collins, but not *that* Michael Collins." My father offered a hand which swallowed the boss's as they shook, but the boss's grip was every bit as firm as Papa's. It was obvious he didn't understand the reference. My father didn't bother to explain.

"Frank Costello and a friend of mine, Jimmy Yalata."

"Costello, is it? Good solid Irish name, but ya know, you surely don't look Irish to me my friend."

Costello pointed to his chest with a sly smile. "I am in here and that's all that matters."

"It truly is, indeed," my father agreed.

"We took one look at you handling those…*amateurs*," Costello spit the word out, "and I said, 'You know, Jimmy, that guy handled those two punks in seconds, and didn't even break a sweat. Mr. Dwyer could use a man like that.' Isn't that right, Jimmy?"

"That's right, Frank.".

"You've heard of Big Mike Dwyer, haven't you?"

"Well, now that we're talking about him, I wish that I did," my father replied.

They looked at each other, caught off guard by this. Jimmy smiled and stopped in front of an old brownstone building. There was a bakery on the first floor and apartments above. Drying clothes were hung on one of many lines that crossed the street. Children screamed in Italian while playing in front of the tenement building.

"Mr. Dwyer just happens to need a man like you. And you just happen to need him more. You're a guy who knows how to use his fists when needed. Mr. Dwyer knows how to give good pay for good work. It's a regular job with regular pay. Interested?" Costello asked.

"Indeed I am."

"My kind of guy. Let's go meet Big Mike."

They walked through the bakery and around the counter to the back. Jimmy knocked on a door that led to the basement.

A peep-door opened and a gruff voice responded, "Yeah?"

"A.R. sent us," Jimmy whispered.

The peep-door closed and they heard a bolt slide back. The door opened to a small landing where the guard was stationed. He was another big man, fortyish and balding. At first, he eyed my father suspiciously but then smiled when he saw Jimmy and Frank.

"Well, hi, guys," he said with a smile showing off yellowing teeth. "How's things?"

"Good, Tommy. Real good," Jimmy replied. "Big Mike around?"

"In his office."

"Big Mike runs this club," Jimmy said. "It's for members and friends of members only. It's got stuff that people want, you know, the stuff that used to be legal that ain't anymore. Things that make a party a real party. Get it now?"

"I believe I do, sir," my father replied. "When a man has a thirst for a good time, he goes to Big Mike's club. A secret club it is, so not just anybody can get in to cause trouble."

"And that's where you come in," Frank said. "Big Mike needs a peacekeeper. Someone who can throw people out *gently*. You know, so they still want to come back the next night. We don't want any fights or people getting stupid on us. They get loud and stupid; you throw them out. They don't want to pay the tab; you *encourage* them to pay up."

"It's a bouncer you want."

"Big Mike don't like that term. He prefers customer liaison."

"It's a customer liaison you want." Papa shrugged. It was all the same to him.

"Yeah, you know, nothing physical unless they deserve it. *We* decide if they deserve it. But if we say so, give it to them and let them know if they come back, they'll be sleeping with the fishes," Frank explained.

"Let's meet Big Mike," Jimmy concluded, obviously growing bored.

The meeting went well and our circumstances changed immediately. My mother stopping working and spent time with us, or more accurately with Julia and Patrick. We moved to a bigger apartment, coincidentally, right next door to Mrs. Carnahan so I still spent most of my time with her.

She considered me her own daughter. She started teaching me to play the violin now that we were so much closer. She had all the patience in the world and had me doing scales and playing simple songs. She even let me take it home and play for the rest of the family. My father loved my playing.

Most mornings, we would have oatmeal cooked in last night's dinner pot of boiled cabbage. We always had boiled cabbage with dinner, and the morning oatmeal always tasted like cabbage. I hated cabbage. So did everyone else. But it was cheap and easy to cook.

After we gagged down the putrid breakfasts, I would play the violin for Papa and then we would go to the neighborhood diner for coffee. This was on the sly because my mother's rule was no coffee for anyone in the house under 13. And since Papa preferred the diner's coffee to my mother's, we had our together time—just the two of us. He drank his black so he could enjoy the bitterness, while I poured as much sugar and milk in mine as the cup would hold. And he enjoyed my company and the coffee. As I recall, he never had a bad word to say about my mother, but never said a good word about her coffee.

Mrs. Carnahan gave me that violin at my seventh birthday party. It was a monumental gift for such a little girl. My mother was speechless. I don't think she enjoyed my squeaky beginning, but my father was proud as punch. I always had to play a song for him at least once a day when he was home. That meant a lot of practice. And I loved practicing because Mrs. Carnahan always praised everything I did. I even showed Julia how to use the bow and she was asking for lessons.

Oh, and Frank Costello and Jimmy Yalata were also at my party, along with some classmates of mine and Mr. Costello's business partner, a small man with a big smile named Meyer Lansky. Many negative things were said of these men, probably all true. I can only say they were kind to me. Mr. Lansky brought a cake and Jimmy gave me some hair ribbons, which I profusely thanked him for, even though I already had hundreds.

The cake was particularly appreciated, since the last two times Mama baked cakes, they were not well received. The first was black like charcoal. The second looked nice on the outside but was raw batter on the inside.

Frank got me a small stuffed bear, who I immediately named Little Frankie, and it was the perfect size for a seven-year-old girl. They were such good friends to my father and they treated all of us like family.

It didn't take us long to figure out that Jimmy was never going to be much more than what he was now—a little man in a big city. Frank and the diminutive Meyer Lansky ran the show and they were wildly successful. They operated several gaming tables in or around the speakeasys. Gambling was not entirely legal in those days, but my father figured that so long as nobody was being dragged into the club and forced to drink and play the tables, the law be damned.

"Hey, Little Amy," he said to me one day while Julia and Patrick were in the other room playing marbles. "I was thinking it might be time for me to be teaching you how to play poker."

"What?" Mama almost screamed, "Are you crazy? Poker?"

He ignored her. "Your mother thinks games like poker are a CARD-inal sin, so to speak," his eyes twinkling, "But I think you should learn the basics. Now, what do you do if a big red bird lands on the table and tried to steal the cards?"

"I'd poke her?" I already had a feel for my father's sense of humor and enjoyed our bantering.

"Ha, ha," Mama said. "I'm serious, and bad jokes won't get you anywhere."

"That was a great joke," he replied, taking fake offense, then he looked at me. "You and me love to play on words, but your poor mother finds them to be an absolute punishment, so to speak."

She went to the other room to see how the marble game was going while Papa showed me the basics of five card draw.

As the money flowed in, Mr. Dwyer invested in legitimate businesses and slowly left the unsavory world of prohibition behind. Frank Costello bought out his booze and speakeasy businesses. He was now a big man in New York City. Maybe not the big boss, but someone you'd want to be on side, or at least not against you.

Not long after that birthday party, Mr. Costello gave my father a different job that paid even more. He drove a truck from New York to Buffalo with Jimmy. Papa told me that they transported whiskey from the Canadian border to the city.

"It may be illegal," he said to me, "But in my mind, it's the Volstead Act that's really illegal."

The Volstead act was the law that made alcohol illegal.

"Michael, I don't think this conversation is appropriate for her. What if she says something?" Mama asked.

"I won't," I promised.

"She won't," Papa agreed. "What happens at home never leaves the home or the guilty ones leaves the home. Never to come back."

"Still…"

"Don't you go worrying about her. She needs to know. Something might happen. I don't want her to be surprised. It's gainful employment and life will be better for us all."

Then his eyes lit up, "Besides, it's the grains I'll be transporting, not the grapes."

"What difference does that make?"

"I should think you wouldn't *whine* about it."

She laughed in spite of herself and the subject was dropped.

We saw a lot less of my father after that, but our lifestyle changed even more for the better. There was always money left over at the end of the month and my mother treated us to ice cream quite a bit that summer. By the end of August, my parents were talking about leaving Manhattan and buying a house in Buffalo. It made good sense since my mother grew up on a farm and lived in a house her whole life until she moved to New York City. She never liked apartment life, especially after we kids came along.

"The walls shrink with each little child," she told me. "You'll understand, some day."

My father would have preferred to stay in the city but figured he would be happier if his wife was happier. Since his job was driving from Buffalo to Manhattan, he could just as easily make his home on the lake. Why go to a park when the park could be your own backyard?

It was decided. My father had no runs to make on the week of Thanksgiving, and when he went to Buffalo again, he would look at neighborhoods and see what Mama would like. Julia and I were a bit apprehensive about leaving home and I cried at the thought of leaving Mrs. Carnahan behind, but she assured me that she would only be a train trip away, and my mother agreed a week every summer would be manageable.

The Monday after Thanksgiving started out so happy. Before my father left, I played him *Danny Boy* on my violin without a single mistake, and when I was done, he pulled me close and said, "If only we could move to Ireland, you would be the star of the whole island. Everyone from every county would come hear you play and forget everything bad. The whole country would be unified, if only they could hear you play."

"They'd love you in Faucette, too," my mother added, which made it a really special moment for me, since she rarely complimented me. I was beaming with happiness.

It was spelled Faucette but pronounced *fo-shay*.

"That because it's French, sweetheart," Mama would say. "It's a very romantic language."

"Hmm, it's really because the French can't speak or spell," my Papa clarified.

Mama poked him in the ribs with her elbow, not entirely playfully. "Just because you couldn't make friends there."

"I had some. It's just that there's not many there worth being friends with."

"You just didn't give them a chance."

"I gave my southern belle a chance and a ring, right? And how far did we have to run to get away from your family?"

Poke. Poke. Poke.

Faucette was a small town compared to New York, but was big enough to support a theater, which doubled as a cinema. There was a library and a dancehall that was once a tavern. Its main employers were a timber company and a sawmill, both owned by the same family. Various other businesses grew around them to provide multiple goods and services.

Mama's grandmother and her sister, Cassie, owned a restaurant there where Mama was once a waitress. Apparently, she showed so little aptitude for cooking that she was banned from the kitchen at an early age. This lack of capability followed her into her adult years as well. She never showed any proclivity for stove-work that I can remember. Since her grandmother owned a restaurant, the implication was that she was a serious disappointment. Compliments from her mother were rare and criticism plentiful. I understood that quite well.

She did well enough as a waitress, though her stories and remembrances seemed to focus more on flirty encounters with the local boys than serving tables. She rarely mentioned her home or family to me with any tenderness.

I had heard stories of her family and wanted to meet them but, times being what they were in those days, such an extravagance would always be postponed. Travel was both time consuming and expensive. Besides, Papa had a low opinion of her parents and made it clear that he would not travel with us. But still, they lived on a farm with a pond and big aromatic pine trees surrounded the house. Live oaks covered in Spanish moss dotted the large meadow of their front yard.

Aunt Cassie was the second wife of Paul Villians. Both Mama and Papa met him, but they didn't speak about him very much except to say that his first wife was a southern belle named Francine Scott. They had four children before she died of the flu in 1919. So, I had a lot of step-cousins down there.

Mama spoke several times of sending me there for a summer, but nothing ever came of it. However, she loved her family in spite of their flaws and harsh ways and did want me to experience the quiet surroundings of the country. She seemed less enthusiastic about such an excursion for Julia.

New York City offered nothing that would encourage

folks with rural roots to thrive. Mama longed for a calm, peaceful kind of lifestyle again. Buffalo offered a similar (colder) lifestyle with acreage, trees, water, and fields for us to run around in with friends. Mama was overjoyed that Papa was searching for a home upstate. Whatever he found, she would transform into a wonderful and loving home for us all.

Best of all, Buffalo was on the lake. That meant sailing, canoeing, and fishing. Mama could execute some poor fish and behead it, de-tail, scale, gut, and filet it as good as any man. It was her job back home to take a living thing and turn it into something cookable. After that, her job was finished since God only knows how she would cook the poor things. The fish would peer down from heaven and think they died in vain after my mother rendered them inedible.

Her grandmother and the cook, on the other hand, could actually turn them into meals by frying, broiling, baking, or stewing the tasty little corpses. But they were in Louisiana. If ever I went down south, maybe I could learn to cook. As it was, all I had to do was look at what Mama did and do the opposite.

Anyway, Mama was going to be happy in Buffalo. We would bring back a stringer of fish every day and she would expertly transform them into wonderful, tasty fillets before turning them into smoking, crispy charcoal. She said it would be like Faucette only better, since it didn't have any snakes.

But we never stepped foot in Buffalo. Michael Collins drove off with Jimmy Yalata to make a run. They made it there without incident, but they didn't come back.

CHAPTER 3

A FUNERAL AND A WEDDING

The police found the bodies a couple of weeks later just south of Albany, right after Julia's seventh birthday, but before my eighth. They were murdered by other bootleggers who stole their precious cargo of Canadian whiskey. There was a lot of money to be made smuggling alcohol in those days, but it came at great risk. The so-called 'great' American gangster of the twenties inspired many Hollywood movies, but most bootleggers were men like my father who just drove a truck. There is no glamor in shipping illegal booze or perishing while defending it. My father and Jimmy Yalata didn't even make the front section of the paper.

Their demises were reported not quite on the back page with a 'crime doesn't pay' viewpoint. The snarky little article contained an excess of sanctimony and scarcity of empathy. It was obvious that the writer thought they got what they deserved. I didn't think that at all. Nor did I think our family deserved what happened next.

There was a gigantic funeral with a substantial amount of vehicles that drove from the funeral home to the cemetery on that clear but frigid January afternoon. At the time, I thought my father had lots of friends in the bootlegging business, but the funeral was really a statement to put the killers on alert.

My father's employers were not going to let this go. There was going to be revenge. Whatever happened after that was beyond my years. As far as I know, nobody ever found out who killed them. The police never cared enough to investigate the murders.

But we were devastated. Mama was devoted to her husband. We were all dependent on him. We all knew that whatever the future held for us, it would not be as good for us as it could have been. After he disappeared, my mother spent the week in her room crying while Mrs. Carnahan and I cared for and consoled Julia and Patrick. No one comforted me. Mrs. Carnahan was very tired by the end of the day.

Mama regained her composure after the bodies were found and attended the funeral without making a show of grieving. Greif was a personal and private thing to her. Sobbing, crying and fainting in public was to be avoided at all costs.

She had me stand with her at the reception line when the mourners paid their respects. I was now old enough to observe how this sad part of life needed to be handled— with dignity and grace.

The men kissed her hand as they passed and whispered how much they loved and respected her husband while handing her little envelopes filled with cash, anywhere between $50 and $500, to help us settle into our new lifestyle. Their wives hugged her by pressing their cheeks to hers and saying things like, "You poor dear" or "Let me know if I can help you." Some of them hugged me as well and I hugged back, but the whole thing was creepy and made me nervous.

Frank Costello, Meyer Lansky and Big Mike Dwyer were there, and a great many strangers I never saw before. The most memorable guest was a tall, almost impossibly thin, man named Giovanni Corelli. His smooth swarthy skin practically stretched over his skull, but he still had an easy smile that showcased perfect teeth. I noticed the smile was only on his mouth and never reached those cold, dark, calculating eyes.

Mama never discerned the evil behind those devious unblinking orbs or wondered what malicious schemes they gave away. She just noticed the pleasant face, no hair out of place (because he used more oil than a kerosene lamp), smooth complexion, and white teeth, all perfectly aligned when he smiled. Unlike most of Papa's Italian friends, he spoke quietly, with a smooth cadence and no accent, since he was born in Rhode Island.

Mama must have noticed his neck as well, although she never mentioned it. Julia and I spotted it immediately. It seemed like he grew an extra vertebrae, stretching his neck out so it was extra-long and graceful, almost like a swan. In fact, his Italian friends called him Gio the Giraffe. The problem was, a giraffe has a certain elegance and charm. Giovanni had no grace or charm, at least, not that I saw.

Sadly, my mother did see something in him. Maybe it was his appearance. He had the face of an angel. Maybe it was how he dressed. He wore a neat pinstriped suit and blue tie that resembled a successful businessman.

Neither Julia nor my mother ever saw the evil in his eyes. Cold demonic orbs that spoke of unspeakable cruelty. I could see the reptilian soul that lurked behind his irises. And when he taunted me with those malevolent stares, I shivered. I knew he was a man who loved to hurt people for fun. It was a shame that only I could see it.

I hoped to never see him again after the funeral. I didn't like the way he leered at me with those eyes. He just stared, occasionally licking his lips. I hoped he was just one of many well-wishers who came to a burial service and went back to wherever he came from, never to be seen again. But he came back a couple of weeks after the funeral with flowers for my mother, a purple stuffed gorilla for Julia, and some wooden blocks for Patrick. Nothing for me. He pretended he must have dropped it on his way to our home, but he had already sized up my relationship with my mother and knew my opinion of him would neither help nor hurt his courtship. Therefore, I wasn't important.

"He's creepy," I pronounced to Julia the second time he visited.

"No, he's not and he's very nice. You don't like him because he ignores you and doesn't give you presents."

"I don't like the way he gawks at me."

I was too young then to know it was called a 'wolf-leer,' but I knew I didn't like being on the receiving end of one. More than one, in fact. And I knew Gio the Giraffe was a man to be avoided.

"It's just looks. It's not like he's giving you the evil eye or anything."

"It's not his eyes I worry about. It's the rest of him."

Sadly, by the end of 1928, he became a fixture in our apartment. He arrived a little after five p.m. each weeknight, usually with flowers or gifts, and stayed until after seven when he went home to be with his family. He lived in Brooklyn with a sister and his children from a previous marriage. Occasionally, he brought dinner, bought from some street vendor. I disliked him much less on those evenings since he did rescue us from Mama's cooking.

All we knew about him was that his wife died two years

earlier from Scarlett fever and left him with two daughters. They favored Julia so much they could be sisters. That meant they had heart shaped faces, brown eyes, sculpted cheekbones, and angular noses. Classic beauties. My hair was more chestnut and my eyes were hazel. In those days, I had a soft clear complexion marred by a host of freckles on my slightly turned-up nose. I was not ugly by any means but was easily overlooked when Julia was in the same room. But that didn't bother me. I got my fair share of attention from Mrs. Carnahan and my friends from school.

We met the Giraffe's daughters that Thanksgiving. Mother decided that since Papa's funeral was in January, she could have a 'gentleman caller' over for a holiday meal and celebration, especially with five young chaperons. They arrived at nine that morning—the Giraffe, the evil Isabella, and the oblivious Sofie. The Giraffe's sister had a previous engagement for that holiday, so we missed her. It started off bad and went downhill from there.

Even though Mama's family owned a restaurant in Faucette that made the finest food in all Louisiana (she said), her recipes were unimpressive. The turkey was stuffed with some foul-smelling bread that reeked of wine and tomato, with green olives, beets, and turnips. The bird itself was already turning black, although the juices were still red. The potatoes appeared to be overdone and she didn't salt them anyway. But the worst was okra.

Okra is a southern vegetable that turns into a nasty looking green slime, like what you see in stagnant ponds. It had a foul stench that attacked the nose with putrid fumes. And don't forget to include the fetid stink of her boiled cabbage 'specialty.' Even skunks would avoid our home at mealtime.

Our company was too polite to say it reeked like a

World War I battlefield after a mustard gas attack and talked about how 'amazing' the dinner smelled. It certainly did smell 'amazing.'

Since they did not run away after the first sniff, Mama had us line up in front of her when they came in and Giraffe inspected us. I was first.

He gently stroked my cheekbone with his thumb and whispered, "You are very pretty. When you're older, I can get you a job where I work."

"Where do you work?" I asked hesitantly.

He responded with an ominous grin, "You'll find out."

I glanced at Mama for help, but she didn't quite hear him. He moved on to Julia. He gave her a warm hug, then picked up Patrick and really squeezed him.

"I can only wish I could have a son as limitless as you," he said.

Limitless? To this day, I found that such an odd choice of words.

He stepped back and guided his oldest daughter to him, squeezing her close from behind, his hands covering what would become her lower breasts. I shivered in distaste. No one else seemed to think it was improper.

"Now, this is Isabella," he introduced. She was ten, slightly older and substantially taller than me and may have been the prettiest child I ever saw. Black hair, blue eyes, perfect features, and an elegantly long neck. Her only flaw was her soul. Whereas her father had cold and calculating eyes, her orbs were nothing less than cruel. Cold blue ice surrounded by pits of black pupil. No mercy would ever come from that one.

Oh, but she was charming. She curtsied gracefully when introduced and said, "So pleased to meet you all." She was speaking to us all but stared right at Mama. Those cat-like irises almost glowing with smugness.

My mother motioned for her to come to her and they hugged warmly. Isabella received more affection in that hug than I ever got from her. Julia and I looked at each other, confused. I felt like a henhouse chicken being introduced to my new guard, the fox.

Sophie was two years younger. She also had black hair and blue eyes, but hers were softer. If her soul was cruel, her eyes didn't betray it. She was still in the chubby, slightly awkward stage. When the Giraffe introduced her, she curtsied, but almost fell with the attempt. She was flustered but managed to squeak out a "hello" to us.

Afterwards, we children were sent to our room (yes, the three of us shared one bedroom, and Julia and I shared a bed) to play while the adults talked about grownup things. We had a copy of *Peggity*, which was quite popular in those days since we could play it indoors when it was cold. The players try to put pegs into a board so that they connected five in a row while the other players tried to stop them and connect their own. I got our copy out of the closet but before I could set it up, Isabella stopped me with a hateful eyeroll.

"We don't play baby games like that anymore," she announced.

I was surprised at the sheer rudeness she displayed, but I kept calm and met her carnivorous eyes. "Well, what would you like to do?" I asked politely, while sneering inside.

"Well, what else have you got? Do you have regular cards? We can play *Gin Rummy*."

I shrugged, "They're on the nightstand."

I pointed and started to go get them, but Isabella swooshed over to them and barreled right into me, almost making me lose balance.

"Hey," she shouted, "Why'd you push me like that? What's wrong with you?"

I was shocked. I glanced over at Julia, who was obviously just as surprised as I was at Isabella's outburst. Sophie was next to her, but she was amused and looking at the floor to keep from laughing. This behavior was new to us, but obviously routine for them.

"I didn't push you. You walked in front of me."

"Hey, stop that" Mama's voice commanded from the door, the Giraffe behind her, silent and unsmiling.

"Papa," Isabella cried out, "She just pushed me for no reason. Just attacked me. Can't we just go home?"

"I did not," I cried, "I was getting the rummy cards and she just ran in front of me and started throwing a fit."

"Amy," my mother's voice shot out like a bullet, "don't you dare lie to me."

"I'm not lying. She just…"

"Amy, you have a history of hitting and punching and I'm sorry your father encouraged it, but it stops now. If you can't play nice and behave, then you can't play at all. Now apologize."

I looked at Isabella's smug face and triumphal eyes and couldn't say anything to her, certainly not an apology.

"No," I said.

That refusal altered my life forever, but acceptance of Isabella's conniving trick would also have had had consequences, and who knows what they would have been. Although I didn't think of it at the time, my life changed drastically that day just by meeting Gio the Giraffe's evil family.

My mother made short work of me. She grabbed my ear and dragged me to the living room for a private 'talk.'

"If you can't do the right thing and apologize to your guest, then you'll have to go to a private spot and not play at all. Is that what you want? Now, go do the right thing."

'Private spot' was code word in our apartment. Since it was so small with only two bedrooms and we weren't allowed in our parents' room, there was no privacy anywhere. We went out and sat on the fire escape for our 'private spot.'

Luckily, it wasn't too cold that day, so I went to the coat rack and fumbled for my sweater, under the furious eye of my mother.

"If you go out there, you won't have dinner with us," she warned me with a growl and snarl.

Somehow, not eating a dinner that smelled like an open sewer did not seem to be too much of a punishment. I nodded. I was upset by being so mistreated but missing that dinner more than made up for the injustice.

My book was on the table by the lamp and she let me take it with me. I was reading *Rebecca of Sunnybrook Farm.* Armed with my literature, I climbed out the window and began my exile.

Not being around Mama for the holiday wasn't that bad. Since there was no wind outside, I was comfortable enough. My absence certainly didn't bother anyone. I could hear laughter and singing through the glass. It annoyed me that they could have such fun and I was out there. I got up and walked to the far side of the building so I wouldn't have to hear them.

Just as I was settled in to read, I heard Mrs. Carnahan call me. I looked up and found her waving me over. I climbed over the rails, jumped to her ledge and she gently pulled me into her apartment. Her holiday meal perfumed the air with the wonderful smell of turkey, rice and lentil soup. There was also a pumpkin pie on the counter, half eaten. I was suddenly hungry. After she hugged me, I explained why I was banished from our holiday meal.

"Dear, dear," she clucked, "such a thing to happen, and on Thanksgiving Day. Well, you'll just have to have dinner with me today."

"Really?" My eyes must have lit up.

She laughed and tousled my hair a bit. "Well, of course. But you know, it's just me. I wasn't expecting company. There's plenty for us both, but it's nothing fancy for a holiday."

Nothing fancy at Mrs. Carnahan's was much better than anything from home. We ate until we were totally stuffed, then we listened to the radio for a while. A starvation and isolation punishment isn't effective when the culprit eats a large meal with a loved one. After a couple of hours, we decided I better get back in view or things could get worse.

Mrs. Carnahan was such a wonderful person. I still remember her words of advice when I left.

"Now, remember dear, when a woman loses her husband, she loses the man she loves *and* the security he provides. With three children to provide for, your mother most likely feels she has no other options than to consider the first man to show interest. Most men won't take in another man's children. Finding one who will is somewhat rare. Whatever your mother decides, you should support her in every way possible. Remember, you're her daughter and her family."

"I will," I promised, unaware of just how wrong she was at the time.

So, I left her to go back home. I was lucky. Just as I got settled in on the landing and had my book in hand, the window opened up and Julia called me in.

"We're having a family meeting," she said excitedly.

I squirmed through the window and into the malodorous apartment. It was warm enough that I immediately took off my sweater and laid it neatly on the wing chair. My stomach turned a bit from the cabbage and burned turkey fumes. When I looked up, I was shocked to see the Giraffe and his two malevolent daughters were there at *our* family meeting. His arm gripped Mama's waist and his other hand was entwined in hers. She was gazing up at him with loving eyes while he glowered down into hers with an expression of triumph.

"Children, we have wonderful news for you," Mama said in a joyful, lilting voice.

My stomach churned. I already knew. That lovey-dovey pose said it all. My father was being replaced. Gio the ghastly Giraffe was going to be our stepfather. My mother seemed to absolutely adore him. He looked like a snake who found his way into a rabbit warren. And now we had his two foxlike daughters to deal with. Predators, all.

"Gio Corelli just asked me to marry him. We're all going to be a family together."

Support her in every way possible.

"We'll be moving to Brooklyn."

Not voluntarily.

"Your new father has a house with two extra bedrooms, so Julia, you and Amy will share a room and Patrick, you'll have your own room."

I liked the bedroom we had.

"And we'll all be so happy together."

But we'd be even happier apart.

The other children cheered, ran over to them and got into one of those awkward group hugs. My mother was all smiles. Even the Giraffe's grin reached his eyes. He glanced at me on the other side of the room and waved me over.

Support her in every way possible.

So, I slowly went over to the crowd and hugged Julia and Patrick. I wanted to say something positive and encouraging.

You're marrying a reptile.

But I didn't know how to say anything to Mama that would convey my true feelings of happiness for her.

You just ruined your life and took us down with you.

Mama squeezed my shoulder close and kissed the top of my head. Apparently, I was forgiven for refusing to apologize and missing dinner.

"I do so hope you two will be happy," I said, even though in my childish heart I knew better.

"We will be," she practically sang. "And I want all you girls to be best friends. You're sisters now."

Wonderful. I'll be sister to two Gorgons.

"And Amy, I want you to go ahead and have some Thanksgiving dinner before I put it in the ice box."

I glanced over at the table. The main platter had turkey shaped clumps of charcoal scattered on it. A lonely, untouched bowl of congealed green slime, and cold boiled cabbage sat next to it. The dressing was untouched. The unsalted potatoes were gone. Obviously, the best of a bad lot.

"Oh, no thank you, Mama," I said through a forced smile. "I'm too excited to eat anything."

Especially that.

"I told you she wouldn't touch that goop," I heard Isabella whisper to Sophia. Well, maybe we might have some common ground after all.

The next few weeks were a flurry of activity. The wedding was set for March 21, so it would be a spring affair.

Mama ordered a pastel green wedding dress made of chiffon with a white silk shawl and veil, all tailored specifically for her. Gio spared no expense on the gown. The gruesome twosome, as I nicknamed Sophia and Isabella, were picked as bridesmaids, along with two of their unmet cousins while Patrick was the ringbearer and Julia became the flower girl. I was an 'honored guest' and would sit in the front row for the ceremony.

The Giraffe's sister, Isadora, was more or less in charge of the wedding. For some reason, she reminded me of a ferret. I never actually saw a ferret but there were pictures of them in some of the readers at school. So, she was less fortunate than Gio in appearance. Whereas Gio was handsome and evil, she was ugly and evil.

The kindest way to describe her would be to say she had a hatchet face with dark eyes planted in a bloodshot yellow background. Her teeth were small with extra-large incisors that looked like fangs. She had her graying hair pulled sharply back from her face and knotted in a tight bun. Isadora was proof to me that the more time a woman took to perfectly arrange her hair bun, the less capable she was of smiling.

Gio may have been marrying my mother, but Isadora ran the show. And we soon found out she would be living with us after the ceremony. She was very different from her brother. She was only two years older than Gio, but those years looked like decades. He seemed so much younger than his forty years that I thought he was my mother's age, not twelve years older. Isadora was only forty-two but could easily be mistaken for well over sixty. Gio had an easy, if fake, smile. She had an easy and sincere frown. Gio never seemed to be angry. She was never content.

Both Isabella and Sophia gave her a wide berth and

always looked down when she spoke to them which no doubt was only when they were in trouble. I overheard Sophia tell Julia that Isadora believed in corporal punishment and really enjoyed allocating it to the guilty party.

"You two will be part of the family now," she told us brusquely on our first meeting while loudly tapping a ruler into her palm. "That means you behave properly. People judge us by our children. So, you must be clean, straight, and proper young ladies. Your appearances reflect on all of us. You may have some wild Irish blood in you, but you'll be quiet, dignified Italians when you become adults. You will not embarrass this family."

As she spoke, I glazed directly into her eyes for a moment. They were severe and melancholy. Sad and empty. She had a bleak soul.

"I will let it pass this time," she scowled. "But never look an adult in the eye ever again. It's disrespectful. Children always need to keep the eyes down."

I just knew it was a gesture of great restraint on her part to not hit me with the ruler. She may not have known how to be nice, but she definitely knew how to intimidate.

"Why can't Amy be in wedding?" Julia asked her one day while Isadora was examining potential tablecloths and napkins.

"Everyone and everything in its place. She has no place. Four bridesmaids, one flower girl. No other positions available."

"That's fine with me," I said, trying to let Julia know I liked being the honored guest. The less time I spent with Isadore, the better.

"She could have my spot," Julia offered.

"She's too old to be a flower girl."

"Yes, I'm too old. Honored guest is fine."

"She could play a violin piece before the ceremony."

"We have professional musicians playing. The groom is an important man who will not be having some distant relative play a serious instrument. Only grown men should be playing on formal occasions.

"This is an event that will have everyone watching us and judging who we are. A wedding ceremony is an important community event. It isn't for family."

I did not want to be a part of a wedding that wasn't meant for family. Maybe Isadora sensed that thought and decided I was too independent to have a highly visible role. Maybe there was another reason. She glanced at me with an expression I would see often. Not hostile or friendly. Possibly sympathetic. Maybe sad. She seemed melancholy, as if I reminded her of someone she loved long ago but lost. Someone she would always remember.

"She's sad because her two sons live in Sicily," Sophia explained one day when Isabella was getting fitted for her dress. "They live with her grandparents and they think she's their sister instead of their mother."

"Why is that?" I asked, totally confused.

She shrugged, unconcerned. She had no interest in Isadora at all. Just fear.

It was Isadora who picked out the color scheme, flowers, suits and dresses, candles, and every other thing a wedding had. I think she even told Gio what ring to give Mama as well, or so Sophia told me. Mama never confirmed or denied it.

Isadora also was in charge of the guest list. I remember there was a bit of a fight over the invitations as well. Mama wanted two dozen sent to her family and friends in Faucette.

"Why? We have enough guests who are local," Isadora pronounced. "There would not be any room for interlopers."

"Interlopers? Why is it that my family and friends are interlopers and your family isn't?

"Besides," Isadora continued, ignoring the question, "it would be a waste of paper to send them since so few of your poverty-stricken relatives can spend the money to come all the way to New York. Just send them a letter."

Isadora did not endear herself to my mother.

"I want my family there for my wedding," Mama appealed to the Giraffe. "Why can't anyone understand that?"

"I understand," Gio replied unctuously. "Family is important, of course. But you moved here to get away from them, no? They weren't here for your first wedding. They weren't invited then, why have them now? It's your big day. You don't want to ruin it with family drama and recriminations. Reconcile later. Besides, they would be out of place in Manhattan. And how would they dress? They just wouldn't look right at a sophisticated New York ceremony and most likely would all feel awkward. You see now, we're being kind by not inviting those people."

Mama nodded her head sadly.

The next few months were filled with chaos and stress. Things went well for a while, then little problems (or gigantic catastrophes, depending on who you asked) popped up. All the bridesmaids' dresses came out too dark and had to be redone. I handled the re-order as Isadora was always busy with some other catastrophe.

Julia's pastel gown was too long and she tripped over the hem tearing it. It had to be replaced. I went to a different tailor so as not to overwhelm the one that was redoing the other dresses. Patrick hated his little tuxedo and constantly had to be coaxed into wearing it and doing what he was supposed to do in rehearsals. I was in charge of the coaxing. For my troubles, I got to pick out my own formal dress to wear. Since I wasn't part of the wedding party, I didn't have to follow any specific color scheme, so I chose a nice gray dress with a scarlet hem and collar. It was a warm wool, but not too hot. And it wasn't itchy like chiffon. I was probably the only comfortable one in my family.

During this chaotic time, I also managed to avoid Isabella and Sophie quite successfully. I don't think either of them wanted to talk to me either, which made it easier. I occasionally wondered what life would be like when we all lived at the Gio's house in Brooklyn. We visited his family there a couple of times without incident.

The house was much bigger than our apartment, and it had a bathroom next to the kitchen. There were four bedrooms—one for the parents, Isabella and Sophie would continue to share the one they had, Isadora commandeered one, and the last one was for Patrick since Isadora didn't believe it was proper for girls to share a room with a boy.

"What will people think?"

Gio (who we now had to call Papa Gio), had half the back porch enclosed for Julia and me. During these visits, the gruesome twosome were always nice to Mama and Julia but hateful to me, although I think I might have been friends with Sophie if she wasn't always following Isabella's lead. As it was, I was lucky I was always too busy helping with the wedding to let them bother me.

The only real problem occurred two weeks before the wedding day. The best man, Antonio Dragucci, was shot on a subway platform in Brooklyn. He survived and still made his appearance, though he wore a brace on his leg and moved about very slowly. The whole ceremony moved in slow motion as everyone accommodated his handicap. Dragucci was the Giraffe's business associate and was higher up in the level of command. He was apparently quite respected, although 'feared' would be a more accurate term. He certainly wasn't best man because he was Gio's friend.

None of my father's old friends were invited. The guests were all the Giraffe's family and friends who all spoke Italian and were very old school. The men shouted to one another across the room, yelled back a punch line and the whole room howled with laughter. The women isolated themselves, spoke quietly to one another and occasionally giggled at something. Mama, Patrick, Julia, and I were virtually alone in a sea of bellowing men and whispering women.

In spite of all the minor problems, everything came together for a beautiful ceremony. During the reception, I was in charge of the visitor ledger. I basically gave the guests a pen and watched while they signed some innocuous 'best wishes' comment down and thanked them for coming.

I rather felt like a second-class family member. But considering who the other family members were, I was content. The less the Giraffe and his daughters saw me, the happier I was. The strangers who were fussing over Julia, Patrick and the gruesome twosome seemed revolting to me. I believe it was uncomfortable for them as well, judging by their expressions.

My anonymity was short lived. Isadora introduced me to Dragucci when he signed the book. He was a large man with cruel eyes and several scars on his cheeks. I recognized him because he toasted the couple and mentioned that Gio was robbing the cradle. I didn't understand why that was significant but there were a lot of whistles and catcalls. He then went on in Italian, so I have no idea what he said, although the whole room turned to glare at me once during his speech, which made me uncomfortable.

"So, you are little Amy," he said to me with a raspy voice and a crooked smile as he uncapped his fountain pen. "Giovanni says you will soon come work for me in my club."

News to me.

"Oh?" I said politely, thinking I would still be going to school.

"You will be quite a star attraction there. Won't she, Isadora?"

"A bit young, I would think. It would be unseemly to some people to…*employ* her at this age."

"We can wait a while."

"What kind a club do you have?" I asked hesitantly.

"A…gentlemen's club. You would smile and dance and look pretty for the…gentlemen when they ask for you. You'll be a rich young lady in no time. You'll be so popular. And you can come live there with the other young ladies."

As he spoke, he rubbed a reptilian finger down my jawbone. I shuddered involuntarily at his highly unwanted touch.

"Oh," I said, feeling a little afraid being around this man. "I don't think I'd be very good at that, and I like living at home."

"Wait and see," he concluded, capping his pen.

They walked away to mingle with the other guests, but he did add, "Sometimes, as you grow up, it's the best option."

"Sometimes it's the *only* option," Isadora whispered intently to me.

What a loathsome man. What a repugnant woman.

The wedding and reception both went very well and Mama and Papa Gio were extremely happy. She slipped into our room early the next morning and woke me to say thank-you for all my help.

"You're welcome," I said through sleepy yawns. "I'm happy it went the right way for you."

"Well, it did, and in no small way because of your help. I know things haven't been going well for you through the courtship, but I promise you I want the best for you. No matter what is said or done. I will always be there for you."

"Thank you." My mind was on alert. Something was going on, and it didn't sound good.

"And Amy, I know you felt a little left out."

A little?

"But I'll make sure Gio and Isadora understand you're a part of the family, no matter what."

"Isadora and that man, Gio's boss, say they're going to put me to work in their gentlemen's club and make me live there. I don't want to do that. I want to stay in school. Mr. Dragucci seems to be an awful man and he and Aunt Isadora (*we were instructed to call her 'Aunt' now*) say it's decided. It's the only option."

"You won't be working in that club. There's booze there and God knows what goes on. Remember, there is never an 'only' option."

CHAPTER 4

THE NEW FAMILY

Over the following months, I witnessed Mama being browbeaten and verbally abused by both her husband and sister-in-law. Because Julia and I were both born in the same year, Isadora kept asking Mama if she liked hearing people call her 'Fertile Myrtle.'

Something had to be done. It was embarrassing. And the Giraffe always sided with Isadora. Mama may have been the wife, but Isadora was the mistress of the house. It was a position she refused to relinquish. And she would never tolerate any rival (such as my mother) to challenge that claim.

In fact, Mama was more or less fired from the kitchen. *Which wasn't a bad thing.* She made breakfast for us and shopped for dinner supplies, but Isadora did all the other cooking, which was somewhat better. Before, our meals were usually boiled-to-mush ham, potatoes and cabbage with no spices. As a 'treat,' Mama made 'gravy' to go with these dinners. She would ladle out some of the water she boiled dinner with and mix it with flour and salt, although mixing wasn't her strongest point and occasional clumps of flour would find its way into our mouths. I became adept at relaxing the muscles in my throat and simply swallowing the cabbage-y mess. Although it was a 'treat,' it somewhat failed to impress us. We never told her that because Papa always instructed us to compliment her efforts so we wouldn't hurt her feelings. She had unhurt feelings, but we had severely damaged tongues.

When Isadora became the sole cook in the house, things went from overcooked mushy yuckiness to overcooked pasta dinners with lots of tomato sauce and occasional Italian sausage meatballs (though usually Isabella and Sophia got all the meat) swimming in olive oil and garlic. It was a slight improvement. At least with Isadora's cooking, we thought all we really had to do was tilt our heads up and the spaghetti would slide down on its own, lubricated by all that olive oil. No doubt the garlic kept us safe from vampires, too.

Mama would stay in the kitchen to watch her cook but was not allowed to help unless it was chopping vegetables. Isadora was afraid that Mama could burn the house down if she got too near the stove. *Which was unfair. The house never got burned when Mama cooked. Just the food.*

Isadora was sharp tongued and treated Mama like a housemaid. Sometimes, Gio seemed to treat Isadora like his wife and Mama as some poor relative rescued from the streets. Isadora never was wrong. Mama was never right. The only good thing about it was at least he was gone most of the day and quite a bit of the night, working at the club. He came in at the end of his day with a big duffel bag made of shiny brown leather that he hid in their bedroom, and he'd leave early the next morning, taking it with him. I didn't see him very often. Neither did his own daughters, which may have contributed to their hideous personalities. The only adult figure they had for years was the stone-faced Isadora and her obsession with appearances.

I think that was why the 'Fertile Myrtle' label became such an issue. The family embarrassment. It just rankled Isadora to no end, which meant that she nagged at my mother to no end, like anything could be done about it. The problem was, there *was* something that could be done about it.

"We decided that I'm not old enough to have a daughter your age," Mama told me in June, right after school let out for summer. "So, your Aunt Isadora, Papa Gio, and I want you to start calling me Aunt Mary instead of Mama. And he will be Uncle Gio. Everything else will still be the same, it's just that…it makes things easier for us. You understand?"

No, I don't understand.

I knew what they were doing, but I didn't understand why. Things may now be easier, but nothing would ever be the same for any of us. Mama had traded her freedom and self-respect for security and servitude. And she was letting them isolate me from the whole family. And the true insult for me was that both Isabella and Sofia were by now calling her 'Mama.'

"Well, of course *I* call her Mama," Isabella stated with contempt. "She married my Papa. *I'm* part of the family, but you're not part of this family and don't you ever think you will be. You'll always be some poor orphan cousin in this house. That's why she's 'Aunt Mary' to you and 'Mama' to everyone else."

Sophia always agreed with her. She never really initiated the subject but could always be relied on to repeat whatever malevolent attack her sister initiated. And there were daily insults from them. And they were always supported by Gio and Isadora, who I nicknamed the demonic duo. They could say anything they wanted to me and never be corrected. Indeed, the adults pretended not to notice anything, although occasionally I could see a small, satisfied smile creep over Isadora's lips.

I tolerated all the abuse as well as expected for a nine-year-old. I still called her Mama when we were alone. While the others played games, talked to each other and formed family attachments, I took my violin to the back porch and played my music as best as I could. Out there, no one could hear me. My music drowned out the peals of laughter from the other children. It made me feel less alone when I couldn't hear the rest of them enjoying themselves without me.

Mrs. Carnahan was far away in the city, so my lessons were no more. Mama mentioned to Gio that they should find another instructor and maybe get the other girls to learn to play instruments and we could all play together. Gio told her to talk to Isadora about it. Not surprisingly, she said no. It made for a bad appearance. Making music was for men. Women should only listen and politely applaud their efforts.

Sometimes, I would sit on the bed in our small bedroom and play to my heart's content. I would talk to Little Frankie, but he never spoke back. What can you expect from a stuffed animal?

I imagined my father's loving voice encouraging me. When the music stopped, his voice did too. So, I would start another song, even though I didn't know many. Eventually, I began composing my own melodies, every one entitled *For My Father* to help me connect to him. The music made me remember all the fun we had. Now, fun was forbidden for me and it was replaced with resentment.

It all came to a head one rainy January afternoon in 1930, weeks after my unacknowledged tenth birthday. It had been sleeting for a week and I couldn't play my violin on the porch because it would get wet and I would freeze, so I played in my room, as softly as I could. If I played too loud, Isadora would complain and yell at me and 'Aunt Mary' would come in quietly suggesting that I play at a later hour. Obviously, there would never be a later hour. The violin was just as unpopular in the house as I was.

Julia was always playing something with the gruesome twosome. The two aunts groused at each other in the parlor, usually about how Mama could be a better wife. Only Patrick would come and listen to me play. He was too young to know what was going on, but I think he wanted me to know he loved me.

That day I was playing *Oh Danny Boy* after school. Patrick and Julia were in another room playing marbles when Isabella and Sophia burst into my bedroom with intense rage.

"Stop making that awful racket," Isabella screamed. "You can't play that thing and it hurts everyone's ears."

"Yeah, you just make noise with it," Sophia agreed.

I made the mistake of setting it down on the bed and standing up to her.

"I didn't invite you into my room. Just leave. Just get out of my life," I yelled back at them. By then Julia was in the doorway.

"Come on, girls," she quietly urged them. "Let's just leave her alone. She's not too loud and I like the music anyway."

"Just shut up," Isabella growled at her. "We're not talking to you."

"Yeah," Sophia chimed in, "just let her handle it."

"Just sit back down," I heard Isadora bark out at Mama from the parlor. "Let the girls handle it. They can work it out between themselves."

As if on cue, Isabella grabbed my violin off the bed and raised it over her head, dancing around while I tried to get it back. It was a bit of a struggle and I almost had it but Sophia grabbed my hair and yanked it hard. Isabella had sole possession of my precious instrument and she smashed it against the bedpost as hard as she could. Its death rattle was a flat sound of disappointment and despair as it was demolished. Isabella, the assassin, laughed cruelly at her murderous deed and Sophia let go of my hair.

"What cha think you're gonna do about it?" she sneered. She started to say something else, but my fist smashed into her nose. Whatever vicious thing she thought to state was replaced by a scream of pain. I had inflicted the perfect punch. Papa would have been proud (maybe). I caught her nose right at the tip and followed through with all my weight, aided by sheer fury.

I broke her nose. Her hands covered her face while she howled in agony. At first, I thought it was an act, but as she moved her hands about, I could see a lot of blood pouring through the damage.

"Oh my God," Sophia cried out. "Aunt Isadora! Come quick. Amy killed Isabella."

Obviously, Sophia had been exposed to high drama before.

The two adults came running. Isadora pushed Julia out of the door and she landed on her rear in the hall, unhurt but very unpleasantly surprised. She quickly started to comfort the little villain and coaxed her hands away from her now deformed face. Mama surveyed the damaged bed post and violin and went over to pick Julia up and give her a hug.

"I'll have to take her to the doctor," Isadora announced with a venomous voice. She scowled at Mama. "I'll leave it to you to chastise your vicious little bitch-daughter. When Gio gets home, there'll be hell to pay for this. I want her out of this house."

She took a handkerchief out of her sleeve and pressed it to Isabella's face and they scurried out of the room with Sophia following them like an unwanted puppy.

"Oh, Amy," Aunt Mary sighed, "What have you done?"

"It was the only thing I had."

"I know," she whispered. "I know. Clean your room up and I'll make a phone call."

"You're not mad at me?"

"No," she sounded defeated. "But things have definitely changed here. Isadora won't let you live with us anymore."

"What about Uncle Gio?"

"It's her house."

"It is?"

"It is," she nodded. "Gio's businesses have some issues with the tax system, so he keeps all his assets in her name. He may have bought the house, but legally, it belongs to her. That's why she makes all the decisions."

This made no sense to me at the time, but I accepted it. Julia helped me clean up the room. I cried when I gathered up the pieces of my violin, while she wiped Isabella's blood from the furniture and floor.

Somehow, as I threw the broken wood apart, my anger melted away. So did something else inside. Mama was not Mama anymore. I had no desire to call her anything but Aunt Mary. I realized that I never really had a Mama. A real mother wouldn't have let Mrs. Carnahan raise me. Would have spent more time with me. Would have defended me. Most importantly, she would have loved me. Aunt Mary did none of these things and never would.

Isabella and Isadora were back in a couple of hours. Isabella had a gigantic square bandage covering her nose and cheeks. Her eyes were tired and puffy from laudanum. She went to her room to sleep without saying a word to anyone. Isadora had hatred spewing out of her demonic eyes as she glared at me.

I could her yelling hateful things about me to my Aunt Mary and I heard meek responses of agreement. Seconds later, my door squeaked open and there she was holding an empty carpet bag just perfect for my little hands to carry.

"Your Aunt Isadora is quite unhappy with you. I'm not. I should have stood up for more. I know now I made a mess of things. But I need you to listen and do exactly what I say. It's very important that you follow my directions, no matter what you may think of me. Can you do that?"

"Yes, Aunt Mary. I can."

I saw the hurt in her eyes, but it gave me no satisfaction.

"Aunt Isadora thinks you are too ungrateful to have a bed to sleep in. You'll be on the back porch tonight." She dropped the bag on the floor. "I want you to pack everything you want in here and be ready to leave in the morning."

She hugged me but I didn't hug back.

There wasn't much to take. Just Little Frankie and some underwear, my play clothes that were a size too small, my Sunday school skirt, a faded red one that fell just above the ankles and a frayed blouse with a small stain just below the collar. Sophia usurped my wool dress from the wedding. I only had one pair of shoes, which were a size too big. Aunt Mary liked clothes to last as long as possible so everything she bought was too big so we could grow into things.

I took the bag and walked dejectedly out on the porch with a comforter and sat down on an old wooden

Adirondack chair and watched the sleet turn into snow. I was asleep by dark.

I awoke late that night. Uncle Gio was home. The back porch formed an L shape from our bedroom being added. So, my back was to the bedroom Julia and I shared and I saw through the windows into the living room and master bedroom. The walls were thin enough that I could hear Uncle Gio and Isadora yelling at Aunt Mary about me. About my attitude and disrespect. About hurting Isabella. About my lack of gratitude to them for giving me shelter and food. Under no circumstances could I stay there. I was dangerous.

Aunt Mary reluctantly agreed. I could hear her crying. Isadora called her a failure of a caretaker to me. I should never have been allowed to grow up as mean as I did. Aunt Mary agreed again. Isadora would take Isabella to the doctor in the morning and then come back to get me. I was to move into Mr. Dragucci's nightclub. At ten, I may not have known how bad that nightclub would be for me, but I knew it would be nightmarish. I didn't want to go.

I stayed on the back porch all night. I heard the sounds of agreement and saw the lights go out, first in Isadora's room, then in the master bedroom. I could hear the bed creaking and Gio cooing Aunt Mary. Then all I heard was the wind and sleet. It soon transformed into snow and didn't stop until the wind died down a few hours later. I couldn't sleep any more.

I was thinking about running away. My suitcase was packed after all. Would Mrs. Carnahan take me in permanently? While I considered it, I could hear footsteps in the master bedroom and saw a small light move around. I peeped in through the back window.

I saw Aunt Mary holding a small flashlight over Gio's

duffel bag. It held piles of cash, neatly organized in clumps by rubber bands. She pulled a few bills out and, glancing to the bed, stuffed them in her purse.

She made breakfast and we ate together. It was a silent, miserable affair. Very little was eaten, either because of the oppressive atmosphere or because the pancakes were black on the outside and raw on the inside. Gio was gone. Isadora occasionally sneered at me without saying anything. She followed Aunt Mary to the back bedroom and I heard them talking.

"I know what you're up to," Isadora said softly with no trace of anger in her voice. "You need to remember Giovanni Corelli isn't a good man to cross. Anyone who defies him gets very badly hurt. He is a devil."

"You know I have to try. You have children of your own."

After a pause, Isadora responded, "Yes, I have children. My *own* children. My sons are in Italy. I can never see or talk to them. Or visit or write. They were told I am dead. And I *am* dead to them. It was all Gio's doing. My brother is the devil, but he is all the family I have left who will speak to me. He is your family now. Everyone else is gone. Here and in Louisiana. You don't want to anger him."

"Thank you for understanding," Aunt Mary said, apparently not hearing the veiled threat that I heard.

"There is no understanding. That child is evil. She makes this family appear undisciplined and wild. You will take her to Gio at ten o'clock. They'll be waiting for her. Isabella and I will go to the doctor at nine. You two will make your way to the cabaret alone. They will come looking if you are late."

"We will leave around the same time," Aunt Mary said.

"At least the other two children are more docile. Julia

can grow up to be a young lady much easier with Amy gone. She is a bad influence and I don't think she wants to be a proper young lady. Whatever she wants is not what this family wants. We will be better off with her at the club…or elsewhere."

By nine, Isadora and Gio's daughters left for the doctor to check Isabella's broken nose. Aunt Mary waited five minutes and told me to get my suitcase. When I came out, Julia and Patrick were hugging me and crying their good-byes. We all knew a big change in lives just happened and we didn't know if we would ever see each other again. I was crying also.

"Hurry," Aunt Mary urged. "We can't be here when Isadora gets back. She'll have to warn Gio that you're leaving or he'll suspect her of helping."

And so we left. We caught the subway to Grand Central Station. While on the way there, Aunt Mary told me I was going to Faucette to live with my Aunt Cassie. She bought me three tickets from New York to St. Louis, then to Baton Rouge, finally to Faucette. She also gave me ten one-dollar bills for food. As it was Friday, she figured I would arrive there by Sunday evening.

"Oh, Amy," she whispered, eyes wet from tears she held back, "I'm so sorry. It's all my fault. I should have spent so much more time with you. But Julia was all I could focus on because she was so much younger. And when Mrs. Carnahan offered to help with you, I felt so blessed. Now I wish it had been me to hold you and make you know you were loved, just like I did with Julia. You'll never know how much I regret that."

"But I love Mrs. Carnahan, Aunt Mary. She taught me to read and play the violin. She gave me hers for my very own. I cried over that violin."

"I know, sweetie. And I know you thought you had every right to hit Isabella. She was so mean to you. So hateful. Gio and Isadora don't see that in her. Even last night, Isadora said she had every right to break the violin because it annoyed everyone. But it didn't annoy anyone. They were just being mean. But right now, we have to get you out of here. When Gio finds out I'm sending you home, he'll be furious. I don't know what he'll do."

She paused to collect her composure.

"And your father. If you were a boy, learning how to fight would have been good. But for a girl? Look what happened when you were taught to use your fists instead of your brain. I should have stopped that, but he was so sure he was doing the right thing and he even convinced me it would be good for you to know how to defend yourself. And look where we are now.

"And I needed help. You kids needed a man for fatherly love and support. Gio was so kind and understanding at first. And he had two girls who needed a mother. It seemed perfect. If only I had known about Isadora. She was mother and father enough. But it was my only option."

There's never only an 'only' option.

"But you know what I regret the most? Giving in to their demand to not let you call me Mama anymore. A little girl needs her mother, and that was the ultimate rejection."

Yes, it was. I wasn't just hurt by that. I was wounded. My soul ached when that happened. And the gruesome twosome stepsisters loved to rub salt into that wound. But I didn't tell her that. I didn't say anything. Agreeing would make it worse, arguing would be dishonest.

"Now listen," she changed subjects, "actual respect and politeness mean a whole lot more down there than here. Real respect, not that exaggerated need to keep up appearances that Isadora demands. The adults are always 'sir' and 'ma'am.' Always say 'please' and 'thank-you.' Always curtsy when introduced to an adult. Don't embarrass your Aunt Cassie. She's been through enough.

"She will love you like a mother if you give her a chance. She's two years younger than me and she's married to a war veteran named Paul Villians. She's his second wife and they have a lot of children. Give them a chance. Don't you think they'll be like Gio's daughters. They'll all love you. Every one of them."

She looked behind us, then to the side, like a hunted animal.

"It'll be okay, Aunt Mary." I didn't know what to say but didn't want to be silent. She winced at that name but jumped a bit and glanced behind us before I could correct myself.

The conversation was over now. Aunt Mary was getting more nervous with each passing moment until the train came in. When the doors opened, she hugged me close and this time I hugged her back. I climbed aboard and a smiling conductor led me to my seat past the other passengers. I sat down next to the window and glanced out to see if she was still there.

She was. She didn't see me there and I started to wave but didn't. Mr. Dragucci and Gio were there, obviously yelling at her. Two swarthy men in pinstripe suits were with them, watching the little drama with cruel eyes. Gio's hands were on her shoulders squeezing them viciously. I could almost hear her cry of pain.

Just as the doors closed, they all looked up and saw me at the window. Mr. Dragucci yelled something at me and started to run to the closed door in a vain effort to stop the train. He violently slammed down his hat on the platform as the train picked up speed. Gio's face was flushed with anger while the two strangers calmly looked at each other, then at Mr. Dragucci. Aunt Mary just stared at me. I realized a few things. I was out of danger now, but she was in trouble. And there was nothing more either of us could do.

"Good-bye, Mama," I mouthed to her as the train slowly pulled out.

CHAPTER 5

A TRAIN RIDE

The sky cried ice cold teardrops of rain to match mine. The playful droplets ran from one side of the window to the other, proudly displaying their defiance of gravity as the train sped to St. Louis. I wiped away my own tears. The city was soon far behind me. I never looked back at the skyscrapers and assumed they just vanished in the bleak winter grayness. I was unhappy in New York, but I still didn't want to leave.

New York became New Jersey, and the buildings metamorphosed into bare trees and desolate marsh. Dingy little towns came and went. Garden State indeed. We sometimes stopped to vomit out passengers or swallow new ones. They all chose to sit with each other. I had the whole row to myself and slowly become mesmerized by the silent motion of the transforming landscape.

Little Frankie made a soft enough pillow and, after a snack of roasted peanuts, I leaned into him against the cold window. Just as I could see hills coming our way, I closed my eyes. The lack of sleep and bitter morning took their toll on me and I slept all the way to Pittsburg. When I woke up, the businessmen of New York were all gone, replaced steel workers and miners. The workers were going home.

In a way, I supposed, so was I. They just knew where home was and what to expect there.

After it got dark, Little Frankie and I went to the dining car. I got a cheese melt and cola drink then went back to my seat. Now that I had a full stomach, I fell asleep for the night.

The red of dawn attacked my eyelids and a new day faced me. The next stop was Wheaton, and I realized I slept through Chicago and its various satellite towns. After freshening up in the lavatory, I got an omelet and cola. Mama and Isadora would both agree that a cola was a terrible choice, but they were gone. It was time to make my own decisions.

All the stops between Chicago and St. Louis consumed the rest of the day and most of the night. Black storm clouds blotted out what little moon there was and darkness swallowed any and all scenery. It was well past dawn on Sunday when St. Louis arrived and I was deposited at platform three. It was time for me to leave my temporary home. My ticket said I had to be at line eighteen in forty-five minutes, so I had plenty of time to kill.

The rain had stopped but the freezing cold seemed even worse than New York. Both of my hands were cold and exposed since I was holding my suitcase in one hand and Little Frankie in the other. My hands ached as I walked around the station looking for line eighteen.

The station vibrated with sound. People were talking, sometimes yelling greetings to long unseen relatives or friends. Conductors were screaming out their last calls for boarding. The public address system reverberated an occasional loud announcement nobody could understand. But the trains belched out the loudest noises, from the squealing wheels to the air brakes exploding out steam, to the air horns screeching out their warnings. Somehow, it seemed louder here than in Grand Central Station. Maybe because I was alone here.

When I reached line ten, I saw a pretty little girl crying out for her Mommy or Daddy, but no one answered her. She was no older than six and obviously came from a nice home. Her dress was neatly ironed and she had perfect curls in her blonde hair with blue ribbons tied exactly right. She looked like I did at her age. Who knows? Maybe we had a common ancestor or two in the recent past. It seemed like she was going to church. I went over to her to calm her down a bit.

"Hi there, sweetie," I said, using my most winsome voice to soothe and quiet her. "Are your parents lost and maybe scared without you?"

I remember Mrs. Carnahan using this approach in Central Park a year before and it really worked for her. I could only hope it worked for me. It did.

The girl nodded, quieting down as I scanned around for likely parental candidates. Few blonde people at all and the ones who were there weren't in formal wear.

"I stopped to watch a man walking his puppy. And when I looked up, they were gone."

"I'm sure they're not far," I comforted her, sounding confident and self- assured, even though I wasn't. I sat her down on a nearby empty bench.

"I shouldn't have stopped."

"Oh well," I responded, trying to sound breezy and carefree. "Now you know for next time."

Still no sign of anyone dressed like her. An idea hit me.

"What's your name?"

"Debbie."

"Debbie what?"

"Debbie Polanski."

"Good."

I stood up on the bench, struggling to keep my balance, cupped my hands over my mouth to amplify my voice and yelled to the top of my lungs, "Debbie Polanski. Debbie Polanski here. Polanski."

It worked. About four lines down, a man and woman stopped and looked around. Then they saw me and started back towards us. I waved to them and pointed to Debbie. They hurried over.

After some hugs and mild reprimands, they thanked me for my quick thinking. They were also embarrassed that they didn't keep track of her. I just smiled and told them I was glad to help.

"Where's your family?" Mrs. Polanski asked.

"My father died a few years back and my mother is sending me to live with my aunt in Louisiana."

"They sent you here all alone?" The man frowned. "I guess that's a sign of the times." He shook his head.

Of course, I had heard of the stock market crash. It was big news in New York. I was unaware of its severity or of the looming depression. I didn't know it at the time, but everyone's life changed that year, not just mine. Extra children were shipped off to relatives who could better provide for them. It was a common occurrence.

They escorted me to line eighteen and I obviously found a friend in Debbie. Mr. Polanski asked me if I had money for food. I did, but not much was left after all the sodas, snacks and meals. They boarded my train with me and took me to the dining car. Mr. Polanski asked me if I liked chicken fried steak in front of the cook.

"I can't say that I ever had it," I replied, which was true. Most food in my house was fried until black or boiled until mush, until Isadora took over the kitchen. She was a decent enough cook, but Italian food never consisted of exotic titles such as chicken fried steak.

Both men laughed.

"If you're going to live in Louisiana, you need a sample of the cooking," the chef told me. "And, not only that, I can take you into the kitchen and show you how it's cooked." He looked at Mr. Polanski who smiled broadly and paid for the breakfast, which included potatoes and gravy.

"It's good to have the Polanski's as friends," he told me. "They own Polanski Meats and Poultry, the company that we get our supplies from. They also ship to the finer restaurants and stores. And they're good people. Not just anybody would buy a meal for a girl they just met. Now, store your bag up front and let's give you a cooking lesson."

I put my carpet bag in the kitchen as they said good-bye to me. Debbie hugged me which pleasantly surprised me. I noticed that she had nothing to cuddle with. Since I had outgrown Little Frankie, I handed him to her and told her to love him forever. She was all smiles, and I had a pocket for at least one hand in this cold winter.

I never learned the chef's name, but I always remembered him because he was so kind, and at that point in my life kindness was scarce. He showed me his pots, pans, knives, bowls, and mixing spoons. He showed me his recipe book, though he told me he never used it. The recipes were in his head where they belonged.

Corn meal and flour were mixed with salt, pepper and eggs, and transformed into a golden batter. He massaged a flank steak into the mixture and dropped it into a seething pan of fresh oil. It bubbled and hissed in rage, but its fate was sealed. While it was bubbling away, he scooped out a spoonful of diced potatoes and loaded them into a frying pan to warm them up. Some thick gravy was prepared next. Normally, I don't care for gravy since Aunt Mary's usually tasted like something dead. But this gravy smelled delicious! He left me for a minute to attend other kitchen matters and while I was waiting for him to return, I glanced out the window.

Two pinstripe suits reflected the dim light. Those two swarthy men from the New York station were on the platform, fresh off the express train. They sidled up to Debbie Polanski and tried to guide her away from her parents. One of them took her wrist and was pulling her away from her parents, who instantly started yelling at them and rescued her from their grip. One of the men pointed at Little Frankie while the other nodded in annoyed agreement.

Soon, two other men joined the conversation. The chef had returned by then and observed the platform.

"Something's going on," he said. "Looks like two thugs decided to bother the Polanski's and the railroad detectives got involved."

One of the thugs was gesturing wildly with his hands and the other tried to calm him down while arguing with the other men. I could read his lips from the window.

"That has to be her. That's the bear. She needs to go back to New York with us."

A little later, the calm one pointed to my train. "That train there."

Finally: "No, but we have tickets to New York."

The conversation was over. The two men in suits raised their hands up signifying they lost, and they turned away and left. Their eyes searched the windows of the passenger cars but didn't see me.

Breakfast was ready. The chef guided me and my carpet bag to a table where I ate my first real meal in two days. It was wonderful and I overate which made me realize how tired (and content) I was. After thanking the chef for his time, I went back to my seat. Something caused a delay and I sat there, rereading *Rebecca of Sunnybrook Farm*, thoroughly aware of how similar her situation was to mine. I sat by the window to stare out at the landscape as the train started and stopped, slowly moving south. After a few hours, I was asleep.

When I woke up, it was after ten o'clock Monday morning and I was greeted by a heavy frost on the windows. I was supposed to be in Faucette already and here I was still waiting to get into Baton Rouge. My stomach was upset and churning from that last meal. A ginger ale settled me down, but it cost me the last of my money.

"That's because there's snow two and three feet thick on the tracks in places up ahead so the engineer is pacing himself so when he gets there, it's all cleaned up," I heard the conductor tell some of the irritated passengers. "Can't be helped. Once we're out of the Ozarks, we'll be good."

True to his word, the train sped up after several hours and we pulled into Baton Rouge a little after midnight. All I had to do now was catch the line to Faucette. No wonder *travel* and *travail* are so similar! But the travail was not over yet because the travel was not done.

The train to Faucette didn't leave until eight o'clock Tuesday morning. I was going to be two days late. I didn't have Aunt Cassie's number to call and my money was gone, so there was nothing to do but wait and worry. Would she be mad? Would she yell at me for not calling? I certainly was not off to a good start.

The train left at its scheduled time and I found a seat

next to a frosty window. It was relatively empty. I was to find out later that the commuters packed the train going into Baton Rouge to work every day. Going to Faucette was relatively rare in the mornings. Most jobs were on the oil rigs and barges in the city, but a great many people still lived on their farms and grew their own food. Their cheery little houses dotted the view all the way to my new home.

There was a great view of the pine forest, with tall, majestic trees flowing into the sky over one hundred feet. Beautiful green specimens of the evergreen family, but I didn't care. I just wanted to get to my new home. There was plenty of time to be awestruck of these magnificent green giants. We passed over a seemingly never-ending river of muddy brown water. It wasn't until the engine pulled into Faucette that I realized that I had crossed the mighty Mississippi River and that was all there was to it.

After about an hour, the train stopped for no reason I could see. There was no station. I heard the loud and raucous voices of children in the car behind me. I couldn't hear the words, but the happy tones were soothing for this weary traveler. I thought about going back and saying 'hi,' but I didn't. What if they didn't like me? The train stopped again, almost immediately and the conductor called out "Faucette!" while smiling at me.

I had finally arrived. The children's voices faded away as they exited and I was the last to leave, double checking to make sure I carried off all my precious (if pathetic) belongings.

CHAPTER 6

ARRIVAL

I didn't know what to expect, but it certainly wasn't what greeted my eyes. The station was a simple affair. Two tracks. One east, one west. The station house in the middle. Two drinking fountains were in front of me. One said 'White' and the other 'Colored.' I stepped out on a warped wooden platform and watched the engine journey on eastward. There was a bench facing both tracks outside and it was surprisingly cold. I thought that Louisiana, being south, would have warm winters. I escaped the frosty morning by entering the ticket station.

Two empty benches faced the ticket booth, which was no bigger than a closet. An older man who seemed quite unpleasant stood behind the cage and sneered at me while making a show of putting down whatever he was working on. I think he was trying to smile, but who could tell? His lips were too thin to see and his teeth were too sharp to be completely human. His nose was long, close to a snout, completing his wolfish look. He had a dreadful knife scar that ruined his left cheek entirely and ears that obviously had been battered in his younger days. He wore a billed railroad hat and white frilly shirt with a houndstooth vest. Obviously, a railroad man. The imitation smile disappeared as he saw me cautiously approach his domain.

"Whatcha need little girly?" he croaked out in a guttural voice.

I was taken aback by his tone. He seemed nothing short of hostile.

"Excuse me, sir," I said meekly. "My name is Amy Collins and my Aunt Cassie was supposed to greet me here."

"Well, did you see her outside?"

"No, sir."

"Do you see her inside?"

I didn't answer. The question was an insult and it frustrated me.

"Well, you know, if she isn't here, that means she isn't here." He laughed like he just made some kind of joke. "You'll have to go about town hunting her down or you can go outside and wait for her."

He went back to whatever he was doing as though the conversation was over. I approached him close enough to see his name tag: Durrell Kaker.

"Excuse me, Mr. Kaker, sir. Nobody left a message for me or anything?"

"Not nothing." He didn't even look at me. "You can go outside and wait for them there."

"Excuse me, sir, but it's cold outside. Can't I wait for her in here?"

"Absolutely not," he snapped at me. "Those benches are for paying customers, of which you obviously are not."

I viewed the lonely and vacant pews in front of me.

"But there isn't anyone here. They're empty."

"They're waiting for paying customers to sit on them."

"I'm a paying customer. I bought tickets to get here."

"So? Did you buy them here?"

"Well, no. If I bought them here, I'd have arrived somewhere else."

"That's right. And you're here, *not* somewhere else. That means you're not a paying customer."

I rolled my eyes at the sheer pettiness of it all and walked outside.

The north side of the station was maybe ten yards of barren field that ended at a dirt road. A shabby hardware shop stood next to a stable and feed store on the other side. I could see a beautifully decorated cross at the top of a steeple beyond them. A harsh path of sunken wagon wheel ruts scarred the earth, leading to the hardware store from the station. But even so, the frosty grass and weeds sparkled out a warm welcome to me. The cold seemed to lift up momentarily and I determined: the people of Faucette might be rude and unwelcoming, but the land knew I belonged.

I turned to the other side of the station and saw a mansion. It stood two stories tall in the center with one floor wings on either side. It was freshly painted white with gold trim on the shutters. At least a dozen windows stared out at me and the station. A large round fountain spewed geysers of water straight up into the air. A lawn of twinkling frost glittered at me. I was transfixed. When Aunt Mary said she lived in a farmhouse, I could only hope she meant this.

I stepped off the platform onto a rickety wooden sidewalk to get a closer view. There was some skirting covering the entire bottom of the house that betrayed its existence by being crooked. I could see a concrete support holding the home about two feet off the ground. I had never seen anything similar in New York. I turned around. The railway station was supported off the ground as well.

In fact, all the buildings I could see floated on concrete pylons.

A man was walking on the other side of the station. He was small, with a gray fedora firmly planted on his head and a store-bought cigarette held to his mouth. He stared at me with something more than curiosity, sizing me up for some reason. He was clean shaved and wore nice work clothes, but even so, I took a step back, wanting to keep a distance in case I needed to run. He merely smiled at me and tipped his hat politely without saying a word and kept walking.

A chilly wind softly blew into my face and I felt cold again. There was no place to go and nothing to do so I trudged to the station's bench, sat and waited. There was a little traffic in front of the hardware store. All horse and buggies. To my right, far down the road, I could see a battered, wooden, arrow shaped street sign that said Faucette Avenue. On its corner, I could see a garage with an old beat-up pick-up at its side. The Automobile age hadn't consumed Faucette yet, but it was coming, I was sure.

From my vantage point, I could see the street sign on the other side. The railroad station itself was on River Road. The nearest cross street, opposite of the garage was Thomas Street. Smaller signs advised 'White' on one side of the street and 'Colored' on the other. I could hear a click clock of horse hooves and groaning wheels. I waited to see if it would be my ride.

It was not. A large terribly old-fashioned carriage rumbled down Thomas Street, pulled by two dark horses. A young black footman stood on the running board next to the door and an older black man drove the antique slowly. It was black with bright gold trim and doors on either side and three windows. I could only think it dated back to the French Revolution. My jaw dropped as I felt like I was transported to an earlier century.

An ancient lady rode in the back with her eyes staring ahead. She couldn't have noticed me gazing at her and her carriage with wide eyes and open mouth, but the footman did. He grinned at me and waved. Then he opened his mouth and tapped his fingers to his chin in an effort to tell me to close mine. My head turned to follow the carriage as it clomped on down Thomas Street.

I scurried down the dirt road and watched the carriage shrink into a landscape of old wood shops and sturdy two-story brownstones. I really wanted to explore my new home, but I was afraid of missing my ride, so I trudged back to the train platform.

I leaned my head back against the cold wood of the station house and closed my eyes. The fitful sleeping I did the past few days caught up to me and I was soon laying on the pew with my carpet bag serving as a pillow.

I heard a wagon pull up but my head was filled with dreams and so I slept on. It was the strange sound of clomp/swish, clomp/swish that brought me back into reality. I sat up sleepily, wiping my eyes and looked up. Approaching me was a very big man. He stood at least 6'3" and was about 230 pounds of pure muscle. He wore nondescript gray work clothes and had a few days of beard marring his face. His wide nose protected his thick lips. He wore an amused smile and his brown eyes were warm and friendly. But the first thing I noticed was that he had a wooden leg. As he walked, the peg would clomp on the wooden platform while his foot made the low swishing sound.

I stood up respectfully as he approached.

He peered down at me and over to my carpet bag.

"Amy Collins?" he asked quietly.

"Yes, sir," I replied with one of my better curtsies.

"I'm your Uncle Paul. Your Aunt Cassie's husband. We've all been looking forward to meeting you. Especially me. I like a girl who can hit so hard she sends her enemy to the doctor. Just remember: we don't do that here. Your Aunt Cassie will die of embarrassment. Stand up and I'll take you to meet her."

I was confused. "I am standing up, sir."

"Oh, so you are. I thought you'd be taller."

He reached over and squeezed my upper arm.

"And meatier. When was your last meal?"

"The day before yesterday in St. Louis. And I'm kind of hungry now, sir. And cold."

"I bet," he smiled though he seemed distracted. "Why didn't you wait inside the station where it's warmer?"

"Oh, Mr. Kaker says I had to wait outside because I'm not a paying customer."

"Oh, did he? Wait in the wagon for a minute. I want to have a talk with…Mr. Kaker."

I found an old wooden wagon with two thin horses in the street and climbed in while he went inside the station, closing the door tightly behind him. I could hear them both shouting, though I couldn't make out the words. Then something clanged like a bell. Mr. Kaker yelled out something and then I heard that bonging sound again.

A couple of seconds later, Uncle Paul came out. Before he closed the door he yelled back to Mr. Kaker.

"If you used the inside of your head more, the outside would hurt less."

Without another word, he effortlessly stepped into the wagon next to me and swung his wooden appendage around so it leaned on the floorboard in front of him and urged the horses on. We rode down the firmly packed dirt of River Road past Thomas, towards the garage I spotted earlier.

"Your Mama did tell you your Aunt Cassie and I were married, didn't she? You seemed kind of surprised to see me."

"Oh yes, sir, she did. She didn't tell me you only had one leg though—"

I stopped, completely embarrassed that I would say such a thing.

"I'm sorry, sir. I didn't mean to be rude."

"I wouldn't call it rude," he replied matter-of-factly. "Just obvious. I already knew I only had one leg. Lost the other in the war. Lost my first wife to the flu. Just the way it is. The other children are in school, so I'll take you to the restaurant to meet everyone else. Maybe get some food into your gullet."

We turned left at the garage onto Faucette Avenue. It seemed no different. Hard dirt firmly packed. The first building was a general store with a wooden sidewalk and a hitching post. We drove by it and turned beside the next one where he pulled the horses to a stop in front of a small shed. Two black boys about my age scurried outside to tend the horses and cart while we hopped down. My new uncle took my hand and we walked around to the front.

"If I had directions, I could have walked."

"If you went the wrong way, we'd lose a day trying to find you."

That's why I would need directions.

I chose not to say that aloud. Anybody who could so casually hurt people's heads was not someone I wanted to annoy.

We walked around to the front of the building. I think

it was originally white, but the paint was either mostly gone or faded into a colorless gray. Two lamps jutted out above the front door with their bulbs pointed down. Red covers shaded them so their lights would illuminate an old wood sign that announced "Faucette Café." Two windows flanked the glass front door with matching Coca-Cola signs.

Uncle Paul pulled open a well-worn brass door handle and I followed him inside. It was marginally warmer, though I was not tempted to remove my coat. It had a homey sort of feel to it and was clean but dark. Two men were sitting in a corner booth. They glanced up at me then went back to their breakfast.

A shelf holding dusty candy bars and sealed bags of peanuts completed the picture. A square window showed off the kitchen that I later learned was called "the pass," since that was where the tickets and food passed through. No activity was going on back there. Ten tables dressed in white and red checkered oilcloth were waiting for diners, all with tiny unlit candles standing as potential guardians against the gloom.

Two women stood behind a lonely counter, both wearing aprons. One favored Aunt Mary except she was pregnant. Four months along, I found out later. The other was an older woman with a severe, unsmiling face who had to be in her mid to late sixties. The younger one had dark blonde hair almost the exact color of mine pulled back in a tight bun. She had a full face, even features, and silky skin that almost glowed. Her blue eyes just lit up with joy when she saw me come in. She hurried from behind the bar and hugged me tightly. I was very surprised and almost uncomfortable at such a warm welcome from a stranger.

"Amy" she cooed to me, "I'm your Aunt Cassie. You'll

be staying with us now. Welcome home."

I glanced around the restaurant, a bit confused. "This is home?"

Maybe the living quarters were upstairs.

All three adults laughed.

"She misspoke," the older woman said, also giving me a tight hug. "We have a house you'll live in. I'm your Gramma Morris. Young Cassie's grandmother. I am happy you're out of New York and home here with us. With family."

"Well, Aunt Mary was family too," I argued half-heartedly.

"Aunt Mary?" they both exclaimed at once, giving each other worried glances.

"You call her Aunt Mary?" Aunt Cassie had tears in her eyes.

"Yes ma'am," I reluctantly replied. "Right after she married that man, she told me to call her Aunt Mary because she felt she was too young to have a daughter my age."

"What? Julia's not even a year younger than you. What vanity. I'll call her up tonight and give her a piece of mind," Gramma Morris said, glancing towards the end of the counter, where a phone protruded from the wall.

"No, please don't. What's done is done," Aunt Cassie said. "I'll talk to her on the weekend when the rates are cheaper."

"Suit yourself," Gramma Morris promptly switched subjects and turned her full attention to me. "Now Amy, I want you to know I am so happy to meet you. You'll be living with us and you'll be an important part of this family, like everyone else. Now we all know why you're here and I don't want to know what caused your little spat. Just remember: Faucette was named after Pierre Faucette, our direct ancestor. He started a trading post right along this river and the town grew along with it. For over ten generations, we have lived here and our family battled in every war this country ever fought.

"As such, young lady, you will be proud to be part of our family tradition. That means no embarrassing us with fighting or hitting or breaking noses. You are a genteel young woman and you will act like it. We'll always be there to help you when you run into low-life trash. We'll teach you the proper way to handle situations."

I think I just met Isadora in another form.

At least she had a smile (of sorts). She was obviously fighting a losing war with gravity and her cheeks drooped a bit downward, as did her lips, making her appear extremely severe. Her short white hair was smothered by a hairnet. She wore an extremely old-fashioned black dress with a grayish white lapel and large black buttons. I couldn't tell when such a hideous garment was ever in style. I considered it wise to keep that opinion to myself.

"Well, ladies," Uncle Paul clapped his hands, "I hate to interrupt, but I have chores to get to. I would like to mention that Amy here hasn't had anything to eat since Sunday."

"What?" Gramma Morris exclaimed. "Why didn't you say something?"

"You were too busy reading her the riot act," Uncle Paul laughed.

Aunt Cassie rolled her eyes and guided me to a seat at the counter and Gramma Morris marched to the kitchen door.

"Cici," she called out, "Amy's here. And she hasn't eaten since Sunday."

"You'll love Cici," Aunt Cassie told me. "She's the cook, chef, and mistress of the kitchen. The heart and soul of the café."

Seconds later, an enormous, light skinned, black woman bustled out and walked over to me, a smile the size of Delaware on her face showing off snow white teeth. She wore a blue bandana that gathered all her hair inside, hiding every strand from view. She wore a gray dress covered by a dirty yellow apron. Her wide nose flared a bit because of the broad grin in a disarming kind of way. I liked her immediately.

"I had to come out and see you, little girl," she said giving me a bear hug that stopped my breathing. "You just sit there and wait half a minute. I have biscuits and gravy heating up. You want a Coke while you're waiting?"

"Cici, it's not noon yet," Gramma Morris exclaimed.

"So? We don't want her fainting dead away from hunger now, do we?" She turned to me. "When did you last wash up?"

"Um," I had to think, "On the train?"

"Soap on a train? That'll get you dirtier than no soap at all," she huffed indignantly. "Come with me. I'll show you the latrine."

I looked at Aunt Cassie for permission. She nodded with a smile.

Cici very firmly guided me by the shoulder through the swinging door into a huge kitchen. A large wooden table dominated the room, covered in bowls and decorated with raw vegetables. Pots were everywhere and the sink was filled with dishes. The two black boys I saw earlier were washing and drying them.

She marched me over to them.

"Now Amy," she said, touching the taller one, "This

here's my grandson, Ronald. We call him Thrushy because he *whistles* like a bird. My younger grandson here is Daniel, though he goes by Finchy. We call him that because he *sings* like a bird. They live with me now that their folks died."

Thrushy was taller than me. I guessed him to be about twelve or thirteen. He had tan skin and light brown eyes. His angular nose and thin lips betrayed his white ancestry, and he smiled at me, showing off his lovely white teeth. Finchy was smaller. Younger than me I thought. He was darker than his brother and grandmother, but he still had Anglo features.

They both said, "Hi, how you doing?" and went back to work.

We strode towards the back while I glanced around quickly. The floor was old, yellowed linoleum that curled up in places and it had a spongy little bounce to it. The walls cried out for paint. Neglect left them motley and splotched. Water stains totally discolored the ceiling. The shelves and cabinets were clean and well organized. The stove was just beyond the sink. It was a range, which means a stove top with round plates for cooking that sat on top of an oven. A large ice box stood guard next to it. A solid oak door was padlocked shut next to it. We continued to march through the back door to the back. A large staircase of rickety wood led up to a second floor I hadn't noticed before.

"Upstairs there, that's where Lila lives. She's the night help. Part of her salary, so to speak. Not enough room for a whole family."

Two sheds were behind the café. One stored the horses and supplies, the other housed the generator that hummed a steady noise as it furnished the restaurant's electricity. Both small buildings needed paint.

We walked over the hard packed dirt into a grassy

embankment where a dark stream of muddy water swooshed by. It was about twenty yards back and five feet down a slope. Those magnificent pine trees stood as lonely sentinels swaying in the cold breeze.

"That's Faucette Creek. Loaded with crawdads. Makes good etouffee. Be careful if you get near it. Those cottonmouths don't care who they bite. They just like to bite."

"Cottonmouths?" I asked hesitantly.

"Poisonous snakes. One bite can kill you or make you real sick. And there's plenty in there. When it rains down here, that creek can fill to the top and overflow. Then those snakes will be waiting for you."

It was actually quite enchanting it spite of her warning. Those tall pines dotted the bank on our side, but it was a thick pine forest on the other side. Brown vines slept contentedly away from the roots, closer to the embankment. The water whooshed in my ears and I felt very comfortable. It may sound strange, but I knew I belonged here. The land told me.

The restrooms were clearly marked and just to the right. The men's room was first, followed by the lady's room. It was small, but I was happy it had running water. I freshened up and washed my hands in the rust-stained sink, using extra soap, so I would impress everyone with my hygiene.

Cici was at the stove humming *He's Got the Whole World in His Hands*. She smiled at me when I came back.

"Now, just you go up front and get a table Little Amy. Biscuits and gravy are coming up."

"Thank you, Miss Cici. I love biscuits." I really didn't, because they were always doughy and sometimes unblended chunks of raw flour would pop open in my mouth. But I lied to be pleasant.

Her smile faded a bit as I left the kitchen. My effort to be pleasant must have failed. No time to worry about it though. Aunt Cassie was talking to the two customers and looked up with a smile as I came back in with Gramma Morris behind, nodding her head.

"Amy," she called out softly, "come over here. I want you to meet these men."

I obediently went over and curtsied, lost balance and collided into Aunt Cassie's hip. Her hand steadied me and I recovered, highly embarrassed.

"Obviously, my sister taught her that curtsying is important, but didn't think to teach her how to do it."

Everyone laughed but me.

"I think she may be tired," one of the men said. "Train sleep isn't as good as bed sleep. Those Pullman cars can be lumpy and uncomfortable."

"I wouldn't know. I didn't get one."

"You slept in the seat?"

I nodded.

"She left in a hurry," Aunt Cassie told him.

He was a tall man with a round face and soft blue eyes. He reached down, cupped my jaw and turned my head gently from one side to other, ignoring my flinch.

"Amy, this is Dr. Gannon," Gramma Morris said from behind. "He's just giving you a quick exam. He won't hurt you and we wouldn't let him if he tried."

He quickly glanced up my nose and in my mouth, felt around my neck and throat, then pulled back and released me with a big smile.

"Mr. Mayor," he said to other man, a much shorter, heavier man of indistinct age, "your new citizen seems to be of perfect health."

"That's great. Little girl, I'm Mayor Rich Norman. I

want to welcome you to Faucette. You'll love it here. Much nicer than New York."

"Um, thank you, sir."

"And Cassie," the doctor went on, "she is a bit small for her age, and certainly thin, but a couple of home cooked meals and she'll be fine. Nothing to worry about."

"Thank you, Dr. Gannon."

"Worry?" I asked, totally confused.

"I was concerned. You're so small and thin for a ten-year-old," Aunt Cassie replied. "And Dr. Gannon was right here so it didn't hurt to have a quick look-see."

The men were leaving and said good-bye to me.

"And I'll see you next week," Dr. Gannon told my aunt. She nodded.

He turned to me. "Maybe you can come with her and get a full examination."

I started to curtsy, but Gramma Morris grabbed my shoulders with both hands.

"Don't," she whispered. "You'll hurt yourself or destroy the whole café."

I blushed.

"And don't get your feelings hurt. Everybody has to learn from the beginning."

We went back to the counter. A place setting was waiting for me.

"You'll be getting biscuits and gravy," Aunt Cassie said, with exaggerated happiness. "They're soooo good."

"Well, I like biscuits," I replied.

When they're cooked and not burned.

"And gravy?" Gramma Morris asked with a frown.

"Well, I don't really care much for cabbage, or anything cooked in cabbage."

They were both speechless. So, I went on.

"Really though," I said truthfully, "I just don't like food."

"I wouldn't like food either, the way you describe it. You put gravy on cabbage?" Aunt Cassie asked as if she were afraid of the answer.

"No ma'am. Aunt Mary boils the cabbage with meat and potatoes and scoops up the water and fries it in the pan with flour and salt and we put it on the potatoes to make them taste better."

Both pairs of adult eyes left me at the same time, shooting up to glance at each other in amazement.

Aunt Cassie said to Gramma Morris, "This child is going to bring back my morning sickness."

The silence broke as the kitchen door squeaked open and Cici appeared with a big plate of breakfast. I had never seen biscuits and gravy before, and I have to admit it really didn't seem appetizing. The brown sausage gravy totally obscured any trace of biscuit. And the gravy itself was viscous and tan, like a polluted brown ocean with little chunks of sausage peeking out like malevolent dark icebergs, waiting patiently to sink some unprepared Titanic.

"Well, Cici," Gramma Morris announced, "You have here the challenge of a lifetime. This little girl doesn't like food."

Cici's smile vanished completely as she glared at me. The other women came to my defense, explaining what passed for gravy in New York.

"Don't go talking like that in my restaurant," she warned in a low voice. "That Mary De Montfort was the worst cook I ever laid eyes on. MMM HMMM. That girl wouldn't know a stove from her rear end if you tied it around her neck." She glared down at me. "And don't you go thinking we cook like that down here. You will taste everything we make you and you will like it. I can promise you that. Now get that fork moving. Your mouth is in for a taste sensation."

Taste sensation. I like that, assuming the taste is a good one.

The plate was thrust in front of me and a napkin and fork materialized at my side. The first thing to hit me was that delicious and wonderful smell. Biscuit, sausage and gravy combined to make my mouth water and my stomach growl. For the first time in my life, I could almost hear the food calling to me, telling me to indulge.

I took a dainty bite to be ladylike, then another, larger one. I never ate so much so fast. I went through the whole biscuit and was scraping the dish with my fork.

"Now hold on," Cici laughed. "You can't eat the plate. I can make you another."

"Let her stomach work on this one," Gramma Morris ruled against her. "Too much food on an empty stomach can get her a stomachache. How about you get us all some sweet tea and we'll sit at a booth for a bit. Lunch crowd will be coming in soon."

The three of us moved to a booth and talked for a bit, so I could get a better understanding of our family history. Gramma Morris was born right before the Civil War, which she called the 'Blue Devil Invasion,' and would turn seventy later in the year. Aunt Cassie was twenty-six, married for almost seven years. She moved to Nueville sometime in 1920 and got a job at a restaurant as an assistant manager, which meant she was a waitress/cook/bookkeeper. When Grandpa Morris died, Gramma Morris was overwhelmed and Cassie moved back in with her to help out and before you knew it, they were in business together. There was some tension when Uncle Paul came courting, but it smoothed over. After all, he was a war hero, amongst other less desirable things.

Papa knew Uncle Paul from the war. They were stationed together in Fort Anderson, near Monroe, and on weekends Uncle Paul took the train home. He invited Papa to meet his family one weekend and that's when he met my mother. They went to dances together and Papa became a fixture in Faucette.

Actual discharges were slow in coming after the war as there was a recession going on and the government was reluctant to add great numbers to the workforce. So, Papa had more opportunity to visit. He and Paul became unlikely friends of sorts. But Paul became a Christian during the war and Papa's belligerent ways were a bit off-putting to him, but Aunt Mary and Paul's first wife became friendly.

On weekend visits, my father courted Aunt Mary and he met her parents. My maternal grandfather, Major James De Montfort, was obviously aware of Papa's military indiscretions and my maternal grandmother was a military nurse who loathed him.

My grandparents met while attending Tulane University and it was love at first sight. My grandfather's family had a tradition of being career army and the De Montfort name was highly respected. So, when he was a young cadet with a vision of being a surgeon, he fell for the perfect woman. My grandmother was a no-nonsense top of the class student with as unlimited a future as a woman could have in those days. They were married the day he received his commission and became a second lieutenant. That was in 1901. Women were not part of the army in those days, but as nurses were scarce and demand was high, she was an immediate asset to his career.

As mentioned, my grandparents were unimpressed with

my Papa, as I had heard many times. It was the same with my great grandmother, Gramma Morris. She had lots of two-word sentences to describe him. Big mouth. Cocky attitude. Worthless drunk. Hot tempered. Ignorant Irishman. Know-it-all moron.

"My daughter absolutely hated that man," Gramma Morris told me. "She put up every roadblock she could find to keep him away from Mary. But he was determined and even though Mary wasn't in love, she thought it was love."

"What's the difference between being in love and thinking you're in love?"

Aunt Cassie rolled her eyes at this.

"If I say it's love, it's love. If not, it's not."

"Oh," I said, choosing a safe response.

"But I will hand it to him. He said he would stop drinking and as far as I know, he dropped it cold turkey. Mary did him good," Gramma Morris concluded. "Once he got on his feet, he provided well for you all, and he was a real father. Not necessarily a good one but he always seemed to be there for his family. And Mary never realized she didn't love him."

Maybe because she did.

"Anyway, when it comes to young people, tell a girl she can see any boy but that one and that's the one she has to have. Mary and Michael were an item. End of story. My daughter forbade Mary to see him. My son-in-law refused to talk to him. That's because your Papa punched his commanding officer, who just happened to be James's brother."

And Aunt Mary's uncle.

"He didn't just hit him," Aunt Cassie said. "He broke his jaw with a sucker punch. Luckily for him, he was a war hero. All he got was a dishonorable discharge and no jail time.

"Your Papa moved to Faucette and stayed with Paul and his first wife for a while. Long enough for Mary to forgive him for that indiscretion. But the rest of the family wanted to tar and feather him, so there was a bit of tension. Mary tried to bring them all together, but that wasn't going to happen. The couple eloped to New York by 1919. Our parents immediately disowned her for marrying such a man. They blamed her for our Papa not getting his promotion. An officer who can't run his home, can't run army troops. I went to visit them later that year and spent some time with them…to show support."

She and Gramma Morris glanced at each other for a second.

"During this time, Paul stayed home with his growing family. Sadly, while your parents were making a life for themselves in New York, Paul soon became a widower with four children to feed. His disability pension did not go far enough and his employment opportunities were limited, but he was resourceful. His younger brother, Vincent, helped him convert half of his eighty acres of farmland into pecan groves and the other half was dedicated to raising chickens. He also had a two-acre pond stocked with catfish and snakes, but that's beside the point.

"Since Paul had chickens, eggs and fish to sell, and our restaurant needed food to cook, it was only a matter of time before we found each other. We were married in early 1924, two days after my twentieth birthday.

"And it was the best birthday present I ever got," Aunt Cassie said, squeezing me close. "Next to you coming home."

I was overwhelmed at this welcome. I was not at all

expecting anything like this. We talked a bit more, then I asked her some questions about my new and old family.

"So, Aunt Mary's maiden name was De Montfort?"

"That's right, dear, we change names when we marry."

"I know that. I guess I forgot her original name was De Montfort. I thought it was Faucette."

Or never knew what it was in the first place.

"Oh, yes. It becomes confusing after a while too. Almost everyone in town is descended from Pierre Faucette in some way or another."

CHAPTER 7

WORKING IN THE KITCHEN

"Miss Cassie," I heard Cici yell out. "Time to start preparing for the lunch crowd."

"Okay, Cici. I'll send her in."

I had absolutely no doubt who *her* was. I was quickly guided back into the kitchen by Aunt Cassie, where Cici took over.

"Your family wants you to get used to Louisiana ways before you start school. So, for the rest of the week, I'll be teaching you how to cook."

She led me to the wood table and sat me down in front of two bowls and a knife.

"Now boys," she said to her grandsons, "Miss Amy is going to learn how to cook. And she's going to like it." A mischievous grin crossed her lips. "Or else."

My first lesson was snap beans. They're just regular green beans, still in the pod. My job was to cut off the stems and points and snap them in two, which explains the name. While I was snapping, Cici got a pot of water heating on the stove and salted it. She got out an iron skillet and salt pork and started slicing it up and heating it. She made a point of showing me the meat. It looked a lot like bacon, only in a big chunk instead of sliced up. I handed her the beans and wiped the stems and tops off the table into a waste basket.

"Good girl," she said and handed me some more beans to snap.

I could hear Gramma Morris yell out, "Order up!"

Cici went to the window and retrieved a ticket.

"Red beans and rice," she said to me. "Git over here and I'll give you a lesson in cooking the good stuff."

She moved about the kitchen with speed and grace that belied her size. First, she went to the icebox, taking out a bowl of rice and another of beans. They were dark, red and kidney shaped. I never saw beans like that before. Beans were always green, thin and tasteless. One sniff and I knew they had flavor.

She slid another skillet out and poured some oil and whapped a slab of butter in it as well.

"The whole secret of success in a restaurant is to be prepared. We always cook up some rice and beans when we get here in the morning. That way, it only takes a second to get them heated up for the customers. Remember: most of them commute from someplace and stop here for a quick bite. Most the trains come and go so fast they don't get off at all. We can't make them regret coming here. The eleven o'clock and three o'clock have freight to deliver. They're here for over an hour. That's when we get the commuters stopping by for meals."

The food was sizzling in the skillet in no time and with a few quick turns of the spatula it was done, on a plate and in the window.

"Beans and rice," Cici called out. The plate vanished in a heartbeat.

Back to the snap beans. After I filled the bowl again, I discovered where they were stored and got a refill.

"Now hold on there, Amy," Cici called out behind me. "You got enough there for three days. Such a good worker. Too bad you aren't permanent."

I smiled from sheer joy. I was not used to being appreciated.

"It's time to hitch the wagon, Ma," I heard Thrushy say.

"Okay, you do that and get it up front."

"I can help," I said, eyes wide with enthusiasm.

All three of them seemed horrified at the thought.

"Go on boys. Amy, stay here."

I was crestfallen.

"Did I say something wrong?"

"No, child, you didn't. It's just that you don't know the rules very well. Things are different here. Black folk and white folk have very serious lines they don't cross. The boys are friendly enough and good young men. They're just a little afraid is all. They can't cause you no harm, but you can do them plenty if you ain't careful. White girls ignore black boys, or it's bad. Bad for you *and* them. Always remember the rules."

She smiled, seeing my disappointment.

"But you know, a little bending won't hurt. Run off for five minutes, but when I call, you need to be back quick as a flash."

So off we went. The wagon hitching took no time at all for the experts to do and we walked down to the street so Thrushy could look at cars at the garage. It was an unimposing wooden structure crying out desperately for paint with a hard packed dirt surface serving as a parking lot. A faded red sign swayed silently in the wind. Dupris Garage and Storage. A smallish man in greasy overalls and a discolored straw hat who was wiping his hands on an equally greasy rag greeted us.

"Hi, Mr. Dupris," Thrushy said, pronouncing his name Du-PREE. "This here is Amy Collins. She's new in town."

I curtsied to him, but my lead foot was on a particularly sharp stone, so I shifted weight and came back up with a slight sway. He didn't seem to notice and tipped his hat to me, while spitting out a stream of tobacco juice.

"I am most pleased to meet you Miss Amy Collins," he said, with a pleasant smile that displayed brown stained teeth. "I heard there was a new young lady in town. One who keeps her hands to herself and doesn't hit anyone."

I found this annoying and decided I didn't particularly like Mr. Dupris but smiled and said, "Well, sir, that would be me."

Thrushy twittered out a wolf whistle at a bright blue Packard inside the shop. It was a gorgeous car; made in an era I always remember as the golden age of the automobile.

"That is one fine automobile," Thrushy said, ostensibly to me, but more to impress Mr. Dupris. "It's a 1928 Packard De Luxe Eight. It's powered by a low-compression aluminum head, has a five-person body style, and an L-head in-line eight-cylinder engine. That's why they call it the L-8. It's got a 57.8 cubic inch displacement and an updraft carburetor with fuelizer and nine main bearings and has 85 horsepower. I will have one of those someday," he said, not quite drooling over it, but coming close.

I didn't want to appear rude by seeming disinterested (which I was) but I didn't want to sound ignorant either, so I remembered one of my father's lessons for life. Ask questions. Preferably intelligent sounding ones.

"Horsepower?"

"That car has 85 horses under the hood. Goes fast and smooth, uphill and down," Mr. Dupris said.

"Oh. But does it matter how many horses it has? It can only go as fast as the slowest horse, wouldn't it?"

There was a slight pause, while Finchy and Thrushy glanced at each other with slightly wider eyes.

Mr. Dupris turned and looked over toward the creek and finally turned back to me. His eyes danced with amusement as he spit out another stream of his hideous tobacco juice and said, "They're *mechanical* horses. They all go the same speed. And no harnesses or hay. Or cleanup."

"Oh, mechanical horses. That makes sense."

I may have been successful in sounding interested but failed miserably at not sounding ignorant.

"We got to go back," Finchy said. "We only had about five minutes to visit."

I pretended a quick curtsy and we hurried back. I was in the kitchen just when Cici was about to call.

"Have fun?"

"We did. Thrushy saw a blue car and he really liked it."

"That's nice."

With that, the subject turned back to business. The Tuesday special was coq au vin (chicken in wine).

"Now you know because of prohibition, wine is dear. People still make it, but *good* wine is hard to find. Some folks make it out of blackberries and things. I prefer a hearty red wine made from grapes, but we work with what we have. Blackberry wine adds a rather unique flavor. Come with me and I'll show you our stash."

We ambled over to the locked door. Cici reached into her apron pocket and produced a key. With one effortless twist and pull, the door creaked open into a dank, musty-fumed storeroom. Wooden crates and packing boxes labeled with brand names and descriptions of canned product were neatly layered throughout. We approached the first large stack.

"Canned foods are the ruination of good cooking," she pronounced.

Cici effortlessly slid the stack aside with a gentle nudge of her foot, revealing a trapdoor built into the floor.

"They're empty but serve a purpose."

She pulled up the trapdoor to reveal a crate filled with bottles of red wine.

"It used to be there were two houses here, built close together. We bought them both and fixed them up as one. This used to be a fireplace. Where that wine was, that was the cinder closet. That's where we store the wine and things. It's three block walls and the open area is so dark nobody can see there's anything there to get."

"You mean someone can crawl underneath the building and take it?"

"Only if they know where it is."

"Why do they build the houses so far off the ground anyway?"

"Water. When it floods, the water goes under the house and it rots and molds the wood. And when spring gets here, it'll flood. Not Noah flood-like, but still, lots of water."

The trapdoor was closed and boxes were replaced. The key jumped back into her pocket and we were back in the kitchen. The door was closed and standing sentry to its alcoholic secrets.

"After you learn how to make coq au vin, I'll teach you how to make the best red beans and rice. You can always have a job cooking."

We fired up bacon, sauteed mushrooms and onions, peeled garlic, and carrots, and started to cook things up while the chicken soaked in the wine. The smell alone was worth paying money for. The aroma of all those ingredients as they softened and caramelized was unlike anything I ever encountered. And, best of all, there was no cabbage.

CHAPTER 8

ANOTHER NEW FAMILY

Once we had the coq au vin simmering in a pot, Cici took down another large pot and filled it with water and kidney beans. She had to tell me that was their name because as far as I knew, a bean was a bean. We didn't eat them at home. Aunt Mary pronounced them 'too involved' and Aunt Isadora deemed them to be 'peasant food.' Both crimes carried with them a sentence of permanent banishment from the kitchen. When I explained this to Cici, she decided one aunt was lazy and the other snobbish.

"If you don't eat rice and beans down here in the real world, you're just going to have to starve."

"Cici?" Gramma Morris entered the kitchen, "Are you teaching her some cooking?"

"She's learning to make coq au vin."

"Good. Now take your time and get it perfect so she learns to do it the…Cici way. Not the Mary way. By the way, are you putting in enough wine? It just doesn't taste the same as when I was a child."

"All the wine it needs, Miz Morris," she said with a knowing smile.

There were maybe three pounds of the reddish legumes in the bowl, most of them sunk like stones on the bottom, while a dozen or so floated contentedly on the surface. Cici whisked the floaters up with a slotted spoon and deposited them in a smaller bowl, which she placed high on the shelf.

"Those beans that float give you gas. Not every cook knows that. That's why the commuters stop here for lunch. They don't get all gassy."

After that she got out a cabbage, cored it and shredded the leaves through a grinder and mixed it with shredded carrots. The she got out some white sauce that she identified as homemade mayonnaise and whisked it together with vinegar, sugar, salt, and cream.

"Cole slaw. The secret is the sauce. You ever taste any?"

"No. Are you going to boil that?"

"For land's sake no. Boiling cabbage stinks up the whole kitchen and makes the place smell something awful. Ain't nobody going to step foot in here if they smell boiling cabbage."

I had to agree. And the coleslaw was a sweet and tangy 'taste sensation.' I devoured it. My sample wasn't very big and Cici made it clear I wasn't getting any more.

"You can't make too much at a time cause it goes bad quick. We'll save it for the paying customers."

I can't say I saw a whole lot of commuters. Cici explained that the one o'clock and three o'clock stops carried freight as well as passengers. It took a bit over an hour to uncouple the cars. The passengers would stop by for lunch or coffee. Because of the recent crash, business slowed down because people were afraid of losing their jobs.

While she was explaining all this to me, we started to boil the beans in salt water until they cracked open (that releases the flavor) and put a pot of boiling water next to it for the rice. She manhandled a skillet and started to sauté chopped onion, celery, and green peppers. She mixed in some chopped up red peppers and Andouille sausage. The beans and rice would soon be mixed into the pan for that 'taste sensation.'

When three o'clock came, the café had a few customers straggle in for the coq au vin. Just as the last one left, the door flung open and the front was filled with children's voices. I snuck a peak out the window and the café was bursting with activity. Talking, laughing, jumping children were all squirming at the counter, all of them wearing happy smiles. Four girls and one baby boy surrounded Aunt Cassie, each with a story to tell.

"Time for you to get out of here and meet your new family," Cici urged me.

"All at once?" I was suddenly nervous. Would they be a family to me like Julia and Patrick? Or would they be more like Sophia and Isabella? I was actually rather content to stay in the kitchen and watch them for a bit, but Cici put two meaty hands on my shoulders and guided me firmly out the door.

"All at once," she repeated to herself with mock disgust while pushing me into the dining room.

Not unlike impatient mother birds who throw their unsuspecting young out of the nest to fly or die, I was nudged out of the safe warm kitchen back into the dining area to meet my new family.

I could hear the bits of conversation directed at Aunt Cassie as the other kids peppered her with questions.

"How's the baby?"

"What's for dinner?"

"Guess what I learned today?"

"Is she here yet?"

"She's right here," Cici announced. "And y'all will just love her. You'll see."

The door swooshed behind me and Cici was gone.

"Well, get over here," Gramma Morris urged impatiently. "This is not a good time to be bashful."

I took a couple of hesitant steps forward. It seemed like a great time to be bashful. There were lots of eyes staring at me.

Aunt Cassie pulled me close to her with an encouraging smile.

"Now girls, it's time to meet your new sister."

Sister? I thought I was a cousin at best. But sister sounded better. She must have sensed my confusion.

"Just to make sure we all remember the rules: my house, my family, my rules. No half-sisters, stepsisters, cousins, or anything else. Amy is now your sister and only your sister. The only difference will be her last name. And that reminds me, Amy, you will now call me Mama or Mama Cassie. I don't want you getting the idea you're not as close to us as any of the other children. Same with your Uncle Paul. Papa or Papa Paul, got it?"

"What is her last name?" one voice popped up.

"Collins," she answered brusquely. "And she'll stay a Collins. Name changes cost money. Now Amy, it may bother you to call someone Papa other than your New York father, but it bothers me to hear you call the man who's going to be feeding and sheltering you anything else. Do that for me?"

It may have sounded like a question, but it was a definite command. And it didn't bother me any. I called Gio the Giraffe 'Papa Gio.' And I didn't even like him. I liked Paul.

"Or, if you prefer, I know in the north people use the terms Mom and Dad. That might be better for you since you're working on your third father."

"Yes, Ma'am. Mom and Dad."

Mama and Papa were names that belonged to my Collins family in New York. I was much more comfortable with Mom and Dad.

That conversation was finished. A new one started.

"Now Annette?" The tallest girl stepped forward a bit. She had blue-gray eyes and rich dark brown hair pulled back into a ponytail. She was pretty, with clear skin and a bright smile.

"Hi," she said quietly.

"Nice to meet you."

"Annette is our oldest. She's sixteen and my proxy. That means when I'm not here, she's in charge. She's the oldest and has the most sense. She'll be seventeen in April."

The little boy called out in excitement, "And we're going to have a surprise party with a cake and everything."

"Jason," Gramma Morris said sternly, "it can't be a surprise party *now*. You just let the cat out of the bag."

I looked around, confused because I never heard that particular idiom before.

"There's no cat," Mom said patiently. "It's just an expression."

Everyone else missed that exchange while Annette was assuring everybody that a party was wonderful. No need for a surprise. But there was a need for a cake. Everyone laughed and the ruined surprise was smoothed over.

"Do you like cake?" Little Jason asked me.

"Um…I do. But I like sharing even more. Maybe you can have my slice when it's here."

Deadly silence.

"You don't like cake?" Gramma Morris asked in shock.

"I do. I just like sharing—"

"I heard you the first time and the horse-manure meter went through the roof, and it isn't going down any."

"Well, I like cake when it's made from flour and sugar. Potato, molasses and corn meal cake upsets my stomach a little."

Well, really my tongue. My stomach was fine. The last cake Aunt Mary made was really hard to choke down and the memory would never be forgotten.

"Cici," Gramma Morris called out.

"I hear you," Cici was at the window.

"This child doesn't like corn meal, potatoes or molasses in her cakes. Do you think you can find a recipe that uses flour and sugar?"

"I don't need any recipe to bake a cake with flour and sugar. But I would definitely need one to use corn meal, potatoes and molasses. Nobody I know bakes a cake with that stuff."

"Thank you." Gramma Morris looked at me. "Don't be giving away any food down here until you taste it."

"So now," Mom went on as though nothing happened. "Here's Michelle. She just turned fifteen and she's my big help at the house."

Michelle had a sturdy build with protruding breasts. Not really heavy per se, but big-boned with a round face and mousy blonde hair. She also had the same blue-gray eyes as Annette, but she seemed more reserved.

She spun her arm at the elbow in a circular wave and whispered, "Hi."

"Hello," I smiled. "Nice to meet you."

"Next is Anna Marie, who is ten, your age, but her birthday is next week. You can have a piece of cake to see if you like it then. I imagine you and Anna Marie will get along the best. It'll be like having a built-in best friend."

Anna Marie stared at the floor with a scowl. She was at least three inches taller than me and more filled out. She was going to be a beauty but her brown hair was clumsily braided and it was obvious she didn't care about it or me. I could tell that meeting me was not high on her list of things she wanted to do today. 'Built-in best friend' may not have been the best choice of words.

"Hi."

"Hello," I replied. That conversation ended quickly.

"And last, but not least, we have Holly, who is six."

"And in first grade," she added. "And I like cake too, if you're sharing."

I smiled at her. She had a heart-shaped face with light blonde hair and deep brown eyes. Her smile exuded her confidence in the fact that everyone loved her.

"Whatever food I have to share, I will share. And I'll always keep you in mind."

"And you already met Jason. He was spending time with Lila, our night waitress, while his Aunt Sharon, who usually has him, had an errand to run."

"Hi, all," came a new voice from the kitchen. "I'm here."

What timing. There she stood in a faded black waitress dress with a white lace apron and smart little matching hat that tried to hide her hairnet. She was somewhere around fifty, with shiny gray hair that used to be dark and smile lines deeply etched into her cheeks. She had a slight stoop and seemed world-weary but determined to carry on.

"Well, hi, Lila," Mom greeted. "I was just about to send Annette to fetch you."

"No need for that. I ain't never been late, though occasionally I might not be entirely on time," she modified after observing a roomful of dark stares.

"You must be Amy. Oh dear, my little sweet, but you look like your…Mama." She glanced at Mom.

"Yes, well," Mom replied dryly, "Annette will be staying tonight to help you close. Vincent will pick her up at closing time. Michelle, get that pail of beans and rice. That's our dinner tonight."

To me now: "And you'll eat it and like it."

There was no question she was loving and kind and even less doubt she was the boss. And there was no back talk or questions. When Mom spoke, people listened and obeyed.

There was a chugging and coughing sound coming down the street. I looked out the door and a beat-up Model T pickup truck rattled towards us. Its driver was a jaunty younger version of Dad with two legs. After parking the vehicle, he gracefully stepped out and yelled in a happy voice, "I'm here."

He tousled my hair and inspected me.

"You must be Amy. I thought you'd be bigger."

"Hush now, Vincent" Mom scolded. "She just needs some home cooking and she'll be fine. Amy, this is Paul's brother. That means he's your Uncle Vincent. He drives us home at the end of the day. Everybody in. Jason, up front, with me."

The order was not needed. The back of the truck was already loaded with kids. I was the only one left out.

"Well, get in, Amy," she said, exasperated.

"In the back?"

"Yes," Uncle Vincent replied dryly. "It works better than riding on the hood. Doesn't block my vision so much."

He laughed heartily at this witticism. I could tell by her eye roll that Mom wasn't impressed.

"That would make sense," I said agreeably (though I can't say I liked his sense of humor at all) and climbed in the back with my new family.

Now the pickup trucks in those days were quite small. The very early ones were the Model T cars with the back seat cut off and a makeshift bed attached, which just happened to be what we were bouncing on. It was a clever invention for thrifty farmers as it could haul produce as well as children. Also, as it soon became quite obvious, no investment in shock absorbers was needed.

The bed was slotted wood with four 4x4s affixed on the corners and connected with slats to keep us from falling out, though I was doubtful they would be effective if ever really needed. We all scrunched together to keep warm as the January wind blew over us. The winter was not as cold as New York, but the day never got warmer than forty degrees and with the sun fading behind the pine trees, it was below freezing and the wind made us all miserable.

According to Anna Marie, school already made her miserable. So did her teacher, who seemed to be unpopular with my new family. And since it was a one room schoolhouse, with only one teacher for all grades, all the children preferred ignorance to education.

"She kept me in the room all through recess and made me write 'I will learn my times tables' one hundred times."

"Your teacher sounds mean," I said, attempting to be empathetic.

I always loved my teachers and they loved me back. I think I could have been the shining star of the Manhattan school system if I was a bit more outgoing and assertive. 'Mean' and 'teachers' were not words that went together in my world. But I was raised to accept things and not complain. I was content to be quiet and stay in the background. That way I could avoid getting in trouble for existing.

"Mrs. Porter's as horrid a person as a woman can be. She's Hugo Landacre's sister-in-law, you know."

But she pronounced it LAND-da-cur. I would soon remember how the French spelled words one way but pronounced them another.

"Oh, I don't know what that means. Landacre."

"Well, Mrs. Porter comes from the Wilson line…"

"Wilson line?"

"Everybody here is descended from Pierre Faucette," Michelle took over. "He was a trapper and hunter and he created a trading post way back in 1630. He brought supplies like salt and flour and things up from New Orleans and traded them for furs. After a while, he stopped trapping and just started trading. All his daughters married and of course took their husbands' names. So, when that happened, they just say the new name as the family line. The Wilson line and the Landacre line come from the second family."

"Second family?"

"Pierre Faucette's first wife, Nicolette, had seven children. When she died, he married again. The story goes his second wife, Constanza, was a witch who cast a spell on him to marry her, then he sold all his land to her brother. They both died while fishing on the Malmort river. She inherited everything and when she died, she left it to her three children. Cut the first family completely out of everything. All seven of them."

"So, they're all witch's spawn. Just evil. And Hugo is the devil," said Anna Marie.

And I am going to have nightmares.

"Anyway," Michelle continued with an eye roll, "there

is a serious hatred between Mama and the Landacres. And Gramma Morris, Papa, Uncle Vincent, and all of us. And it's on their side too. The Porter's, Wilson's, Landacre's, and Beaumont's all hate us. And Mrs. Porter is on their side. I don't hardly think any of them are *devils* though."

"Well, maybe demons," Anna Marie offered to compromise.

"Anyway," Michelle went on after giving her a dark glare, "all that was years ago. Most of the lines all get along. Something unforgivable happened a while back that brought it all to the front again. Something between Hugo Landacre and Mama. He really must have insulted her big time. And it was Hugo Landacre's fault. And his wife is Estelle Beaumont Landacre. Our teacher is Blanche Beaumont Porter, her sister. So, it's all in the family. That means they have to hate us, just like we have to hate them."

"So, she hates us because her sister is mad at Mom because she's mad at Hugo Landacre about something we don't know about?"

"We don't have to know why we hate them. It's enough that we do. After all, it's enough for *them*."

My head was spinning. I didn't even know these people and I was expected to hate them.

"It all probably has something to do with math," Anna Marie said sincerely. "I don't understand it. It doesn't make sense, and that horrible witch gave me three pages of homework."

At last, something logical and intelligent, sort of.

"Maybe I can help you. I'm doing pretty well in math."

"Oh? You think you're smarter than me?"

What hostility. Obviously not the thing to say.

"No," I hoped to recover. "My teacher just wasn't a witch."

"You're lucky." She stared off into the gloom. Conversation over. Not much later, so was the ride. We were home.

CHAPTER 9

MY NEW HOME

We pulled onto what I thought was a white gravel driveway but soon learned was seashells. The house was a simple two-story clapboard frame with a tin roof. Four windows faced the street. It may have been a typical farmhouse for the area, but it was a mansion to me. It was much bigger than the Giraffe's house in New York.

"Wow," I said softly, drawing incredulous stares from my new sisters.

By now it was dark. Not the dark of the city, with lights from hundreds of apartments shining down, but an extreme blackness. The headlights lit the way to the front door, which was opened by Dad. A brick fireplace showed off a roaring fire. Jason was out of the cab and Mom was struggling for her freedom as well. Gramma Morris had her arm and when her feet reached the ground, she was fine. Dad was soon there guiding her into the house.

"Thank you, Vincent," Gramma Morris called out and a chorus of good-byes sounded from the others.

I inspected the outside of my new home for a minute while the others all ran inside to get warm. The house may have been warmer than the outdoors, but it was still a bit chilly. All the other children were sprawled in front of the fire with their shoes off, warming their hands and feet. Coats were piled near the fire to keep them warm. As a new family member, I put my mine with theirs, though I kept my shoes on.

The first floor was mainly one big room. Near the door was the living room area with a fireplace, threadbare sofa and a couple of worn chairs nearby to enjoy the warmth. A well-used upright piano with yellow keys leaned against the other wall. The kitchen half had the table, chairs and other expected appliances. The range and icebox were on the far wall, next to an open bathtub with a curtain held up by a rounded pole and rings. Cabinets stood out from the walls, stark and functional, not even trying to be decorative. A phone guarded the wall right beside the last cabinet.

A backdoor exited out to a screened in porch. Another door stood closed behind the fireplace. I later learned this was my new parents' bedroom, sometimes called 'the forbidden zone.' There was another bedroom for Gramma Morris with its own separate entrance through the back porch. It was also off limits to us smaller life forms.

"Who wants to help with dinner?" Gramma Morris asked. The silence was answer enough, so I raised my hand a little bit, unsure of what to expect.

"Amy? Okay, thank you." My volunteering must have surprised her. "We're having fish and red beans and rice tonight. Have you ever cooked fish before?"

"Well…no ma'am," I replied.

Dad laughed derisively at my answer.

"Now ask her if she ever *ate* fish before."

"I have. We had fish and chips every Friday."

"That's good. Your Mama's ability to ruin fish was legendary around town." With sparkling eyes, he asked me, "Did she teach you how to burn the fish?"

"Well, no. But I can learn."

The whole room burst into laughter.

"I mean—"

"That's all right," Gramma Morris came to my rescue. "And it's better this way. We'll teach you to cook fish without having to un-teach you any of Mary's tricks."

And so I learned how to make batter and dip the fish and put it in the pan for frying. After three tries, I even learned how to not get burned while cooking it. The completed fish fillets were placed in a platter and served along with a bowl of reheated rice and beans.

When I looked at the table, it was already set by Michelle and the other children were seated at their places, waiting patiently, whispering quietly.

They sure have their routines down.

This was my first meal in my home with my new family. And it ended up being a disaster.

The food tasted great, but after the spicy gravy that morning and all the tastes of coq au vin, I really wasn't very hungry and my stomach was upset. I tried to get by with a taste of each to be polite, but Mom loaded my plate down with pounds and pounds of food, or so it seemed. She and Gramma Morris made it clear I was to eat it all.

Luckily for me, Dad was an ally.

"Leave her alone. It's all new to her. The food, the water, the time, the people, the smells, and she's nervous for some reason. If she doesn't want to eat, spread her dinner around to everyone else."

"Paul," Mom scolded, "can't you see how small and skinny she is? It's winter and she needs food."

"I know you have good intentions, but you don't want her to get sick. Remember, her parents are smallish people. She's bound to be the smallest girl here."

"Paul," it was a spoken word, but it sounded like a bullet. "Michael Collins was not smallish."

He shrugged in defeat. "Well, he was shorter than me."

"She'll get sick if she doesn't eat."

I was the topic of conversation for the adults during dinner while the children talked about school, friends and interesting things that I couldn't quite hear.

I'd get sick if I did eat. I'd get sick if I didn't eat. Dad was the one who was right. The grease from the fried fish and the spices from the rice dish were very stomach-unfriendly.

But the final word was for me to continue eating, so I picked at my plate for a while more. The other kids were all somewhere else listening to the battery-operated radio when Mom finally said I could leave. I could tell she was frustrated with me. But she had other worries.

"Anna Marie," she called, "have you started your homework?"

There was no answer, but Anna Marie silently dawdled her way into the kitchen carrying a math textbook and some paper. She pulled out a chair, plopped down and opened the book with dread.

"Did you even start?"

Anna Marie shook her head miserably.

"What did you do while we were at the café waiting for Uncle Vincent?"

"Thinking about how much I hate math."

"Clever. Table. Homework. Pencil. Now."

With a put-upon sigh, Anna Marie loaded the table with her schoolwork. The way she walked to her chair made me think of Marie Antoinette being marched to the Guillotine.

"Michelle," she called out, "show Amy around the yard, please."

"It's dark. And cold," she protested.

"Thank you for keeping me informed. Now do what I say, please."

Michelle materialized beside me, shoes on and buttoning up a threadbare cloth coat, a lantern in her hand. I retrieved my jacket and we found the backdoor and the night. There was a tiny sliver of a moon and bright blue stars twinkling overhead, but the dark swallowed the lamp's light with ease. There was nothing to see except night, so I didn't know what there was to show. It would soon be obvious.

The ground had a slight downward slope as she turned left and headed to the side. Cement stepping-stones lined the way reflecting the pale moonlight on their white surfaces. After two dozen steps, I could see the building ahead. It was sturdy and rested on a concrete slab with a couple of stairs leading to the door. The necessary room. Outhouse. Latrine.

"Always take a lantern with you out here at night. If you see anything in the grass, stay away. Also, you'll want to see when you're in the privy here."

She opened the door and shined the lantern for me, showing a surprisingly modern toilet, complete with real toilet paper. I was expecting a catalog. The water tank was over the bowl so gravity would help with the disposal, just like New York, only better as I would only share it with one family—my family. And there was a functional sink with a water faucet for washing up.

"This one's for the girls. There's another one on the other side for the boys. That's Papa, Jason, and Jeremy when he's home. You haven't met him yet. He's eighteen and works on the boats. Two weeks on and one week off. We can use theirs when we have a line, as long as it's empty.

"Papa was going to make us a proper indoor bathroom on the other side of the kitchen, but Gramma Morris had him put it out here. She didn't think it was sanitary to go inside the house."

She shivered a little and stepped beyond the little building. I followed her to the edge of a pond. The water appeared black and menacing in the tiny light.

"That's where Papa caught the fish." She pointed left. "That's the grove where we have pecan trees. When Papa lost his leg, he couldn't rightly farm anymore, so we get a harvest of nuts every year." She pointed in the other direction. "And over there are the chicken sheds. We have two farmhands, Huck and Porky. They take care of the chickens and the pecan trees and keeping the place up. Mama doesn't like them near the house though. She calls them when she needs them. She says they make her nervous.

"The land rises up on the other side of the pond. It's okay to walk around in winter but stay out of that forest in summer. Snakes everywhere. And mosquitoes. The kind that get you sick. Just beyond the rise is the Riviere de Mal Morte. The Malmort for short. Gramma Morris has a story about it. You can ask her about it sometime.

"Lat's go back in. It's really cold out here."

We went back inside, but I came right back out, as my stomach had the final word on my meal. It wasn't staying down. And what had advanced too far down to be thrown up demanded immediate release as well. I spent nearly an hour in the outhouse purging my family's good intentions.

Holly came out to check on me and reported back that I was deathly ill and may be dying. Even at six, she had a flair for melodrama. Gramma Morris came out to see what was really going on and half-dragged, half-supported me indoors. I was given doses of some noxious tasting medicine, obviously designed to poison the illness *and my mouth.* A saltwater gargle completed the torture.

I was then exiled to the hearth to warm up in one of the chairs. A blanket was thrown over me and a cup of hot tea with sweet cream and honey put in my hand. A lamp was put on a homemade table behind me and my copy of *Rebecca of Sunnybrook Farm* materialized in my hand.

Wow, this is almost worth being sick.

Dad was listening to the radio and talking softly to Mom. The stock market crash was now being called a depression. Business was bad and it was going to get worse. I gathered we were lucky (depending on how one defines the word) because we were poor. We had no money in the bank to lose, we grew most of our food, and best of all, we had no mortgage. We may not thrive, but we would survive.

Michelle was playing the piano. Torturing it actually. The tormented cries of agony it made could hardly be called music. She rarely hit a right note, and when she did, I'm sure it was by accident, all the while hitting two keys to create a cacophony of noise that even the denizens of hell would describe as cruel and unusual punishment. She was either playing *Amazing Grace* or *Dixie,* I couldn't really tell, but Jason sat next to her wide eyed. He occasionally made comments like, "You're the best pee-no player ever." I concluded that musical taste is not innate but learned.

Over by the table, Holly was pestering Anna Marie to read to her. She had a book and it looked thick and awkward in her tiny hands. I heard 'please?' and 'no' quite a few times, with more anger creeping into the tone of the no's.

"That evil woman gave me pages and pages of math homework just to ruin my night. And it's all this multiplication garbage that serves no purpose and it's hard."

The two older women settled her down and stayed with her while Holly hovered in the background waiting for her story time.

Finally, I called over to Holly, "What are you reading?"

"The Wizard of Oz." She trotted over to my chair with her treasured storybook.

"I love that book," I said with false enthusiasm. "I read it a few times and I saw the movie five years ago when it came out."

Which was true enough. I remembered thinking at the time that the only thing the book and 1925 movie version had in common was the title. The movie was also too scary for a six-year-old. I really didn't like it very much, but I didn't want to seem critical, so I let it drop.

"Really?" she asked.

I nodded.

"Where are you at in the book? I can read it for you tonight, since your sister has homework."

"Just start it over," she replied, obviously knowing how to capitalize on a good thing.

I opened the book to the first page and showed her the picture and began reading, making sure to adjust the octaves of my voice or to affect an accent so every character voice had a unique sound. Soon enough, she was snuggled in the chair next to me, hanging on to every word. By the time we got to chapter two, Jason was on my other side, the radio was off, and the piano was mercifully silent. When I glanced up, the whole family had gathered around to listen.

My throat was sore from the earlier vomiting and when I pointed to my empty teacup for Holly to fill, Michelle took care of it. Three chapters later, it was bedtime. The door opened, letting in a gale force wind and Annette walked in with a young man who had to be her boyfriend. He was taller than her but much smaller than Paul. He had brown eyes and dark hair cut short. He wore faded overalls and carried a straw hat in his hand. Although he had all the required facial parts, none of them carried distinction. He wasn't handsome or ugly. All I could say is he just was.

"Oh good, you're still up," Annette said to me. "This is my new sister I told you about. Amy, this is Guy Thomas. He took me home from the café so Uncle Vincent could stay home tonight. He lives down the road a ways."

I started to get up, but Mom ordered me to stay seated.

"Amy is a bit under the weather," she explained. "All the change and the new food really was too much for her."

Guy seemed to understand. He smiled a shy sort of smile and said 'hi' to me. He and Annette started to whisper a little and then she announced Guy was going home and she would walk him to his car.

"Your Papa can do that," Gramma Morris said sharply, an amused twinkle in her eyes. "He can even give him tips on how to park without losing his car and needing someone to walk him to it."

They both blushed, him with embarrassment, her in anger. They marched through the door and down the steps, letting the screen slam hard against the frame.

"Now Amy," Mom told me, "I got you a toothbrush the other day. I didn't know if you brought yours down or not. Might as well start with fresh things, I say. You can use the kitchen sink. It's easier. I was going to have you sleep upstairs with Holly and Anna Marie, but I want you down here in case you need to use the facilities. We'll put a couple of extra logs on the fire and I got out some bedclothes for the couch. Anna Marie will show you the room and you can get your nightgown on up there."

Anna Marie, who must have defeated the homework demon, silently guided me to what was going to be our room upstairs. A double bed hung off the floor surrounded by a bookshelf, chest of drawers, and dresser, lightly covered in toys, dolls, and a couple of children's puzzles. A small butane heater was on the floor with its gas line disappearing into the wall just next to the door. No pictures hung on the walls. No decorations of any kind, other than a small accumulation of dust at the threshold. I changed into my flannel nightgown and returned downstairs.

A threadbare sheet and a couple of blankets now covered the couch waiting for my return. Michelle added a few more logs on the fire before she retired for the night. The extra fuel added warmth, light and cheer to the dreary room. Annette returned and went straight upstairs after whispering 'Good night,' to me. The cold she let in made me shiver for a second. A southern winter may be nicer than a northern winter, but it was still winter.

Only Mom was left by now. She spread the blankets and sheets over the sofa for me and kissed my forehead goodnight, pulling me by the shoulders to arm's length to look me in the eyes.

"Feel better. Tomorrow, we'll go see Dr. Gannon. I love you and I love having you here with me. By the way, I set out our old chamber pot next to the couch in case you need it." She pointed to an ugly, discolored crock near my feet. "It'll be too cold to go outside."

"Okay," but I thought about it for a second. "Michelle said that Dad was going to build the latrine into the house but didn't because it's unsanitary. Why would anyone think that?"

She sighed.

"Some questions have no answer."

Life was going to be different in the country.

CHAPTER 10

THE FIRST DAY

It was dark when I woke up for maybe the fourth time. Although it was nice to have the pot close by in case I needed it, I used the outhouse instead. I was as quiet as a mouse and nobody could possibly hear me step out and back. This time I could hear soft whispering, so I knew other people were getting up. I had time to use the flush toilet so I quickly dressed and headed out to avoid any lines that might form.

Enough light shone through the tall pines for me to see the chicken sheds. I saw water from the pond lapping around the edges. It made a spooky sort of sound that I found somewhat unnerving. But I just went straight to the latrine and back, feeling a sense of relief when I was back in the warm house.

"Oh, I thought you'd still be asleep," Mom greeted me from the kitchen. "Why didn't you just use the pot?"

"I thought it'd be less messy to use the flush toilet."

"Makes sense," she agreed. "Gramma Morris and Paul are up. We only beat you by half an hour. They're taking the wagon to the café with supplies. Just some eggs, and a couple of plucked chickens. Then Paul goes on down to the river to fish and crab."

"Crab?"

"He sits in the boat and drops little nets that sink to the bottom and he lifts them up every so often to see if he got a crab."

"Really? If we were in New York, my Papa could make a betting game and lay odds on his catch."

She appeared horrified and for a moment she was speechless.

"We don't play games like that down here," she said slowly. "And please don't ever talk about betting games or odds or gambling to anyone ever again. Down here, gambling is a vice to be overcome, not a game to enjoy.

"Now grab a few eggs and we'll make breakfast."

What she called breakfast would be a feast anywhere else. Pork chops breaded and fried in lard with scrambled eggs and toast and jam. At the first sizzle of meat cooking, I could hear thumping from upstairs. Obviously, cooking food replaced alarm clocks down here.

Jason was down first. He rushed through the kitchen with a quick 'hello' and headed outside.

"Paul," Mom yelled out.

"Got it," came his loud reply.

"He still needs help," she explained to me.

I already figured that out, having my own little brother, who I was beginning to miss already.

The girls all tumbled down and headed out. Holly stopped long enough to hug her mother and then me.

"Are you going to read to me tonight?"

I looked at Mom for help, but none was coming.

"Well, I can, but wouldn't Anna Marie feel bad if I came in and just took over her job? We wouldn't want to hurt her feelings. But if she prefers to have a rest from it, I would love to."

Mom smiled brightly while she deftly flipped the chops. Somehow, I must have passed a test of some kind. Holly ran off when Jason came back in. A glance out the window showed both sides of the outhouse were in use. Soon the meal would be ready. The pork chops, being small, were finished and Anna Marie had plates scattered on the table and was laying down forks. I cracked the eggs and mixed them for their heating. Gramma Morris and Dad were in by now, washing up while the meals were dished out.

Breakfast was different. All the plates were filled by Paul and Gramma except mine.

"The girl needs to eat," Mom argued.

"You said that last night," Dad pointed out. "She might not be hungry, like last night."

"Maybe a piece of toast?" I contributed.

"Toast? That's all?" Gramma Morris harumphed, "If you're going to go on a hunger strike, have a cause. I don't want to see you waste away to nothingness."

Dad pointed out, "Vincent won't want her to throw up in his car."

While the debate raged, the chops and eggs slowly vanished. All that was left was a half piece of toast. I managed to secure it in my hand and took a bite.

"Debate over," Dad laughed. "All the food's gone now anyway. There's no time to cook anymore, and we have to get going. The girls have school you know."

The two older women glared at him darkly but knew defeat when they saw it. Gramma Morris took Anna Marie to the fireplace and started to arrange her hair while Mom helped Jason get ready for his babysitter. Annette and Michelle washed the dishes. I had nothing to do so I stepped out on the porch with Dad.

He had lit up a corn cob pipe and was quietly smoking

while the family noises sounded behind us. The green grass spinked with frost seemed to fascinate him.

"Different down here," he said. I couldn't tell if it was a question or statement.

"It really is."

"You'll be fine. I already get that you're useful. And smart. Just make the adjustments you need as fast as you can. And don't forget, we're here to help."

He turned towards the door. "Hey, Louisa. It's 6:30," he called out.

He turned to me. "The restaurant opens at six o'clock. Cici should have enough eggs to get started, but she'll need more. The mill shift starts at eight and we better get there or they will find somewhere else to eat."

Gramma Morris stepped out, dressed to go in her winter coat.

"Your first name is Louisa?" I asked innocently, having never heard anyone call her that before.

"To some," she replied tartly. "To you, it's Gramma Morris."

They each gave me a quick hug and off they went. A couple of wagon lanterns were lit up and they slowly moved down the driveway to the road. I watched them as the lanterns faded and the sun started to turn the dark night into purple dawn.

I went back inside to find the other children dressed, washed, brushed clean and bright, ready to face another day. Anna Marie explained their routine to me, which was a surprise since she was the least friendly so far.

"It used to be that we walked down the driveway to Lasalle Road and turned right and went over the bridge to New Paris Road to Faucette Street, but the bridge over Faucette Creek washed away. The creek was too deep. The winter was too cold. The water was too wet."

Makes sense.

"But fortune smiled on us, at least for now. The railroad agreed to stop for us and take us to the station. It would be easier if they let us walk over the railroad bridge, but they really don't want that and will charge us with trespassing if they catch us."

"I remember the train stopped right before Faucette and I heard a lot of children," I said.

"That was us and the other children who live west of the creek. You should have said 'hi' or something. We didn't even know you were there."

"Well," I looked down, "I didn't know you then."

"How do you get to know people if you don't talk to them?"

Some questions have no answer.

And they were gone. I got a hug from Holly as they left for their learning adventure. I rather wished I was going along with them which reminded me of an old quote from Mrs. Carnahan: Be careful what you wish for. It may come true.

I would soon learn how true that was.

CHAPTER 11

GOING TO TOWN

Mom had unpacked my clothes and frowned at me.

"Is this all you took?"

I nodded; afraid I was in trouble.

"One skirt, one blouse, one nightgown, and some rag that used to be a dress?"

"I brought underwear," I defended.

She rolled her eyes.

"This is too small for you. This skirt has seen better days. This blouse is close to the ragbag. You can't go out in public only in underpants. Didn't Mary help you pack?"

"Well, not really. She just told me to."

"And this is the best you could do?"

That stung. I was close to tears. "Well, I didn't know what to bring."

She sighed, "I'll see if there's anything Anna Marie outgrew we can get for you. We can't worry about it now. Change into your blouse and skirt."

Once that was done, Mom, Jason and I walked to the road, heading in the opposite direction from the children's path. After a few hundred yards, we came to another driveway and followed it to a farmhouse similar to our home. The model T pickup was parked by the side and

Uncle Vincent was just getting in. He saw us and smiled a greeting. A woman stood beside him and waved to us. Jason ran over to hug her.

"Auntie Sharon," he cried out, "we have a new sister."

"I heard, Jason," she said with a smile. She hugged me tight when I was close enough.

"I'm your Aunt Sharon, dear," she said sweetly. "And if you need anything from me to help you adjust down here, you let me know. Family makes life better for family."

"Thank you," I said with a curtsy, but my shoe found an unexpected depression in the grass and I gracefully rescued myself by grabbing hold of the car. They all laughed.

"They should have named you Grace," Uncle Vincent said.

I scowled at him.

Jason was deposited with Aunt Sharon for the day and the three of us headed north down Lasalle Road (not that I knew this; Uncle Vincent mentioned it). The trail led over the railroad tracks into a forest. Tall, majestic pine trees towered over us and crowded the road. Even with the windows closed, I could smell the pine scent and loved it. I was only here a day, and already knew I found home. Soon the trees dissolved into a lush meadow on the left, while the forest continued tall on the right.

We drove for quite a long way and came to a stop sign at Forest Road. It headed to what suspiciously seemed like nowhere in both directions. We continued to where the road forked a few miles down and headed right, through even more densely packed forest. The left side was downright spooky, with trees covered in what they told me was Spanish Moss. It grew in large clumps of gray netting and intimidated trespassers by invoking images of ghosts or worse.

Lasalle Street ended at State Highway 188. There was some traffic here, though not much. We turned right and drove a few miles down through more forest, though I could see water on both sides of the shoulder. We drove over the creek and continued until we reached Thomas Road and turned south.

"Isn't this the road that goes by the train station?" I asked.

"Good observation," Uncle Vincent remarked. "A few miles down there'll be houses, then the doctor's office. Down further, River Road, and from there, the café, and from there, food."

I was still unimpressed with his sense of humor.

After a bit, the forest thinned out dramatically, exposing lush green meadows. The frost had faded away and the leftover dew sparkled like diamonds in the morning sun. It was like a fantasyland.

Smoke escaped from several chimneys on a magnificent three-story mansion. It was a somber gray with dark blue shutters and wood shingles, with over a dozen windows of various sizes reflecting morning sunlight. This was by far the largest house I ever saw in my life. A carpet of perfectly trimmed grass ran to the road, while a paved driveway led around to the hidden back.

I stared in awe, jaw agape.

"If you don't close that mouth, a fly can get in. And you just don't know where that fly's been," Uncle Vincent warned.

"Wow," I said, ignoring his humor.

"That's the Thomas House," Mom said. "It's the biggest house in the parish."

"Parish?"

"Louisiana doesn't have counties," she explained. "We're broken down into parishes. We live in St. Columba Parish. After the Civil War, Morgan Thomas married into the wealthier side of the family and from that beginning they became the richest family in the parish. He was a carpetbagger from the north, appointed by the Yankee governor to help keep order in these parts.

"The next house you see belongs to the most…eccentric lady I ever met. They call her the countess."

"Does she ride in an old-fashioned carriage like Cinderella?"

"That she does. She doesn't like automobiles. She thinks they're too loud, fast and smelly."

"I saw her when I arrived, riding in it. It was so keen. Like it just pulled free from a storybook and transported itself into reality."

Uncle Vincent chuckled. "Land, the way you talk. You are so…" a pause while he searched for a word, "educated."

Her house was obviously the next one. White columns rose from the ground, blanketed in what I thought was ivy but in reality, was wisteria. Dark windows scowled at the street and the yard with large clumps of clover standing high above the unevenly trimmed grass. But it was such a wonderful house. Shake shingles that looked like vanilla wafers covered the two-story mansion and brown paint faded from sunlight gleamed like slightly melted chocolate.

"I bet that looks like Cinderella's house too. A house that looks like gingerbread and cookies, just waiting for some unsuspecting children to wander in for dinner," Uncle Vincent remarked, showing off his total ignorance of perfectly good fairy tales.

"Same book of stories, anyway," I replied politely.

There were other stately mansions all down the road, some larger than the countess's home but none quite as enchanting.

"Is she really a countess?"

"No," Mom replied. "France executed all their nobility in the Revolution and we don't have such things in America. She married into the De Pilord family. Originally, they were rum runners from New England, but something happened and the family came here and started a sugar plantation."

The magical house faded into the background to be replaced by another antebellum mansion. This home was even more elegant than the countess's but lacked the fairytale charm.

"Eventually, one of his daughters married into the Landacre line and their family merged with ours. A couple of generations later, their descendants hired a young woman as governess for their children. She eventually married the oldest son and became the next countess, although back then, she thought the title was silly. She refers to herself as Mrs. De Pilord, which is sensible enough, but folks round here still call her the countess."

Another crossroad loomed up ahead with a quaint wooden sign announcing it as Main Street. The first building was a non-descript, one story, wooden structure with a green tin roof. Uncle Vincent stopped in front of it and Mom nudged me out of the truck.

We walked up a couple of wooden steps and I saw a shingle swaying from the vibrations of our movements. I recognized the name: DR. NOAH GANNON.

Mom opened the door and we walked into a waiting room that smelled of medicine. We apparently were the first patients of the day and a pleasant woman smiled at us. It turns out she was Dr. Gannon's receptionist, who served double duty by being his wife. She ushered us into an examination room.

This resembled something out of a mad scientist movie set. A stark table of wood and a stool. A cabinet filled with medicines and chemicals with frighteningly long names. Bandages, wraps and gauze pads were in the next cabinet. And the worst of all were these little tools that lurked next to the bandages that obviously belonged in a medieval torture chamber. An ancient clock hung sadly on the wall dutifully ticking off the seconds.

Dr. Gannon bounded in with a quick smile and set me on the table with ease. Soon, a bitter tasting thermometer was in my mouth and a cold stethoscope on my breastbone. He thumped, pinched, twisted, and poked. He hit my knees with a little hammer and asked me questions about New York—what I ate, what exercise I got, sleeping habits, and other things I'd rather not discuss. After he was done, he smiled at me and let me readjust my clothes.

"Do you want the short diagnosis or long one?" he asked Mom.

"The short one, please."

"You're feeding her." He started filling out a chart commemorating my visit.

The clock ticked six times before I heard Mom say (through clenched teeth), "What's the long one?"

"You're giving her real food with spices and peppers. Her diet in New York was serviceable. It kept her alive, but it was all boiled meat, potatoes, cabbage, and carrots. What passes for gravy up there is criminal. Black pepper and salt were the only seasonings. It changed a little bit to boiled pasta and tomatoes with garlic. You're giving her spicy food with rich gravy, fried fish, and red beans and rice with hot sausage. Her system rebelled. She can't eat that stuff yet, but you're making her eat it anyway. Of course, she got sick. Give her toast, oatmeal or boiled rice for the rest of today. All she can eat. No bacon, sausage or gravy. Tomorrow, she can have a biscuit, if she wants, with a teaspoon of gravy for breakfast and rice with a tiny bit of sauce for lunch and dinner. A little more regular food each day and by Sunday, she can eat real food, like what people eat."

Then he said to me, "By Sunday, you'll be sneering at boiled dinners. You'll wish you never tasted them."

Good prediction. I never liked them anyway.

"Your height and weight are just fine. You're just smallish. But that's natural. Your parents were smallish and your Mama here is comparing you to the Villians. They're big people."

"My New York father was tall. He was as tall as Dad."

The doctor shot a dark look at Mom and sighed.

"When you're young, you think the adults in your life are giants. Michael Collins was taller than average, but Paul Villians is just as tall and bigger around. Way more muscle. And then you have your petite mother here. That's that. If you enter a tallest woman contest, you'll forever be disappointed."

I was sent out to the waiting room while Mom and the doctor talked some more. He recommended that she start her privacy, which meant she should stay home until the baby is born. It was supposed to keep her off her feet and many women didn't want to be seen with their bellies extended outwards. A secondary reason was to keep the mother as quiet as possible and to limit her exertions. I remember that Aunt Mary went through privacy went she carried Patrick.

I was pleasantly surprised that so many people called Mom my mother instead of my aunt. Usually, people can be determined to thwart basic wishes in the name of total honesty.

We soon left his office and she made me admit the visit was not so bad. As far as I could remember, it was my first visit to a doctor. Papa Michael, as I was beginning to call Michael Collins, had the theory that visiting doctors was unhealthy because of all the sick people. Julia and Patrick went once a year, but he saw no need for me to see one.

I took a quick look at the town center. Dr. Gannon's office was on the northwest corner next to a dilapidated building that housed a dentist. A fabric and seamstress shop was next to it. Visible in the distance was a movie house that appeared like it would fall over any minute now. A bridge was beyond it.

Mom said, "That's the Atchafalaya River over there. It sort of marks the end of town, but folks on the other side still think of themselves of Faucette citizens. So do we. The town just never incorporated that land into city limits.

"The land here is like a peninsula between the Atchafalaya and Malmort Rivers. Goes all the way south to where the rivers join. The swamp is too dense for people to live in after that."

Across the street was the gas station and post office building. Two rusty pumps stood in a bed of asphalt with corpses of last year's weeds between the cracks. Two bays stood empty with the doors open, hoping for business. A few men were out talking. They watched us go our way with a kind of sinister curiosity. That man I saw at the train station was with them, his gray fedora pulled down over his eyes, like he was hiding his face from us.

Across the street stood a three-story building with

officious letters announcing: FAUCETTE CITY HALL. It was the offices, courtrooms, meeting places, and conference rooms for the whole parish. It also had a small chamber that was lent out to the phone company for their operators to use.

And right across the street was the sheriff's office. A cardboard sign was taped to the window: *Out on official business. Be back soon.* This was certainly not New York.

We continued down Thomas Road where I eventually saw the railroad tracks and knew where we were. A few steps more and a turn and we were at the restaurant. Thrushy was out front sweeping the sidewalk and picking up large cabbage leaves.

"Delivery this morning," he said quietly. "Finchy keeps forgetting to pick up the spills and things. If these leaves get wet, they get slippery and folks could fall over."

"And we appreciate your efforts," Mom said to him absent-mindedly as we walked into the café.

Dad was at the counter, perched on a stool with his wooden leg planted firmly on the floor for balance. He was engaged in conversation with a deputy. Mom strode over to join Cici in the kitchen and they started talking.

"Come back here, sweet pea," Cici called to me. "I'm going to start a biscuit for you, but I got a little chore for you to do first. These clean plates and tableware need to go up front under the counter right by where your pa is talking to Depjim."

"Depjim? What kind of name is that?"

"Well, it's sensible. He's a deputy and his name is Jim. Depjim. So many people here named James or Jim, we need something to tell them apart. Wait'll you start counting all the Cathys."

She gave me a cart of clean plates, bowls and glasses. I

was able to see where they were supposed to go and wheeled the cart up front and started working. I was close enough to the deputy and Dad to hear their conversation.

"It's a matter of respect, Depjim. He made that little girl stand outside in the cold just to be mean-spirited and petty. He knows she's my family and I won't tolerate that. He needed a lesson and I needed to teach it. That's all. It's not like I *really* hurt him. Just his pride."

The deputy, a handsome young man of maybe twenty-one with cold blue eyes and a Valentino mustache, stood a solid half foot shorter and about ninety pounds lighter than Dad and stared back at him in disbelief.

"Paul, you reached through the bars of the ticket booth, grabbed his shirt and yanked him into the cage iron so hard it cut his cheek. Then you did it again to give him a nosebleed. Just because you didn't kill him, doesn't mean you didn't hurt him. And not just his pride.

"Now, there's a lot of things about my job I just don't like. Following up on a complaint like this is high on the list. Especially an issue between you two. I mean, you couldn't solve this peacefully? Think of me for a minute. Do you think it makes my job easier? Did you really have to hit him twice?"

"Well, no. But it was so much fun the first time I couldn't resist the next one," Dad said with a smile.

Depjim sighed. "Paul, I don't understand it. You and the Kakers were friends at one time. You rode together. Hunted together. Broke laws together, though I'm not here to discuss that. You went to war together. He was the lieutenant you served under."

Broke laws together?

"That's the problem. He was a snitch. Walked around with a little notebook writing down every rule infraction he could find. Wanted to make captain without fighting. And he thought he could snitch his way to the top. I'd have made Sergeant if it wasn't for him writing all the infractions. More money for my family."

"Could you have just not made the infractions in the first place and made Sergeant that way?"

"Not when I was that age."

Depjim shook his head, bemused.

"The army could have given me a lot more support, you know. I lost my leg in battle."

"I heard you lost it when your illegal still exploded."

Dad pulled back a sleeve, showing off a viscous scar that ran across his forearm. "*That* was from the illegal still. The leg was from the battlefield. The guy next to me stepped on a mine and I got the flak. Surgeons decided it was easier to cut it off than save it. Regardless, that little girl is my family. He wants to treat her like that, I'll treat him like *that*."

Depjim sighed and shook his head again. It was then that he saw me so close. Whatever else he was going to say died on his lips as he glanced down at me with those menacing blue eyes.

"And are you listening in on this conversation, young lady?" he groused at me.

Well, of course. Obviously, they were talking about me and of course I would want to know what they were saying.

"Well, not intentionally. I was putting dishes away. I could look away while you talk but I couldn't hear away."

I wished I had more time to think about my reply. That really wasn't one of my better efforts.

"I suppose not," he said dryly, then to Paul, "Is this our new resident?"

"That she is. Miss Amy Collins, meet Deputy Jim Walker. We call him Depjim for short."

I stood up and curtsied. This one might have been perfect, but I was too close to the counter and banged my knee on the shelf with a loud whapping noise. Depjim winced at the cracking sound, but it was more loud than painful. Two unkempt young men I hadn't noticed before were a few seats down the counter drinking coffee and did not hesitate to laugh at my discomfort.

"Hush now," Gramma Morris scolded. "Amy, these boys are Doug and Scott Tanner, my great nephews. By marriage, of course."

'By marriage' obviously meant they weren't really family.

"They drive the trucks from The Landacre Lumber Mill to the rail station."

I didn't bother to curtsy to them as they appeared dirty, unshaven and hungover (a look I had seen on the Giraffe). Besides, they laughed at me. How much respect did they deserve?

"Hi, Amy," Doug said pleasantly enough and then went back to his coffee.

"Hey, little lady," Scott leered. "Come visit me in a few years. I'll make sure you never get lonely."

Doug snickered loudly at that remark. I was embarrassed to no end and escaped to the kitchen while Gramma Morris whapped the counter with her hand.

"Now you see here, Scott Walker Tanner. If that was supposed to be funny, it failed. If it was supposed to be vulgar and low class, it worked."

"Just joking around, Aunt Louisa," he said, his eyes down.

"Joke around at work. Some trees are just dying to meet you."

They were finished anyway and tossed some coins on the counter and walked out.

"And come back tomorrow. The lesson in manners is free."

Cici smiled, "Amy, I have your biscuit here."

I zoomed to the table, where a cloud of absolute taste sensation was waiting for my attention, steaming hot on a plate. But wait, no sauce.

"Um, Cici? The doctor said I could have a spoonful of the gravy with my biscuit." I hopefully held up the largest serving ladle I could find to help her.

"The doctor said a teaspoon," Mom said firmly. She produced a tiny little spoon you'd need a microscope to see.

The gravy was spread evenly across the biscuit like butter. No sausage chunks. But still, it was a better meal than anything I ever got in New York.

CHAPTER 12

NEW FRIENDS AND A NEW STORY

When breakfast was done, I went back and finished putting away dishes. Dad and Depjim were gone. Gramma Morris was at the counter reading the day's newspaper, while two customers were at the breakfast bar, munching on their orders. A loud airhorn blasted from the back and I looked up to see what was going on.

"Go on out back," Gramma Morris said. "See what they want."

I obeyed, not knowing what to expect. The back door was propped open to let the cold air mingle with the hot kitchen and I saw a houseboat on the creek.

It wasn't very large, so it was obviously shallow enough to stay afloat. It was moored near the general store. Thrushy and Finchy were tying the lines on a small cement landing I hadn't noticed before. It was complete with posts, called piles. A small gangplank was already connecting the boat to the landing and two not quite elderly women were cautiously inching their way to the solid earth. They were both heavyset with hair set in loose buns.

I thought they might be twins, they looked so much alike with the same heavyset build and facial features. The only difference was in their clothes. One wore a gray full-length dress with a white bodice and cross shaped pendant and a happy smile, while the other opted for a dark blue print and a pearl necklace and seemed annoyed.

"Those are the Farley sisters," Cici said from behind me. "Don't know why anyone calls them that. They ain't sisters and their names ain't Farley."

"That's kind of unusual. And one wears a cross. The other looks cross," I observed, enjoying the pun.

"Word of advice. That sort of thing may sound clever in New York, but it'll just get you in trouble down here."

Once the two women were assured of their footing, they glanced around and waved when they saw us. Cici waved back so I followed suit. The one with the pendant pointed towards the general store then stuck out five fingers and pointed to Cici. Cici flashed an okay sign and nodded with an exaggerated smile.

"What did that mean?"

"They're going to load up on supplies and stop by for lunch in five minutes. You'll get it. You just have to learn to speak southern."

That was speaking?

I finished up the dishes and gathered the dirty ones the customers left to bring to Cici. When the counter was cleaned and dry, the women came in.

"Well, Helen and Reba," Gramma Morris welcomed, "It's been too long. Have a seat."

They hugged and fake kissed while Mom endured the same ritual.

"We can't stay long," Helen, the pleasant looking one said. "We just have to load up on supplies and be on our way. We have a load of formula to bring down to friends in New Orleans."

"Oh dear, the formula," Mom's voice hardened a bit,

"Amy, come here please. I want you to meet our dear friends, the Farley sisters."

I walked over and started to curtsy, but Gramma Morris grabbed my shoulders. I looked around at her and she said, "Now."

I curtsied perfectly with her support.

"You are so pretty," Helen said. "You look just like your mother did at that age. You know, we were there when she was born all those years ago. 1904 I believe."

"1902, ma'am," I said automatically. "My Aunt Cassie was born in 1904."

Both Farley sisters seemed confused.

"1904? Isn't that right? I don't understand," Helen sputtered to Reba.

Gramma Morris suggested that we go get some coffee while Mom entertained them. Back behind the counter, she whispered to me, "Never contradict your elders. See her now? She's all confused over nothing."

"But 1904 is—"

"Listen," she said in a this-is-final tone, "if she forgets to put on a dress, you tell her. If she gets a decades old birth date wrong, let it go. Adds nothing to the conversation."

Back to the table with the cups, saucers and coffee pot. I gracefully placed them down without making any noise and Gramma Morris filled the cups. I took a deep breath of the forbidden black brew.

"You like the smell of coffee?" Reba asked me.

"I do. My Papa, my real Papa used to take me to a diner in the city all the time and we'd get a cup."

"Your real father being Michael Collins?"

"Yes, ma'am."

"Then your…Aunt Mary didn't make coffee?"

"She did. But she wouldn't let me drink it until I'm

thirteen. That's why my Papa and I went out for it. Besides, he didn't like her coffee."

"Oh? Why not?"

"He said he didn't like chewing coffee."

I thought I saw the twitch of a smile. The other women studiously looked everywhere but at each other.

"I can't say that I blame him," she said dryly. "I hope you learn how to make coffee better than that. Learn to make it like this. I can taste the pride your grandmother puts in this."

"Yes, ma'am."

As good a response as any.

"And by the way," she continued, "Some girls can be very…difficult to be around, whether it's here or New York or anywhere. You should kill them with kindness. Make them love you. Turning an enemy into a friend might be a bit more difficult if you smash her face in."

"Yes, ma'am."

"Helen and I were in Vaudeville in our younger days. The Travelling Farley Family. We were surrounded by very mean and selfish people, but we always acted like ladies and always overcame all our torments with words. We never hit. All our other sisters may not have loved us, but they knew better than to vex us."

"You have other sisters?" I asked being polite and feigning interest. The we-never-hit part grated on me, since so far, no one asked why I hit Isabella in the first place.

"There were sixteen of us.,"

"Sixteen? Your mother must have loved children."

She paused.

"We were adopted. The Farleys only had two girls. They hunted down the rest of us from orphanages, poorhouses or families with too many daughters and not enough food.

Taught us to sing and dance and put us on stage. When they died, we all went our separate ways."

We talked a bit more about their careers and life together. They never brought up the hitting incident again and spoke to me as if I were an adult until Thrushy called out from the kitchen that their hardware order was all loaded on the boat. They placed a dollar on the table and hugged and faked kissed again, including me this time.

"The creek's dangerously low nowadays," Helen said before leaving. "I don't know when we'll be up this way again. But when we are, we'll be sure to visit. And I hope to see you again, sweetie."

"Me too," I replied. I decided I liked her after all.

I walked out back with them to say good-bye. They each gave me a quick hug and headed towards their houseboat. As I turned to go back in, I saw the man in the gray fedora watching us from the hardware store. He turned and disappeared around the corner when he saw me glance his way.

"I can't imagine it," Gramma Morris said when I got back inside. "Living like that. That's all they're going to do with their lives is live together on a two-bit houseboat and float up and down swampy rivers. What if they get sick? Or have an accident? Who'll help them? You'd think they'd know better than that."

"What would you have them do?" I asked.

"Find a man, get married, buy a house, make a home, have a family, though it might be too late for that, go to church regularly, and be solid citizens. Instead, they galivant down the rivers and streams, making their cheap whiskey."

"Lots of money in the 'cheap' whiskey," Mom corrected. "Besides, they also make blackberry wine. And they darn sure don't give *that* away either."

"Now, how would you know that?"

"Where do you think we get the wine Cici cooks with?" Mom smiled.

"Oh," there was a long pause, "I guess that explains why the coq au vin doesn't taste the same anymore."

And the conversation went on. They talked about the Farley sisters and their wine, and about coffee. They liked Aunt Mary's rule. No more coffee for me until my thirteenth birthday. We all talked, getting to know each other.

"Michelle told me you have a good story about the river," I said to Gramma Morris. "Will you tell it to me now?"

"The Riviere de Mal Morte?" she was amused.

"I thought it was the Malmort."

"That's its full name. It's French. *Riviere de Mal Morte.*"

"Wow, that sounds so romantic," I gushed while Mom smirked a bit.

"It might be in French, but not so much in English. It means 'The River of Bad Death.'"

"Oh," I was disappointed already.

"Roughly sixty years ago, when I was about your age, I remember my father would always tell us children to never go beyond the top of the hill. The *solid* ground is soft enough to sink in, there are quicksand pits, poisonous snakes and spiders, and it's just a place of disease. Some geologist explorers said the hill is manmade by some ancient native tribe, maybe as a border with another tribe. But my father said it was built to keep in something monstrous.

"Idle superstition of course. But children thrive on legends. And little boys have to impress little girls with their boldness. And little boys don't know the difference between bravery and stupidity. And so, one spring day my sister, Cosette, and I were with my brother, Jed, and his best friend, Jethro. Now, Jethro was sweet on Cosette and at that age he just had to show off.

"So, we went to the top of the hill, through the blackberry vines, which were thick with thorns but thin on berries thanks to those thieving birds, and Jethro challenged us all to a race to the river's edge and back.

"By a three to one vote, the challenge was declined, but he still had to show off. He walked a few feet towards the river, just looking for some reason to be brave. And he found it.

"'Hey, look over there,' he yelled to us. A quiet forest echo followed, 'Over there…over there.'" She quieted her voice on the first echo and was barely more than a whisper on the second.

"We looked but all we saw were pine trees, mud, brambles, stagnant water puddles, and mosquitoes. Lots of mosquitoes.

"'On the ground. Ground…ground.' He ran about thirty feet down and toward the left of us through the dark shade of the thick pines. We didn't know where he was going and weren't about to follow him. Even if we missed the mud and quicksand, and avoided the spiders, what's to keep a hundred snakes from slithering out of the river and turning us into dinner? Not to mention alligators.

"He disappeared behind some trees for a couple of seconds and then returned. He had a reddish stone-looking thing in his hand and an expression of triumph on his face.

"'It's an old Indian arrowhead,' he exclaimed. 'I bet it's ancient. I bet a museum will pay thousands for it.'

"It was definitely an arrowhead. How old it was, I couldn't tell, neither could Jethro, though he wouldn't admit it. We each held and inspected it for a bit. It was still rather sharp, and with the proper honing could be turned into a deadly weapon again.

"'How did you even see it all the way back there?' I asked.

"'It kind of glowed when the sunlight hit it.'"

"I looked at the spot where he got it from. Deep in the shade and dark as night. No sunlight.

"'Good for you,' Cosette told him, 'Now you better put it back.' 'Back…back.'"

That echo surprised me because I didn't think she said it loud enough to create one. In fact, it seemed the echo was louder than her voice.

"'No, I'm going to keep it.'

"No echo replied at all. By now it was obvious that Cosette noticed something wasn't entirely right either. We looked at Jed for help.

"'Put it back, okay?' 'Back…back' 'This is making the girls nervous.'

"Him too, but he was too much of a boy to admit it. Anyway, Jethro was adamant.

"'I will not put it back.' 'Put it back…put it back.' 'I found it.' And in a last-ditch effort to prove it, he yelled loudly in desperation, 'It's mine' 'It's…mine.'

"But this time, it was different, the echo. It wasn't the voice of a child, but a grown man, and the inflection was different. It was confident and quiet, like a patient father explaining something to an excited son. We all turned to look at the river, but it offered us no clue.

"Jethro was angry, but he should have been afraid like the rest of us. We ran as fast as we could to get out of there. After about thirty feet, we all stopped and turned back. Jethro had the arrowhead in hand and threw it as hard as he could in the direction he found it.

"'It's not fair,' he yelled at the swampy air. 'It's fair…it's fair.'

"We all went home after that and stayed inside and quiet. When we went to school the following Monday, we learned Jethro was sick with the Yellow Fever. He recovered after a few weeks, but he was never the same. Always sickly, always melancholy. Said if he ever looked at that river again, it would kill him. Well, the river flooded over the hilltop ten years later in the worst flood ever known hereabouts. Water covered every bit of ground. Good thing the houses were built so high up. Jethro got the fever again and died, just like he said he would."

I am really going to have nightmares.

We talked about the River of Bad Death until the next customer came in, about an hour later. She strode in alone, a determined look about her. It was obvious she was a woman used to being in charge and would tolerate no backtalk. Actually, if I could ignore the tightly sealed thin lips and frowning eyes, she was quite a handsome woman of maybe fifty years. She wore a gray checkered dress with pleats so sharp they looked like deadly weapons. A gray and white wide brimmed hat was pinned tightly on, the pink heads of the hatpins not quite concealed along its sides. Her steely blue eyes circled the room until they found Mom, who stiffened as they made eye contact.

"Good afternoon, Mrs. De Montfort," Mom said to her formally.

"Mrs. Villians," the older woman nodded, "You look well." She glanced down at Mom's swelling belly. "And coming along, I see. I heard you were going to have another blessed event. I am happy for you."

Her tone of voice sounded more angry than happy. I

started to wiggle out of my chair and go to the kitchen to see if Cici needed any help, but that woman's gaze caught me at my first movement. She looked me over, like she was inspecting meat on the hook. My hair, face, blouse, skirt, shoes, and whatever else were quickly noted and disapproved of by her. I tried to hurry out faster, but Mom protectively put an arm over my shoulder.

"Mrs. De Montfort," she said with a haughty air, "My daughter, Amy."

I started to curtsy, but she squeezed me closer to her, so I nodded solemnly to her.

"Daughter or niece?" the older woman said with a raised eyebrow. "You make it hard to keep track."

"My house, my daughter, my rules."

"Amy," Cici called out from the kitchen, "I'm going to poach you some eggs now for lunch."

"Okay," I replied happily. I nodded and started to leave, but Mom held tight and Gramma Morris was blocking the exit.

"She'll be right in," Gramma Morris pronounced.

"Okay, but if she wants to learn about poaching those eggs, she better hurry."

"It's okay if they're not poached," I said helpfully. "My Papa from New York said poaching is against the law in some places."

All the older women laughed at that, even the severe Mrs. De Montfort, though it was clear she would rather be cranky than amused.

"Wrong definition of poaching," Gramma Morris said, tousling my hair.

"It would be the definition that man would give her though," Mrs. De Montfort said with a little disgust, obviously referring to Papa.

Then I remembered several conversations from the past.

"Mom, isn't your and Aunt Mary's maiden name De Montfort?" I turned to her, "Are we all somehow related?"

There was a deadly silence, then Mrs. De Montfort shook her head. "Everyone here shares an ancestor somewhere down the line. But sometimes it's so distant, it doesn't count. Just because we have the same last name doesn't make us family."

"But you will still be polite to her," Gramma Morris said firmly.

"I will," I replied, curious as to why she thought I wouldn't be.

"And I will be to you, my non-family friend," Mrs. De Montfort said to me.

Strange conversation.

"Now Amy," Gramma Morris said, "Mrs. De Montfort is the town librarian and the head of the school board. She was a nurse in the Spanish American War and the Great War. Her husband was a Major and doctor in the army. There's a statue of him in Faucette Park down the way."

She tilted her head to the south, where I hadn't had the opportunity to explore yet. "Faucette Drive curves until it meets Thomas Road. Where they meet is Faucette Park. Statues line the Thomas Road front, while a few cement boat ramps are on Faucette Street, while Thomas Road straggles on for some reason until it ends in a little unincorporated village called Foytville."

"And you never go there for any reason," Mom added. "That's a dangerous place and the only reason I can think of for you to be there is if you're being driven through it for your funeral."

After some discussion, they all agreed that if I were

dead, it would most likely be all right to visit Foytville. Even so, there were better places to go after one dies.

"Amy, your eggs," Cici called out putting a plate on the pass. "I'll teach you poaching later. You need to spend time with your family."

"Poached eggs for lunch?" Mrs. De Montfort looked at me askew for a moment.

"She has a delicate stomach," Mom defended me.

"She was sick all night. Made half a dozen trips to the outhouse. Woke me every time. It's a wonder she didn't trip over the chamber pot she kept jumping over," Gramma Morris added.

I picked up my plate. Two little white blobs on toast. No gravy. No bacon. No butter. I sighed to myself. What good is learning to enjoy tasty food and not being able to eat it? I started to sit at the counter but was motioned over to the table.

"When it's just one customer, you should join us," Mom said, although I didn't think she really meant it.

I dutifully sat at the table, but I already knew I wouldn't enjoy the conversation.

"Why is she a customer?" I asked innocently enough. "She didn't order anything." And then I said to the town librarian, "Are you a family friend?"

"Coffee, please," she replied pleasantly to Gramma Morris. "Black."

She stared at me. Not a hostile stare, but certainly not friendly. She was finalizing her judgement of me. I already failed the appearance test. Now, I was sure I was about to flunk another.

The coffee arrived and she sipped it for a bit looking at me.

"So, you are going to school by Monday?" she asked.

A fair question. She was on the school board, after all. I nodded since I was eating. Cold eggs aren't as good as warm ones.

"Good. I wanted to go over some of the rules down here."

The other women rolled their eyes.

"I think we went over this with her…," Mom started.

"Children need reinforcement. Sometimes, you think you taught them well, the next thing you know, they ruined their lives and made a shambles out of yours. Now, Amy, I only know you by reputation. Not a good one. This is not some jungle like Chicago or New York. This is civilization. You are a pretty young lady and you will behave accordingly. There will be no fighting at school…or home or anywhere else. Young ladies do not provoke or start issues, arguments or disagreements. Is that understood? And they walk away when antagonized."

I nodded. The eggs were gone. They were sort of bland and tasteless. Anyway, I wasn't hungry anymore, and if I was, this conversation would have killed any appetite.

"There will be no back talking or disrespect."

I got away from Aunt Isadora, only to find another version of her.

I nodded again.

"You're done with your food. Please give me a verbal response."

"Yes, ma'am."

"Yes what?"

Yes what? What was the question?

"I'm done with my eggs."

Mom started giggling, while the other women appeared frustrated. I obviously answered the wrong question.

"Are you a young lady who refuses to get in fights and will walk away when provoked?"

"Yes, ma'am."

"Yes, ma'am what?"

Stumped again.

She sighed out, "Yes, ma'am, I will avoid fights at all times."

I dutifully repeated it, hoping we were done. But we weren't.

"Just remember this: Women are the foundation of society. Good men respect us because they know that little fact, although you'll never find one who'll admit it. But you have to earn that respect and maintain it. Because once it's lost, it's gone forever.

"And when respect is gone, civilization crumbles. It'll be chaos and pandemonium. People fighting over anything. Killing and murdering each other in the streets. It'll be like New York or Chicago. And we won't have you bringing in that kind of Sodom and Gomorrah down here."

"No, ma'am."

"Well," she said with a now-that's-done tone, "I have to get back to the library. I closed it long enough to meet our new citizen." To me now, "And Amy? I hear you're quite the reader. *Rebecca of Sunnybrook Farms* was one of my favorites when I was your age. Good choice. I want to see you at the library at least once a week. There are worlds to explore in literature. I won't have you miss any of them."

"Mrs. Villians, you should take her."

"I would, but I'm starting privacy next week."

The older woman looked down at her tummy. "Yes, that would make sense. Stay off your feet and get plenty of rest." She glanced around at the empty tables. "I don't think it's critical for you to be here these days anyway."

She got up and left, leaving behind a full cup of cold coffee and a dime.

"Is there really a library here?" I asked after she was safely gone.

"Oh yes," Gramma Morris answered. "It's on Main Street, down past Doc Gannon's office."

"Can I go there sometime when she's not there?"

No other customers came in that day. The other children arrived from school and we waited for Uncle Vincent to take us home. Gramma Morris would stay until seven o'clock. My second day went well enough, I thought, at least I was beginning to fall into the family routine.

CHAPTER 13

THE TROUBLE WITH MATH

The ride home was cold. The bitter wind seemed to come from Alaska. If that wasn't bad enough, the poached eggs were not digesting well.

My new sisters barely spoke to me. Annette was reading a mystery and didn't say a word. Anna Marie just stared at the scenery. Michelle and Holly made a few comments about how lucky it must be to get to stay at the café all day instead of going to school.

But after a glance inside the cab, Holly squealed with delight, "Oatmeal. You know what oatmeal means?"

"A mushy breakfast cooked in last night's cabbage pot?"

"No, silly. Oatmeal cookies. I don't see any raisins though."

"She probably hid them from you to keep you from eating them all," Michelle teased.

"I don't eat them all. Just…some."

"All," Annette contributed from behind her book.

Anna Marie sighed and complained about math. Her homework came back with a grade of twenty-six percent, which was bad enough, but for some reason, Mrs. Porter decided to announce the highest score was one hundred percent, by Chuckie Landacre. Everyone who had scores of under eighty percent just weren't trying. And Ella and Dora Foyt, along with Anna Marie Villians all got under thirty percent. What does that say about their intelligence?

Wow, the teachers in New York never said anything like that to me. *But then I never turned in a twenty-six percent assignment.*

"Did she really say that? In front of the whole class? That seems kind of mean."

"She did," Anna Marie was adamant.

"She did," Michelle agreed.

"She did," Holly confirmed.

"She did," Annette said while turning a page.

This reminded me of Gramma Morris's echo-in-the-swamp story.

"When we get home, I'll look it over for you. Maybe together we can get that grade up," I told her, then I remembered her hostility from yesterday. "Not because I'm smarter or anything, but I had different teachers. Maybe the way they taught me will work better for you."

To my surprise, she nodded and said, "Okay, let's give it a try."

Well good, maybe if she's not all upset by math, we can relax and be friends.

"Hey," Holly exclaimed, "you're supposed to read to me, like last night."

"I am? I thought that was Anna Marie's...privilege."

I almost said 'job,' but I caught myself at the last second. The last thing I wanted to do was hurt her feelings by implying that it was a chore and not something I wanted to do with her.

Michelle smirked, "It's yours now. You read better than anyone we ever met. Papa told us listening to you is better than the radio."

"He did," Annette said while turning a page. Her eyes were on the book, but her ears obviously were focused on us. "Now, it's your…privilege."

Was she mocking me?

"I'm surprised they didn't tell you."

So am I.

"Well, that's good," I said. "After *The Wizard of Oz*, we can read *Rebecca of Sunnybrook Farm*. That's the book I'm reading now. I always seem to get interrupted."

"No," Holly was quite animated. "Mrs. De Montfort has the whole set of Oz books in the library. All fourteen. The next book is *The Marvelous Land of Oz*."

"Fourteen?" I repeated, dismayed. "There are fourteen Oz books?"

"Not counting the ones written by Ruth Thompson. She writes one a year. Ten, so far," Annette added.

"Twenty-four? Oh my gosh." I did a quick calculation, "Twenty-four chapters per book. Two hundred forty. Times two. Four hundred eighty. Five hundred eighty. Five hundred seventy-six chapters. If I read three chapters a night, that's…one hundred ninety-two. That's over half a year of Oz books," my voice faded as I glanced up.

They were all staring at me. Annette was looking from over her book. Holly was open mouthed. Michelle was frowning. Anna Marie was glowering.

"What?"

"How'd you do that?" Anna Marie asked in hostile wonderment.

"Do what?" But I knew 'what.' My mental calculation impressed them. And not favorably.

"One hundred ninety-two nights?" Annette asked, shaking her head. "You just made that up, right?"

"Sure," I replied, happy for an escape.

"No, she did it all in her head," Michelle inferred. "She's some kind of Einstein."

"Are you a witch?" Holly asked, wide eyed.

Wonderful. The little Oz fan just compared me to the most villainous character in the book.

"Or just a freak," Michelle concluded.

The cold. The stress. The riding backwards. And now, the poached eggs wanted out. Deep breath. Close eyes.

"I am not a witch. I did it in my head. And it's simple multiplication. And I'm going to be sick."

Michelle and Annette immediately banged on the back window, which must have been some kind of signal because Uncle Vincent pulled over. I hobbled down and rejected lunch on the roadside while Mom hovered over me, more concerned than ever. These things just didn't happen in New York.

I rode the rest of the way back in the cab with the adults. The other girls were quiet now that I was gone. They must have been happier without me.

Mom had me sit in the middle and Uncle Vincent told me it's rather common for children to get sick in cars. Just something that happens, nothing to worry or be embarrassed about.

"How about being called a freak? A witch? An Einstein? And that's my so-called family. I just want to go home," I was crying now and hated myself. What a baby.

"We're almost there," Mom soothed. "Then I want you to lie down while we sort all this out."

I didn't want to go home *there*, but home, *New York,* would be even worse. I really had nowhere to go and I knew it.

"And I want to know what happened. We'll all get

together after dinner and we'll find out who said what and deal with it. I can tell you right here and now, there is no reason to call anybody a freak. Whoever said it will have to apologize."

"Please don't. An apology that's forced doesn't mean anything and they'll resent me even more for being a stoolie."

"A what?"

"Tattletale."

"I still need to know what happened so we can make it right. And please don't talk like a mobster."

I knew from the tone that the conversation was over, which was just as well since the truck pulled into the driveway. There was a thank-you or two to Uncle Vincent as he pulled off, but everyone was quiet. Mom seemed a little angry and the girls were unusually silent as we entered the house.

I went to the living room, snatched up my book and slunk out onto the back porch while everyone else began their regular routines. Anna Marie was at the table, first setting it for dinner, then spreading her homework out. Michelle was in the kitchen helping with dinner. Beans and rice with leftover coq au vin. I had no doubt I would get rice, while everyone else got food with flavor. It looked like Holly had homework too, which she had spread out on the floor in front of the fire.

I got through a few pages, then realized that I was just gazing at the words. No comprehension. My eyes were tired and heavy. I decided to just close them for a minute to rest them, and when I opened them again, it was dark. The poor piano was being tortured again. Michelle obviously hated musical instruments.

I went to the outhouse and when I returned, Vincent's

truck was disappearing down the drive. Dad was hobbling into the house and I heard my name being called for dinner. Jason was back from Uncle Vincent's house and was already at the table, telling Mom about his day.

The meal seemed more like a feast. The coq au vin looked scrumptious. The beans smelled wonderful. Extra bacon was sizzling in the background, smelling extra delicious.

Of course, I got salted rice. At least I was given child size portions this time.

Dinner was over when the food ran out, which was quickly. Food that tasted like that had short life span in this house, I soon learned, and coq au vin never lasted long.

The three older girls cleared the table and Anna Marie wiped it down while the dishes were washed and dried with quiet efficiency by Michelle and Annette. I started to get back to my book, but Mom shook her head firmly.

"Family time," she said grimly when we were all together.

All the children were looking down at the table, so I thought it would be wise to follow suit. Dad seemed a bit confused but said nothing.

"So, who had the bright idea to call your new sister a freak, or a witch, or an Einstein? You made the poor child cry. Imagine traveling all the way down here just to have your own family call you names. *I* am embarrassed about that. The poor thing has a delicate constitution and is obviously quite sensitive, so we have some things to get straightened out...now. Let's start with freak. Who thinks she's a freak?"

Wonderful. Their *delicate* and *sensitive* new sister just got them in trouble. Maybe I could move into the chicken shed. At least the birds might like me.

"I said 'freak,' but I didn't call her one," Michelle confessed. "She did that math trick thing in the truck and I said she's Einstein or a freak, meaning unusual, not weird or creepy. I admit it was a bad choice of words, but I think her reaction was a little overdone."

"What math trick thing?" Dad asked.

They all started talking at once. I heard phrases like 'calculator brain,' 'math genius,' and 'just a bluff.'

"Stop," Mom raised her hand, "I started this wrong…"

"Well, I'm home," Gramma Morris called out from the door while taking off her coat. "Am I interrupting a family meeting?"

"You're early," Dad said with surprise.

"The mill discontinued the late shift. No more workers coming in for sandwiches. Just an occasional diner here and there. Lila can handle it without us. We'll only need someone there on Fridays for a while. The rumor is the trains won't stop here anymore. Too many folks have their own cars these days."

"Well, we'll have to see," Dad said. "No use in worrying about things until they happen. Besides, Governor Long will make it right. He's the only politician who cares about us working folks."

"True," Gramma Morris said. "And right now, we need a good man like him to help us through this crash. Best governor we ever had in this state."

"And we're having a family discussion right now," Mom interjected. "Something happened on the way home that caused a stir, and we're trying to figure it out. So, Amy, why don't you tell us what happened from the top. Just what happened. No opinions on what was meant."

I explained it from my offer to help Anna Marie to when the girls got hostile.

"And she just said a bunch of numbers randomly then the answer," Annette concluded. "I just thought she was bluffing to look smart."

"Or make the rest of us look bad," Anna Marie chimed in.

I scowled at her.

"So, you can take any two-digit numbers and multiply them in your head," Mom said. "That's a really nice talent…" She pulled out a piece of paper and pencil. "One that will really come in handy. Let's try thirty-three times fifteen."

She started to write the equation.

I figured it in my head.

"Three hundred thirty. Four hundred thirty. Four hundred ninety-five," I said with finality.

"Wow," said Annette, "she got the answer before you even wrote down the problem."

"Hush. Let me finish."

A second later she confirmed, "Four hundred ninety-five. Maybe that was too easy…"

"Too easy?" Michelle and Anna Marie said in unison.

"Sixty-six times sixty-six," Mom tried again.

I sighed. "Now I really am feeling like I'm part of a freak show."

"Last one," she snapped back at me.

"Six times six is thirty-six. Times ten is three hundred sixty. Add thirty-six…three hundred ninety-six. Add four. Four hundred. Times another ten is three thousand nine hundred sixty. Add four hundred is four thousand three hundred sixty. Remove the added four equals four thousand three hundred fifty-six." I even told them how to do it this time.

"She beat you again," Holly observed.

"Hush. Let me finish…four thousand three hundred fifty-six."

I felt fourteen eyes on me. Just looking. It made me feel like a zoo animal without the cage.

"It makes me nervous to have everyone stare at me."

"Holly, take your sister out back and show her…something," Gramma Morris ordered and the two of us slipped out back.

It was dark and the moon wasn't out so the only thing she could show me was night. The only light leaked out from the threshold. We fumbled around until we found the chairs and sat. It was cold, but not miserable, at least there was no wind.

"There are good witches in Oz."

"Huh?" That caught me off guard.

"When I asked you if you were a witch, I didn't mean to hurt your feelings or make you cry. I see the older kids having problems with smaller numbers, and there you are, solving it faster than it takes Anna Marie to walk to the chalkboard. It was so amazing. I thought you might have powers."

"No. No powers. And Oz isn't real. It's all just stories. It's not a real place."

"So is Cinderella, but there's a carriage, and it's real."

"I know. I saw it yesterday," I said.

"Will you forgive me?"

I reached over and after a bit of searching, I squeezed her hand. "I already have."

The door opened and Annette ushered us back inside. Anna Marie was still at the table with her math. Michelle was behind her.

"We're sorry," they said cheerfully. "We acted badly."

"I thought the Einstein and freak things were funny, like

a joke," Michelle apologized. "But they weren't. Once you get to know me, you'll understand my sense of humor, but, after all, you've only been here two days. Friends?"

I nodded. A little caution never hurt anybody.

"I shouldn't have doubted you," Annette said next. "I just never saw anything like that before. I certainly didn't mean to make you cry or get you sick."

"I think riding backwards is what got me sick," I lied.

"I should have seen you were hurt and protected you. From now on, I'll always be there for you. Sisters to the end. Forgiven?" Annette continued.

I nodded. She might make a good sister, but I had my doubts.

"Good," Mom said while clapping her hands twice. "I'm glad that's over and done with. Now Amy, I want you to sit next to Anna Marie and get her up to speed on her homework. And I want her getting all A's in math from now on."

"In one night?" I asked. I had seen enough of Anna Marie to know she would rather complain about math than do it. This was not going to be easy.

"You two can do it. Together, you can do anything."

"And if we can't?" I asked.

"You'll be sleeping with the chickens."

"Oh," said I sadly, "but I guess It's better than sleeping with the fishes."

There was a stunned silence, before Dad started to laugh.

"You've got another Al Capone over there," he said.

"Huh?" Michelle asked.

"That's what those gangsters say when we turn on the radio. When they kill somebody and throw their bodies in the river, they're sleeping with the fishes."

"Never mind, do the math. Holly, watch what they do. You'll be learning this stuff soon enough."

The first problem was two times three and her answer was five. I wanted to sigh, but that would start things off poorly, so I went to the kitchen and got out all the tableware. I set up two piles of three and explained that multiplication meant adding the piles, not the pieces. So, one pile of three plus one pile of three really meant three plus three. She knew it was six and I moved on. Problem after problem, we used that three-dimensional approach with her translating multiplication into addition. I had Holly set up the piles for us because she seemed to enjoy doing that sort of thing. Once we hit the sixes, I saw her eyes flash for a second, like a light bulb spark.

"So, seven times six is just seven added six times." She got it. "That's why it's called times instead of something else."

Actually, I didn't think of that, but it made sense.

"But I can't take all this stuff to school with me."

"You don't have to. Memorize what you can and add the rest. Say you don't know seven times six. You remember seven times five?"

"Thirty-five."

"You add one more seven to thirty-five and what do you get?"

"Forty-two," she said after a pause, no doubt counting one by one to get there.

"Good. Do the rest of your homework and show it to me and I'll double check it for you."

"Mama, Amy's all done. Can she read to us now?" Holly was nothing if not enthusiastic.

"Oh good," came the reply. "Yes, Amy come on in here. We decided that one of your family contributions will be to read to us after dinner."

"I heard," I smiled, resigned to half a year of *The Wizard of Oz.*

"I was hoping for another cup of that wonderful tea," I hinted. "It would make my voice sound better."

All eyes turned to Michelle, who silently hurried to the kitchen. We waited for her to come back and I began.

And so another three chapters down. Anna Marie showed me her homework and all the answers were correct. She sat on the floor by the fireplace and listened to the story while Michelle refilled my tea. Lights were dimmed at seven o'clock while we all shared the sink, used the outhouse and dressed for bed.

Tonight, I was upstairs, sharing a bed with Holly and Anna Marie. Holly was in the middle, so she got the extra body warmth, but it was still better under multiple blankets with two warm sisters than on the couch. Dad came in and kissed each of us and turned on the gas heater to a sadly low flame. Both of my new sisters told me how happy they were that I was now part of the family and we talked a bit before sleep overtook us.

Chapter 14

Back to Town

I woke up first and gently eased out of bed without waking my sisters. Sausage was cooking. I could smell its wonderful spicy scent. I was hungry at first whiff. The stairs met my tromping feet and I was soon in the kitchen, putting on my coat for a trip to the outhouse.

"Put on boots," Mom called from behind me. "It rained last night, don't want you getting your shoes muddy."

"I don't have boots."

Heavy sigh.

"Wear mine. The black ones in the corner."

When I came back, I found a rag, wiped them clean and went into the kitchen. The other kids were filing out by now. Who needs an alarm clock when there's food cooking?

Five plates were set out and we all sat down. Annette sat nearest the stove, followed by Michelle. Then Anna Marie on the other side, followed by Holly. I squeezed in next to Holly near the end of the table. Mom walked around the table with a big iron skillet and loaded the plates with scrambled eggs and that wonderfully aromatic sausage. First Annette, then she worked around the table, emptying the pan on Holly's plate and went back to the stove.

I looked at the empty pan and my empty plate, willing for some food, but my ability to wish food into existence was limited and my plate stayed empty.

"What about Amy?" Holly asked. "I can share some of mine if there's not enough."

All the others agreed there was enough to share, but Mom was back with a small pan and bowl.

"Amy has a delicate constitution and has to gradually get used to our kind of cooking." She set the bowl on top of my plate. "So just especially for her, I went to the store and bought some oatmeal just like what she ate in New York."

She lovingly plopped a large spoonful of the mush into the bowl. I smiled as best I could and croaked out a "thank you." I made an unsuccessful effort to not watch everyone else's plates and slowly ate the grainy paste.

"Does that mean no cookies?" Holly asked plaintively.

"That's what it means. I hope the oatmeal tastes good," she said to me. "I normally don't make it for meals."

"It's better than Aunt Mary's," I said, trying (and failing) to sound enthusiastic. "You didn't cook it in cabbage water, at least."

"Oh, come on," said Annette, rolling her eyes. "Mama, was Aunt Mary really that bad a cook? That doesn't seem possible."

"I never said she was a bad cook," I defended. "I only said I don't like food."

"Have some of my eggs," Michelle offered her plate from across the table.

"Michelle Villians, did you just hear me say she gets oatmeal and offer her something else? Knowing she gets sick easily?"

"I don't think she meant it that way," I intervened as

she pulled her plate back. "She meant I could have some of her eggs when my stomach's better."

She stared at me while I mustered up the weakest sincere smile in human history. She turned to Michelle, who had the second weakest sincere smile in human history.

"You two are as thick as thieves," she said, suppressing a smile, but we knew it was there. "But I like the way you stick up for each other. Now eat. And Amy, stop with the starving dog eyes. Look at your own plate."

I was glad that conversation was over.

"Is Amy coming to school with us?" Holly asked.

"Not until Monday. She needs clothes. She only brought undies, rags and some lounge clothes that might fit Holly but won't fit her. We're calling Mary on Saturday and ask her what she was thinking of, sending that child down here like that. We'll be going to Betsy's to get the material and some thread. She needs at least two more dresses. And shoes too. I want her to have something nice to wear to church on Sunday."

"Sounds like a busy day," Gramma Morris said. "You and Betsy finally talking to each other again?"

"No, but this is business and we'll have fun, won't we, Amy?"

"Yes, we will," I practically sang out, trying to sound enthusiastic. But deep down inside, I could think of roughly a thousand things I would rather do.

Jason soon left with Dad and Gramma Morris; the girls left to catch the train minutes later. The sprinkling rain sounded loud on the tin roof, but it was barely coming down as we waited on the front porch.

"It's nice that it's just the two of us for a while," Mom said.

We talked, getting to know each other. Uncle Vincent

came back a bit later and drove us to into town. We drove to main street and turned left, going past the doctor's office and the dentist. The next building was obviously a house, though it had a shingle above the door facing the street: *Betsy's Sewing and Supplies.* Mom assured Uncle Vincent we could make the walk to the restaurant when we were done so he drove off.

"What does Uncle Vincent do for a living?" I asked.

"He's a distributor."

"What does a distributor do?"

"He distributes."

I gave her a sideways glance.

She sighed. "People make things for other people. He sees to it they get them. Timber to New Orleans. Shrimp to Baton Rouge. That sort of thing. He owns a couple of barges and has crews that do the work. He gets the jobs other people don't want to do."

"He's a bootlegger?"

She seemed annoyed, "He distributes valuable medicine that has traces of alcohol in it."

"Like rum?"

Her eyes were spitting out daggers at me. It was time to drop the conversation.

"We got you out of New York just in the nick of time, before you're old enough to start dating gangsters."

"Oh, no worries there," I replied. "I would never be a mobster moll."

"A what?"

"A gangster's girlfriend."

She shook her head. "Either just in the nick of time or maybe too late."

That was a long way to get a short answer.

The seamstress' shop was unlocked and we strode right

in. The room had a dress form mannequin on a sturdy table and several dresses and blouses in various stages of completion. A counter was unmanned and a closed door was to the side. Large cubbyholes were behind the counter carrying rolls of cloth.

"Aren't we walking into someone's house?"

"No, dear. We're walking into her store. Her house is behind those doors."

"And they are not for the public to enter," came a cold voice behind us.

We both turned to see a thirtyish woman with long black hair pinned up haphazardly, in contrast to the neat and perfect styles I had seen since moving here. Most women with dark hair would have brown eyes, but hers were sapphire blue. Her even features were complemented by a delicate bone structure and perfect skin. And her figure was what Papa would have called 'shapely.'

"As I was explaining to the child," Mom responded in a fake-friendly voice. "Amy, this is a distant cousin of ours, Betsy Devereaux. Betsy, my new daughter, Amy Collins."

I curtsied as usual and it was perfect, except my knee bumped into the table holding the dress form. It only wobbled a little, but I still winced.

"Ah, she is just as graceful as advertised, I see," Betsy said with an unfriendly smile.

"Yes, well," Mom said briskly, "practice will help."

The door quietly opened behind us, but I didn't see anyone there. The adults were too busy talking to notice.

"Amy, when we were in school, Betsy and your Aunt Mary were the best of friends. Her brother, Ashley, and Mary were quite the item, until she met Michael Collins. Your father," she added quickly.

"I think she knows he was her father," Betsy said.

"Although, she was lucky enough to look more like…her mother."

"Are we really related?" I asked, uncomfortable with the conversation.

She stared at me for a moment. "Your Gramma Morris was my grandmother's first cousin. That would make us" a slight pause to calculate, "third cousins once removed."

"Will I be as beautiful as you when I'm old?" I asked hopefully.

Her demeaner changed instantly.

"I am not old. I am full grown," she smiled. "But in my younger days, I did have dinosaur eggs for breakfast." She obviously wasn't offended.

Mom' head fell a little bit, but she propped it back up with her fingers.

Betsy reached under the table and scooted out a small stool. She picked me up, put me on it and mock inspected me.

"Hmm. Hair's too light, eyes green but the same hue. More robust bone structure. We have the same nose…"

"We do?"

"Same shape nose. But mine is in my head and yours is in yours. Well-shaped ears."

She squeezed my upper arm and pressed her hands on my rib cage.

"You will be the loveliest young woman in every room you walk into, but in a different way than me. You'll be younger and…" she squeezed my arm again, "starving. Don't they feed you?"

"She keeps throwing up."

"Oh, well, that will do it. So, what brings you here today?"

"I need some material. She came down with nothing but

rags to wear, so I'm going to make her some dresses this weekend."

"You? Sew?"

"I've made clothes before," Mom said defensively.

"No, you've wasted cloth before. I tell you what. Family needs to stick together. You buy the material; I'll make the clothes."

"Why Betsy, thank you."

"For her."

"For both of us?" Mom persisted. "I made a mistake and I've paid dearly for it. Can't we just get past it and be friends again?"

I said, "I think that would be nice."

Betsy frowned at me, but it faded into a smile.

"Why not? It all over and done. You won and you lost," Betsy replied. "And I supported my cousin." She turned to me. "My other cousin. That's who was really unhappy with your mother here."

"I couldn't agree with you more. I don't know what I was thinking," Mom said quietly.

"Neither does anyone else. But who cares? I've been thinking about it for a while now. Why throw away tomorrow over what happened yesterday?"

While they were talking, I looked at her sewing machine. It was big and intimidating. It reminded me of a horse with a wheel instead of a head. Its manufacturer's name was emblazoned on the wheel.

"Are you in a church choir?" I asked.

"No, why?"

"Because you have a Singer sewing machine."

She groaned appreciatively and turned to Mom while tousling my hair.

"We have to be friends again. She has to visit me and

tell me more jokes."

Then to me, "You're pronouncing it wrong. It SINGE-er. That's because, when I sew, I'm on fire. If you get to close, you'll get singed."

I was delighted. Mom was shaking her head with an almost suppressed smile.

"I thought you were cured of all those bad jokes."

"No, I never had an audience intelligent enough to appreciate good humor. Now I do."

They reached over and hugged each other, making those fake kissy sounds. It made me happy to know we had a new friend in town. Then Betsy turned to me, stretched my arms out and took measurements.

"Now, young lady," she said.

I sighed inwardly. Everything after 'young lady' was always bad.

"You do know that your behavior tells us how beautiful you really are. Hitting another little girl is just never acceptable, no matter what she says to you."

I think I heard this one too many times, and just blurted out, "She broke my violin."

"Excuse me?"

"That's the 'no matter what.' She came into my room and smashed it on the bedpost and broke it into a dozen pieces. That's what she did. And it was the only thing I had."

I was fighting back tears. Mom swooshed over to my side to hug me.

"You never told me that," she scolded gently.

"You never asked."

"I wished I did. Mary made it seem like something trivial."

"Was it a toy?" Betsy asked, while positioning me back for more measuring.

"No, my babysitter gave me hers because she wanted it to go to someone who would take good care of it. And I…failed."

I started to cry again and hated myself. But they were understanding. Mom held me close, and Betsy measured my legs on the sly. After I calmed down, I heard a tapping sound from behind us and we turned towards the counter.

There she was. The oldest woman I ever saw in my life. She was thin, slightly stooped over, and watching us. Her dry skin was pulled tight over her skull and showed hundreds of lines and creases. The wrinkles dominated her desiccated neck which was barely thick enough to support her head. Her thin wispy hair was white as snow and she *did* appear old enough to have cooked dinosaur eggs.

She wore a black dress with an aged white bodice that was so old fashioned it could have been used as a stage costume. A black bonnet completed the antebellum look.

"Countess," Betsy greeted, "I didn't hear you come in. Let me finish here and I'll be right over."

The old woman nodded absently. Her eyes were on me.

"Who is this young lady?"

A nudge to my side from Mom.

"My name's Amy Collins, ma'am," I said. I started to curtsy, but four hands grabbed my hips and knees.

"You're on a stool," Betsy hissed impatiently.

The countess graciously ignored the activity.

"Amy Collins. Cassandra De Montfort's daughter."

"Cassandra Villians."

I was impressed that so many people knew to refer to me as her daughter instead of her niece. Mom must have some really good pull in town.

"So, you played a real violin, did you now, Amy Collins?"

"Yes, ma'am."

"What are the four string notes?"

"G, D, A, and E."

"What pieces did you play?"

"Greensleeves, Danny Boy, Amazing Grace, Love Lifted Me, Just As I Am…"

"Just the melodies?"

I nodded. I obviously failed a test of some sort.

"Cassandra, I would like to take her home with me for an hour or two to see what she can do. She needs to play music. It wounded her to have her instrument destroyed. I can see it in her eyes. Music soothes the soul and gives her spirit strength. Gives her a change of scenery too."

Both women seemed completely mystified. After a couple of seconds, Betsy nudged my mom.

"Yes, of course. But you know, she doesn't have a violin anymore, and we really couldn't afford one."

"Yes, violins are in meager supply here. But I happen to have one that might work for her. Just don't let any jealous sisters destroy it. Betsy, are you done with your measuring?"

"Yes, Countess."

She held up a spool of thread and a coin.

"This is what I came in for. Cassandra, would you like a ride to the cafe?"

We rode in the Cinderella carriage back to the restaurant. Thrushy and Finchy were open mouthed when they saw us. The black groomsman solemnly opened the door and helped Mom out, then got back on the side bar and grinned ear to ear at their amazed looks as we left.

"Tell Cici that Fredrick says 'hi,'" he told them.

The countess and I went back to her fairytale home. The lesson itself was a pleasant review. She gave me a very nice violin and we played a duet of *Oh Susannah*. Then we talked for a while in her parlor. The drapes were open to let the light wander over the antique furnishings and Persian rug. The room was a little dusty but obviously maintained, at least somewhat.

"Are you really a countess?" I asked. Even though Mom said she wasn't, I hoped she was. I never spoke to royalty before and wondered what made them different.

"I would say 'no.' But so many people here want to have someone important about. I used to correct them, but it was no use and my late husband, Henry, liked to be called the 'Count.' You see, his great-great grandfather, Hugh De Pilord, was the count of Mon Aloneux. He and his oldest sons and daughters were all killed in the French Revolution. His youngest son, who was named Hubert, was in Boston, either on business or in exile, since the rest of the family couldn't stand him. So, he assumed the title and changed his name to Bourbon."

"I thought he imported rum."

"Bourbon was the family name of the French king. He took the name to make himself appear legitimate.

"Well, anyway, he convinced a great many foolish women to invest in his crazy schemes to reconquer France and restore the royalty. When he saw he stood no chance to succeed, he abandoned his plans, but kept the investments. Built up a rum import trade. Then he had a run-in with pirates. Pirates just infested the waters in those days.

"Being that he was a businessman, he made a deal with them. He gave them the routes and destinations of the ships of rival businesses and they shared the spoils. That worked well until it came time for him to get his share. He just barely escaped with his life.

"He went to the authorities and told them where those evil pirates or clever business associates, however you want to phrase it, moored their ships on Cat Island. Cat Island was a large sand bar two miles offshore with no natural cover. The Navy simply surrounded them one night. Those poor, evil men never had a chance. The boats were all sunk within minutes of battle and survivors were left to swim two miles to the mainland. The Navy had no casualties; the pirates, no survivors.

"Hubert De Pilord wasn't a dumb man. He was very sly. He knew where the treasure was and went out and dug up the buried gold and jewels. He lived quite the life for a while, until some of the victims realized he had their jewels.

"He left in a hurry and wound up here in Faucette. Bought huge tracts of land and planted sugar cane and cotton. Married a local girl from the Landacre line in 1796. Had a large family. They all had large families in those days. His children understood the value of money, that is, it's better to keep it than spend it. And after Hubert died, his eldest son, Eugene, at least changed the name back to De Pilord, but kept the title of 'Count.' Even his brother, Bartholomew, snickered at him behind his back because of it. Americans never did respect the aristocracy.

"And then the war hit, Eugene was too old to fight but he had three sons who fought under General Kirby Smith. When they came home, there was hunger and poverty everywhere.

"The De Pilords did better than most, though. The Northern army didn't come through here to plunder because it was too far out of the way, so the property was untouched. And they never exchanged their gold for confederate money. That made them the only family who had anything of value: land and gold. Well-hidden gold.

"During reconstruction, all the other branches of the De Pilord family moved out west to escape from the Yankee rulers and scalawags. After Eugene passed on, the family business was run by Mr. Charles De Pilord and his two grown sons from his first marriage, Jeremiah and Henry. Mr. Charles had seven children and a pregnant wife with consumption. He hired a governess. Me.

"I was an orphan who was lucky enough to be adopted by the Johnson Family Traveling Musicians. My new parents taught me the violin. We played on street corners at first, then in real venues and halls. We were in Chicago when they died and I went on to St. Louis and gave violin lessons. Ten cents per hour. I sometimes performed, when asked, and was paid. I lived modestly enough and was happy, until the most wretched man entered my life.

"He was a widower named Richard I. Karp and he decided that I was to be his next wife. His idea of courtship was to order me around like a servant girl, and then get angry when I ignored him. Apparently, he was wealthy and powerful enough that he didn't think I had a choice in the matter, but he found out that I was quite capable of survival without him or any other man because I could play and teach music. So, one day, my students and I were performing on the palisade by the riverside, and he grabbed my violin and threw it into the Mississippi River. There was a policeman standing right next to us on the sidewalk, and you know what he said?"

I shook my head, waiting for her to continue.

"You should be more careful, ma'am."

She shook her head and continued. "Well, hard as it may be to believe, this is not a good method to winning a girl's heart. I ran like hell, pardon the expression. Packed my bags and caught the next train out of town, going anywhere. Wound up in Baton Rouge.

"There was a church near the train station, so I went to service and by chance met the pastor and told him my story. The next thing I know, I was a governess of two children in the home of a high-ranking government official. The war had just ended a couple of years earlier so the northerners were running the State. The reconstruction government was unpopular and so was I. But at least I was employed.

"By the summer of 1870, my employer moved back home to run for office. He offered to retain my services, but his hometown was St. Louis, so I declined. With his references, I was hired by Mr. Charles to attend his young children and his poor wife here in Faucette. His older sons flattered me with attention, but I never considered them serious suitors. I was just an orphan girl. Mr. Charles wouldn't have allowed either of them permission to court me. He had their lives all planned out for them. He probably had the amount of children and their dates of birth prearranged as well, knowing his need to control.

"The house was always quiet and dark in the odd belief that darkness was good for the patient. The children weren't allowed to make noise of any kind. Any running and playing was always done outside. Mrs. De Pilord was in a race. Would she give birth before she died or would she and the child die together? It turned out that they both died together in September. Mr. Charles was devastated. The children were to remain in a dark, quiet and somber house to respect their mother's passing. I did what I could to make their lives happy and cheerful. I took them outside as much as possible and we played games. We fell into a routine as Mr. Charles left his grief behind.

"Well, things were going well enough until my adopted brother, Danny, visited. He represented Selbs, a rum distillery in New Orleans that wanted to buy sugar cane. Danny was a young, socially inept, and impetuous child when we separated five years before. Since then, he went from a skinny little sixteen-year-old boy cultivating fuzz to full grown man, complete with a full greasy-looking beard. I didn't recognize him when I answered his door knock. But he recognized me.

"'Susan,' he called out in a happy, louder-than-needed voice, right in front of Mr. Charles, Jeremiah and Henry, who were all looking on with amused interest, 'Susan Johnson. Don't you remember me?'

"'No.'"

"'Danny Johnson. Your brother. The Traveling Johnson Family Musicians. I played flute and sang. You were the best violinist in the New World.'

"We hugged each other awkwardly, at least for me. The three De Pilords were listening quite intently and were obviously very interested. I made a sharp head move towards them and introduced him to my employers, who quickly kidnapped him and led him into the study. When they were done, I was called in to see Danny folding up a standard contract.

"'There she is,' he exclaimed. 'So, you married into the De Pilord family?'

"As before said, he was socially inept.

"'Miss Johnson serves as our governess,' Mr. Charles said coldly.

"'Your children are lucky. Are they getting violin lessons as well?'

"I angled over to the side and was gesturing for him to stop bragging about me. It was embarrassing and immodest. But he was blissfully unaware of my efforts.

"'No, I was unaware of her talent in that regard,' then to me, 'Is there something wrong, Miss Johnson? You seem to be going into spasms.'

"I relaxed. Danny wasn't taking the hints anyway.

"'Oh, yes,' he went on, unaware that I was seriously considering disowning him. 'She was the star of show. They wouldn't let her sing because they wanted her instrument in every song. She's the best violinist in the world.'

"'Oh, please. They wouldn't let me sing because I sound like a toad, and as far as the violin goes, I can barely put two notes together.' He gave me a dark look.

"'I'll compromise with you. I'll stop over-complementing you if you stop being over-modest and say you're very good. Deal?'

"I gave him my best if-looks-could-kill glare and said, 'I'm very good.'

"'Why didn't we know this until now?' Charles seemed quite exasperated.

"I said, 'It never came up.'

"Danny said, 'Sis, you didn't mention it in your interview?' I told him to look around the room. 'Violins are scarce. Why would I bring the subject up?'

"The following week, they weren't scarce. Each child had a violin and teaching music was added to my duties. The curtains were opened to let in light to help them read the sheets. Music became the favorite part of the day and a big part of life at the house.

"That Christmas, Mr. Charles gave me a stock certificate for the Bank of New York which began my investment history. Jeremiah was in New Orleans courting his lady love. Henry bought me a violin. It was very expensive though he never admitted it. He told me he took lessons years before and promised that we would make beautiful music together when I got him up to speed.

"I kept giving him easier music sheets, but he just didn't follow the score. After a while, I suspected the only reason he knew a violin's strings go on top was because he watched me give the children lessons.

"'Did it ever occur to you that you can play the music the way it's written?' I asked him one day in exasperation.

"'Did it ever occur to you that I can't read music?'"

"What did you do?" I asked her with a laugh.

"What could I do?" she replied helplessly. "I fell in love with him."

By now it was past lunch time. The countess had the carriage pulled to the front and the three of us, Susan De Pilord, myself and my new violin, headed to the café. Both Mom and Gramma Morris were happy to see me and shocked that the countess brought me back herself *and* came into the restaurant for the first time. Her family married into the Landacre line after all, and the Landacre line was not friendly to the Morris line.

"But remember, I married into the De Pilord line only sixty years ago, and the De Pilords married into the Landacres in 1796. Long after the bad blood happened."

"The original bad blood is long forgotten. It's the recent bad blood that we're worried about," Gramma Morris harrumphed.

"Amy," the countess commanded, ignoring the remark, "get out your new violin and play *Oh Susannah* for us."

I played it well, I thought. A few unwanted squeaks cried out here and there, but not bad, considering how rusty I was. They all applauded my effort, I even heard clapping from the kitchen from Cici and her two boys. I smiled.

"Don't curtsy," Gramma Morris said sharply. "Just put

it away so the countess can take it home.”

“Oh, no, Louisa. It belongs to her now. I gave it to her; on condition she plays it and comes back for lessons.”

“She doesn’t need lessons. And if we can’t buy her a violin on our own, she doesn’t need one.”

“Gramma Morris,” I cried out, “what are you saying? Mom?”

“Amy,” said the countess gently, “would you go back to the kitchen and…cook something for a minute please?”

I left for the kitchen, went to the pass immediately and crouched down so they didn’t see me but I could hear them. Cici nodded her encouragement.

“Louisa, why did Amy leave New York?”

“She got in a fight with her stepsister and broke her nose. And it seems like the whole town knows that.”

“I certainly did. Do you know what the fight was about?”

“No, something silly I would think. You know children. And Amy seems to be a bit more high-strung than most.”

“Gramma,” Mom said gently, “Amy owned a violin in New York. Her stepsister broke it. Deliberately.”

“Did you think I’m such a great teacher that she played that piece so well after one sitting? We just reviewed. I have seven violins at home. Six, for now. Do you really think, down in your heart, that it’s better for me to have seven of them collecting dust and her not having even one?”

“It’s not good just to take things from other people, no matter how good the intentions. She’ll start to expect gifts all the time.”

“Is that all? Then we can make an arrangement. Have her over first thing every Saturday morning. She can dust, wipe things down, sweep the floors for an hour. Then I’ll give her a lesson. No gift. Business arrangement. Amy, I know you're listening. Be at my house first thing in the morning. I have housework and violin work for you."

I jumped up from my hiding spot.

"Yes, ma'am," I sang out. "I will be there."

Gramma Morris scowled. She lost this one and knew that if she presented another objection, she would look petty.

CHAPTER 15

MORE MATH

It was too late for lunch and dinner wasn't even a thought, so Cici gave me a slice of cornbread and some hot tea to 'keep body and soul together.' We found a table and I told Mom and Gramma Morris about my day with the countess while I nibbled. Mom wanted me to play another song on my new violin, but the door swooshed open and a customer came in.

She was maybe fifty, with her hair swept in a bun and iron gray bangs covering her forehead. She wore spectacles that enlarged her gray eyes and crow's feet. Her nose was angular and she had the thinnest lips I ever saw.

"Dianna," Mom called out softly, "come on over. Talk to us."

She accepted the invitation, saw what I had and ordered the same.

"Well, dear," she said to me, "my name is Dianna Wilson and I'm the phone operator here in town. My sister, Debora Devereaux, is the other one. I work nights when it's quiet. I like quiet. Debora works days. So, if you are ever playing on the phone, one of us will tell you to get off. Remember: it's a party line. Everybody in town needs that line. Phones are serious things. Not toys."

"Had a rough night?" Mom asked her sympathetically.

"Some people just shouldn't be parents. All the way until eight o'clock, the bell kept ringing, but no one was there. Just kids giggling. And people use their phones for emergencies. It's just a crime."

Then to me, "We work from five to five, Monday through Friday. I just don't know how that weekend staff can stand it."

"Maybe it's not so bad, with the whole family together and all."

"No, it's worse. Kids everywhere, and that's when the adults are trying to make their long-distance calls. If they don't control their children soon enough, people just won't have a use for the telephone anymore and we'll be out of work."

"I don't think that will happen any time soon," Mom replied dryly. "Speaking of which, we plan on calling my sister, Mary, this weekend. What do you recommend as a good time? We always have bad luck."

"I would say around four a.m. The little monsters are still asleep or in the plotting stage. It'll be five New York time. Those Yankees always think they have to be a little bit ahead of us decent folks. You should have some time."

"So, dearie," she addressed me, "I suppose someone's mentioned to you about how young ladies don't hit down here."

"We have," Mom said.

"So has everyone else I met."

Well, not the countess. Maybe that was why I liked her so much.

"Then I won't. Everybody wants to help parents when they have wayward children, but sometimes it isn't helpful and can be downright annoying."

"It certainly can," Mom said pleasantly, her eyes boring into the operator like death rays.

Mrs. Wilson soon paid and left, while my family shook their heads. It wasn't long after she left when the rest of the children started filing in the café and we all knew something was wrong.

Holly went to Mom, snuggled for a second and said, "Mrs. Porter just doesn't like us." Then she ran to the kitchen for a snack before Mom could react.

Michelle was next. She smiled and put her hands on my shoulder. "You tried," she said and started for the kitchen.

"Tried what?"

"Let her go," Gramma Morris said. "The not-so-innocent ones always slink off to the kitchen when someone else is in trouble."

Whatever that means.

Anna Marie's head was buried in Annette's shoulder while she whimpered and moaned angry, wretched, loud, sobs of anguish.

"My Lord, sweetie," Gramma Morris exclaimed, "Whatever happened?"

Anna Marie tried to answer, "Waugh, I tuond eeen mmm pypaeer in Meez Poormean sees…"

"Deep breath, sweetheart," Mom said, offering her a handkerchief and taking over the comforting. "Annette, what happened?"

"Well, the good part is that she turned in her math homework and got all the questions right," she said while nodding, then she started shaking her head. "The bad part is that she got a zero on it."

"Well, how did she get a zero on a hundred percent?" Gramma Morris was confused and getting angry.

"Mrs. Porter said she cheated. Nobody goes from a

twenty-six to one hundred overnight."

"It's all your fault," Anna Marie lashed out at me. "If you didn't butt in, I'd have gotten some points."

I knew that Anna Marie and I would never be close at that moment.

"Then I'll never help you again."

I got whapped on the back of the head with a teaspoon by Gramma Morris.

"You're not the adult here. I'll decide who helps who. Go to the kitchen and cook something."

"That's what the countess said," I accused, while making a point of not rubbing my head from her sneak attack.

"Well, I liked it, and you'll be hearing a lot more of it. Now, go cook something."

I went.

"Whatcha think you're going to cook with no customers?" Cici asked, shaking her head.

So, I sat at the table with Holly and Michelle who were quietly nibbling on cornbread and milk while trying to listen in on the conversation in the dining room. Knowing I could hear better at the pass, I got up and started to get closer when Cici's hand clamped down on my neck.

"What are you, some kind of little snoop? This isn't about you. Go sit down. You want some cornbread?"

"No, thanks."

I went back to the table and we waited. After a while, Annette joined us.

"They told me to go cook something," she said matter-of-factly. "Mama and Mrs. De Montfort and Mrs. Porter are talking on the phone. No telling how many others are listening."

"What does that mean?"

"It's a party line. You pick up the earpiece and turn the handle to get the operator. She makes the call for you. We know it's for us by the rings. At home, it's four long rings and two short ones. Here it's five long and one short. Once the ringing stops, anyone can pick up and listen in. We're not allowed to use the phone, so we don't get accused of eavesdropping."

Anna Marie came in. She was calm now, though her eyes were red.

"They told me to go cook something," she said sullenly.

"Try cooking up an apology to Amy," Cici suggested.

"Don't bother," I responded. "You said what you meant."

I got up from the table and went out the back door and over to the creek's edge. The stream poured by and I walked as close as I could without falling down the incline. The whishing nose of water sounded friendly and pleasant. The towering pine trees that dotted the waterside swayed gently in the soft breeze. The shadows grew longer as twilight was approaching and I was thinking if I were the only person in the world, this is where I'd want to be.

I soon heard a skirt rustle behind me and turned to see Annette there looking almost shy.

"It's time to go," she said. "And Amy? Anna Marie was just upset. And she lashes out at people when she's upset. I wish she didn't, but it's how she's made. It would be better if you forgave her."

"Fine. I forgive her," I said expressionless.

"Well, that's a start. A little sincerity would be better."

I gave her a sideways glance and we went back in. Everyone was there waiting for us and they were all staring at me.

"Something going on?" I asked, still a bit sullen over

Anna Mare's unwarranted accusation.

"Mrs. Porter was taken aback by Anna Marie's sudden improvement in math," Mom said. "And knowing there was a new girl in the house, she wrongly assumed that Amy did the work for her. So, we made a deal. Friday is quiz day. Anna Marie will get a full one hundred problem test. The times tables, one through twelve. If Anna Marie gets a perfect score, everybody's lowest test score will be dropped.

"The whole class is rooting for you and Anna Marie," Michelle said.

Anne Marie didn't look too happy. "What if I don't get a hundred?"

"Then the other children will be disappointed," Mom added. "Don't worry. Amy will help you study."

"I will?" I asked, still unhappy. "So she can blame me if she misses a couple?"

"Anna Marie, didn't I tell you to apologize?"

"I tried but she just walked out the back door."

"She did," the other three snitches sang out in tattletale harmony.

"What are you? A bunch of ratfinks? Rat. Rat. Rat." Pointing to each one. "And she's not apologizing if you make her say it," I replied. "She's following directions."

There was a hearty laugh from the pass.

"You're not an innocent little ten-year-old girl," said Gramma Morris. "You're a thirty-year-old little cynic. However, Little Cynic, I don't like name calling. They were just helping to answer a question."

Mom interrupted, "And I won't make you 'follow directions' but I would hope you apologize to everyone?"

"For what?"

"For calling them rats," Mom hissed through clenched teeth.

"I'm sorry you're rats."

"AMY."

"I'm sorry."

"Anna Marie."

"I'm sorry. Truly. Can you find it in your heart to forgive me?"

"Okay, I guess it's better than being mad all night."

"And you'll help me with my studying tonight?"

I'd rather have nails pounded through my knuckles.

"Can't Gramma Morris help you?"

"No, child," Gramma Morris responded. "I spent my time helping my mother raise six other children, then raised five of my own and helped with my grandchildren and now my great-grandchildren. I never had the time to learn books and numbers. But when I saw my brothers both lose their land signing contracts that didn't say what they were supposed to, I vowed my children would all get the book learning they needed and wanted. So, I can't help her with what I don't know."

"Mom?"

"I have dinner to cook. Besides, you can get the answers quicker in your head than I can write down the questions."

That's a problem I can fix.

"And don't go thinking that's a problem that needs fixing."

Mind reader.

"Come on, Amy," Anna Marie pleaded. "I said I was sorry."

"So? If you do good, you do good. If you do bad, it's all my fault and everyone will hate me before they even met me."

"I just lashed out. You were just there."

"Couldn't you 'lash out' at your teacher?"

The room went silent.

"Young lady," said Gramma Morris, "down here, children never show their teachers disrespect. If you have a problem, you come to us. You never confront your teacher."

"Did you ever lash out at one of your teachers?" Holly asked.

"No," I admitted. "They weren't lash out-able."

Uncle Vincent soon arrived and we sped home. Michelle and Annette helped Mom with dinner while Anna Marie and I reviewed her math. Holly and Jason were destroying a checkers board while trying to play. Dad was watching them while listening to the radio.

Mom was on the phone while the girls were preparing Cajun breaded steaks. I wished I was in the kitchen learning to cook. It would be a nice skill to have if I ever had to go back to New York.

"Mama," Michelle called out when she heard the phone hang up, "we're missing steaks."

"What? We should have ten. Did you find both packages?"

"Uh-huh."

Mom started over to help them when Michelle called out, "I found a couple."

Mom sat in a chair next to us, watching Anna Marie work out her problems, all correctly. The steaks were sizzling noisily, filling the room with their aromas, though tonight's dinner didn't smell as good as anything we cooked before.

"That was Dr. Gannon," Mom said happily. "He says the breaded steaks should be mild enough for you to eat.

Now, why don't you two put that away and get to setting the table?"

A real meal at last. I was so happy.

I was beginning to like Dr. Gannon.

Dad, of course, got the largest steak, but Mom's was pretty good sized too. Everybody got a steak and a heaping spoonful of rice and beans. Mom served everyone from the pan but ran out right before my plate.

"Oatmeal again?" I asked sadly, remembering this morning's breakfast.

"No, there wasn't enough room in the skillet for yours and Holly's steaks. They're coming right up."

Gramma Morris was behind her with the smaller pan, fishing out our steaks.

"Go sit down, Cassie, these little devils should be serving you."

"I'm sorry," I said, looking down. I felt bad, not really knowing why I was being groused at.

"Now Amy," Mom said softly, "you're not a 'little devil.' That was just her way of having some fun. Adult humor."

"That's right, little girl," Gramma Morris nodded. "When I'm mad at you, you *will* know it. So don't go thinking I'm some kind of monster. It's my job to keep you from getting a big head, doing stupid things and getting hurt. Because if you ever get hurt, body, soul or heart, I'd feel real bad... After I stopped dancing."

"Gee, I feel better now."

"This meat tastes awful," Holly changed the subject. "I don't like it."

I tasted a bite of mine. It was the worst meal I had since moving down south. Everybody else just shook their heads in confusion.

"It's as good as ever," said Annette.

Holly wasn't convinced, "It's the worst ever."

"Fine," said Mom, pretending to be nonplussed, "just eat your beans and rice. Someone can have your steak tomorrow with breakfast. Someone being me."

"Fine."

"Fine."

"Good."

"Good. And you'll need to go to bed early to conserve your strength."

"Can't I stay up until Amy reads *The Wizard of Oz?*"

I ate the rest of my meal while those two struggled for the last word. I enjoyed the beans and rice, but the steak immediately started my stomach rolling.

"I'm tired tonight…" I started.

"We all are," Dad said. "Go get settled in and get the lamp going. I'm going to step out back for a bit, and everyone else can get the dishes going. I want an early evening tonight."

And so, in less than five minutes, I was in my chair with Holly snuggled up to me and the whole family listening to me read more about the adventures of Dorothy. By the end of the first chapter, I could feel my abdomen swelling and twisting. The nausea came before the end of the next chapter. I shut the book quickly, which startled Gramma Morris and Michelle, who were both dozing off.

"Move, Holly," I whimpered. "I'm have to go outside. I'm going to be sick. No time."

Everybody cleared a path, but Mom yelled out, "Without any shoes on? Stop right there."

I turned to see her holding that awful chamber pot. I had no more time, so I grabbed it and fell to my knees on the floor while my stomach unloaded everything, with geyser-like intensity. Liquid missiles of partially digested food poured out at tremendous speeds, splashing out of the pot and splattering my face, the wall, the floor, the couch, and chairs. The pot was almost full before Gramma Morris thought to get a mixing bowl for the excess.

Mom was on the phone, frantically talking to Dr. Gannon, who apparently agreed to make a house call. All my sisters had towels or rags in hand wiping things clean. Dad was holding Jason and comforting him as he seemed to be very scared. Gramma Morris had taken the chamber pot away for dumping.

I lowered my head for a round of gagging and dry heaving, panting for breath, while my intestines started twisting and spasming. I staggered up from the floor, pointed to where the outhouse was and started for the door. Mom was on one side and Annette on the other, dragging me out the kitchen while the others watched.

The outhouse was too far away and I started gagging again. There was no chance and, to my embarrassment, I soiled my clothes. Annette had to carry my shameful garments in the house for washing and soon returned with an oversized robe and a pair of slippers. I shivered in the cold. Mom wiped me down as best she could and I was dragged back into the house. The bathtub was half full of warm water and I was unceremoniously dumped in it. I was soon dried and wrapped in the robe while Mom pinned a small hand towel on my backside.

"A diaper?" I was humiliated.

"Do you need to wash out your own dress and panties to prove you need one tonight?"

I gladly lost that argument and was led to the couch to lie down, the scoured chamber pot next to me, now my favorite ceramic piece.

"We're not sharing our bed with her tonight, are we?"

Anna Marie asked in a worried voice.

"If I had more energy, I would hate you," I muttered.

"Of course not," Mom snapped. "I want her down here near the plumbing. Now, get off to bed, all of you. You don't know if this is her sensitive stomach or something catching."

That emptied the room. You can have great friends when you're reading or helping them with their homework, but when you're sick, you're alone.

Gramma Morris inspected the room for any missed puddles or spots and, when satisfied, sat next to me and rubbed my forehead.

"Cassie, she has a fever now. Probably got a chill. Do you want to go to bed and I'll wait for the doctor?"

"No, she's my daughter and I'll handle it."

My daughter.

I don't think Aunt Mary ever said those words to or about me. And they were so nice to hear. I drifted off to sleep.

The doctor was there, poking and prodding me when I woke up. He attacked my eyelids, forcing them open, holding a candle too near.

"What exactly did she eat?" he asked.

"Just breaded steak and rice and beans. No dessert. Just what we talked about on the phone."

"Was there any leftover?"

Gramma Morris said, "Holly didn't eat hers. I wrapped it up for someone's breakfast."

The doctor somehow had it in his hand, unwrapped.

"Smell this," he ordered flatly.

"Oh, my," Mom said, aghast. "Michelle, where did you find the last two steaks? Weren't they wrapped?"

Michelle tumbled down the stairs in her nightgown.

"Yes, they were. There were three packages. Two on the top shelf and one on the bottom. Remember, we couldn't find them all? Then I looked on the bottom shelf."

"There were only two on the top shelf."

"No, there was a package of two on the bottom."

"Oh, no," Mom exclaimed, "I bought those for Amy on Saturday because we expected her no later than Sunday. Nobody cooked them? Just left them?"

"I remember someone saying she was going to step back a bit and let the girls learn how to run their own household. They ran it into the ground," Gramma Morris pronounced.

"Well, you have to monitor what they do," Dr. Gannon said. "It's good for them to be cooking and cleaning, but someone has to keep track of the food and how long it's been there."

"But she had to know it was bad when she tasted it," Michelle offered.

"No, she didn't. She not used to this kind of food. She probably thought it was supposed to taste that way. And Cassie, if she's not eating the exact same thing everybody else is, I suggest you taste hers, just to be certain. She's probably not going to want anything tomorrow, other than tea or toast. Let her have as much as she wants, have her down it slowly. See how she does. Bland food diet, as usual. When she wakes up, give her some bicarbonate and ginger to keep her settled."

Soon enough I was alone while the fire chased off the dark. My angry digestive system was growling at me most of the night, but I was too tired to care. Sleep whisked me away from my discomfort and the most bizarre dreams trespassed in my slumber.

CHAPTER 16

AN IMPROMPTU PARTY

It was a little after nine o'clock when I woke up the next morning. The room had a pleasant gingery scent. Mom had me take off that hated diaper and inspected it before tossing it in the basket of dirty clothes that slept just out the door on the back porch. Then we had breakfast, which was a tiny bowl of oatmeal, no more than two bites with a small glass of water. She sat down opposite of me while I ate. I finished in less than a minute, since the quantity was so miniscule.

"Tummy sore from all the throwing-up?"

I nodded.

"Then I have a happy surprise for you. I used the last of my ginger to bake you some cookies," she started, which explained why the room smelled so good.

Mrs. Carnahan always made wonderful gingerbread cookies. She used freshly minced ginger and lots of brown sugar and honey. Her cookies were delightful, like a little piece of heaven in every bite.

"Dr. Gannon says ginger does wonders for an upset stomach. I normally don't bake ginger cookies. The children all seem to prefer oatmeal cookies or molasses chews."

"I love them all," I said. "And I really love ginger cookies."

I took a bite into one to savor that gingery tang, only to find a dry, sandy texture that held a bitter gingerroot spicy taste that almost burned my mouth. I chewed as best I could and used the water to help moisten this blob of refuse.

"There's no sugar in these, is there?"

"Well no. Dr. Gannon wants you on a bland diet for the weekend. Gives you time to recover."

I was beginning to develop a real dislike for Dr. Gannon.

I put it down, patted my sore stomach and said, "I don't want to get too full, just in case."

"I like that. Now normally, if you take something to eat, we expect you to eat it. 'Take what you want but eat what you take.' But don't eat it if it tastes bad."

This had me confused.

"You always load my plate for me. And everyone else."

"That's true. When it comes to food, I put the most I think you can eat on your plate. Eat what you can and say, 'I'm done.' Someone will finish it for you, I'm sure. If I don't put enough on your plate and everything's gone, then you're out of luck. 'Those who linger are lost.' And you have all the marks of a lingerer."

"But I don't take what I get. You give me what I get."

"And you take what I give," she said triumphantly.

I wasn't sure how to respond to that. Luckily, the clip-clop of horse hooves coming down the driveway ended the discussion. We looked out the window to see a one-horse shay clomping towards the house. Two young women were in it, their long black hair freely flowing from under pink bonnets and black wool coats crowned with raccoon obviously kept the chill away. The shay seemed a bit unstable on the driveway, but from what they tell me of shays, they were always unsteady. That's because a shay is a simple carriage on only two wheels, instead of four.

"Oh, my goodness," Mom exclaimed. "It's Brigitte Nye and Darlene Charon. I haven't seen them in years, since before you were born. Put your coat on and run get Huck and Porky to tend their horse and shay."

"The farmhands?" I asked, vaguely remembering Michelle telling me about them.

"That's right. They'll be in the chicken sheds out back."

I put on my shoes and she stared at them for a moment.

"Those shoes are way too big for you.

"I know," I said, while pulling on my coat. "Aunt Mary buys things large so we grow into them."

"That doesn't work on shoes," she said slowly through clenched teeth. "That's why you don't curtsy very well. We'll have to get that taken care of. Meantime, go get the boys. The ladies will need help."

I nodded, and asking a logical question for a city girl, "Huck and Porky. How will I know them?"

She gave me a long sideways glance. "They'll be the only two things in the *chicken* shed that don't look like *chickens*."

Not such a logical question for a newly minted country girl, apparently.

It was a short jaunt to the sheds and I was calling out both names when they appeared from around the corner. A tall unusually thin man with rapidly disappearing blond hair who was running head on into middle age and a muscular younger man, substantially shorter also with thinning hair, a ridged forehead and wild blue eyes. Both were past dirty and entering the land of filthy.

The taller man faked a smile and said, "You're the new girl in town. Amy. Not as tall as I expected."

"Kinda puny, truth be said," the other one added.

"Truth don't always need to be said," the thin man said. "My name's Tom Landrieu, but they all call me Porky."

"Porky?" I repeated in disbelief. The man was maybe five eight and weighed no more than one hundred pounds. He had barely enough skin to cover his bones. Indeed, he was little more than a tree stalk with eyes.

This time the smile was real.

"I used to raise pigs. Had a nice business too but ran into some bad luck. I went to Little Rock and sold a whole herd. When I came back home, I found that my wife ran off with my partner."

Considering how dirty he was and how much he smelled, I couldn't say I was surprised. I wondered if Porky's nickname was really due to his former occupation or his odor.

"They took all the livestock with them," he continued. "Every animal in the barn except the rodents. I was wondering if I should start over when a tornado flattened everything I had left, except me and the mice. Then the bank called about the mortgage, so I told them they could have it and here I am."

"I'm sorry you had such a run of bad luck," I said.

He shrugged.

"I'm Huck," the other one said. "I work here too."

He stared at me intensely and licked his lips while rubbing his hands together. A leering grin showcased his yellow teeth. I shivered. I could see why Mom kept them at a distance.

"My real name's Finn. That's why they call me Huck. Huck Finn. Get it?"

"I do, and it's good to meet you," I said politely if untruthfully. "We have visitors at the house. Mom wants you to help them with the horse and shay."

"Yes, Little Miss," Porky smiled at me. "Let's go, Huck."

"Looks like there's two carriages," Huck commented. Sure enough, another one was next to the first, the reins lightly wrapped around a porch rail.

"And Miss Sharon walking over from across the street," said Porky.

I waved to her when Porky commented, "Hey, isn't that that countess lady's carriage?"

There it was also heading into the drive.

"Y'all are having a regular party," Porky concluded.

"Yeah, a real hen party," Huck started laughing at his own unfunny joke, while rubbing his hands together like he was getting a favorite meal. "You ladies should come down to the sheds. There's a whole bunch of hens who can join you."

Porky thumped his ear.

"Behave," he said firmly. "If you don't want your job, don't be messing with mine."

They went off to tend to the horses while I followed, keeping a distance between us.

Betsy was there with a big smile, holding up a lovely Sunday go to church dress, green and white, complete with frilly white inset on the bodice. I almost completely ignored everyone else when I saw it.

"It's so beautiful," I said, while holding it in front of me. "I never got to wear anything this pretty since my Papa died. Thank you so much."

"Well, try it on," she laughed. "Let's make sure it fits."

"*After* you greet our other guests," Mom said with a note of exasperation.

"Oh," I said, "I'm sorry, I was just..."

"We understand, Amy. I would be excited if I received a dress that pretty too," said one of the guests. Her pink bonnet and coat were off. She was young, about Mom's age, and very pretty with bright brown eyes which matched her dark dress. She wore a pink decorative scarf that matched her bonnet.

"Oh, yes," said the other one with a pleasant smile. "It's a shame that when we grow up, we can't wear clothes like that anymore."

"Amy," Mom said to me with a surreptitious eyeroll, "meet my two friends, Brigitte Nye and her sister, Darlene Charon. We've been friends since our school days."

"Well, I can't speak for Darlene, but please call me Brigitte while we're here. Auntie Brigitte is not correct and Mrs. Nye too formal. Save that for church and town."

"Well, now Amy," Darlene laughed, "Brigitte just spoke for me."

I curtsied to them but lost balance and fell on my side. I was unhurt but embarrassed. Mom and Betsy were there instantly to help me up when we heard thumping at the door.

"The countess," I told them.

Mom gave me a sideways glance and hurried to the door. Betsy helped me up and over to Mom's room, while Brigitte followed, holding the new dress.

"Why Countess," Mom greeted with sincerity, "I am so happy you called. Please do come in. Do you want me to call my hands to help with your carriage?"

"Oh, no, my servants can get it all done. They're real experts at maintaining it."

Which was true. The carriage was in better shape than her house.

"Very well," Mom sounded relieved. "But it's close to

freezing. Amy can invite them inside when all is secure."

"Servants inside?" the countess said doubtfully. "They have warm blankets, but if you want. Have Amy go out and tell them to go through the back door into the back room. That is very generous of you. In my day, they just stayed outside. I remember when I was young, I thought it was quite cruel, then I didn't think about it. It was just the way it was. It is so good of you to mention it."

"Amy?"

But I was already back in my sweater and hurried out. They were hitching the carriage to the post. The horses already had feedbags over their muzzles and were obviously content. Heavy wool blankets covered their backs, and the bridles and reins were already disconnected.

"Hello," I called.

"Why, hello, Miss Amy," one replied. He was tall with very dark skin, a long, angular nose and thin lips. He looked like a white man with black skin.

His friend nodded with a huge smile. He was the man I saw on the carriage's side when I was at the station. His smile never seemed to leave.

"The countess wants you to come inside and sit on the back porch where it's warm when you're done."

"We're done," the younger man said with a grin. "Your timing was perfect, Miss Amy."

I stopped. It made sense they knew my name because they heard the countess use it on my last visit. But I didn't know them at all. They just seemed to blend in the background, which, I found out later, was the mark of a good servant.

"Well, I feel remiss. I don't know your names, but you know mine."

"Well, we wouldn't want you to feel remiss," the older

one said with some amusement. "This here young man is Fredrick."

He bowed very ceremoniously. I remembered he said it to Thrushy and Finchy at the café.

"And they call me Killy." He also bowed.

"Well, I'm happy to make your acquaintance. Mr. Fredrick and—"

"Please, now, Miss Amy," Fredrick interrupted, "no Mister for us. It won't do for the white girl to call the servants Mister. Just Fredrick is all I need."

"And Killy for me," said the older one firmly.

"How did you get a name like Killy?"

"It's short for Achilles, but I don't go by that name. It makes me feel like a heel."

I giggled my approval and we talked on the way to the porch door. They were quite amiable and friendly. Killy had worked for the countess for over forty years, Fredrick for twenty-five. They felt very lucky to have such an employer who paid well and treated them with respect. Fredrick also mentioned that I knew his aunt.

"I do?" I asked, puzzled.

"My Aunt Cici, from the kitchen."

"She's your aunt? I'll be sure to tell her I met you."

"Oh, don't do that. We haven't spoken to each other in thirty-three years and counting. When Aunt Cici gets mad at you, then she's REALLY mad. She has a heart of gold," he smiled. "So much gold there's no room left for forgiving."

"You haven't spoken in thirty-three years?"

"No, little miss, not a word."

"What happened?" I asked, unaware I was getting into personal territory.

"Well," he said sadly, "she baked up some cookies for

her shop. She had a bakery back then instead of a fancy restaurant. And I took a whole bowl of them and shared them with my friends, not knowing they were for a customer. When they came looking for their cookies, they weren't there. That was a problem. They were paid for in advance and she used most of the money for special ingredients. That was a bigger problem.

"Those folks were MAD. But not like she was. Threw me out of her shop and said never come back. Wouldn't forgive me for nothing. Then her and my Mama got into it and they stopped speaking. Didn't talk for twenty years until my Mama died. Didn't talk to me even then. Never said nothing when my family all died when our house burned down. She and those boys are my only living relatives and we don't talk. All because of a bowl full of cookies."

I felt sad for him, but his smile returned.

"But some day, the Lord will lock us up on a cloud together until we put it all behind us."

I opened the door to let them in. They pulled up a couple of chairs by the portable stove.

Fredrick said, "Now, you go in and enjoy yourself. You made us very happy just by listening and talking to us and inviting us into the warm."

The dress was waiting for me patiently, but the ladies were not so patient.

"Next time, just invite them in. You don't have to show them where to sit or make them a meal," Aunt Sharon teased me. "We want to see you in the dress."

"Yes, go ahead and try it on," Brigitte told me. "Even if it needs a little altering, you'll impress everyone to no end."

Betsy nodded so I ran into my parents' bedroom and quickly changed.

I heard the voices in the main room talking while I inspected myself in the full-length mirror. It was perfect. It didn't need any adjustments. I entered the main room and instead of a curtsy, lifted the edges of the dress slightly and nodded. Another tumble like that could cause some serious damage to my already battered ego.

"Bravo," clapped the countess. "You are the loveliest child I think I ever saw. And I'm so glad you didn't curtsy. They're painful to watch."

I blushed.

"I just found out her shoes are too big. She's probably sliding around in them," Mom defended me.

"Well, she made the perfect adjustment," the countess said. "I heard she was very sick last night and came over straightway to make sure she was recovering. She looks fine. Just beautiful in that dress. Betsy, you are a wizard at the sewing wheel."

Brigitte Nye spoke, "Well now, I can't say I can compete with that wonderful dress, but I heard you were low on ginger, so I brought a couple of roots for you." She turned to me, "Minced ginger in cookies is soooo good. Do you like ginger cookies?"

"I do when they have sugar in them."

All eyes turned to Mom, who frowned at me and simply said, "Rat."

The other ladies were quite amused by this.

"Hey," I replied, indignant, "you said we can't call each other that. You made me apologize."

"You are right. One hundred percent right. And when you're right, you're right. I apologize. I'm sorry you're a rat."

The whole room burst in laughter.

"Why, Cassie," said Betsy. "Cookies without sugar? You

and Mary are such…sisters."

"You can feed then to the chickens, maybe they'll taste exotic," Darlene said. "The chickens, I mean."

"Did they taste good?" Betsy asked me, trying to sound innocent without success.

I scowled while I shook my head no.

"Whatever were you thinking?" the countess asked as the laughter played out.

"Well, Dr. Gannon said she needs to be on a bland diet, but he said ginger would be good for her, so I tried to follow doctor's orders."

"Well, yeah," said Brigitte. "Give the sick child the worst food possible. It stops them from faking it to get out of chores. Won't have any medicinal value."

"Same thing with castor oil. A child who willingly takes castor oil isn't *pretending* to be sick at all."

And so the conversation went. It was decided that I was over my food poisoning. Dr. Gannon's dietary advice was suspect. I would enjoy school. My school dress would be ready tomorrow and we'd pick it up at church. I could play the violin.

"I heard," Brigitte said, "she's not bad at all for someone without formal lessons."

"I heard she played like an angel," Darlene said.

"I didn't know she played," said Aunt Sharon. "How come I'm the aunt and I'm last to know?"

"We just found out yesterday at Betsy's. Apparently," Mom said giving me a momentary glare, "Amy thought it was state secret. But I'm glad you found out. Maybe we can get her to play for us."

"I would love that," said Darlene. "Pastor Josephson told us you played like a bird. He's hoping she might play at church, especially on the holidays. Perform for us, Amy."

"Who's Pastor Josephson?" I asked.

"From the Baptist Church, the one we go to," Mom replied, frowning. "How did he even know she played?"

Darlene shrugged, "He must have connections. I learned it from him."

Brigitte nodded, "I was there with her. I thought you called him, Cassie."

"No, not me. Seems kind of disturbing that so much happens here in the house and everybody in town knows about it," she shook her head and sighed. "But that's the modern world, I guess." She turned to me. "Play something for us."

I played my usual pieces—*Greensleeves, Oh Danny Boy, Nearer My God to Thee,* and *Amazing Grace.* I could always tell when I did well because the countess flashed a contented smile. She winced when I missed a note or two.

"We love it," they said, applauding my efforts.

I started to acknowledge their clapping by putting a foot back.

"Never curtsy when holding your instrument," the countess warned me.

"If you play at the church, you should wear that dress," Darlene said, while the others nodded in agreement.

"And you look lovely in it. I think you should hang it up so I doesn't get wrinkled," Betsy smiled at me. "I'm afraid the pinafore will be much less elaborate."

I changed back to my old dress and was back in no time.

"The pinafore will be fine. All we want is something that fits and keeps her covered and comfortable," Mom was saying, "with as little trouble as possible. We've had enough trouble over the years."

"We have. What with our husbands being so obstinate and all," Brigitte said.

The countess asked, "What does Amy know of your…family's history?"

"Well, nothing, it's been hectic since she's arrived," Mom replied.

"With the two wives here, it might be a good time for her to find out. You can correct each other's…misperceptions."

Brigitte shrugged and looked at Mom, who began, "Paul was the fifth of six sons and two daughters. Now to say his father was meaner than a rabid dog is an injury to rabid dogs everywhere. He came from the east, Georgia, I think. Paul never talks about him, but then, Paul was two when he died. His name was Clay Villians. Said he was somehow related to the Faucettes, though they never allowed his claim.

"Well now, old Tom Ridgeway had quite a bit of land west of the Malmort and was in his last years. When he was fifty-five years old, his wife Mary had a baby girl, named Matty, but she died in the birthing process. Tom and his sister got her raised to past her sixteenth birthday. Tom was past seventy and in his declining years when Clay Villians rode in seeking work. Old Tom hired him and things worked out for a month or so, then Clay decided to marry Matty. Tom wouldn't hear of it. Some drifter with no prospects? He fired him on the spot and told him to leave.

"So, Clay picks him up and throws him in the pig pen. Chases him away from the fence every time he tried to crawl over. Matty was frantic, crying and yelling for him to stop, but he wouldn't until he got old Tom's blessing. Which he got. And he pulled Tom out and tossed him in a horse trough to clean up. Matty was screaming for him to go away. She'd never marry him. He said, 'Oh yes, you will.' And dragged her to the pig pen, but she consented to be his wife before he threw her in."

"Where was Depjim?" I asked.

"Not born yet," Mom replied. "And the sheriff back then was a carpetbagger from the north. He wasn't really a sheriff anyway. More of a tax collector.

"The 'Old Ridgeway' place became known as the 'Villians Place,' anyone who called it the Ridgeway house got a mouth full of fist. But I guess he was good enough to Mattie. Never hurt her as far as anyone knows. Anyways, Tom died soon after and her two brothers came to get their inheritance Clay met them with a shotgun and said the only thing they were getting is buckshot. So, they left. They knew better than to go to the sheriff. And that was the last anyone heard of the Ridgeways.

"Now Clay was not a good farmer, but he had a friend named Antione Nye who was worse. Antione was Brigitte's father-in-law."

"Who I never met."

"Who she never met," Mom agreed. "Antione and Clay were two of a kind. They were long riders."

"Long riders?"

"Bank robbers. Always robbed out of state banks, which were long rides. They were operating for over forty years. Brought their sons into the occupation. Antione's brother-in-law worked for the railroad and would tell him where cash shipments were going. He'd round up a crew and they'd get the money. They never went big. Always robbed enough so that each man's share was just a bit over $100. That way they were just annoyances, not a threat."

"It worked well too," the countess said. "They had a gang of over two dozen ne'er-do-wells. Antoine and Clay always made sure it was a different group for each job. That way, no one suspected it was one big gang. Just some random bank robbers who got lucky. But still, the banks thought robbers were a serious problem and the Pinkertons fixed serious problems, usually with bullets. So, it wasn't always a safe journey. Clay Villians died in an 1894 robbery when the townspeople started firing back at them."

Mom took over the story. "Then, right before the great war, Antoine decided on one big last hit. His brother-in-law retired and they were both well over seventy by now and wanted their last days to be comfortable. There was a cash payroll of over half a million going to Edgewater, Arkansas. Paul and all his brothers were going to go. Angus Nye, Brigitte's husband, and his brothers went. And the Kaker boys."

"Like Durrell Kaker, the mean railroad man?" I asked.

"That would be him. And there were others. Rob Longley became the most well-known of the bunch. But the days of the bank robber was over, at least on horseback. Eighteen men rode into Edgewater. Three rode out. Fifteen long riders died, as well as five townsmen and a deputy. Over two dozen more were wounded. Angus Nye, Durrell Kaker and Rob Longley got away."

"What about Dad?" I asked.

"He didn't go. Anyway, Rob Longley was captured and hanged. The posse wanted him to name the others, but he wouldn't. He only said, 'You know, I look around here and see a whole lot of hate and mighty little love.' That line made him famous. It was in all the papers. And the story stayed there until we entered The Great War a week later."

"Why wasn't Dad in the raid?" I asked, fascinated.

"He was in jail, luckily for him. Mattie died earlier that year and Vincent came to town with his lawyer to collect his and his sister Deborah's share of the inheritance. Paul thought they were northern carpetbaggers. He drew his gun on them and told them to get out of town and never come back.

"Well, they came back, with deputies and an arrest warrant. Paul got thirty days in jail and while he was cooling his heels, the raid happened."

"Deputy Wheeler, who was here before Depjim, was able to convince Paul that Vincent was indeed his half-brother and they made peace. They worked together and got Paul's family all situated. Now Vincent could read and write and fixed it so everyone got their fair share of inheritance. Most of the family moved to Baton Rouge and Deborah introduced them around the city.

"Well, lawmen were everywhere by now. Looking to solve every unsolved crime in the state by pinning them on the boys, even though everything they did was out of state. So, the three desperados decided to join the army."

"I thought Rob Longley didn't give their names," I said.

"Well, he didn't, but some of them burned their names on their saddles. That gave everything away. They weren't planning on a wall of bullets when they got there."

"I don't think they planned much of anything," the countess said dryly.

Mom continued, "Well, Paul blamed the other two for the raid turning out so bad. Said they could have done more for the others when the bullets started flying. The only thing they could have done is talk the others out of going in the first place. And I think that was unreasonable on his part. But his resentment just festered. To this day, he has nothing to do with Angus Nye or Durrell Kaker."

"And it works both ways," Betsy added. "Durrell Kaker thinks he should have been promoted to captain when he was in the army. He distinguished himself very bravely in battle and has a drawer full of medals, but an officer has to lead men and Paul wasn't going to be led by Durrell Kaker. Angus was lucky enough to be assigned to artillery, so he wasn't involved in their disputes, but he and Paul had already developed a healthy hatred for each other. And it looks like it will never be resolved."

Brigitte said, "And that's why Cassie and I used to be close friends but hardly talk to each other now. Our men both forbid us from socializing. Doesn't stop us but makes things unsettled in the home. At least mine."

"Paul prefers me not to see you but respects my wishes. I can keep my friends. He just doesn't want to be around when you're over here," Mom replied.

They did that pretend hug thing adults do.

"So, when Uncle Vincent helped Dad plant pecans and raise chickens, it wasn't here?" I asked.

"It was their family homestead," Aunt Sharon replied. "Vincent bought out the widows. That left Paul and Vincent with all that land. Just a few dozen acres went to Buford Lawton, their nephew, Matthew's oldest son. He does some kind of business in New Orleans. They planned to grow sugar cane, but Paul came back wounded and Vincent knew he'd never farm again, so he turned the land into a pecan grove. It was a brilliant idea. Then Paul met Cassie and the rest is history. We made a bit of money on those pecans, moved over here and had the chicken sheds built."

"So, we own land on the other side of the Malmort?" I asked.

"We do. Paul and Vincent go over there a lot to tend the trees and keep it up. There's also a house and a barn. We thought Vincent and Sharon would move in when they left Baton Rouge, but they wanted to be closer, so Gramma

Morris sold them their house and we all became neighbors."

"That house was Gramma Morris's wedding present," Mom added. "Her parents gave them the land and Blackjack Morris, her father-in-law, had the house built. When her parents died, her husband and she moved back over here so they could tend to her younger sisters and start their own family.

"That was so wonderful too. My parents were stationed all over the country, so I was raised in this house, mainly by Gramma Morris. She likes to think of herself as crusty and stern, but inside, all mush. When Grampa died, she was old and alone, so I moved back in. Then I married Paul and his family moved in, and now it's all of us."

"And it was all so romantic," Darlene said. "The two social outcasts found each other and became pillars of the community."

Mom glared at her for a second and the subject quickly changed to my school dress and how lovely it would be, my rapidly approaching first day of school, and all the new friends I would have.

Soon, Betsy had to leave to finish my dress. The countess to take a nap. Brigitte and Darlene to get dinner ready.

"It was so much fun to see you again," Brigitte said while Darlene nodded enthusiastically.

"Yes," said Darlene, "we should do this much more often. Now that you're in privacy, we should stop by to see what we can do for you while you get more fat and helpless."

"We have to go," Brigitte said quickly. "Let's hop on, Darlene."

"I would love that," Mom said insincerely. "Some adult

conversation is so welcome to me now that I won't get out much. But please don't let me be a bother."

"You? A bother? Never," they laughed and their shay cantered down the drive.

We waved when they turned on the street and they could catch a glimpse of us. Mom put her arm around my shoulder and squeezed and we went back inside.

Aunt Sharon was waiting to say good-bye.

"I wonder about that woman sometimes," she said to Mom. "Doesn't seem to know what she's saying. I think it's women like that who kept us from voting all these years."

"I could vote all my adult life," Mom shrugged.

They did the hug and fake kiss thing and soon it was just Mom and me.

"Were you really a social outcast?" I asked her.

"Now really," she replied, "but sometimes people do things other people find unforgivable even though it doesn't concern them."

"Oh? Like what?"

"Oh, just things. We'll talk about them later."

"Why not now? We're family. Shouldn't we discuss things like this?"

"You're right. We should. And we will discuss it. I just don't want you in the room when we do."

I learned a lot from that party. I had three fathers in my life. One was a rum runner, one worked in an illegal speakeasy, and one was a reformed bank robber. I had two mothers who both were disowned by their parents. Not every young girl could brag about a family like that. But then, not many would want to.

Chapter 17

New Encounters

We cleaned up after our guests and Mom took a nap while I dusted and generally found something to do. I got out the violin and started to play again. Music brought out a melancholy in me. It felt like I was playing to an invisible audience who enjoyed my efforts but couldn't let me know it. I felt strangely and sadly content.

After maybe thirty minutes, I put the instrument away, wrapped a sweater around myself and walked outside. It was brisk, but not cold and I made my way around the dark water of the pond.

Beyond the oak was the pine forest, rising up where the meadow ended, almost like a wall. It blessed me with its wonderful pine scent. The fragrant air was delicate and reminded me of Christmas, when my father would bring a fir tree in for us to decorate.

But this was different. The pine mingled with fresh air, seasoned with a slight, almost imperceptible tinge of death. I was going to look at The River of Bad Death, after all.

After quite a few steps, I could hear the rush of water leading the way. Scraggly pines and dormant oaks slept peacefully as I trudged upwards to the hilltop. Leafless briars and thorn bushes guarded the forest floor. Beyond them all was the river, flowing smoothly, barely moving at all. The shoreline where the river rock and driftwood gathered was where the swooshing sounds emanated as the water flowed over and around those barriers.

The rocks were gray survivors of bedrock being worn away by the water and smothered in yellow and dark green moss. A rotten potato sort of odor drifted my way. Sulfur, I was told later. The Malmort flowed through the Sulfur Hills of Arkansas, an area loaded with the yellow mineral.

"People are afraid of it."

I turned around and there was Huck, rubbing his hands together and leering at me, while liking his lips. He winked and I shivered with revulsion.

"The river. It smells bad. It lures you onto it with promises of massive fish, but you don't eat the fish. They eat you." He started to tickle me. "Bite, bite, bite, bite." He said as he poked my ribs.

I wrenched away from him yelling, "Leave me alone. Get away."

His mocking laugh filled my ears. I ran about ten feet and turned to glare at him. He was still there, staring at me.

"Don't you like to play? I have other games we can play. Just for two."

"You just stay away from me."

He laughed.

"Stay away in the day. Come close at night. I know all about it."

He took a menacing step towards me and I turned and ran as fast as I could. He didn't follow me. He taunted me one more time.

"Play hard to get, Missy, but I always *get* when I play," he called out behind me while laughing gleefully.

I was out of the woods and into the meadow. I looked

behind me, but Huck wasn't following me, so I slowed down to a more-or-less casual walk while catching my breath. The house was about a hundred yards in front of me and Uncle Vincent's truck was pulling out of the drive.

Everyone was home when I entered the door. Mom was awake and everyone was talking at once. Holly whooped when she saw me, and Michelle and Anna Marie rushed over to hug me.

"I got a ninety-two on my test and Mrs. Porter dropped everyone's lowest test sore," She was jumping up and down with excitement.

The other girls were dancing along, except Annette, who was too mature for such things.

"Good job, Anna Marie," I said, trying to put some enthusiasm in my voice.

"And it's all your doing. You're ten times the teacher that old Mrs. Porter is," she replied.

"Well, I wouldn't get carried away. You were the one to take the test, not me."

"That's so right," said Gramma Morris, squeezing both of our shoulders. "You two make a great team. Just don't be so quick to blame someone else," squeezing Anna Marie's shoulder extra hard, "And don't be so quick to take offense. And forgive easier." Squeezing my shoulder.

"And for the ladies of the hour," Mom said brightly, "Anna Marie's favorite dinner: pork chops and rice with gravy." She raised her voice in falsetto, "Yaaaaaaay."

There was a half-hearted joining in.

"I like pork chops," Anna Marie said, "but my favorite is fried catfish."

A much more enthusiastic cheer rose.

"Well, maybe tomorrow," Mom said. "Maybe you can take Amy fishing when we get back from town."

"NO," I said, a little too loud, "I don't ever want to go near the Malmort again."

"I meant in the pond."

"There either."

I walked out of the front door to end the conversation, but I could hear them asking each other what just happened here. They didn't understand and I couldn't explain it. After all, he didn't hurt me or threaten me. He just bothered me. What could I say? I'm afraid of being tickled?

I sat on the porch swing and swayed back and forth for a while when I heard footsteps and the door open. It was Annette. She sat next to me and rocked gently, following my rhythm.

"He was out there, wasn't he?"

I looked at her for a moment, then nodded.

"He won't hurt you. He just doesn't know how to talk to people. That's his way of playing. To let you know he likes you. He doesn't know how awful he sounds. But you live here. This is your home. You should be able to walk the property any time you want without him bothering you. You want to tell Papa? I'll go with you if you want."

I shook my head no.

"It wouldn't feel right if I got him in trouble. I'm so new here. I just need to find my way is all."

She nodded and squeezed my hand. Then we rocked for a bit, until Uncle Vincent's truck pulled up to the house. As if there was an invisible cue, she stood up.

"Time to help make pork chops," she said.

And they were good. Mom pan seared them and let them cook in broth until they were tender, done and tasty. The rice and pork gravy were superb. I feasted that night. No worrying about anything (except maybe Huck), and everyone was happy. Dad was proud that Anna Marie did so well and happy that I helped. And I was happy too.

When dinner was over, I was sent to the couch and I read to everyone, with Holly firmly planted next to me with her head on my shoulder. It was nice being a part of the family and having such an important role. The official reader.

We discussed the book together when I was done reading. Then we all went to bed. I slept in the bed again with Holly and Anna Marie. That evening was one of my most cherished memories.

The next day was not so precious. It started off while we were waiting for breakfast. Annette and Michelle were put in charge of making pancakes while Mom took me to the back porch with Gramma Morris.

"What did she do?" I heard one of them ask as the door closed behind us.

"Now Amy," said Gramma Morris, "can you tell us what happened when you left New York? Just the part of you leaving."

I went into detail of how we hurried to the train station and I was on board when Papa Gio and Mr. Dragucci confronted Aunt Mary while the other two men watched. How he grabbed her shoulders and how Mr. Dragucci chased after the train. And I added where the two other men followed me to St. Louis but were turned back because I gave the stuffed bear away and they caught the wrong girl.

"Quite the adventure," Gramma Morris commented. "That explains a lot. Why you packed so little, how we didn't know anything was wrong until we were told you were coming. Good thing she got you away from there. Good thinking on her part to send you here."

"Amy," Mom said, "we called New York to let Mary know you got here safely. I spoke to your Aunt Isadora.

Mary fell down a staircase and broke her ankle and arm. And she's going to have a baby. And the girls are squabbling."

"I thought Julia, Isabella and Sophie were all friends."

"Not anymore."

"They want me to go back to help?"

"Over my dead body," Gramma Morris said forcefully. "They lost. We won. You're here."

"But it would be nice if you wrote her a letter saying you miss her and are thinking of her."

It was a short letter. I wished her a speedy recovery and thanked her for the train tickets. I said hello to Julia and Patrick and wished them well. The rest of her family I ignored. As Papa Collins said, 'If you can't say anything good, don't say anything at all.'

After the note was sealed in an envelope and stamped, we ate and got ready to go to town. I was getting shoes that fit and little ribbons and ties for my hair that matched Anna Marie's outgrown dresses I inherited.

But the first thing for me to do was visit the countess. One hour of dusting. Ten pounds of dust. But the furniture shined by the time we got out our violins. The lesson went well. We learned some pieces by Dvorak and a few church hymns. By ten o'clock, we were done. I packed my instrument and music away and Fredrick drove me to meet Mom at the ten-cent store.

I stepped down onto the dingy yellow wood plank sidewalk and walked into the store, but Mom wasn't there yet. After a cursory look around, I stepped back outside and waited. A sweet-tempered girl roughly my age skipped up to the door and started to open it but stopped and looked at me.

"Hi," I said.

"Hi, yourself," she responded with a smile. "You passing through town?"

"No, I live here, across the creek."

"I don't recall ever seeing you here before. You go to the Catholic school?"

"No, I just moved here from New York. My name's Amy Collins."

"Oh, my. I'm not allowed to talk to you at all. If my mother sees me with you, I'll get in bad trouble—"

"Laura May Sauveterre, get over here this minute," a woman yelled out.

"Yes, Mama," Laura said quickly and ran over to her.

They both turned to look at me. They favored each other except her mother's face, while possibly pretty at one time, was twisted and red in her fury while Laura appeared more curious than anything else.

"You stay away from my daughter, you…you *thing*," she yelled shrilly.

She yanked her daughter by the hand, storming off in righteous rage, leaving me hurt and confused, with tears in my eyes.

"What was *that* about?"

I turned and there were two blonde girls in Catholic uniforms staring at me. They were roughly as old as me. It was hard to tell as I was about two inches smaller than most girls my own age.

I shrugged while taking in a deep breath to calm down.

"I don't rightly know," I said with a steady voice. "She asked me my name, and that was her reaction."

"What is your name?"

"Amy Collins," I replied, braced for more rejection.

"Well, hi, Amy Collins. My name is Meredith Baxter, Merry to my friends and I hope you'll be one. And this is

Lizzy Farrell."

"I heard of you," said Lizzy. "You just moved here. You live with your mother and her husband, Paul Villians. You're in fourth grade. And you're not Catholic."

"Well, actually, we did go to Sunday mass. My father was Irish and my step-father was Italian, after all."

"Did you go to catechism?"

"Well, no."

"Then you're not a Catholic."

"Oh."

"That's all right. God loves all people, even if they're not Catholic. I think."

"We have to go," said Merry. "Our choir is singing in the Mardi Gras celebration down in New Orleans. We have to go practice."

"Oh," I replied, "I was wondering why you were wearing your school uniforms on a Saturday."

We said our good-byes and I waited a few more minutes before Mom showed up. I told her about Laura and her hostile mother, and she just lowered her head and shook it sadly.

"Laura May's mother is Catherine Landacre Sauveterre. She's Hugo Landacre's older sister. We used to be friends years ago. We were a whole gaggle of young girls, just giggling away at nothing for years. Then, there was an…incident and everything changed. We weren't friends anymore and realized we never were and would never be again."

"What happened?"

"It's not something we should talk about on the street where other people can hear."

"Oh. Well, how about at home?"

"It's not something to discuss in front of the other girls."

"Just you and me on the back porch?"

"It's not something to discuss in front of you." She circled her hand in front of my face playfully and tapped my nose on the 'you.'

"Now, if you want to talk about something, we can talk. Did you and your Aunt Mary have *The Talk*, yet?"

"*The Talk*?" That sounded ominous.

"Obviously not. Well, you're young yet but it's time you know how life works for girls and women. The downside of femininity, so to speak."

And so we had *The Talk*. On the street where other people could hear, although, if I must be fair, she was discreet and stopped talking in mid-word if anyone was even near close enough to hear. When she was done, I was overwhelmed a little bit.

"Is all that really true?"

"It is. I started when I was twelve and nobody had told me anything. No warning at all. I thought I was dying."

"Oh. Why is it we could have *that* conversation on the street but not the other?"

"Some questions have no answer."

We reached a small building with no sidewalk and a faded shingle swaying in the slight breeze: *Dupree Shoes and Repair.* She shushed me and we walked into the claustrophobic little shop.

Trevor Dupree was an old man. A civil war veteran, I was later told, which made him roughly the countess's age.

"Well, now, Mrs. Villians and the newest Villians. How do you do?" he said, as we walked through his little kingdom of shoes. He had shelves of boots, moccasins, formal shoes, lady's shoes, children's shoes, and any other item a person could put on their feet. A few small oil portraits graced the wall behind his work bench.

He was very formal, but polite, like he felt he was talking to someone of highly inferior status. I didn't think I would like him.

"Amy here needs a pair of shoes that fit better," Mom said primly.

"Well now, Little Amy. I thought you'd be bigger. What with Michael Collins being your father," he said politely, glancing slyly at Mom, who didn't seem to hear as she pretended to shop.

"Someone has to be the shortest," I said defensively, remembering one of Papa's life lessons.

"And do you know what being the shortest means?" he asked, then answered his own question. "It means you're the smartest."

Now, I thought I *would* like him.

"Your name is almost the same as Mr. Dupris who runs the garage," I ventured.

"Almost," he agreed while measuring my feet. "We live in America, so my branch of the family Americanized the name. He keeps it the French way. With an 's' you don't even pronounce."

"So, you're the same family?"

"Only by blood," he replied.

How else?

"You see, way back in 1750 or so, our ancestor, Jean Dupris came here because he heard there was a need for a leather worker. He became quite successful here. And he had lots of children but two sons in particular showed promise. Jules was the shoemaker. Claude made saddles and bridles and everything else. That way they wouldn't be rivals.

"But they soon became bitter rivals. You see, a peddler and his family rode through town, selling metalworks, you know, pots and pans and things like that. This being a trading post, he was in heaven. Decided to settle down.

"He had the most beautiful daughter who ever walked on this earth. Her name was Angelique. The perfect name. She was mostly French, as all the truly superior people are, with hair as blonde as the sun and eyes of sky blue. And she was royalty, of sorts. She liked to brag that she was 1/64 Choctaw Indian. Descended from a real princess. Both brothers had to have her. Jules, my great-great grandfather won her hand and married her.

"Claude went insane with rage. He yelled and swore and eventually was forced to live on the other side of the Malmort. Well, he just left town for two years. When he came back, he had his own bride and she was really pretty too, so I heard, but he still sought his revenge. He found some old man who came to town saying he knew the family.

"He said she was not descended from Indian nobility, but by a black slave. To some people, it didn't matter. To some, it did. That's her."

He pointed to one of the pictures behind the counter. It was a blonde woman with excellent hair and perfect features. She was absolutely stunning with her laughing blue eyes and aquiline nose.

"Jules was so angry with his brother he changed the family name and disowned him and his family. He even hired a lawyer to do her family tree. Came back inconclusive. No Indian or black could be found.

"The Indian princess story was just something she was told and innocently repeated. The black slave story was all lies. No one in my branch ever had anything to do with those people ever since. Victor Dupris can go buy his shoes out of a Sears catalogue as far as I'm concerned."

"You've been feuding ever since 1750?" I was speechless.

"No. Feuding means to bother each other. We leave each other alone. After all, he is just some peasant. I come from royalty."

"1/1024th royal blood?" I asked after a quick mental calculation.

"You know another way of saying 1/1024th royal blood?" he asked with a smile.

I shook my head no.

"Royalty."

He found a pair of leather shoes that fit perfectly.

"Here you go, Little Amy. Shoes meant for a princess."

"I never saw him talk to anyone like that. Now I know why he thinks he's better than most everyone else in town," Mom said as we walked out of the shop, carrying my old shoes in her handbag while I squeaked along beside her in my new ones, "but nothing equalizes people more than a purse full on money."

"That's filled with money?" I asked pointing to her slightly fraying bag.

"Don't be so literal. It's filled with your old shoes now. But we have a little left for some ribbons for your hair."

We walked back to the ten-cent store. It seemed everybody stopped in mid motion when we entered, then turned to watch us intently.

"Well, don't mind us," Mom said lightly. "We're just here for some hair ribbons and ties. You can go back to staring at each other in just a bit."

The clerk hurried up to the counter and we examined ribbons for maybe a minute.

"I like the red one," I said hopefully. It was a big one that would be centered on the back of my head. It reminded me of Christmas.

"Of course," said the clerk. "All the girls like red. But with those hazel eyes, don't you think a dark green would look wonderful? No one could miss those little peepers with a dark green ribbon like this."

There were no other words spoken by either the clerk or Mom. Everyone else in the store was sullen and avoided eye contact. The green ribbons and ties were safely in her purse and we headed back to the café.

"I've decided to put off going into privacy for another week," Mom said to Gramma Morris and Cici over coffee in the kitchen, while I drank tea with sweet cream. "I think I need to be close in case Amy needs me, at least for her first week in school. It certainly can't hurt to be near."

"You off your rocker?" Cici asked incredulously. "She's just going to school, not a war zone. You need to stay home, knit some baby socks or something and get fat and content till the baby comes. You stay on your feet all day and no telling what will happen." She pointed at Mom's bump, "That baby in there needs a whole lot more care than Amy does.

"Not to mention the fact that you're too tired to be much help anyway. All you do is sit at the counter and hand out menus and say, 'hi,' when people walk in. And dream about what your life would be like if you never met that disgusting pig, Hugo Landacre."

"I'd be with Paul," she said distractedly. "And Amy would be his. And his children would mine. But you know who I feel sorry for?"

"No, who?"

"Estelle Beaumont. She married him."

"I thought Dad married a woman named Francine Scott from New Orleans."

"Hugo Landacre married her."

"Francine Scott?"

"Estelle Beaumont. Paul married Francine Scott.

Too difficult.

"Oh," I said politely. The rest of the conversation was just words to me until it was time to go.

"We don't need you here, Miss Cassie," Cici said firmly.

"Amy does," she claimed just as firmly.

I agreed with Cici but knew Mom well enough by now to know any argument would be a lost cause.

And on that note, we went home, leaving Cici shaking her head.

CHAPTER 18

SUNDAY

Sunday was my last day before school started. Breakfast
was pancakes. There were no pockets of raw flour lurking
in them, which was good, and there was butter and honey
as well. I preferred maple syrup from New Hampshire, but
quickly adjusted. The quality of the food more than made
up for that little disappointment.

It was church day and we all wore our best clothes. We
took our baths the prior evening, after dinner so we would
be ready and at our cleanest best. Although that was
debatable. The tub was in the kitchen, next to the sink. We
attached a sluice from the water pump to the tub's side and
pumped, while Mom set a couple of pots on the stove to
heat up. When the waters were mixed, they were clear. We
left the kitchen while Dad and Jason took the first bath.
Then Mom and Holly took a turn. Anna Marie and I were
next.

"What about Annette and Michelle? They're older," I
said, while eyeing the slimy soap filmed water that waited
for us.

"They're taking sponge baths," Mom replied.

"I can take a sponge bath."

"You need a full cleansing bath. How clean can you get

with only a sponge bath?"

"Cleaner than soaking in this. River water looks cleaner."

"Amy!"

"I just don't understand why some of us get to take nice clean sponge baths and I have to swim in…this."

Gramma Morris stepped in, "Michelle and Annette are going to stand in this very same water and sponge down. Right now, they are in an overabundance of femininity. That's why."

"What does that mean?"

"Amy," said Mom, obviously at the end of her patience, "you remember *The Talk?*"

"Yes. Oh." I thought for a second, "How about I take a sponge bath with them to show sympathy for their situation?"

"Get in the tub. Now."

Reasoning with my new family was pretty close to a lost cause.

So church was calling us. We were clean (sort of) and wearing our nice, well-ironed, Sunday best. I wore my new dress. Everyone else looked very pretty, in a practical sort of way, with a ribbon on every head, at least for the girls. Porky and Huck wiped all the dust and dew from the wagon so we would stay that way.

Uncle Vincent and Aunt Sharon drove Mom and Jason there because the car was less bumpy, easier to get in and out of and Mom was getting bigger every day. Dad drove the wagon with the rest of us, his wooden leg pointing just outside the splashguard, appearing completely comfortable in his skin.

"You'll just love my friends," Anna Marie said to me. "We've known each other our whole lives and we've always been friends. And they'll just love you too. We'll all be like sisters to each other."

More sisters? I have Annette, who doesn't mind that grown man who is nothing short of creepy. Michelle, who called me a freak. Anna Marie, who is only nice sometimes. And Holly, who's a little clingy. If I count Julia, then I have one who always sided with the evil stepsisters when they moved in. I don't want any more sisters.

But I smiled as she droned on about their adventures in discovering life, games and things they did together. Also, they seemed to stay after school a lot. Not their fault, of course. It was that mean teacher. Quite the trio. Her friends, Martha and Maureen Davenport, were ten and twelve, and Anna Marie would be eleven tomorrow. Their father was a lawyer who met their mother during the war and married her within a week. As their mother's parents were invalids, they stayed here until they died. When he wanted to move back to New Orleans, she convinced him to stay. After all, they had a house and yard of their own now. And the children belonged in Faucette. It was home.

"How romantic," she gushed at the end.

I would have called it practical, but it was not an important difference. What *was* an important difference was reality.

We got off the wagon and Anna Marie called the girls. They turned around with unmistakably unfriendly faces and waited for us. I pulled back a little in case the hostility was directed at me.

"Hey there, Maureen, Martha," Anna Marie said, blithely unaware of their stone-cold stares. "This is my new sister, Amy Collins, from New York."

Maureen nodded and Martha said, "Hi."

"Hi," I said pleasantly, though I had a good idea from yesterday where this was headed.

"We can't play with you anymore," Maureen said firmly.

"Our Mom said we're too grown to be around any Villians."

"She did," Martha agreed. "She doesn't want us to be friends with you anymore."

"That doesn't mean we don't like you," Maureen added quickly. "But we'll get in trouble if she finds out we talk to you unless it's strictly school or church."

"Girls," an adult voice called out harshly.

I turned around and there was a large-boned woman marching towards us.

"What did I say to you?"

"We were just saying good-bye," said Martha.

"Well, you said it. Now, get to your class." She pushed their shoulders around and pushed them inside the building, leaving Anna Marie open-mouthed and gaping at them.

"Your friends seemed nice," I said, trying to soften the blow. "But their mother could scare Mad Dog Coll."

"Who?"

"Never mind, let's go."

Our Sunday School class was mercifully small, fourth and fifth graders, so it was just the Davenport girls, Laura May, a boy named Robbie Lee, Anna Marie, and myself. Our teacher was Mrs. Gardener, a middle-aged no-nonsense type with hair parted down the middle and a net holding each captive strand in place. I was sure if she ever smiled, her face would break.

Anna Marie introduced me and we started in prayer. Afterwards, Mrs. Gardener asked me some questions about New York and then asked me if anything impressed me about Faucette. It was not an easy question to answer because I felt like I had stepped back in time, which would not be a polite way to start things off. So, I mentioned

Gramma Morris's creepy story about the echo on the river. Mrs. Gardener suppressed a smile while the other children laughed out loud. Anna Marie lowered her head like she wanted to crawl away.

"That story came over with Christopher Columbus," Martha said.

Laura May nodded, "They've been telling that story ever since they found the river."

"Yeah," said Robbie, getting excited. "It's so old, it's got dinosaur manure on it."

Only he didn't say manure. Mrs. Gardener whapped his knuckles with a ruler, then sent him out to sit with his parents in the adult service.

"He'll get a double whipping," Laura May said to me. "One for saying that word and one for getting sent to the main service. Parents hate to have the whole church know when you've been bad. He'll hate you forever."

"Laura May," said Mrs. Gardener, "I highly doubt he'll hold a grudge against *her* for what *he* said."

However, Laura May was the one who was right that day.

The main sermon focused on judgement, love and the church community. How ironic. I certainly felt judged, unloved and not part of any community.

Betsy had my new school dress and proudly showed it off to me after the service. I smiled and thanked her.

"Don't you like it," she asked, obviously a little hurt.

"I love it. But I don't like it here. I'm not wanted in this church."

"Of course, you are," came a man's voice from behind us.

I turned to see Pastor Seth Josephson behind me, flanked by Dad and another man I had not met. I curtsied, a bit too far left, but Betsy caught me.

"Sometimes, when you're new, people have to warm up to you," he continued, ignoring my stumble. "That's all. Now Amy, I want you to be an integral part of this church. I want you playing your violin once in a while, and I want you to be happy and smiling. Once folks get to know you, you'll be just fine. You hear?"

I nodded.

"You'll be fine here," said the other man. Just give things a chance."

"Thank you, sir," I replied.

Dad took my hand and we went back to the wagon.

"Not a bad first Sunday," he said, as he waited for us to get situated on the wagon. "You met both pastors. Seth Josephson and Martin Thomas, his apprentice."

"Apprentice?"

"He just graduated from Bible college and is doing intern work here before he gets his own flock. Just let people warm up to you and you'll fit in so tight, the whole town won't want you to ever go away."

But my experience was no different than my sisters'. My new family all had the same story. One-word answers. Conversations stopped or subjects changed when they were around. All any of them got was 'hi' and 'bye' from their friends. The church was not a warm and friendly place for any of us.

We rode home in silence, each in our own thoughts. I knew that we got the silent treatment because of me, but I didn't know why. I tried to ask Annette, since she was the oldest, but all she said was, "Give it time. They don't know what a wonderful kid you are, yet." Then she looked me straight in the eye and said, "But they will. And when they do, they'll surely feel ashamed."

Lunch was chicken salad with extra vinegar. I normally don't like vinegar in my chicken salad, but I didn't complain because I didn't have to spend half an hour picking out bones.

Dad and Jason went to see Uncle Vincent, Mom laid down for a nap, and the other girls were doing their homework at the last minute. This was a perfect time to finish reading *Rebecca of Sunnybrook Farms*, but I was restless. I put on a sweater and told Annette I was going for a walk around the pond. She nodded, but I wasn't sure if she heard me or not.

The air was brisk, just the way I like it. Winter in Louisiana was so mild. I loved the whish, whish of my shoes breezing through the grass. When I got to the wood line, I looked around to make sure Huck wasn't there and edged in closer to see the river.

It was as it was Friday. Just as dirty as the bath water, perhaps a *little* cleaner with a tangy, unwholesome smell. Still and quiet in the middle, with all the waves and babbling along the shoreline. It seemed peaceful. *I could spend a lot of time here*, I thought, and just contemplate the world, or at least my little piece of it. In fact—

"Came back to play some more?"

I whirled around and there stood Huck, leering at me while he casually leaned against a tall pine.

"No," I stammered. "I think I have to get back home now."

"No, you don't," he grinned, revealing his yellow fangs. "How about we play a game? It's called 'slumming.' It's where the boss's daughter kisses the hired hand."

"That's an awful game," I said and ran to his right, but he got in front of me and I almost ran into him. He grabbed my shoulders.

"Can't wait huh?" he said, leaning down. "Just like your mother."

My fist shot up fast and hit him hard on the bottom of his chin. It stunned him enough that I could shake loose and run all the way home.

"What's the matter with you? We were only playing."

I was scared and out of breath by the time I made it onto the back porch. I started crying. When I was done being upset, I calmly got up, walked inside and washed my face. Then I went back to the porch and finished my book. Although Annette told me she would back me if I complained about him to Dad, I was afraid. Huck was here for who knows how long? If no one believed what happened, I would always be looked at with suspicion. There was really no one to talk to about it.

By the time we started dinner, I was over it. Mom suggested that I was acting strangely but accepted that I was only tired. Dinner was delicious and I read enough to finish *The Wizard of Oz*. Gramma Morris called Mrs. De Montfort right afterwards and told us the second book, *The Marvelous Land of Oz*, would be at the desk for pick up.

How wonderful.

We all went to bed early. Tomorrow was school and none of us knew what to expect any more.

After we got in bed, Holly snuggled up to me and said, "I'm glad you're here now. It just wasn't complete before you came. I didn't know it before, but I do now."

"It's good to be here with you," I said squeezing her tight for a moment.

Anna Marie turned down the lamp and got in the bed. She didn't say a word.

CHAPTER 19

GOING TO SCHOOL

The next day was a whirlwind of activity for me. I quickly got dressed and ready for my first day of school. I was the first child up, as usual, and missed the wait for the outhouse. Breakfast was sausage, eggs and toast, though I noticed I got slightly more toast and less sausage. When all teeth were clean and heads brushed, we went out and down La Salle Road to the train tracks.

Other children merged with us, kept a distance, talked to themselves a little, and ignored us. The sky threatened rain with a slight chilly breeze. Holly hung back by me while the older girls were a few yards ahead of us. She nattered about the train and soon the bridge would be fixed and we'll just walk to school. She said the school was small and the teacher mean at times and the older kids would be moved across town to their own school. Anna Marie occasionally looked back at us, unsmiling, as always.

A few other children, including Laura May, were at the crossroad. Anna Marie's former friends, Maureen and Martha, were there also, as well as their other two sisters. Robbie Lee was there, along with a couple of older kids.

We got on the train in silence, listening only to Holly's happy chattering about nothing. Anna Marie tried to talk to her friends but was rejected immediately. The rest of us accepted our isolation stoically. I tossed a few words at Holly to keep her encouraged, since the car would be quieter than a tomb if she ceased her nattering.

The ride lasted maybe twelve hundred yards. We were only to use it to get across the creek, after all. We disembarked at the train station. We headed towards the garage and turned north, in the opposite direction of the restaurant. Two houses, old, weather beaten and neglected were to our left, and two more stood on the other side on the creek obviously abandoned with their roofs collapsed.

The one-room schoolhouse and play yard loomed over us at the next turn. I saw a swing set in the back with a matching slide and see-saw, hemmed in by a handsome picket fence. No children were using the playground equipment. It turned out that it was for exercise only. Playing was forbidden.

The school was a rather big building, cheerfully whitewashed and well maintained, by country standards. It was obviously a converted church, with an unused steeple above. If it ever held a cross, it was gone now, along with the bell it must have once had. It looked pleasant, rustic and comfortable, with two big oaks guarding it on each side. Their roots rose above the ground in a search for air and Spanish Moss swayed in the slight breeze which gave them a haunted, spooky appearance. The steeple stressed its dominance of the yard—tall, sleek, white, elegant, and empty.

Good place for bats.

"Squirrels get in the steeple all the time," Holly said. "Hunters try shooting them for squirrel stew or soup or something. Depjim always chases them off, but they usually get a couple big ones before he gets there."

Not a good place for bats. Even worse for squirrels.

With one last glace at the empty playground and cloudy gray sky beyond, we stepped into the building. The stale, heavy air had an unexpected smell of soap, chalk and a slight undertone of body odor. It seemed the first rule was that smiling was forbidden. The students who were there turned to look at us with frozen zombie faces. As students entered after us, their animation and childish joy vanished.

Dark brown desks stood perfectly lined in rows. The children sauntered over to their assigned places in silence while I stood awkwardly near the door.

"Amy, sit here," Michelle whispered, pointing to a desk next to her.

I sat down quietly.

She whispered again, "Nobody sits there anymore. She goes to the Catholic school now."

I nodded thank you as I took in the classroom. White, sturdy, plaster walls closed us in. It was a large room, both wide and deep. A clock was right above the entry, showing 7:58, with a silent second hand slowly spinning. It was heated by a propane unit, so the front windows were slightly open to let the fumes out. A few more students silently dragged themselves in before the dreaded eight o'clock bell.

At the front of the room sat the teacher's desk, large and forbidding, neat as a pin with a dime store vase holding paper flowers on one corner and a globe on the other. An American flag drooped on its golden pole in one corner and what I presumed to be the Louisiana State flag in the other next to an old wood door leading to the teacher's office. Behind the desk, a blackboard filled the wall, some words written in yellow chalk for the younger grades. Green shingles of the alphabet were posted above it, showing both printed and cursive letters. Rolled up maps were right below them. A portrait of President Hoover graced one side, another of a nice-looking man I had never seen before on the other. Michelle whispered it was the picture of Governor Huey P. Long.

The side walls had shelves built in about three feet high, loaded with textbooks. Elongated windows, pointed on top, spoke of the building's religious origin. Between these glass portals were posters representing the four seasons and a few posters of dinosaurs hung on the back walls for the boys.

The office door opened and my new teacher walked in. I expected a pointy chinned harridan with a foot long nose with warts and yellow, wolfish eyes and a mouth and chin covered in the blood of some small animal that she was eating while it was still alive. In reality, Mrs. Porter was rather pretty. She couldn't have been more than thirty with light blonde hair pulled back in a tight bun and bangs covering her forehead. She had sparkling blue eyes and full lips, with a classically angular nose. I thought she could be movie-star-gorgeous if she smiled. She wore no jewelry, although a whistle dangled from her neck. She carried a stack of papers in one hand and a long block of wood in the other.

"Is that a two by four?" I whispered quietly to Michelle, who stared straight ahead.

"Yes, it is," said Mrs. Porter with a low, throaty voice while frowning at me. "A two by four for knocking some sense into the heads of naughty children who speak without raising their hands. Who ask questions to each other instead of me. I have sixty young minds that need to be filled with knowledge, wisdom and respect. Can't have anyone disregarding the rules, being loud and obnoxious, or otherwise causing disruption. Makes it harder for everyone to learn."

She lifted the two by four like a club.

"When you're good, this won't hurt you. When you're bad..." She slammed it down on her desk, the noise almost as loud as a gunshot, reverberating around the walls and ceiling. A clicking-clacking clattering sound of a dozen squirrels running for cover sounded above us. "...it's the consequence for your actions."

She smiled at me, or more accurately, showed her fangs. No wonder the room was so unearthly quiet. Childish joy needed to be stamped out. Learning was serious stuff.

"And you, young lady, are Amy Collins. You are student sixty-one. You are in fourth grade, but you're sitting with the sophomores. Think you're quite a bit smarter than everyone else, do you?"

I gulped. Even the wicked witch of the west was nicer than her.

"Well, no," I replied, trying to not look as scared as I was. "The seat was empty, and I didn't know who sat where, so I thought."

Whap!

"Don't think. You should have come to the front desk and waited for me."

"I told her it was okay," Michelle said calmly, with her arm raised. "I didn't know that rule."

"Neither did I," Annette said with her hand up as well.

Mrs. Porter sighed, making a show of staying calm.

"On the first day of school, where do the first graders go?"

"In front of your desk. You seat them by height."

"Wouldn't it be logical and reasonable for the new students to go there as well?"

Silence.

"Very well then. Michelle and Annette, practice up on your thinking skills."

She turned to me and displayed her serrated teeth.

"Now Amy," she said with a voice of honey, "I want you to get to know your classmates. The best way I think for that to happen is for you to call roll."

She pulled out her gradebook and folded it along the seam so I wouldn't see the actual grades.

"So come up to my desk where you should have been all along and I'll let you play 'teacher' for a bit."

And so there I was on my first day, standing in front of the other children, some who were really adults to my way of thinking. I was totally uncomfortable, but I think Mrs. Porter knew that. So I began:

"Rodger Arquette."

"It's Are-kett," he groused at me.

I glanced his way. He was an older boy who silently rode the train with us that morning, sitting near Annette.

"Sorry. Catherine Beaumont," I went quickly. I heard the name pronounced earlier and guessed on the spelling, which worked out well.

"They call me Cathy One," came a long-suffering sigh from the girl next to Annette, "because there are so many of us."

"I'll remember that," I said pleasantly, and called out four more Beaumonts: Donald, Grant, Jacque, and Zachary, all scattered throughout the room, all sullen and resentful.

"Maggie Brisbois."

"Bris-a-boys," she snapped, happy to be unpleasant.

I nodded. In her case, I didn't think it mattered much because I would avoid her at all costs.

"Barbara Cloutier." I tried to pronounce it as 'Frenchy' as possible, but she still corrected me in an unfriendly way. I looked up at her. She was Michelle's friend from the train.

I got Davenport right four times with Camille, Katherine (Kay), Martha, and Maureen.

Oh, no, I thought when I saw the next name.

"Marie Desrosiers." I dropped the 'iers' and pronounced it with a long 'a' sound. She was unimpressed and corrected me, but I didn't hear much difference. Another one to avoid.

I never saw Betsy's last name spelled but guessed it on the next three: Danae, Donna and Danielle Devereaux.

The next name was Foyt. There were eight of them who were big, rugged and obviously came from the worst poverty imaginable. Anita and Calvin were the first two. Calvin sat behind Annette and Anita was with the seniors. The others were Cecil, David, Noreen, Dora, Ellen, and Mary. I had heard of inbred families before, of course, but now I was seeing one. They all had larger than average heads that swayed on impossibly long thin necks. (Gio the Giraffe would lose his nickname in a heartbeat if his friends met any of the Foyts.) Their eyes were too close together and bulged out, like insects. They had upturned noses, almost like little snouts. But what I noticed the most was the shape of their heads. They bent back at an impossible slope right above the eyebrows and angled back so that the backs of their heads were unusually thick. They all answered to their names with a blank dullness, like they were aware they were in the world but didn't really care.

Gaspard Gagneux was next. I almost got his name right, but the second 'g' was silent. Ga-no.

Then came the Kakers: Wilbur (Will), Wilfred (Fred), Wilhelmina, William (Billy), Wilma, and Wilton (Willy). I thought such similar names might be confusing to their family, but like Durrell Kaker at the train station, they were wolfish and hostile, with snarling smiles and sharp teeth, so I didn't care.

The next family name was one I had heard many times, though I didn't recognize the spelling.

"Catherine Landacre," I called.

'Land-ah-KERR," came a chorus of six voices. They were a large family of cousins. There was Cathy, Charles (Chucky), Elenora, Margaret, and Tommy. They were an interesting family. They all favored each other, with light brown hair and green eyes, except for Tommy, who was dark.

Ricky Lawton and Robbie Lee had easy names. I got Louis Lemieux right, which proved I was learning.

Albert Levesque's last name was pronounced le-VASK, so I got it wrong, but he didn't seem to care. In fact, he was kind of nice about it.

Charles and Catherine Maison's last name was three syllables. He was quiet about it but she was offended. She also let me know she was to be called Cathy Two.

There were four members of the Porter family: Cathy Three, Katherine (Kate), Beauregard, and Tim. They all said 'here' loudly and when I glanced up, they all had scowls. I smiled back at them, though I think it might have looked like a sneer.

"Joey Richard."

"It's Ri-SHARD. Get it right."

"Sorry," I muttered.

Sorry I ever met you.

I suppressed a sigh as this torture went on.

"Mary Ri-SHARDS."

A friendly laugh as I looked up.

"'A' for effort, but we're American. It's Richards, just like it's spelled."

Now a real wave of anger and discomfort went through the class as the children tried to start a debate on what made an American. It ended with a crack of the two by four and squirrel claws running away on the roof.

"Sherman Richards."

"Here."

Brother and sister obviously, with auburn hair and dark complexions. She was probably three years older than me. He sat with high schoolers, near Calvin Foyt.

I already met Laura Sauveterre and got her name just perfect. She was unimpressed but I could see that Holly was.

Stephan Tanner was about my age, very dark, almost Cuban looking.

"Anna Villians."

"AMY," she cried out as if in pain while the class laughed hysterically, "you know it's pronounced Vee-YAN."

"I did, I do. I didn't know it was spelled that way. Besides, it just says Anna and I know you as Anna Marie."

Another bang on the desk to settle down the children and scare the squirrels.

"That's good to know if we get another Anna in here," Mrs. Porter said sternly. "Go on."

Last five names: Catherine Wilson (Cathy Four), her three brothers, Derrick, Franklin and Georges (pronounced Georgsh), and a cousin named Katherine (Katie).

Yay, I was done. Papa Collins was right. The French can't speak or spell.

"Not a bad job, Amy. Your next job will be to learn

which name goes to who. There are nine Catherines in various forms. Those will be the toughest for you to learn, I would think."

I moved my desk to the fourth-grade area under her harsh guidance and sat between Robbie Lee and Tim. Billy sat behind me. Stephen and Laura were in front of me. We were the entire fourth-grade class.

Since we were given no time to get to know each other and whispering seemed to be forbidden, I sat quietly in my place, listening to Mrs. Porter explain things quickly and efficiently to each grade before giving out assignments. She started from first grade and worked up giving us all a review of each subject.

Unfortunately, it was a little too basic and the words droned on and on while I daydreamed of what life would be like if Papa Collins were still alive. We would be happy together in Manhattan and Aunt Mary would still be 'Mama' and we would be getting ready to move to Buffalo where she would take cooking lessons and—

"Amy," Mrs. Porter sternly grabbed my attention.

I looked up and she was glaring at me while the other kids were either snickering or suppressing laughs.

"Ma'am?"

"Daydream less, pay attention more," she snapped. "Your problem is twenty-six times fifteen."

I quickly multiplied twenty-six times ten to get two hundred sixty, added half of that sum in my head and said, "Three hundred ninety."

She closed her eyes in that give-me-strength attitude authority figures are so good at doing.

"Go to the board and work it with the other fourth-graders," she said slowly with an over-abundance of forced patience and melodrama.

The tittering in the classroom was getting a bit louder until the two by four came down on the desk, not as hard as before, just enough to be a warning. Even the squirrels didn't react.

I went to the board. The other children were working the problem already, except for Robbie, who was leaning back to spy on anyone else's work and use as his own. Naturally, the only open space on the board was next to him. I found a piece of chalk, wrote the problem down neatly and then the answer. He rolled his eyes in frustration.

Mrs. Porter stopped us to examine our work, sending everyone but Robbie and me back to their desks.

"Robbie, you need to study harder. You couldn't get the answer at all, even cheating, which we all saw you do. Even after Amy blurted the answer out in class, you still didn't get it. You'll never get a job without basic arithmetic skills. And if you rely on your cheating skills for a living, you'll starve to death. Go sit down."

Robbie gave me a dagger's look and stormed off to his seat. I tried to follow him, but Mrs. Porter stopped me.

"I noticed you didn't show your work."

If the school system were the legal system, I just committed a felony.

"Would you like to tell us how you got the answer so quickly?"

No, I really wouldn't.

"I would love to," I replied with a smile, and explained my mathematical logic.

"Interesting," she said, looking at the board behind me. "In celebration of our new student, let's take an early recess. I'll whistle for you when it's time to come back. And Amy, the whistle calls you back into class. If I see misbehaving or roughhousing, I blow it in long, loud blasts. That means everybody stop and return inside. The longer I have to use the whistle, the worse the punishment will be for the perpetrators."

The students got up and filed out one by one quietly, although once out of the threshold I could hear cheering and breathless talking as they found their freedom. I was the last one out, as there apparently was a system for leaving. The back row first, followed by the next until the front row. I didn't want to deviate from the order. Mrs. Porter seemed to thrive on order. She and Aunt Isadora should have been sisters.

Once outside, the children were animated and acted like children again, losing the zombie-like blank stares and silent apathy. I could see where each group of friends set their territories. Sherman sat near Annette, trying to engage her in conversation, while she tried to read *The Mysterious Affair at Styles* by Agatha Christie. I wondered why he was trying to pursue her when she was obviously not interested. Maybe he didn't know about Guy Thomas.

Michelle and Anna Marie were as isolated as they could be from anyone else, just like church. Anna Marie shot me a hateful look, so I decided to stay away. My fourth-grade class was together near the swing set so I went over to try to be friendly, though I didn't think it would be reciprocated.

And I was right. Billy was the first to sound off.

"How did you even know that?" he asked angrily. "That's a stupid way to do math."

"Yeah," agreed Robbie, "Mrs. Porter sure wasn't impressed with that. You can't just work problems in your head. That's just dumb."

"If you don't show your work on paper then you can't check it to make sure you're right," Laura said diplomatically.

I smiled and walked away. I didn't need to be around them. I searched for Holly and saw her skipping rope with her friends. I aimlessly walked around, avoiding everyone as much as possible.

"We can't be seen with any of you," I heard a girl's voice say.

I turned and saw her talking to Anna Marie.

"My mother laid down the law. If she even hears that I'm speaking to any of you now, I'm in big trouble."

"But what did *I* do?" Anna Marie was almost crying. "No one will talk to me at all."

"I don't know. Mama won't say. I just don't want to get in trouble. Maybe this will all blow away soon."

She was talking to Cathy Two. They both turned when I approached and Cathy Two left hurriedly. Anna Marie followed her, but I knew there was no point in it. Even if they could be friends again, they wouldn't be as close.

I walked over the edge of the ridge overlooking the creek and stared at the pines. I could hear the water rush by, but there was too much vegetation to actually see it.

Too soon, the whistle blew. All happiness and joy were pushed into a figurative box to languish until lunchtime. Even though no one was enthusiastic about returning to class, I was still the last one in.

All first through fourth grade students were sitting cross-legged on the floor beside Mrs. Porter's desk. Calvin was standing impassively behind them. Everyone else was silently reading. Mrs. Porter waved me over to her desk when I came in.

"We're doing our reading time now. *The Wizard of Oz.* But I want to pair you with Calvin here, since you've already read it and saw the movie. He has a little trouble with multiplication, so I want you to tutor him. We want to see if you can tutor him as well as you did Anna Marie."

I glanced at Holly who looked away. *The Wizard of Oz* at home and here. How much of one story can she stand? And how did the teacher know I saw the movie? The whole town knew what was said and done in our house. Was Holly their source of information?

"Go out on the front stoop and work together. I've taught here for eight years and Calvin has never gotten higher than a twenty on any quiz. The only reason he got that high was because I gave an extra two points for the students who spelled their names right.

"He's seventeen years old now and will be out of school after next year. If we can get his math skills up a bit, then at least he can handle his own money and finances."

I nodded. What else could I do? Being alone with him was nothing short of creepy to a ten-year-old girl. He was two feet taller than me and weighed at least one hundred eighty pounds of pure muscle. Besides his elongated neck and misshapen head, he had dull, gray, mean, angry eyes. His ears were too big and his corn cob yellow teeth were crooked. His nose was so upturned the nostrils almost resembled a pig's snout. He may have had a winter tan, but I suspect he was just plain dirty. I could smell a little body odor on him in February so how bad would it be in summer? He had a gray shirt on under overalls that once upon a time were blue but would never be anything but gray ever again.

I sat on the porch and waited for him to sit next to me, but he just stood there, looking down at me. I thought maybe he was embarrassed. After all, there I was a fourth grader tutoring an eleventh grader. I patted the stoop next to me as an invitation and smiled up at him.

"Sit down, Calvin. Let's see what we can do for you."

He sat. His eyes seemed to lose some of the anger and meanness.

"I only want to help you. I know this might be a surprise to you. It was to me. So, let's see what I can do to help you with your times tables."

He stared at me. Perhaps it wasn't meanness I saw in his eyes. Maybe suspicion. Maybe he thought all I wanted to do was laugh at him. I tried a different tactic.

"You know, people in town don't seem to like me much. I think this is some way to get everyone to laugh at us. I don't like being laughed at. Do you?"

He shook his head.

"So, let's fool them to no end. Let's make you the best math student in school. Sound good?"

He nodded.

"Let's see where we need to begin then. What do you know?"

"If one of the numbers is zero, then the answer is zero. If one of the numbers is one, it's always the other number."

Well, that would explain why he consistently gets some right.

"Good, that's excellent. How about the twos? Just double it. Like four plus four equals eight."

"I don't know that."

"You don't know how to add?"

I'm teaching him to multiply when he can't add?

"See? I'm too dumb for this."

"Who said you're dumb? I didn't. Listen, it's just a matter of what you're taught. No one ever taught me how to fish. Can you fish?"

He nodded.

"Kill snakes?"

He laughed, "Of course."

"Hunt?"

"I got a shotgun and a .303. That's a rifle."

"Do you bring home game?"

He nodded. He obviously thought of himself as a very good hunter.

"Well, if you can hunt, fish, and kill bad things like snakes, then you're not dumb, are you? I can't do those things, at least, I've never tried."

"Hmm," he said, his mouth opened a bit while he tried to think. Then he sneered, "Maybe I'm smarter than you."

He sounded downright hostile.

Oh my gosh, he really is dumb.

"Calvin, we're not having a contest on who's smarter. Not if you want to be my friend."

"Friend?"

"Don't you want to be friends?"

He nodded. Good. I never thought of it before, but he might have been dangerous. At least he wasn't hostile anymore.

I had to think quickly before he got bored. One of the tools Mrs. Carnahan used was music. I remembered an old nursery tune and changed the words for our situation.

I began singing in a minor key, sounding almost sad but it was catchy and easy to learn. "Two times two is four. Two times three is six. Two times four is eight. Two times five is ten. Three times two is six. Three times three is nine. Three times four is twelve. Three times five is fifteen."

I started again and got him to sing along. Croak like a frog might be a better description since he sang like my Aunt Mary cooked. After a few times, we on to the next verse. Although we didn't know it, the classroom could hear us and everyone was staring out the window, completely mystified.

We broke for lunch after that. I followed my sisters out

to the yard. Annette produced peanut butter sandwiches from her bag and we ate by the fence.

"Why are you singing to him?" Michelle asked, mystified.

"Nothing else is working."

"Oh," she seemed satisfied.

"It's like everything in life," Annette said philosophically. "If it works, it's ingenious. If it doesn't work" her voice lowered in an imitation of Mrs. Porter, "why don't you think?"

We all laughed in agreement.

The afternoon classes were science, history and music, then we were dismissed for the day. Three girls stayed back talking to Mrs. Porter, probably asking for flying-on-broomstick lessons. It drizzled earlier and the grass wore sparkling layers of water. My family was waiting for me at the road and I started to catch them when Billy blocked my path. He looked angry and evil. He was at least two inches taller than me and a little heavier and I really didn't want to have any problems with him. I just met him today and hardly said a word to him. I tried to sidestep him, but he mirrored my move, so he was still in front of me.

"Think you're smart, huh," he sneered. "Showing off to the teacher how you outshine all us country hicks, huh. Well, I don't think you're smart. Not at all. I think you're just a little strumpet, just like your mother. What do you think about that, you worthless Yankee?"

"I think you're a worthless pig," From the corner of my eye, I could see Annette and Michelle hurry towards us, while Anna Marie hugged Holly to keep her away.

"You're the pig," he snapped back.

He shoved me back. I slipped on the grass but recovered balance quickly enough and swung my fist as hard as I could, aiming for his nose, but I was too low and hit him square on the mouth, splitting his lip open. Annette and Michelle squeezed between us while Sherman pulled Billy back and examined his bleeding lip.

"You'll be fine," Sherman diagnosed. "But let's get a cloth on it to stop the bleeding."

Sherman guided Billy away from me, while Billy shot me a murderous glance. I had an enemy. In fact, as I saw other Kakers coming back, it seemed like I had a lot of enemies.

Mrs. Porter was out the door in a heartbeat and I was called back into the building, while everybody else was sent home. Billy was sitting at his desk with some napkins on his face to staunch his bleeding. It seems he bit down on his lower lip at the same time I hit him, which was the cause of most of the blood. Mrs. Porter had me sit at Michelle's desk while she called Mom at the café.

Billy's mother got there first. She was a large-boned woman with a round face and ski nose who looked like she ate lemons all her life. She brought a damp cloth and washed his face in front of us, to Billy's discomfort and embarrassment. She glanced at me impassively and whispered to her son while he nodded back.

Mom arrived a couple of minutes later with Gramma Morris.

Mrs. Porter started right away. "In all my years of teaching, I have never seen such an unprovoked attack by anyone of my students."

"Unprovoked? He first called me and my mother strumpets, then he pushed me. I almost fell."

"Really? Do you know what a strumpet even is?"

"Well, no. But it has to bad, the way he said it."

"Billy, what's a strumpet?"

"I don't know."

"But you called her one."

"No, ma'am. I surely did not."

"Liar," I yelled.

Mom's hand held me to my chair. "Be still."

"I assume no one else saw or heard this?" Gramma Morris asked ruefully.

"Oh, I'm sure if we called all the children in nobody saw or heard anything, like always. Billy, you know if it turns out you are lying, it's the paddle. Amy, that paddle works for you too if I find out you're lying. Now, since Billy's the injured party here, Amy, you need to apologize for hitting him."

"What? I will not apologize to him at all. He needs to leave me alone. I didn't bother him. He started the whole thing."

"Mrs. Villians?"

"Amy," Mom said firmly, "you shouldn't have hit him. Apologize."

"No," I was hurt that no one believed me or would even consider my feelings on this. "I defended myself. My father taught me not to be anyone's punching bag."

"Looks like Billy was the punching bag," said his mother in a raspy voice. "He's the one bleeding."

Good.

I sat quietly.

"Amy," said Mom with a warning in her voice.

"No."

Gramma Morris took my earlobe, yanked me over to her and whispered, "Two choices. Smart and dumb. Smart: apologize and there's no punishment at home. Dumb: sit here any longer and we tell Paul what happened and how uncooperative you were. Paul's your big friend right now.

He makes a bad enemy. Your decision."

Some decisions are easier than others.

"Billy," I growled to him, "I am sorry I hurt your lip."

He had a smug annoying expression.

"I was aiming for your nose."

There was a loud braying sort of noise next to me. I turned to look. It was Gramma Morris laughing her head off.

Uncle Vincent was waiting for us outside. The other girls were all in their places and I joined them.

"Nice punch," Michelle enthused. "You really let him have it."

"Yeah, that was great," Holly agreed. "How much trouble are you in? Will you have dinner with us tonight?"

Annette looked up long enough to roll her eyes, then went back to her book. Anna Marie glanced at me sympathetically but didn't say anything.

"Well, he did push me first," I defended.

"Doesn't matter," Annette commented. "Papa says we never hit unless it's life threatening. He'll handle it or he'll handle us. One or the other. And when he handles it, it's bad."

I was silent for the rest of the ride home. When we pulled into the driveway, it was misting again, making the winter air bone-chilling. We thanked Uncle Vincent and went inside.

CHAPTER 20

JEREMY

Holly was the first to get out and run inside.

"Jeremy's here," she yelled out.

The rest of the girls hurried in. I, the doomed one, was last. I got in as the noisy excitement was fading away.

Jeremy resembled Paul, only younger with both legs. The other girls were all over him with hugs and stories. I wasn't sure what to do so I started towards the kitchen. Mom stopped me and turned me around by the shoulders.

"Jeremy," she said, "this is Amy, our new addition to the family."

"Hi," I said.

"Hi. Y'all were kind of late so Dad and I fried up some catfish."

I smiled, though I felt sad. After all, I was meeting him right before receiving a horrible punishment.

"Mind your manners with her," Anna Marie said. "Billy Kaker pushed her in the schoolyard and she just walloped him."

"What's this?" Dad asked, frowning.

"It was just a little wallop," Holly defended me.

Jeremy smirked a little. "Little wallops can take a guy by surprise."

His eyes were soft brown to match his hair. He had a bit more hair than his father and there was no gray sneaking in. His mouth was always curved in a smile. (Smart ass grin, as Gramma Morris described it.) Although I was only ten, I knew instinctively that he had no problems getting the girls.

"You should have seen the look on his face when she smacked him," Michelle was telling Dad. "He never expected her to fight back at all. He was more surprised than hurt."

"Yes, and a good thing," Gramma Morris said. "If he was expecting it, he'd show her no mercy, girl or not. But that's not the best part."

She repeated the conversation we had after school. Everyone howled in laughter, except Mom and Dad. Jeremy seemed amused. Dad did not.

"We'll talk about this later," he said, resigned that I got away with this one.

Everyone gathered in the living room around Jeremy while Mom and Gramma Morris made a quick salad to go with the fish. He told me that he dropped out of high school and went to work on the oil rigs near Bossier city, in the western part of the state. He worked two weeks on and one week off. This was his week off, so here he was. I loved to listen to his easy laugh and he seemed impressed that I won a fight on my first day of school.

Dinner went without incident. The big conversation was the economy. Fewer and fewer people had any money. No one was buying anything. Nothing was being made because there was no demand and people were losing jobs. Because there were fewer jobs, fewer people had any money.

Only Huey P. Long could keep the poor folks of

Louisiana from starving. He was the governor and a saint. In our house, he could do no wrong.

After dinner, we cleaned up and Mom brought out Anna Marie's birthday cake. It was a simple white cake with plain frosting. No decorations or sugary 'Happy Birthday' written on it. Jason got most of my piece as I promised. I got maybe two bites, only after the adults insisted that I try it. After I tasted that heavenly chunk of birthday confection, I knew I made a big mistake.

"Going to think about it a bit before you give something away from now on, aren't you? Going to at least taste it," Gramma Morris gloated when she saw my face.

"I surely will," I nodded sadly.

After a birthday song and a couple of presents, we got our homework done quickly. Dad wanted me to read to show off to Jeremy, who seemed quite impressed.

"Your reading is better than anything on the radio," he said when I was done.

The whole family stood up and applauded. I was happily embarrassed.

The next day was Tuesday and I was already entrenched in my new routine: Breakfast, walk, train, school. There was some talk at breakfast, mainly reminders of how 'young ladies' are supposed to behave, and 'young ladies' don't get in fights. 'Young ladies' never refuse to do what they're told, like apologize for fighting.

Breakfast wasn't a happy time for me that day. Neither was the walk to school. The other girls walked ahead of me and talked quietly, no doubt saying mean things about me. At least there was as much blue sky as there was gray clouds, so most likely, no more rain. Holly skipped back to me, interrupting my thoughts, and asked what I thought of Jeremy. I said I liked him.

"Would you like him to be your boyfriend?"

"I don't like him that much. Are you trying to marry us off?"

Holly replied innocently enough, "Well, I love having you for a sister. You would be great sister-in-law as well."

"Maybe you should try for a slightly more adult 'great sister-in-law.' Like older than ten. After all, Jeremy is seventeen. He might want a seventeen-year-old girlfriend."

She seemed content with that answer.

CHAPTER 21

BACK TO SCHOOL

When we reached the train stop with the other girls, I said, "You know, if we're supposed to be a big, happy family, it would be nice to be included in the conversations. I'm shut out at school and now I'm shut out at home. I'm just some orphan girl from the city. Do you really think I'm that bad?"

"Nobody thinks you're bad at all," said Annette with fake patience. "We're family and we all love you very much. You are *not* just some orphan girl from the city."

"Yeah," said Michelle. "Listen, as far as I'm concerned, you're my new little sister."

Holly and Anna Marie nodded their agreement, Holly with more enthusiasm, which was expected.

"Yes," said Annette again, "and you are not shut out. It's just that you don't know everybody yet. Or the town and the places we go. Or really our history or who we are. We just don't have anything in common, yet. Give it time."

Same house, same people raising us, same town, same siblings, same school, same class, same teacher, same classmates, same church, same restaurant to go to. Yeah, nothing in common.

The train ride was short and quiet for us. The other children were cheerful and talkative.

The school looked different. It was bleak and forbidding. Sad and menacing. The white of the building was starkly colorless against the blue sky and gray clouds. How I ever thought it appeared pleasant and cheerful yesterday was beyond me.

I sat in my assigned desk and waited for the day to end. Of course, in order for it to end, it had to begin. So, I waited for Mrs. Porter to come out of her office, looking pretty and pleasant. But I would never be fooled again. I knew there were bodies of murdered children in there, along with tortured animals and who knows what other horrors. I shuddered to think of all the terrifying possibilities. And for a ten-year-old girl with no friends, there were a lot of possibilities.

The door opened and out she walked, carrying her gradebook in one hand and her two by four in the other. She stood by her podium and scowled out at us, her evil eye gazing at Billy and me the most.

"As a friendly reminder to you all," she began, obviously unaware that no one considered anything about her to be 'friendly,' "we all have to be here to learn and we are to be pleasant to everybody else at all times in this school or on the playground. Nothing must interfere with any student's opportunity to better themselves."

WHAP, went the two by four on her desk.

"There will be no name calling, pushing, hitting or anything at all like that. It embarrasses me to have to call Mrs. De Montfort over some petty little thing that should never have happened in the first place. Is that clear?"

"Yes, ma'am," we all said in dull unison.

Mrs. Porter took roll. At first, I thought she forgot to add my name, but she called it last and obviously out of order as though I were an afterthought. But I have to say that the second day was not as bad as the first. I answered every question she asked me and never volunteered a response. That seemed to work out best.

When reading time began, I was sent to the porch with Calvin again. He was wearing the exact same clothes he wore the day before and was just as dirty. At least he didn't say mean things.

A pair of doves fluttered down from the cloudy sky and landed on the fence. Coming from New York, I wasn't used to seeing birds in winter.

"Look at the birds," I said enthusiastically.

He glanced up, unimpressed.

"One pair of birds," I said more calmly. "One times two is two."

Another pair followed down and landed near the first ones.

"Another pair," I couldn't control my excitement. "Two pairs. Two times two is four. Get it?"

"Get what?"

"What we're doing. Two birds times two birds. Four birds."

"So?"

"So, what's two times two?"

"I don't know that stuff."

He can recognize numbers, but he doesn't know what they mean.

"Yes, you do. Remember the song we sang yesterday? Two birds" I pointed to the first pair, "times two birds equals four birds."

We sang the song again, this time working into the fives. When we heard books closing inside, I asked him again, "How much is two times two? Think back to the song."

It took a depressingly long time, but he got it right. I almost felt sorry for him, but I knew he didn't want pity.

He was seventeen-years-old and couldn't read or do basic math. The only thing I could hope for was for him to understand how the song could help him if he could make the connection.

Annette opened the door for us just as we got there. We put our books in our desks and got ready for recess, which wasn't any fun. Billy made sure of it.

He sang, "Calvin and Amy sitting in a tree. K-I-S-S-I-N-G. First comes love, then comes marriage. Then comes Calvin with a baby carriage."

Calvin heard it, I'm sure but just walked away and joined his family at their spot, where they whispered to each other and stayed away from everyone else.

But the chant was coming from everywhere. Everyone not in high school was taunting me, except Holly. Even Anna Marie. I knew she was going along to try to win her friends back, but it still hurt.

"What's it like to be in *LUUUUV?*" Robbie asked hatefully, while giggling.

"Wow, you really like older men," Maureen yelled out to me.

"Is a baby coming?" called out her sister Martha, only to be thumped by their older sister Kay.

Those were the worst, but by far not the only catcalls. I was in a bad position. I didn't want to hurt Calvin's feelings and tried to say that he was nice to me, but no one could hear what I had to say with all the jeering. I was happy to hear Mrs. Porter blow the whistle.

Being inside was only minimally better. Our assignment was to write an essay on one of the Civil War generals. In a spectacular display of bad judgement, I chose General Grant. Mrs. Porter said that was a good choice. Everyone else chose Robert E. Lee. That was obviously a better choice. It turned out that Robbie was named after him.

Everybody in the school (including me) had a relative who fought for the confederacy. Not only did I write about a Yankee, I *was* a Yankee. If my classmates didn't have a good reason to hate before, they had one now. I wished I was in high school, where they were reading *The Scarlet Letter*.

Billy made sure I knew my status had sunk even lower. While I was writing my paper, he kicked the legs of my chair and shook it as hard as he could, destroying my neat handwriting. I slid my chair up so it was out of his reach. But he matched my effort and shook it again, causing my paper to be an unreadable mess.

I got up and moved to the back of the room, but Mrs. Porter sent me back to my desk.

"All the children need to be in their places," she said. "And that means you."

I can think of a whole lot of places I'd rather be.

I got out a fresh sheet of paper and started again, only to have my desk quiver under the earthquake-like tremors of Billy's overactive shoes. I looked up at Mrs. Porter, who was watching the whole episode, but she examined the papers on her desk while Sherman discussed *The Scarlett Latter* and the value of accepting blame for our sins instead of hiding them. I was confident *Rebecca of Sunnybrook Farm* was the better read.

And so the day went on. Lunch came, and while other kids were playing and having fun, I ate a cold sandwich and worked on my paper and other homework. With little effort, all my homework was done. At last, my favorite time came—getting out of that building, leaving behind my tormentors and going home.

CHAPTER 22

UNSETTLING PEOPLE

A beat up old black Ford was parked in front of the restaurant, behind a badly abused Oldsmobile. Scott and Doug Tanner were sitting in a booth with two unsavory men. One of them was obviously a Kaker. The high long nose and sharp teeth made *that* obvious. The other man was a bit older, with an elegant black mustache and professional haircut. He had deep set brown eyes that noticed every detail and movement. His intensity was off-putting, at least to me. He seemed angry, not at any one thing, but at the world in general. The others were in awe of him, which he seemed to think was his due.

A worn out middle-aged man was at the counter picking at a hamburger steak sandwich, while a tired woman sat next to him sipping coffee. Apparently, they were just passing through, but Mom made sure they were given the best service possible, in case they ever came again.

Lila was on her way to the table with four bowls of gumbo. The aroma made me hungry and I went to the kitchen to see if Cici would give me a taste. I got a tablespoon of rice and a little bit of sauce. She was making less each day as business kept getting smaller due to the market crash. But still, it was very good.

I went back to the dining area and sat near the others. Lila whispered to me, "You see that one with the blonde hair drinking the iced tea?"

"The one that looks like one of the Kakers?"

"That's right. He is a Kaker. That's Harvey Kaker. He's the mean one in that family. And they're all mean. He just got out of prison for bank robbery. He'll slit your throat in a heartbeat just to have fun."

"Oh."

"He can say the nicest things, but he's unsettling to be around."

Good person to stay away from, like all the other Kakers.

She started to talk to the couple at the bar, nodded her head and went to the kitchen.

Harvey Kaker called out, "I would like a refill on my tea, please."

Since Lila was busy and the tea was near me, I picked it up, walked over to their table and poured him a refill.

"Why thank you, sweetie," he said with a leer. "I can safely say, of everywhere I've been, you have the sweetest tea."

"What?" Doug Tanner exclaimed and they all laughed, except the mustached one.

I nodded and immediately returned the tea to the bar. I knew I was the butt of a joke, but I didn't understand it and he made me nervous.

When I replaced the pitcher, the Tanner brothers and Harvey Kaker were still cackling with laughter. The fourth man smiled indulgently, but I could tell he was quite unimpressed with their humor.

While all this was going on, the other girls told Mom how the day went for them. She shook her head.

"I just can't believe Blanche Porter would allow that."

Annette shrugged, "She can't force people to be friends or play together, not if their mothers forbid it."

"Still," Mom said to her and Gramma Morris, "you'd think school would be neutral. That would never happen when Mr. Benson was the teacher."

"Who?"

"Old Mr. Benson was the teacher when I was a little girl. He stepped down about fifteen years ago because he was losing his sight. Mrs. De Montfort took over for a year or two until Blanche Beaufort took over. She became the teacher right after her wedding. She's Hugo Landacre's sister-in-law."

"And that's why she's letting it happen," Gramma Morris said with finality. "Jealousy and spite."

"Uncle Vincent's here," Michelle said, looking out the window.

I was ready to go home. All the anger, frustration and hurt feelings took a toll on me. I just wanted peace and quiet. As we left, I felt uncomfortable. I turned back and Harvey Kaker was watching me with that wolfish leer. He said something softly and the Tanners laughed loudly. I hurried outside.

The trip home was silent and I almost fell asleep in the back of the truck. I was the last out and while the others all hurried in, I decided to take a walk out to the river. I looked toward the chicken sheds and saw no movement. I checked the tree line for any sign of Huck. He was nowhere to be seen, so I walked over to the river.

I wondered why I liked being near the rushing water. It smelled bad. There were thorns. The water had a nasty, unwholesome appearance, yet watching it go its way and listening to its song made me feel peaceful. I could understand why the Farley sisters lived on a houseboat. I thought I could, too.

It heard a snap behind me. I whirled around and there was Huck, smirking.

"I knew you'd come to me," he said quietly and confidently. "You know why?"

"I didn't come to you," I said backing away, trying not to show my fear.

"Oh, yes you did," he replied knowingly. "I can tell a thing like that. You love me as much as I love you. That's why you came here."

"What?" I was stunned.

"That's why you came here. To be with me. Make no mistake, little girl, we're going to be married one day. And even better, we can pretend to be married right now."

I turned and ran as fast as I could. I looked back and saw he wasn't chasing me. He was following me, but only walking with that expression of supreme confidence still on his smirking face.

"Yes, I'm still here. I'll pursue you to the ends of the earth, Amy. You're the one I want. It's destiny. We're a pair and we'll be together forever."

I turned and dashed back home in record time. I was exhausted, but safe. I scurried onto the back porch and sat on the little couch to catch my breath. Then I started to cry. I tried to be quiet about it, but Gramma Morris heard me and was out in a heartbeat.

I thought she would grouse at me for being too old to cry but she did no such thing. She sat next to me and pulled me close to her, whispering that everything was going to be all right. She felt good and soft and loving. So different from the harsh, no-nonsense disciplinarian I was used to.

"So, what's this all about?" she asked after I calmed down.

"It's everything," I said, trying to be calm and failing. "Everyone hates me. They barely talk to me in church. They laughed at me when I told them your story about the echo at the river. Said I should have known it was just a story as soon as you said it. Everyone's family tells that story to *little* kids. I just met you. How was I supposed to know you'd lie to me like that?"

She stiffened. "It wasn't a lie. We were told that story when I was young. I embellished it; I suppose. I tried to make it something you'd relate to better."

I looked at her.

"Okay, I hoodwinked you."

"Hoodwinked?"

"I deceived you. I lied," she admitted, "but not to make you look bad. I never thought you'd repeat it to anybody."

"Well, I did. And they laughed at me. And I wanted to believe you, so I went over to the top of the ridge and yelled at the river. And nothing. And I like going to the river and listen to it try to talk to me. But Huck comes up to me and he bothers me. He scares me. And every time I go there, he's there and he gets worse. I'm afraid to leave the house."

"How does he bother you?" I could hear cold steel in her voice.

Was I in trouble again? It didn't matter. I needed to talk to tell her my feelings.

"He wants to kiss me, marry me. He wants to pretend we're married. He says it's destiny."

"Wait here," she ordered and stormed into the house yelling for Paul.

A minute later, Dad and Jeremy were in front of me. I had to repeat my story to them. They looked at each other briefly and Jeremy headed over to the shed. Annette came out and sat next to me with her arm around my shoulder.

She confirmed that she had a similar run in with Huck while Dad angrily shook his head.

"How did you two expect me to solve a problem like this if I don't know there is a problem like this? What if this had been Holly? I need you two to think better."

"Yes, sir," we said in unison.

Jeremy and Huck stepped onto the porch. Huck took off an old beat-up slouch hat and held it in his hand. His smirk was gone.

"You wanted to see me, Mr. Villians?" he asked, his head down and eyes to the ground.

"How old are you, Huck?" Dad asked quietly.

"Twenty-five. Twenty-six next month."

"Amy is ten."

"Oh, that," he looked up hopefully. "Well, I was just joshing. You know, playing around. I didn't mean anything by it."

"You don't 'josh' like that around here. This is my family, and no one thinks you were 'joshing.' Least of all me. You're through here."

Huck looked up; his humble act gone. His lip curled up in a snarl.

"Well, what the hell," he spit out. "She'll be wanting it. Wants it now. You know it. She's just like her mother—"

Dad's fist connected to his chin. Huck just stood there for a second, his head weaving in little circles. Before he could recover, Jeremy grabbed his collar and belt and threw him off the porch onto the grass. Annette picked up his hat and tossed it on the ground next to him while Dad threw some coins at him.

"Be on the next train out of town and don't come back. For any reason. Ever."

He slowly got up, a bruise already forming on his chin.

I thought he was going to make an idle threat, but he just took the money and his hat and started walking. Annette went up to Dad and put her head on his shoulder.

"Thank you, Papa," she said.

I was too uncomfortable to cuddle up to him, but I did say 'thank you' as well.

"I'm so glad he's gone," Mom said when we came back in. "He always made me nervous."

"Me too," Michelle concurred, while Anna Marie vehemently nodded her agreement.

"Well, I'm glad I made everybody happy," Dad said. "Now, let's try to remember that I can't fix problems if I don't know about them."

With that, we sat down to a dinner of beans and rice. No meat or fish because income from the café was down. I didn't mind. Being around family more than made up for it.

I helped clear the table afterwards and read aloud a couple of chapters about *Oz*. All the excitement and stress, followed by a nice dinner made me sleepy. I was first in bed and barely noticed Holly getting in beside me and cuddling her head up on my shoulder. I put my arm around her and slept until dawn.

CHAPTER 23

A BETTER DAY

I woke up wishing it would be my last Wednesday of going to school in Louisiana but wishes only came true in storybooks. Michelle and Annette were trying to sleep in like it was the weekend, but Mom wasn't having it.

"Wake up, get up, clean up, eat up, and continue to grow up," she called out to us. The words sounded playful, but her tone did not.

Breakfast was scrambled eggs and toast. Not a sausage or bacon slice in sight. The other girls grumbled a little, but this was still better than anything I got in New York.

A little bit of fumbling for books and things and we left for another day of school. Michelle and Annette waited for me and we walked to the train together, with Anna Marie and Holly in front of us.

"You know," Annette said philosophically, "maybe it's a good thing all this happened. Now we know that all our friends will drop us like we have the plague without hesitation. Barbara will talk to me on the train, but not in school. She thinks Mrs. Porter will call her parents if she's acting friendly in school."

"At least your friend talk to you," Anna Marie whined. "Martha and Maureen won't talk to me anywhere. They say they don't associate with bank robbers like Papa or his kin."

"Papa was a bank robber?" Holly asked, her eyes wide.

"Not really," I said, giving Anna Marie a dagger's look. "He's the kin."

"Really?"

"Papa is a war hero," Michelle took over. "That's how he lost his leg. He'd look pretty silly walking into a bank with Tommy gun and robbing it with a wooden leg."

"Yes," said Annette, "pretty silly. But we had some uncles way back before the war who we aren't very proud of. But there's a skeleton in every closet."

"There's a skeleton in my closet?" Holly's eyes were even wider. "I never saw it. Can it hurt me?"

"It's a figure of speech," I said. "It means that we would have preferred no one know about our uncles, so we kept it a family secret. Obviously, we'd rather not have anyone know if we have a skeleton moldering under our clothes hangers."

Icy glares from Annette and Michelle indicated my explanation was unwanted.

"The smell might scare people off," I added helpfully.

Colder icier stares.

When we reached school, nothing terrible happened. Mrs. Porter chose not to call on me for anything and I reciprocated by not volunteering. No new social mistakes on my part at all. No new reasons for them to hate me. Although, the fact that I still was breathing was reason enough for Robbie and Billy to loathe my existence.

I sang with Calvin during our tutoring session while the rest of the children read their assignments. Anna Marie was reading aloud to the class. She had a halting, monotone voice that made me glad to be outside, even if it was with Calvin. We were up to five on the multiplication tables. I gave him problems to work and he did very well. The other kids stared at me strangely when we came in, but no one said anything about it.

For recess and lunch, I sat alone near the edge of the embankment. I could see Anna Marie on the other side of the yard, looking miserable and lonesome. She was just as ignored as I was, only it bothered her a whole lot more. She could see that I was just as lonely, but she stayed where she was, hoping for someone to sit beside her. Holly was surrounded by friends as they played hopscotch and jacks. Annette was reading and Michelle was talking to Barbara, although it wasn't quite apparent if Barbara was listening.

Just before the end of the day, Mrs. De Montfort marched into the room, wearing her usual frown. Mrs. Porter was obviously surprised by the visit but kept her composure as the older woman breezed to the front of the room.

"Good afternoon, children," she said.

We all responded out of unison.

"I have some good news for you today. The board has decided to partition the building into two sections, which will separate the high school children from the lower grades. There will be two teachers starting next month. Mrs. Porter will handle the upper grades while the elementary levels will be taught by Miss Jenny Du Lin, who most of you already know."

There were mostly cheers and some discomfort amongst my classmates.

"Miss Du Lin comes from Faucette and just graduated from Southeastern Normal School and will be a wonderful addition to our staff. We do expect Mrs. Porter to remain close to help keep things running smoothly.

"The reason for this is because we now have sixty-one

students. We expect seven more first graders next year, while only five seniors will graduate, provided their grades allow for that.

"Right now, we're thinking of purchasing a plot just north of the Old Cemetery."

"By the Catholic Church?" Mary asked.

"No, that's the Catholic cemetery."

Ricky piped up, "So the Old Cemetery is for old people?"

"Only if they're old and dead," Georges called out.

"Yeah, it's better to bury dead people. Live ones might put up a fight," Derrick replied.

WHAP, echoed the two by four on Mrs. Porter's desk. The squirrels retreat sounded in the belfry overhead.

"Need I remind you children that we're in a place of serious learning?" our now scowling teacher asked.

Mrs. De Montfort looked at Mrs. Porter for a moment then down at her wooden block and shook her head.

"When we have the new system in, Mrs. Porter will have a whole lot fewer children to deal with and she can retire that noisy little gavel."

The class erupted in cheering and it was time to go home.

Guy was waiting for Annette at the restaurant and they drove off in his Model T to Faucette Park, just south of the Baptist church where they got together with their friends before Wednesday night service. Papa didn't feel like riding in the wagon that far in the dark and since Wednesday was Uncle Vincent's Knights of Columbus evening out, we stayed home.

I was happy to stay home. I really didn't need more rejection and venom thrown my way. I was content with a dinner of beans and rice with iced tea to wash it down. I enjoyed helping set up and clear the table. It was something useful to do and Mom always thanked me afterwards. Feeling appreciated was important to me. But reading to the family was my favorite part. It was what really made me feel connected.

That night I went to bed and Holly was instantly snuggled up to my shoulder. I enjoyed that. Julia was more my age and needed me less, especially after we moved in with the gruesome twosome. Holly was everything I could ask for in a younger sister. She accepted me and that was important.

Anna Marie flounced on the bed next to us. I imagined she was jealous that she lost her little shoulder-warmer of a sister.

"Amy?" she asked.

"Mm hmm?"

"Today was better, wasn't it?"

"I think so."

"Good. Maybe the worst is over."

"We can hope."

Sometimes hope is overrated.

CHAPTER 24

THE END OF THE WEEK

The next day started off well enough. We had pancakes for breakfast. They were fluffy and tasty, with no cabbage residue in them, so I was happy. The others grumbled a bit because there was no more honey.

"That's because you girls ate it."

"Huh?" Holly asked, confused.

"You eat everything. You see, if you didn't *eat* the honey, we'd still have it. But you ate it, so we don't."

Annette started to play along, "So if we don't eat it…"

"Then we have it. And we have it because you don't eat it. So, if you don't eat it, we won't buy it because, after all, why buy something we don't use?"

"So, we have it if we don't eat it. And if we don't eat it, we have it. And we don't need to buy it if we have it. And there's no need to buy it if we don't eat it. So now we don't have it because we ate it."

"That's right," Mom said brightly.

Anna Marie wasn't happy with this.

"So, when are we buying more honey?"

"We're not for a while," Mom was serious. "We're in a spiral right now. Business is bad at the café. We have to cut corners. Mr. Prejean, that's who we buy honey from, Amy, will lose business, at least ours, and he'll have to cut corners. And then the people he buys from will lose business and they'll have to cut corners. And a restaurant is an easy corner to cut."

"That means no more honey?" Anna Marie asked, obviously not happy.

Mom hugged her from behind.

"You're so smart," she said. "That's why I love you so much."

"Honey isn't that important," I said to Anna Marie on the way to the train. "You should be thankful the pancakes are mixed right and cooked right and don't taste like boiled cabbage."

"Hmm," she responded, "everything tastes like cabbage to you."

"Not down here," I replied cheerfully. But that cheerfulness was short lived.

The other riders were at our makeshift train stop before us. Maureen and Martha stood there confronting us.

"Well," said Maureen, "it's the Amy half of the 'Calvin and Amy singing duo.' Soon, you'll be on stage."

"Step right up folks," Martha took over. "Here they are. He sings like a frog and she looks like a toad."

Annette's hands were on my shoulders pulling me backwards, but I still glared at them. Their older sister, Danielle, smirked and looked down, but Kay, who was in Michelle's grade, interceded.

"What are you thinking?" she said as she dragged them back by their collars. "Live and let live."

"Why are you being so mean?" Anna Marie was shocked.

"Just telling the truth," said Robbie. "Everybody knows she wants to marry Calvin Foyt, but don't worry, Annie," he added to Anna Marie, who seemed to hate being called 'Annie,' "you won't have to be an old maid. Donavan Foyt's still available.

"Donavan Foyt?" I whispered to Annette, a little too loudly.

"Calvin's father."

"And Uncle," Maureen screeched in laughter.

They all laughed at that cruel joke, except for Rodger, who rolled his eyes silently. The rest of the conversation was drowned out by the arriving train.

"I can't believe they turned on me like that," Anna Marie said sadly when we were seated on the train.

I winced a bit, waiting for her to blame me for our treatment, but she didn't say anything else. The rest of the day went by without incident. So much of our lives were spent doing useful and necessary things, but our brains rebel at the thought of remembering them.

It was the next day, Friday, that was truly memorable. It started with a sweet surprise. Honey was on table for pancakes.

"I thought we weren't going to get any more," Anna Marie happily exclaimed.

"You can thank your dad," Mom said cheerfully. "He made a deal with Mr. Prejean. Four dozen eggs for two quarts of honey. Who needs money?"

"Sounds like a honey of a deal," I commented. Holly giggled while the rest groaned.

"And good thinking too," I continued, "He can make other swaps. I bet the parish is just honeycombed with potential traders."

Hooded eyes glared at me in the deadly silence that followed.

"This kind of humor give you hives?" I asked in my best innocent voice.

Annette chuckled and Micelle suppressed a smile while Anna Marie rolled her eyes.

"Maybe I could BEE-come a comedienne on the radio with some stinging barbs and drone on about bees and BEE famous."

"Maybe there'll be a lot of buzz about you," Annette laughed.

"Enough with the bee jokes. You have school," Mom commanded.

"Those were jokes?" Jason asked.

"Yes, they were," I said with a smile. "Those type of jokes are called play on words. Some people love them, like me. Some folks think they're a real PUN-ishment. So to speak."

"Out," Mom yelled with a laugh. "Go torment your teacher."

"Amy, I was so surprised at your jokes today," Michelle said on the way to the train. "I didn't think of you as a jokester kind of girl."

"Me either," Annette agreed. "I hardly ever see you smile. You look so pretty with a smile. Why didn't you do things like that before?"

I shrugged. "I guess I was a little more relaxed today."

"I like you better relaxed," said Michelle and the others all agreed.

But Friday was test day. Who can relax with all that stress? We talked and laughed with each other like a family of sisters and walked into the building where we turned into a silent family of zombies.

Mrs. Porter glided out of the office with stacks of papers, all sorted out by subject and grade. After rollcall, a quiz was passed out and a one-hour timer set. When the first one was called in, she started grading it while we went on to the next quiz. They had one hundred questions each and took almost the whole hour to finish. Then we had to wait for the slower ones to finish. We were lucky because there were only three quizzes or the whole day would be ruined while we were sitting, writing, and waiting. Fidgeting, of course, wasn't an option.

The first quiz was history which was rather unchallenging since I had it before in New York. The next quiz was reading. I read *The Wizard of Oz* twice now in six months, so it didn't require much thought. The last was math. We had to show our work on paper, which slowed me down a little bit, but I finished first and sat there, staring straight ahead.

"Did you check your work, Amy?" Mrs. Porter asked.

"Yes, ma'am, I did."

She quietly slid to my desk, took my paper back up to her desk and graded it. She brought it back with my history and reading quizzes. All had a hundred written on them in neat red ink. As other students finished theirs, Mrs. Porter had them bring them to her. She graded them at her desk and sent them back to their seats. Some were happy, some not so happy, but most seemed totally indifferent.

When the third timer rang, we were sent to recess. I wanted to ask Calvin how he did, but he was with his intimidating family, so I decided to wait.

"Good idea," Michelle told me. "If Huck thought you liked him without you even talking to him, think how bad it would be if one of those decided you liked him."

I shuddered at the thought.

We quietly strode back into the schoolhouse when the whistle blew. Mrs. Porter sternly surveyed us until the last one was at her desk.

"Well now, class," she said cheerfully, "I have an announcement to make to those of you who think you can't succeed at something. Mr. Calvin Foyt passed his math quiz with a sixty-five percent That is over three times his previous high score."

She started applauding and we all joined her. Calvin sat in the back looking embarrassed, but happy. He obviously had no idea what to say or do. This was possibly the first compliment he ever got in school, or anywhere else.

We pulled out our science books when Anna Marie raised her hand.

"What about Amy?"

I wanted to whisper that I didn't mind not getting credit, but it was too late.

"What about Amy?" Mrs. Porter asked.

"Well, she helped him all week like there was no tomorrow. And some of the other kids were making fun of her. She deserves some credit."

"She does," Mrs. Porter smiled. "A round of applause for Amy."

My sisters clapped hard for me and there was some polite noise from the older students, but it was obvious that I had no friends here. Even Calvin remained silent.

"A teacher's job is thankless," Mrs. Porter told us, almost sadly. "All we can do is build a firm foundation of knowledge and take pride in the success of the people we help. Right, Amy?"

I nodded.

"Besides, who can name Michael Faraday's teachers?"

"Who's that?" Billy asked.

Before thinking, I said, "He invented the electric dynamo."

I regretted saying it the second the words left my mouth, because I knew what was coming next.

"Who asked you, you little know-it-all?" he sneered at me.

WHAP, went the two by four. Clitter, clatter, clitter went the squirrels.

"Billy Kaker, you're jealous. And if you only did the work you're supposed to do, you'd be smart too. You might try being kind to Amy and maybe she'll help you with your grades. You can stand a little tutoring yourself."

That was not helpful.

She gave each class their assignments and pulled the first graders to her desk for their reading review. The second her back was turned, my desk started shaking from Billy's feet on the back leg. I was annoyed but ignored him.

However, when lunch came, he was impossible to ignore. He intercepted me as I went to see Annette and started yelling at me. Everybody turned to watch the show.

Elenora, one of the third graders, was swinging high on the swings, bouncing the chains, but she slowed down to see the show. Although she was from the Landacre family, our mortal enemies, the real hostility towards me only came from Billy. He pushed me back and I almost hit the swing set but regained my balance before my head hit the metal frame.

"You think you're better than everyone else. Think you're smarter than me," he shouted.

Well, the smarter part was true.

"Go away," I whispered loudly.

He frightened me. He seemed to lose all control. His oldest brother, Willy, saw what was going on and yelled at him to knock it off, but Billy was focused on me.

"You think your ugly face is anything we want to see?"

"Ugly?" I retorted. "You? Calling anybody ugly? If I were casting a werewolf movie, you'd be the lead. And you wouldn't need make-up."

He pushed me again, just as I heard Mrs. Porter's whistle. But I stepped back to catch my balance and Elenora Landacre swung right into me. Her foot caught the back of my head and I went down hard. Elenora was on the ground next to me, crying. Her arm was bent in a wrong place, obviously broken when she fell from the swing.

The whistle was still blowing.

"Hey, that's my friend," Calvin yelled. He grabbed Billy, turned him around hard and hit him square in the nose. An explosion of blood spewed out of his head as he screamed and went down on his stomach, holding his snout in his hands.

The whistle was still blowing.

Annette and Michelle were shepherding Holly into the building. Anna Marie and Maureen were wrestling on the ground, with Martha jumping around them, giving Anna Marie a kick when possible. Margaret was by Elenora's side comforting her little sister.

The whistle was still blowing.

Willie was fighting Calvin, but other Foyts were joining in, as were other Kakers. Beaumonts and Porters were also attacking Foyts while Noreen Foyt grabbed Martha from behind and viciously threw her into the wall. Mrs. Porter grabbed them both and dragged them inside before coming back outside to break up Anna Marie and Maureen, all while blowing the whistle.

There must have been bad blood from a long while back between a lot of people. Sherman was fighting Beauregard. Derrick somehow got Mrs. Porter's two by four and clobbered Andrew. Mary was scratching at Louis's face and getting punched as her reward.

And the whistle kept blowing.

There was so much activity. I was disoriented and groggy. I decided I needed to get away from all the fights and staggered to the back of the building. I figured I would just go around to the other side and go inside. I was wobbly, but I made past Calvin, Will and Billy and made my escape. No one saw me go, so I was safe from everybody. As I progressed to the back, I tripped over one of the safety wickets and plunged over the embankment, landing on the muddy creekbank, almost into the water.

And the whistle kept blowing. It was not as loud now. More like background noise.

The embankment was too high and steep for me to climb back out, but I remembered it seemed to have a friendlier slope near the restaurant. I followed the water, walking upstream. It was a relatively easy walk, but I was getting tired.

While I was lost, the whistle was still blowing. The fights were finishing up. Depjim arrived and roughly waded in and separated the culprits, sometimes by throwing them off of each other. Mrs. De Montfort arrived a little later to survey the damage.

"That whistle sure has been blowing," Mom said to Gramma Morris in the café. "Maybe I should see what's going on."

"A four-month pregnant woman should be home in privacy, not getting in the way of things down there," came the harsh reply. "Besides, if they need you, they'll call. The whole damn town knows something's going on. They don't need a crowd. And as big as you're getting, you're almost as big as a crowd."

"Ha-ha," Mom replied. "But all the girls are there. I

can't imagine what's happened."

Gramma Morris glanced at her, "I can imagine that whatever it is, Amy's right in the middle of it."

While she was stating this vote of confidence, I was getting tired *and* sleepy. I glanced over the creek and there in the middle was a large flat rock sticking out of the water. It was gray and mossy and perfectly Amy-sized for a short nap while I got my bearings. I waded through the cold water and laid down on my stomach using my arms as pillows. Soon, I was spinning into a deep sleep.

The whistle was silent by now.

At the school, Depjim and Mrs. De Montfort were joined by Doc Gannon. It was a busy afternoon for him. Luckily, Mrs. De Montfort was a retired nurse and rendered quick and efficient assistance. There were two broken noses, five broken bones to set, and various cuts and bruises to stitch and mend. After the medical necessities were complete, it came time to find out what happened.

"Billy pushed Amy into the swings and Elenore kicked her in the head and Calvin walloped Billy good," came the answers. Billy tried to deny it but the whole school agreed he was the one who started it.

"Amy looked real hurt and Elenore was worse."

"Where is Amy?" Depjim asked Mrs. Porter, obviously annoyed at her.

"Amy?" she called out., "AMY?"

Soon everyone was calling me. But I was sleeping.

CHAPTER 25

ANGUS NYE

I was part of a crowd of people on the dock waiting for 'Foxy,' the mysterious lake creature that people see occasionally at Foxkill Lake in New York. I was with Aunt Mary and Papa Collins. Julia and Patrick were there too. All were silent. It was not quite cold, but my feet were damp and that made me uncomfortable. I did not say anything because everyone else was quiet. We listened to the water as it surged around us.

The water bubbled up about twenty yards away and the serpentine head and neck of the ferocious monster raised up, looking straight ahead, ignoring our cheers. Its scales were perfect. Its posture was unmoving. Its eyes reflected the fading sunlight like iridescent paint. It was plywood, plastic and rubber. It glided in front of us, then to the side where it disappeared underwater, leaving behind a mighty wake of gray-green water that attacked the shore.

We turned to leave. Mama and Papa talked about how scary the imitation serpent was. There are things in life that are unreal, but we pretend they exist anyway. We need illusion to ease the pain of reality.

We left the dock and went back to the inn. We were staying at a place that needed the illusion to exist. No one would go to Foxkill if not for the monster that is a fraud.

"Amy," said a voice near me.

I turned to see a man wearing a hat. I'd seen him before at the train station. He motioned for me to join him.

"I can't," I said. "I'm with my family."

"They are not your family anymore. You do not belong with them. You do not belong in New York," he said expressionlessly. "Come with me and I'll show you the secret of the Foxkill Monster."

I followed the stranger, even though I knew I wasn't supposed to. Mama and Papa would get upset. But they didn't notice I was gone.

It was a short walk to where the monster disappeared. We entered a cave and walked a short ways. He flipped a switch and a dim ceiling light came on. Of all the things I left behind in New York, I missed electricity the most. We could see the Foxy at the end of the small grotto. He was a mechanical beast. I saw the track he rode in on. It was oval and he followed it around, first underwater until it built up the needed speed to make its dramatic emergence and disappearance.

"This is the monster Billy built. People don't see Billy anymore. Just this. It is made from materials Billy is very familiar with. Anger. Hatred. Bitterness. Resentment. His grandfather was a bank robber who died at Edgewater. His father carried on the tradition. But not very well. He just came home from prison."

"Harvey Kaker."

"The same," the whole time his expression did not change. "Like father, like son, like grandson."

I walked over to the nicely built contraption. I saw a movement from the corner of my eye. It was another monster. Bigger, more animated, and rhythmically moving, as though deep in slumber.

"He built another one," I commented.

"No, he couldn't have," the stranger replied.

"Come see."

He stepped over the first serpent and paused for a second, then continued to the other. It had a bluish tint and glistened with the damp. I felt the damp. The thing was about twenty feet long and thicker than the man and me combined. It stirred a bit as he approached.

The man put his hand on the leviathan and it slithered into great coils. Its head was enormous with giant teeth that gleamed white and sharp in the gloom. Its reptilian eyes focused on my guide.

"You see?" he said calmly as the monster's forked tongue jetted in and out., "Billy didn't build this monster. This one is real."

It struck as fast as lightening. The man was gone and the beast's head turned toward me, its teeth dripping red.

It was a dream I would remember all my life. Billy Kaker made a monster in his cave and then became the monster. I think we all have little caves somewhere in our minds where we make things. Not everybody creates bad things. We can create friends and be friendly. We can create wise teachers and become intelligent. But if we create demons with our anger and hatred, they will become real and devour us.

It was twilight when I completely woke up. The sun was low in the trees and the shadows were long. I was lost, cold, damp, and disoriented. I was stiff and my head ached from where Elenora accidentally kicked me. As I looked around, I realized I should have traveled downstream, not upstream. The embankment looked just as steep as it did before. I had to figure out how to get out of the creek bed or else spend the night on this cold mossy rock.

I stretched, as best I could since my muscles were so sore and started to stand up when I heard a quiet little splash in the water behind a shrubby pine tree. Another little splash and I realized it was an oar spattering in the water. Someone was out in a rowboat, even though the creek was shallow.

"Hello, little mermaid. What's your name?" cried out a man's rough, smoky voice.

"I'm not a mermaid. I'm a little girl," I replied to the shadow.

"Hello, little girl. I bet your name's Amy Collins."

A small, obviously home-made canoe pulled around the stunted pine. A tall, muscular, middle-aged man rowed towards me until the boat lightly tapped onto my rock. He wore a deer-skin jacket that must have been left over from the Civil War and he had a few days of gray beard on his chin with some black tobacco juice escaping his mouth and dribbling down his chin. A wide brimmed hat covered his eyes. His nose obviously was on the wrong end of a fist more than once. As he pulled closer, I could smell bay rum cologne, the kind Papa Collins wore. I thought it odd for him to smell so strongly of after-shave

I nodded. I couldn't see through him, so I concluded he wasn't a ghost. Yet he knew my name without ever meeting me, which was spooky. He didn't moan and groan or laugh maniacally, which was good. But the long shadows of twilight obscured his face which made me cautious.

"I thought you were a mermaid because you were laying on a rock. That's what mermaids do, you know. They lay on rocks and look pretty, luring lonely sailors to them with promises of love. Then when they get close enough, those sirens grab them and drag them to the bottom of the ocean and eat them after they drown."

"Oh," I said politely, not sure how I was supposed to respond, "no, that's not the sort of thing I do."

"Ah," he chuckled, "but you must do something. You are the most famous child in Faucette. In St. Columba Parish by now."

"I'm famous for drowning sailors?"

"No, anyone can drown sailors. Just get them drunk enough. Besides, that's not the sort of thing you do. You're famous for coming home."

"I am?"

"Well, of course. Before you moved here, nobody knew you because we never met you. But you came here and we met you. Now, we know you and that makes you famous, at least in these parts. And now you're even more famous because you're missing."

"I'm not missing. I'm right here," I was getting flustered, probably because of my headache.

"Oh," he said a bit too agreeably, "so you're found and everybody else is missing. I guess that means you can't be famous, can you?"

"Well, yes, but maybe in the future, and for other things. I'd rather be famous for being popular and friends with everyone."

"Oh, well. That's different. That has to be earned."

"I'm trying."

Is he going to help me get home or just talk?

"That's good. Try by not disappearing after the whole school has some kind of riot. Gets people worried. Then we have to go find you. Even if you think you've appeared and everyone else disappeared. That's why I'm out here searching for you. Did you forget to answer people when they were calling?"

"I didn't hear them. I fell asleep on this rock and just woke up——"

"Oh yes," he chuckled again, "a rock. People don't appreciate just how comfortable a damp rock can be sometimes. Especially the mossy ones. Of course, now, your mother or aunt, or whatever she is these days, won't like having to clean the moss and dirt off. But she might be so happy to see you're still alive that it won't matter. Might not, but we can always hope."

Made sense. At least, I couldn't argue with it.

"So, hop on in my boat and I'll take you home," he concluded.

"Thank you, sir. You never told me your name, please. After all, you already know me."

He gave me a sideways glance as he moved the boat to its side so I could get in.

"There you go," he said as he took my hand and helped me into the seat. "Keep your weight even or we'll capsize and that might damage this here fine sailing vessel…"

Sailing vessel? A canoe?

"…and this is a boat I made myself. Proud of it, I am. Cut up an old pine log, burned out the center, and chiseled through the rest. Put some thick tar on the bottom to insulate it and here we are. Much cheaper than those store bought ones and it works just as well. Still, it can capsize, and that would be bad.

"Not to mention that if we end up in the creek, we can get soaked. Water can be pretty wet, you know, when you fall in it."

"So I've heard," I responded dryly, hoping this was his sense of humor.

"And it's Nye. Angus Nye. Pleased to meet you. Please don't curtsy in the boat. I hear you're a disaster."

I ignored the last part. Who'd curtsy in a canoe anyway?

"You're Angus Nye? Brigitte Nye's husband?"

I was surprised. Brigitte was young like my mom. Mr. Nye was old enough to be her father. He could have been handsome for someone his age if he had a haircut, shaved and paid some attention to his tobacco-stained teeth. He seemed so rugged and unkempt to be paired with Brigitte, who was dainty and sophisticated.

He gave the oars a good pull upstream.

"I am," he said gruffly. "What of it?"

Whoops, I must have asked that a little too incredulously.

"I met her last week at my mom's house. And I call her Mom, even though she's my aunt. Brigitte's so pretty and kind. I really enjoyed being with her."

He looked at me seriously.

"Well good. I enjoy her company too."

"So does my mom. They're really good friends. Wouldn't it be nice if you and Paul, who I call Dad, could all leave the past behind and become friends? You used to ride together for years, until Edgewater. You fought in the war together. Wouldn't you like to be friends again? I think it would be just great."

He stared at me until I fell silent under that withering gaze.

"I just rescued you from becoming some wild animal's dinner. Now I'm taking you home. Isn't that enough?

"Besides, Brigitte and Cassandra were always friends and I never tried to put an end to it. Paul did. That's point one. Edgewater was a disaster. My father could have planned it better. It was supposed to be our biggest and last raid, so we'd all be flush for life. That's why so many of us rode in. Paul wasn't there. That's point two.

"I have had nothing to do with Paul or Durrell Kaker since the war. Haven't spoken to them since 1917. I don't see much need. Durrell thinks he's a respected man who works for the railroad, but everyone in town knows him for what he is: a bank robber. A reformed bank robber, but still, it's not a profession that's held in high regard. Paul became a Christian man and goes to church, but still has that temper. Ask Durrell. Paul yanked his face into the teller cage the day you came to town. Twice. So, he's a good violent Christian, who's also a former bank robber. He just avoided Edgewater because of his temper.

"Me? I'm like them, a former bank robber who was famous for a day. I'm also still wanted for bank robbery, attempted bank robbery and murder up in Arkansas. Trick is: we robbed a bunch of banks up that way, so I'm guilty. I attempted to rob the bank at Edgewater, so I'm guilty. Murder? Nobody knows whose bullets went where that day. Besides, we were the ones being mowed down. What we did was self-defense.

"But I tell you what," he said with an evil smile, "Brigitte and I will take you home, Little Mermaid. He wants to be friends again; he can make the first move. He owes me and Durrell big apologies for saying we didn't try hard enough to get the others out. He can start by doing that."

"So Billy Kaker hates me so much because of Dad's issue with Durrell Kaker?"

"No, Billy hates you because his father hates Paul."

"Harvey Kaker."

"Yes," he nodded, then paused. "How did you know that?"

I dreamed it.

I shrugged. "I guess I just heard it somewhere."

"Harvey Kaker wants to start his own gang, like what we had. Kind of a next generation thing. Durrell and I politely told him no. But Paul slapped him around, trying to knock some sense in him. Harvey won't ever forget that. He lost his father and all his uncles but two. Durrell and Preston. And Preston don't count. He never rode with us and disowned everyone after Edgewater. At least Durrell tries to help his nephews and nieces. And he's got a lot of them. Every Kaker in that school is a nephew or niece of his."

"Why are they all named Will-something?"

"Oh that," he said dismissively. "Durrell's father,

William, somehow came into money, dishonestly, of course. He gave each of his children a twenty-dollar gold piece if they named his grandchildren after him. He felt that with everything he achieved in life his name should be around forever. He died a few years ago, so there won't be so many Wills and Bills around."

"What did he achieve that was so great?"

"He did a great job of filling up the outhouses."

We both laughed loud and long at that. I liked Angus Nye.

"Isn't Harvey kind of young to have a son that's ten?"

"That's a sad story. There was a young woman who lived on the other side of the river. Irma Willie was her name. And she was touched," he pointed to his head and made circular motions. "She was maybe sixteen, big as a horse, and too slow upstairs to be with the other children. So, of course, they bothered her. Pestered her to no end. Made her feel terrible. Harvey was just under thirteen at that time and he was the worst. Then one day, she was alone in their backyard and he came up to her and promised to be her best friend."

"Oh no," I said, knowing how the story would end.

"That's right. That's how Billy got to be born. But the Willies and Kakers worked it out. Harvey had an older brother who died in the war. They used that birth certificate and got them married off. William Kaker struck it rich by then and bought the Willie's homestead and they moved off. Irma was sent to Mandeville immediately afterwards. Billy was raised by his aunt and uncle. He doesn't know any of this. And don't go telling him, either."

"I won't. What's Mandeville?"

"That's the state hospital for people like Irma. That way they don't meet people like Harvey."

The Kaker family made me shudder.

"Did you ever meet my father?" I asked, thinking of Papa and missing him.

"Well, of course," he laughed. "I watched him grow up."

"In New York?" I asked.

"Oh," he said, his tone changing, "Michael Collins. Oh yes, I met him a few times. We never were friends or anything. He was Paul's friend. He was one of those people who was always right and would get in fights if you disagreed with him on anything. Didn't bother Paul any, but Francine was afraid of him."

"Francine?"

"Paul's first wife, also my sister. Stepsister actually. From my mother's first marriage. They came from New Orleans. Old-fashioned southern belles." He pulled the boat to the side of the creek where a mooring post stood waiting.

I couldn't even think straight for the moment.

"You mean all of Paul's first children, Jeremy, Annette, Michelle, and Anna Marie are your nephews and nieces and you haven't even spoken to them in thirteen years?"

"We had a serious issue."

We landed by a dilapidated pier and he helped me out of the boat. The embankment was sheer, but a series of earthen stairs had been carved out and we made our climb. Their house was a bit lopsided, but most were, except for the ones on Thomas Street. The back yard was dominated by a dormant pecan tree. A couple of gigantic mystery breed dogs came running up to us, friendly to Angus, nuzzling and jumping around but barking furiously at me, no doubt waiting for permission to turn me into dinner.

"Don't be afraid of these guys," Angus smiled at me

while rubbing one of their necks. "They usually don't bite."

"Great," I replied bravely.

He laughed.

"Harley," he called and the larger dog, black with a tan face, woofed back.

"Here, show him your hand," he ordered.

I hesitated.

"He won't bite. He likes to sniff to make sure you're okay."

I reached out and he sniffed, then licked my fingers.

"Go ahead and pet him. He likes to be scratched around the ears."

I did as directed. Harley immediately started to nuzzle me, his head pushing into my waist so hard I had to step back. His tail was wagging at an impossible speed while I gently rubbed my nails on his ears.

"See? Friends for life. Let's get inside."

It was only a few more feet to the door and he called out for Brigitte when we entered the mudroom.

"Hey woman, we have company."

"Did you find her?" she called out from inside.

"Indeed, I did. She's right here with me. Can you call the Villians and let them know she's all right, more or less? She's got a big bruise on the side of her head."

"I'll be right out."

We went in and he motioned me to an old, stained couch. I politely sat at the end and Harley jumped up and laid his front paws and head on my lap while I continued to scratch his head. I must have been scratching just right because he moaned with contentment.

I want a dog.

Brigitte entered the room after maybe a minute. She eyed Harley on my lap and mock-frowned. "Some guard dog you are."

She turned to me, "Did he show you where we keep the silver, yet?"

"Well, no. I would never ask him to."

She tousled my hair, then frowned when she saw my bruised face.

"Doc Gannon will be meeting us at your parent's house to examine that. Do you hurt anywhere else?"

"Everywhere else."

She smiled and pressed her cheek next to mine as Angus walked into the room with his hat off. He had sapphire blue eyes that lit up the room with their intensity.

Brigitte turned and surveyed him with a frown. Those magnificent eyes made no impression on her. She stood up and walked over to him sternly.

"Can you shave before we go?" she asked while reaching to grab his stubble. He stood half a foot taller than her.

"I think they want her home as soon as possible. They might be worried."

"I suppose," she sighed. "At least wipe that disgusting tobacco juice off your face. And change your jacket. Wear the nice cloth one. That deerskin is older than dirt. You may *want* to look like Daniel Boone, but you actually look like some unemployed Hollywood actor begging for attention."

"Yes dear," he replied in a long-suffering voice. He returned to the back room and we could hear the pump squeak and water splash.

She looked at me with a knowing smirk and we giggled.

The Nyes had a new looking Model A parked in a cramped garage They rode together in the front seat and I got in back.

I was asleep when I got home. Brigitte had to shake me pretty hard to get me on my feet. The other children were shooed upstairs when I walked inside. Doc Gannon gave me a quick examination with Mom sitting beside me. I was diagnosed with a concussion, but no broken bones or other serious damage. A warm bath and bland diet were ordered.

My dress was confiscated for immediate washing and Annette was called down to start boiling water and filling the tub. A cup of hot tea was put in my hand, with no sweet cream as it was expensive now. A blanket was thrown over me while various cuts I didn't know I had were treated with iodide, causing extreme pain for questionable benefit.

"It was good of you to search for her and bring her home," Paul said to Angus.

"Well," Angus seemed to be at a loss for words, "I suppose it wasn't much of a problem. All I had to do was look where no one else did. Besides, she says she wasn't lost. Everyone else was."

"I don't think that's quite what I said," I protested, but they were all laughing too hard to hear.

"And I guess we could say that I was a little unfair to you and Durrell about what happened," Dad went on. "You were there. I wasn't. I'm sure you did your best."

"We did. Our time was past. How did that reporter say it in the paper? We threw away our tomorrows by thinking yesterday was the today."

A clomp of familiar boots shook the porch just as Annette came out of the kitchen.

"The cold water's in the tub and the stove's cooking the rest," she announced.

The door opened and Jeremy walked in.

"You found her," he said. "Where did you run off to? Every husband in Faucette needs a hiding place like that to escape from their wife's nagging and—"

He stopped when he saw Angus.

"Uncle Angus?" he whooped and ran over and hugged the older man.

"Uncle?" Annette asked, confused.

Dad sighed.

"Michelle. Anna Marie. Get down here. Family meeting," he hollered.

They tumbled in the room immediately, along with Holly, making Dad raise an eyebrow. Anna Marie had a black eye. Michelle wore a gauze bandage around an elbow.

"You haven't been eavesdropping, have you?"

"Oh, no sir," came out three guilty sounding voices.

"Yeah, well, just listen."

A family secret was shared. Angus Nye was promoted from Mr. Nye to Uncle Angus. He was family. He received an abundance of hugs and squeal of delight. The same with the newly christened Aunt Brigitte. Thirteen years of bad blood was cleared up, though Dad and Uncle Angus were only polite, not cordial.

After Doc Gannon left, taking our undying gratitude home instead of a cash payment, we all talked. We told Angus and Brigitte all about our adventures that day, who we were and wanted to be. There was so much for everyone to learn about each other but soon it was time for them to go.

"I want you two to visit much more often," Mom said to Aunt Brigitte.

"Every week, if you want us," came her enthusiastic reply.

"Yes," Dad said unenthusiastically, "we'd love to have you."

It was a start.

I was freshly bathed with my washed hair drying near the fire while Mom brushed it when Gramma Morris came home from the café with Uncle Vincent. We all were contentedly quiet and happy the thirteen year grudge was over. Grama Morris was surprised at knowing that Angus Nye and Dad were talking again. She hugged me close but pulled away with a stern expression.

"The whole world is upside down now that you're here," she exclaimed, not angry, just incredulous. "I thought even Jesus Christ wouldn't be able to get those two talking to each other again.

"And the whole town was in an uproar today. That was a full-scale riot. Calvin Foyt was arrested and taken to jail for hitting Billy Kaker. Broke his nose *and* cheekbone. Depjim released him to his father. Said if Billy didn't push you in the swing, none of this would have happened in the first place. So now the Kakers are mad. They want him locked up for life.

"Doc Gannon had to work on two broken noses. Elenora Landacre has a broken arm that had to be set. Three boys have cracked ribs. Noreen Foyt found out where to kick a boy where it really hurts and was kicking every boy she found, just to be mean, until Derrick Wilson pounded her with Mrs. Porter's two by four. Now, she has a dislocated jaw."

"Serves her right," Jeremy commented.

"Everyone got hurt, just about the whole school. You can just look at Anna Marie and Michelle, and they came out better than most."

She looked at me contemplatively.

"And from what I understand, Billy pushed you right into Elenora's swing and that's what started the whole thing. Then, if that's not bad enough, you go wandering off

God knows where. The whole town was searching for you, except for the Kakers. And Porters. And Foyts. And Wilsons. And those who had shops to run or jobs. And those who didn't have phones and didn't know what was going on. And those who were too far away to help. But everybody else went searching for Amy, the new girl who doesn't have enough sense to get inside when a riot breaks out."

"I'm not used to riots. They don't happen in New York."

"That's true," Dad said helpfully. "Just a bunch of crooks shooting each other in the streets."

Thanks Dad.

"Then it's good you came down here," Gramma Morris conceded. "If you can't avoid a swing, how can you miss a bullet? And considering the type of man your Aunt Mary is attracted to, I would image you've seen more bullets than swings.

"Mrs. De Montfort was livid with Mrs. Porter and the school board just had an emergency meeting. Miss Du Lin will be starting a week from Monday now because it was decided Mrs. Porter had too many students. And do you know what everyone is saying? These things didn't happen until Amy Collins moved to town. First, she gets into fights, then other people get into fights because of her.

"My goodness, Amy, you're like a little tornado."

CHAPTER 26

MORE CHALLENGES

Holly wanted me to blow us to Oz, but all we could do was pretend to go there during bed rest and quiet time. But being with Holly was the best medicine for me. She enjoyed my company and if her friends left her behind because of me, she never said anything about it. Unlike Anna Marie, who never let me forget her new status of social outcast.

My violin lesson with the countess was cancelled due to my injuries. And since her great-grandson was coming to visit with his new baby, she wanted some family time.

On Sunday, Mom started worrying about my face because the bruises were the ugliest purple and green imaginable. I made the reasonable suggestion that I stay home from church and school for the next couple of weeks for my convalescence. My brilliant idea was rejected without the slightest hesitation. We compromised. I would miss church on Sunday but go to school on Monday.

"Oz would be much better than school," Holly added to our conversation, unsuccessfully trying to be helpful.

"Perhaps," Mom said agreeably. "But Oz isn't real. Therefore, it's not important. School is real. Therefore, you're going."

Saturday, we read a little longer than usual and finished

The Marvelous Land of Oz and started *Ozma of Oz*. There was a bit of a debate on whether we should start something else. No other suggestions were offered so I started another Oz book, mentally kicking myself for being too timid to advocate for some (any) other book.

Sunday was one of the last pleasant days I would have in a long time. The others all went to church, except Mom, but after we were alone, she decided to take a nap. While she was sleeping, I walked to the river. It was so peaceful listening to its quiet roar as it attacked the apathetic shore. It had a slight yellow tint, probably from its travels through the Sulphur Hills. As always, it had a bad smell, but it didn't bother me. The river was beautiful and calming. Somehow, the irrational thought took hold in my mind that I would always be safe near these waters. At least now that Huck was gone.

I don't know how long I stared at the Malmort, but a cool breeze brought me back to reality and I hurried back home. Porky was just leaving from the back porch. Too far to yell 'Hi' to, so I waved. He waved back and pointed towards the back door. I nodded and hurried inside.

Two blobs of feathers defiled a folding table sitting on top of some old newspapers. Mom had a chair pulled up and was dunking a third one in a pot of steaming hot water.

"Porky was so nice today," she said happily. "He killed three roosters for our dinner tonight while culling the flock. All we have to do is gut and pluck. He even put the water on the stove for us."

I looked down at the carcasses of the murdered fowl. Their lifeless eyes stared back at me from twisted little necks.

"I think I'm going to be sick."

She giggled a bit.

"Now Amy, how did you think we get our chickens down here?"

"Buy it at the butcher shop?"

"We *sell* to the butcher shop. How do you think it gets turned from bird to food?"

"Someone else does it?"

"You are such a *city* girl," she laughed at my squeamishness. Then her voice turned hard, "Sit here and take this bird and dunk it in the water."

I did what I was told, somewhat hesitantly. She looked at me while she furiously ripped out feathers from her bird.

"Like this," she said, firmly gripping my hand and dunking and swirling the body around a few times. She lifted it out of the water and repeated the process, lightly tossing the wet, smelly thing on the table with a soggy thump. Then she handed me the last one.

"Do it without any help," she said pleasantly enough but in a tone that forbid debate.

"I think I'm going to be sick," I tried anyway.

"Do it."

And so I scalded my first chicken (all the while hoping it would be my last). I helped with the plucking. The smaller feathers were the most difficult ones for me to pull, but Mom tore through them like an expert. Then we removed the feet, oil gland, and all the various parts of their disgusting digestive track. What was left was quickly quartered and turned in to parts I was familiar with, though I didn't think I'd ever want to eat them.

I wrapped the various leftover pieces up in the soggy red and pink paper and took the whole mess to the pond. I threw it as far as I could and watched as the evidence of our crimes sank below the surface.

"Don't worry," Mom said. "It won't hurt the water. It'll

feed the fish and make them big and tasty. You like fish, right?"

"Not anymore."

She laughed.

"You are such a *city* girl," she repeated while hugging me. Normally I like to be hugged, but I wondered if she wiped all the blood and gore off before touching the back of my dress.

"But you're in the country now. And though I think you are as pretty as pretty can be, you have to be more than a decoration. That means you have to work and contribute to this family so you'll know how to take care of your own. No man is going to want to marry you if all you can do is read."

"What a shame," I said dryly. "That sounds like a sweet deal."

She gave me a warning glance.

"Have you ever been introduced to the curved end of a tablespoon?"

"More than once," I nodded.

"Keep it up and it'll be more than twice."

She was smiling when she said it, so I knew I was in no danger of being assaulted with a deadly utensil. Instead, oil was boiled, chicken was breaded, and the frying began. The chicken feet were put in stock pot for soup. After a while of watching the bubbling pieces start to turn golden brown, I forgot about my part in the gory dissections.

"I may have a slight talent with the violin," I offered. "But I don't think I have any *talon* when it comes to chickens."

Her eyes quickly hooded.

"Was that a *bird-brained* thing to say?"

She sighed.

"Too bad you don't like puns. I could really *crow* if you started to laugh."

She glared at me.

"Well, people enjoy being around witty girls, don't they? I'm just trying to *feather* my *nest* a little. You want me to find a *hen-some* young man, don't you? One who makes an *egg-cellent* beau? Or does that sound too *cocky* for you? Too bad *yolks* don't grow in the ground. I could pick a *peck* for you, like Peter Piper. You're not laughing. Did I just *lay an egg?*"

She raised her hands up. "I surrender. Stop the torture."

Soon the others were home. They were sufficiently impressed with my bird-dismembering skills if not my bird jokes. We sat at the table, gave thanks for the opportunity to slaughter helpless animals, and ate. Fried chicken with soup and snap beans were passed around and devoured.

Since I was sick the last weekend, I missed the Sunday tradition in my new home. The day of rest meant exactly that. Dad described the church service to Mom while she helped Michelle crochet an elaborate red and gray afghan. Annette read another mystery in her room. Holly and Anna Marie played *Old Maid,* while Gramma Morris watched and played Solitaire. Jeremy cleaned his rifle on the front porch. I took my violin to the back porch and played a couple of hymns.

Before long, I was called inside and Mom played piano with me while the others sang along. It took a while to get used to Mom's no-discernable-rhythm style of playing, but it was fun. Guy came calling for Annette and he was quickly drafted into the choir. It was more noise than music, but it was the most fun that I had in years.

The next morning was another school day. Mom put my hair in a long French braid with a new blue ribbon. The bruise on my face was fading. My sisters silently displayed their battle wounds for all to see.

The dark, cloudy sky matched my mood exactly. The train ride was deadly silent. We spoke softly to one another while the other students ignored us entirely and spoke to their own friends. That was fine with us. After all, we had each other. Who needed them, anyway? I decided to start a new book. After all, recess and lunch would not be socially fulfilling.

There was a surprise waiting for us at school. Mrs. Porter was sitting at her desk as we entered the room, talking to Mrs. De Montfort. She seemed tired and subdued. Her wooden bludgeon was nowhere in sight. By the time the clock struck eight, I could tell the student population was culled by almost one third. All the Foyts and Kakers were gone, as well as a few younger students.

"Good morning, class," Mrs. Porter began.

"Good morning, Mrs. Porter," we sullenly chanted back.

"I was putting the quiz grades in the book when the fight broke out, when I obviously should have been in the yard, watching you."

She observed all our various wounds.

"I expected the older children to watch the younger ones to see that there would be no trouble. That was a mistake. Although that system worked for nine years, it failed and some of you got hurt. I do not blame anyone for not doing what I expected. I expected too much and I apologize. The blame belongs to me."

"I would disagree a bit on that," Mrs. De Montfort said. "The blame belongs on the children who acted badly. We had a girl pushed into an occupied swing and a subsequent brawl. But even if Mrs. Porter was out there watching all sixty-one of you, she could easily have missed that while occupied with someone else. There's blame for everyone, especially the children who participated in the fighting. One teacher was not enough for a class this size.

"As you know, we've asked Miss Du Lin to join our school staff as soon as possible. I will be observing today to see how I can help Mrs. Porter until then. I also want to make the transition to being a two-teacher school move as smoothly as possible."

There was some polite applause and worried looks but the day went on. The seating arrangement was changed and the room consolidated. Steven sat in front of me, Laura behind. I figured things would go well today with Billy gone.

I figured wrong. I didn't put thought into it when I first heard the chewing and chopping noises behind me. I knew Laura was chewing gum and I knew that was forbidden at school, but I saw no reason to report her infraction. No one wants the reputation of being the schoolhouse rat.

However, there *might* be benefits to being the schoolhouse rat after all. Just as the third hour began, I felt Laura slap the back of my head. Hard. The other students started laughing hysterically. I turned around to see her smirking and defiant. I rubbed my head where she hit it and there it was. Roughly three sticks worth of chewed gum just above the braid.

"Special delivery from hell, Amy," she said with an evil smile.

I saw red at that moment and jumped over my desk, leaving it crashing on the floor. I swung a roundhouse right at her, but she ducked and jabbed my bruised face. It hurt, but I had enough adrenalin in me to ignore it and swing an uppercut with my left hand, barely catching her chin, but not enough to do as much damage as I wanted.

And it was over. Mrs. Porter pulled me away and Mrs. De Montfort had Laura in a chokehold until she was calm. After the show was over, we were taken to the office so the adults could figure out what happened.

The gum was obviously there and Laura was the only one who was within reach. Guilt was not in question. My reaction was not acceptable according to the two modern-day Solomons. Her action was even less so.

"Why did you put your gum in her hair like that?" Mrs. Porter asked with a sense of betrayal.

"I chewed all the sugar out of it."

"Oh my, you really think that's a good answer?" Mrs. De Montfort asked incredulously.

Laura shrugged, obviously unafraid of consequences. "Mrs. Porter gets mad if she finds it under the desk."

The two adults looked at each other.

"Amy," Mrs. De Montfort said calmly, "go to the café and have Cassandra get that out. Stay there until tomorrow. I will call her tonight."

I nodded and started to leave.

"And Laura," I heard Mrs. Porter say just as the door closed behind me, "this looks like the first time you'll be meeting the paddle."

Good. Served her right. I went to my desk and gathered what I knew would be my homework and headed to the restaurant. Maybe I could finish it at the café.

When I straightened up, Holly was behind me. She almost scared me; she was so close.

"See you after school," she said and hugged me.

I nodded. The rest of my family stayed in their seats as I left.

The sky seemed to be darker. Gray clouds were trying to block out the sun while sprinkling cold rain on me while

I walked south. Just as I was passing the garage, I saw that man in the gray fedora getting into an Oldsmobile. He paused when he saw me walking, then continued his descent into his enormous automobile. Mr. Dupris, his mouth filled with tobacco, was behind him talking about something mechanical and waved to me with a curious expression. I waved back but didn't stop.

There were some customers in the café that morning. Harvey Kaker was drinking coffee with Scott and Doug Tanner. Pastor Josephson was talking to Martin Thomas who was still nibbling on some toast. A couple of rough looking men were at the register while Gramma Morris rang up their orders.

She frowned at me and rolled her eyes to the heavens when I entered the café, then jerked her head towards the kitchen, towards Cici.

"You didn't just leave school and come here, did you?" Cici didn't sound happy.

"They sent me here. Laura Sauveterre put gum in my hair." I was fighting back tears of sheer anger and hatred "It's as big as baseball."

"Turn around," she sighed.

After a quick inspection, she pronounced, "Well, child, I can see you haven't seen too many baseballs. They're a whole lot bigger than that."

"That doesn't make me feel any better," I sighed with exasperation.

"I start with what I know."

"Whatever are you doing here?" Gramma Morris entered the room, obviously not in a good mood. I could tell from her body language.

"Mrs. De Montfort sent me here—"

"What did you do?" Her eyes flashed with an intense

anger I hadn't seen before.

But I was angry too.

"I sat in my desk. That's what I did. I sat where I was told to sit. Then Laura Sauveterre stuck her gum in my hair. Then Mrs. De Montfort sent me here so you'd get the gum out."

"Well turn around, let's see what we're working with," she turned my head away from her, none too gently, I might add.

"Well, that's all the way to the scalp," she diagnosed. "You didn't feel her wedging that in?"

"She didn't wedge it in. She pounded it."

"That evil little girl hit you in the back of the head after you got a concussion?"

I nodded. I didn't know what a concussion was, but it sounded bad.

"Hold still," she commanded while undoing my braid.

"This is as big as a baseball. Does that girl chew gum by the pound?"

"Neither one of you ever saw a baseball," Cici said, rolling her eyes. "We need to get it out before it dries. Do you need some tomato juice to get that stuff out?"

"Tomato juice? She wasn't sprayed by a skunk. That won't do any good."

She led me out to the dining area and sat me at the bar. Cici was hovering behind.

"Hey, little darling," I heard Harvey Kaker call to me, "How 'bout some tea?"

"What?" Doug Tanner said loudly, and they all laughed.

Gramma Morris was pretty much out of patience by now. "Don't you boys have trees to cut somewhere?" she said sharply.

"No ma'am," Doug replied. "We were laid off. No need

for trees because The Landacres aren't getting any new contracts. Next week the mill's laying off."

"They're closing the mill?" Pastor Josephson asked from his table.

"No," came the reply, "but only family members and long-time employees will stay working. At least while they have contracts. Then who knows?"

Pastor Josephson and his protégé dropped a couple of bills on the table and hurried out, calling out a quick "God bless you."

Gramma Morris sent the Tanners and Harvey Kaker out with a dagger's look and reminded them to pay when they seemed to 'forget.' Then she directed her attention back to the important business of my hair.

"Do you think kerosene will do it?" she asked Cici.

"That child doesn't have lice."

"Egg whites?"

"Makes the hair shiny and bright."

"What about the gum?"

"We can try it," she went to the kitchen and came back with a couple of egg whites whisked together.

I *did* see a nice shine, but the gum was still there.

"Maybe salt water?"

"Why not? It works on leaches."

We found out that it doesn't work on gum.

They called Mom at home. After her initial anger, she suggested bleach. Now I had an unnatural blonde spot to go with the gum. But that was okay with them. Mom had a nice big floppy sun hat I could wear so people wouldn't notice the embarrassing spot and that resilient wad of gum. It never occurred to them that a big floppy hat that went out of style twenty years ago might be worse.

Pine tar was next. Gramma Morris figured we could put

the tar in the gum and brush it out. It didn't work. The brush got stuck in the pine tar. Now I had gum, pine tar, and a brush stuck in my hair.

After the last valiant, if ill-advised attempt failed miserably, Cici looked at Gramma Morris who sadly nodded. I was marched to the back deck and sat down while Cici, the hair-executioner, cut, snipped, pruned, chopped, and hacked. She got it kind of even. I went to the ladies' room and viewed my new look while they cleaned up the follicle corpses. What was left of my hair was almost as short as a boy's hair. I reminded myself of the chickens we plucked yesterday. I cried for a bit, mourning my lost tresses, then washed up and went inside. It was done and couldn't be undone. And it was only hair. It would grow back.

Dianna Wilson, the operator, was sipping on some coffee at a table with Gramma Morris when I came into the dining room. She smiled at me and waved me over. After the required commiseration, she inspected the new coiffure Laura inflicted upon me.

"You know, it's such a shame you didn't have any vinegar and peanut butter here. The vinegar dissolves it and the peanut butter makes it so slippery that the gum becomes slick and off it goes."

I looked at Gramma Morris, who seemed mortified.

"I wish we knew that," was all she could say.

I wish we knew that too.

"You're still cute and adorable," she told me. "I'm sure your great-grandmother told you."

I looked over to Gramma Morris.

"I didn't need to. She spent twenty minutes in front of the mirror looking at herself. She knows she's as pretty as a picture."

I accepted it as a compliment, but I could recall my school field trip to the art museum in New York with the works of Picasso and Matisse proudly displayed. 'Pretty as a picture' obviously didn't mean as much now as it did when Gramma Morris was young.

"All you need is a little snip here and there to make it even and I can put a wave in it. People will think it's supposed to be that way."

"How can you put a wave in it?" Gramma Morris asked.

"You have a wooden spoon?"

We went back to the deck to make a little more hair disappear. She knew how to cut hair, whereas Cici only knew how to cut out gum. The hair was wrapped around the spoon handle and held over steaming water until the wave magically appeared. It looked like a flapper bob. Better than before, but it wasn't me. Even so, it was as nice as it could be at this length.

"Dianna, you should run a salon," Gramma Morris exclaimed. "She looks just like a little Christmas elf."

Wonderful.

"I don't want to look like a Christmas elf," I said petulantly. "Besides, they have pointy ears."

"That's no problem," Cici said happily. "We have some bone shears in the kitchen. I can make them sharper than a pair of needles."

My face must have registered my shock and horror because all the adults laughed loud and long.

"She was just kidding," Gramma Morris said. "She would never hurt you like that, and I wouldn't let her if she wanted to. Don't take things so exact."

The day was slow. I finished my homework and was left with nothing to do. It so happened that Porky delivered a few dozen eggs to the café in the late morning and I rode home with him. I sat as far away from him as possible because he obviously never bathed. He was caked in dirt and his smell was horribly unpleasant. I felt sorry for him because he seemed like a nice man. Maybe he could find a blind woman with no sense of smell.

That night, I was the star of the show. Jason was disappointed that I didn't bring home my murdered tresses for him to use as rope while my sisters all fussed over my new haircut.

"That is so adorable," Annette told me.

"I absolutely love it. That wave really showcases your pretty face," said Michelle.

"It'll make washing it a lot easier," Anna Marie offered, being a bit more practical.

"I don't like it because you don't like it, and Laura shouldn't have done it in the first place," Holly defended.

There was an explosion of talk after that. Laura's mother was Catherine Landacre Sauveterre. She's Hugh Landacre's oldest daughter and Hugo Landacre's sister. I wondered why those names were always brought up in conversations.

"Mrs. De Montfort gave Laura the paddle and called her mother to come and take her home for three days," Annette said. "Now, Mrs. Sauveterre wants to remove Mrs. De Montfort from the school board for spanking Laura. She didn't think she did anything wrong. She even called Depjim to have her arrested, but he told her Laura should just leave people be and he's not the school disciplinarian.

"Mrs. Sauveterre was livid. She said to Depjim, 'I'll have your job.'"

She lowered her voice to imitate Depjim's, "'You? You couldn't do this job.'"

"We all just died from laughing," Michelle continued

because Annette couldn't stop laughing. "And Mrs. Sauveterre just grabbed Laura and stomped off home."

"'And after three days, I want a letter of apology before she comes back,'" Anna Marie cried out excitedly, imitating Mrs. De Montfort.

"Yes, we know," Mom said patiently. "That's her method."

Gramma Morris shook her head.

"All you did was go to school. Now we have someone threatening to have Depjim lose his job and Mrs. De Montford thrown off the school board. Mrs. Sauveterre's mad as a hornet and here you are with your hair cut off. I swear, they shouldn't call them whirlwinds. They should call them 'Amys.'"

After we were done laughing at it all, we went back to our evening routine and then went to bed. Having a family to back me up on bad days made the pain of being unaccepted so much better. Holly's head was on its customary place on my shoulder and we drifted off to sleep, the telephone's ring carrying a gentle rhythm in my ears.

We woke at the usual time and breakfast was scrambled eggs and unbuttered toast. Dairy was going to be limited due to business being slow. We figured this would change soon as we had plenty of chickens and eggs for trade. Of course, so did everyone else, but we were sure Dad would find and make a good deal with someone.

Just before we left, Mom gathered us together.

"Okay girls, just to let you know, Amy will catch the train with you this morning but won't be going to school right away. Mrs. De Montfort wants to see Amy at the library."

She turned to me with an encouraging smile. "She'll be waiting for you there."

"Why will she be waiting for me there?"

"Because she's the librarian. That's where they work," she giggled at her annoying attempt at humor. "Do you remember where the library is?"

I nodded. "Go to Main Street, turn right and go all the way to the end right before the Atchafalaya River, right across from the movie house."

"That's right," she nodded. "So go straight there. No dawdling or side trips. And do what she says and do it the best you can. You're the only one in town getting this opportunity. Don't mess it up."

"What opportunity?"

"When opportunity knocks, don't ask questions. Now go."

"But—"

"You'll find out, either it's good or it's bad."

None of the other girls knew what was going to happen either. We concluded it must be good or Mom wouldn't let me get involved with it. Of course, it could be that it wasn't good, as Mom did say that was possible too. But even if it wasn't very good, it probably wouldn't be fatal—I hoped.

My mystery meeting with Mrs. De Montfort was the only thing we talked about. Whether it was good or bad, I was missing a day of school so my stress level shouldn't go up as much as usual. As far as I was concerned, there was no downside to this.

My sisters all gave me a hug at the school entrance and I headed to the library. There was some traffic around the gas station, which seemed to be a gathering spot for the men in town. I saw a red Oldsmobile turning out onto the road towards me. That man in the gray fedora was driving. He looked my way, his hat covering his eyes. He waved to me, so I waved back.

CHAPTER 27

MRS. DE MONTFORT

The library was a simple one-story, gray building that was obviously once a house. It had a green corrugated roof that exploded with color. A paved pathway led to the door and went out the back to what was evidently the outhouse. The grass was neatly clipped and maintained, with an oleander hedge blocking out the view behind it. All in all, a charming place for reading.

Mrs. De Montfort was unlocking the front door just as I strolled up. A faded green valise was tucked under her arm. She greeted me with a friendly frown, opened the heavy wooden door and motioned for me to go into the shadowy blackness first. Dark rectangles of bookcases stood silently around us, with neat aisles that faded into an eerie black.

'A phantom would love it in here,' I thought with a shudder.

When we were both inside, she turned on the electric lights, which turned the dark into a cozy gloom, and we proceeded to a large roughhewn table. She motioned me to pull my chair to the end.

She sat, pulling her chair towards my corner, opening her valise and pulling out a folder full of papers. I could tell they were tests. Intimidatingly thick ones. And there were a lot of them.

"You know," she said, "if what I hear about you is even remotely accurate, I think part of the problem is you're in the wrong class. So, I called your mother last night, or aunt or whatever she wants to be, and we agreed to let you take the fourth-grade final. Do you know what you will get if you pass?"

"I'll go to the fifth grade with Anna Marie and her class?"

"No, you'll stay home the rest of the school year. I'll give you reading and other scholarly assignments to do to keep your brain working so you'll be going in to fifth grade with a little jump on the others.

"Meanwhile, there will be more time for the town to get used to the fact that you're here and give you a better chance to fit in. So, let's get started. The library opens at ten and I want to get as many of these done as we can."

Math was first followed by history. English and reading comprehension were next. We had to pause for a bit for her to open the building to the public by wedging the door open a crack and opening the blinds. The sky was a gray blue with dark clouds meandering towards us but even so, the room brightened up considerably. No patrons came in, so we went on to general science. After a few questions on art and music, we were done.

"Are you reading anything now?"

"No, ma'am. I just finished *Rebecca of Sunnybrook Farm*, and I'm reading to the family one of the Oz books, but I haven't started anything else yet."

She may have smiled, or had the beginnings of a toothache, it was hard to tell, but she stood up.

"Wait here. I'll find you something that will expand your horizons."

She went down an aisle but was back in a heartbeat carrying an ancient, thick, blue tome.

Florence Nightingale. I browsed through it. No illustrations.

"It looks a little old for me, don't you think?"

"No, I think you read books that are too young for you."

I opened it to the title page. On the bottom, it said, "Recommended for high school readers." I read that part out loud to her, but she seemed nonplussed.

"Just because you don't go to high school doesn't mean you can't read like someone who does. So go over to the reading area and I will commence grading."

I got to page two when I had to ask her what 'pharmacology' meant. I was given a dictionary and sent back to the chair. I think I was in the dictionary more than the book. But as I continued reading, I was grasping the subject matter. I just didn't find it interesting.

"You will," she told me with utmost confidence. "This is the book that convinced me to become a nurse. Read."

I read. Mrs. De Montfort tolerated no dissent. And she didn't need a two by four or wooden spoon for intimidation.

After another ten minutes, she went over to the phone and made a call. Then another. I knew she was talking about me, but I didn't want to risk inching any closer to listen.

Who knows? Maybe eavesdropping was a capital offense here.

"All right, Amy. You passed in flying colors. You have officially graduated fourth grade. Technically, you are still a student in Miss Du Lin's class. When she arrives next week, we'll make a point to introduce you to her. You'll like her.

"In the meantime, now that you have some free time to give to the community, I have someone for you to meet. First, we need to get you a library card and your book. Run down the aisle there and pick up the copy of *Dracula*, please."

Armed with two books that I would never consider reading on my own, we left the library, leaving a 'Be Back Soon' sign on the door. Just behind the oleander hedge was another one-story house. It was in need of paint and a carpenter. One of the front shutters was hanging on one hinge. The support posts were cracked, displaying their rotten interior. The cement stoop leaned to the right, lopsided and crumbling, inviting us up to a waterlogged front porch of gray planks of dubious strength. An iron knocker in the center of the neglected door displayed a rusty horse's head. The lawn was brown and seedy.

And I thought the library was a haven for ghosts.

"Have you ever met Mr. Benson, dear?"

"No, ma'am."

"He is a wonderful old man. He wrote a lot of stories in his younger days. He used to be the teacher before Mrs. Gilroy, who was replaced by Mrs. Porter. He recently turned ninety-five years old and his goal is to make it to one hundred. He does seem to have a little problem with his eyesight so I thought it would be so kind of you to read to him for maybe an hour. He likes spooky books, so you'll make a nice impression on him with *Dracula.* Come on up. I'll introduce you. Be mindful where you step."

If I was mindful where I step, I wouldn't step up there at all.

The concrete stairs held firm, the porch groaned and the door was filthy, but everything held together and we survived the climb. The house echoed a hollow, almost mournful sound when she knocked. It was answered by a muffled greeting of some kind. Maybe annoyed, maybe hostile. Not particularly happy.

"He can sound pretty gruff sometimes, but he's a sweetheart," said Mrs. De Montfort.

The door opened wide and there stood the oldest human being I ever did see. He was stooped over so far his back was shaped like a question mark. His hair deserted the top of his head, but his beard was thicker than a horse's mane. He seemed frail and starved but was quite spry. His dominant feature was his eyes. An unhealthy milky white coating of cataracts rendered them almost useless.

A little problem with his eyesight?

"Mr. Benson," Mrs. De Montfort said, rather loudly, "we are here now."

"Oh, good, good," he cackled, staring straight ahead with his eyes pointed towards her mouth. "I've been so wanting to meet the girl."

His head slowly swiveled in my direction and his eyes fixated on my forehead. He must have thought I'd be taller.

"So come in, I made coffee. Do you drink coffee, Missy?"

"I do," I said, hoping Mrs. De Montfort didn't know I wasn't allowed coffee.

"She doesn't," came her quick veto.

"Not down here, anyway," I said pleasantly enough, ignoring her dark look.

The old man laughed.

"Children never change," he said. "Come on in. Sit down for a spell."

He motioned us to a faded striped settee. The place was neat and spartan, which made sense, since he had 'a little problem with his eyesight.' A little oval throw rug bounced out clouds of dust when we stepped on it. The overhead candle chandelier was grimy. A settee and matching stuffed chair were gritty on my skin. What had obviously been a door that led further into the house had ben plastered over, but a rectangular outline betrayed its existence.

It didn't seem to bother Mrs. De Montfort. She plopped down on the settee and motioned for me to join her. Two clouds of gray dust poofed up into the air as we sat. Mrs. De Montfort gave me a conspiratorial wink to remind me to stay quiet.

"So, you're the famous Amy Collins," he said to me. "I have heard so much about you. Strong fighter, weak stomach, bad temper, good reader."

"That she is," Mrs. De Montfort said. "In fact, that's why we're here. We thought it would be nice for her to read to you a little bit every day, now that she has so much free time. I figure about an hour each morning. And knowing your fondness for…unusual literature, we brought you *Dracula*, in hopes you haven't read it yet."

"I have, but it's such a good book that it can be read over and over. Reminds me of my own writings."

He turned his eyes in my direction. "Yes, indeed I was a writer. I have published over one hundred fifty stories in my lifetime. Think Edgar Allan Poe without the pretentious wording. All my stories were true stories, except for the ones that were fiction."

"They were all fiction," Mrs. De Montfort said firmly. "Really, Mr. Benson, you'll give the dear nightmares. Especially when she starts reading your works." Then to me, "Nightmares in storybook form."

"Stories are diversions, nightmares are real."

"Oh, Mr. Benson," Mrs. De Montfort practically gushed, "you have such a way of phrasing that makes your unsurpassable wisdom just shine in your words."

What?

I whispered discretely, "I didn't understand the unsurpassable wisdom."

"But the wisdom he expresses is glorious. It's your comprehension that's weak."

"Oh no," the old man said graciously, "we forget the age of our guest. You see, Amy, a story tells your mind something terrible until you learn something. And if you don't like the story, you don't have to read it to the end. A nightmare brings you into something terrible, and it keeps you there until you wake up. If a story gives you nightmares, it touched something inside of your soul. Something you have to resolve within yourself. That's why I write stories to scare you, so you have some experience facing your fears. Your *real* fears."

"Oh," I said politely, not understanding.

They laughed, knowing I didn't understand.

"*Dracula?*" he said, changing the subject, "Why don't we get started? Let me make some tea for you, since you don't drink coffee anymore. I'm sorry I have nothing to put in it. Then we'll see if the story gives you a nightmare to face."

And so we began our first reading session. I thought I did a serviceable job, considering that the book had a slow start and a creepy feel to it. After an hour, Mr. Benson was nodding off and we snuck out of the house and back to the library. It was there that I was told I had a new job of reading to him daily, as well as keeping him company, and dispatching mountains of dust. The job paid a dime every week and would be paid to Mom to help with my expenses. I was happy to contribute. Afterwards, I would go back to the café if needed or stay out of sight if not.

All my sisters wanted to see if they could take the finals and stay out of school as well, but they were disappointed with the answer. The idea was to get things at the school back to normal which would never be achieved if I was there. And since I didn't want to be there anyway, everybody was happy, except my sisters. However, I would probably be jealous if one of them escaped that classroom and I was still stuck there.

CHAPTER 28

MR. BENSON

I spent more time talking to Mr. Benson than reading, which was good, because Count Dracula was a frightening literary figure. As each day passed, I gave thanks that we didn't share our world with such creatures. After all, dead things need to stay dead. It would be unpleasant if undead beings walked the streets with us. It would also smell bad.

"Not necessarily," Mr. Benson laughed, "I had a chilling experience one time, years ago and I smelled nothing more than what I would have expected. You know right after the war, me and Billy Hardy, Jack Vance, and Cliff Lee were coming back home when we happened on a Yankee soldier going the other way. We were just north of St. Louis at the time. That Yankee reminded us the war was over and we could be friends again.

"Well, I was just fine with that but now, Cliff Lee? Not hardly. He lost a bunch of family between Shiloh and Vicksburg. We had to keep talking sense into old Cliff. So this Yankee, he tells us how we're all soldiers, we all lost something dear to us, and none of us was going to get anything to take back home anyway. Let's take home friendship."

"Friendship?"

"Yes, that's right. Friendship. Now this Yankee, Horace Goode was his name, he was educated well beyond us. He knew what he was talking about, or he thought he knew, anyway. So he tells us that people become friends because they share an adventure together. That's why war buddies are buddies for life, just look at the adventures they share."

I nodded politely and said, "I can understand that. I read *The Red Badge of Courage* last year."

"Perhaps not the same thing, Deary," he laughed. "Now it was obvious to me that he had something up his sleeve with all this talk about 'adventure,' and it wasn't friendship. So, I said to him, 'Okay, Mr. Horace Goode, I already know you have an adventure in mind. Instead of feeding us more words, why don't you tell us what kind of adventure you got planned?'

"Now he could fake a hearty laugh, but he couldn't fake sincerity. Sounded like a witch's cackle, it did. Downright creepy. He asked us, 'You boys know why we had to take almost four years to win this recent unpleasantness?'

"Now Cliff Lee always had an answer to that kind of question. He said, 'Yeah. One rebel fights like ten Yankees.' And the rest of us all agreed, including Mr. Horace Goode.

"So here was his plan. Real simple. Those Yankees were getting paid in gold in two days and going home in four. Payroll was coming in by train. We rob the train.

"Well, we all agreed to his scheme, not much to lose and a whole lot to gain. We jumped on the train when it passed under some tall trees. We hid in and made our way to the safe. Took the guards by surprise and Billy Hardy tied them all up. We told the pay master to unlock the safe if he didn't want to watch his friends get gutted. Then we shoveled up paper money and gold coins into burlap bags, tossed them out the windows and jumped off after them. Horace Goode was waiting with horses and we got away with it.

"But we were too close to the union camp. The soldiers saw enough to figure out they weren't getting paid and they gave chase. We had good fresh horses and put some distance between us, but they were relentless. Lucky for us, Horace had a back-up plan. We rode through some heavy woods until we came to an old collapsed church. It had one wall that was sticking up five feet from the ground, but we rode on by that into the graveyard. It was old and neglected and we rode over who knows how many graves. Behind a bunch of trees was a dilapidated mausoleum with an iron gate hanging by one hinge.

"There we stopped and Horace Goode told us, 'Serenity was an old town. They settled it before the revolution as a kind of religious utopia. But an injured woman and her daughter stumbled into town one day, looking for shelter. Her daughter was eventually killed by one of the town elders and he got off with no punishment. He said it was an accident. The woman was some kind of witch and she released evil spirits from beyond hell and directed those demonic forces to destroy the entire village, starting with the church and town hall. The elders got sick first and died. Then everyone else got sick and suffered. Most everyone died, including the witch who brought it all down. The ones that survived left it all behind for the evil spirits. No one comes here anymore. I don't think anyone knows it's here, but me.'

"'The money's safe here, but we're not. Those soldiers will track us to hell and back. So, we'll just split up. They'll be looking for five outlaws loaded with gold and money, and we'll just be poor confederate soldiers going home. They'll search us and our horses for the loot, but it'll be safe here. And if we try taking it and get caught, we won't be hiding in trees, we'll be hanging from them. We'll meet back here in three days. That'll be Monday and then we'll split it up for good.'

"We all agreed and took the bags to the mausoleum door and set them in, just out of sight. Never forget that either. I just knew I was being watched. Somewhere, hateful eyes were staring at me. Somehow, I knew I was in danger. But nothing happened and we rode away, each going a different s route.

"Well, I was stopped more than once but my story never wavered. I deserted six months before and stayed with my Quaker cousins in Iowa. They took me in and hid me so I wouldn't be captured by either side. Now that the war was over, I wanted to go home. They did too, even more so. The soldiers and lawmen asked me if I saw five men riding by. I did. They went west. They not so politely told me to keep going. They didn't want rebels around there.

"By dawn on Monday, I was back at the mausoleum, just like I was supposed to be. The sky was turning dark purple when I got there. I was tired and just wanted to pick up my money and go home. I dismounted and called out to the boys, but no one answered. I walked around the building and four horses were there. Not even tied up. Well, that's not a good thing. They can wander off or get hurt. I got the reins and tried to tie them to the back of the mausoleum, but they weren't going anywhere near that home of the dead. So, I tied them to a couple of saplings that were growing close by.

"By now the early morning sky was bright red. *Red sky in morning, sailor take warning.* The clouds formed human looking figures of how I imagined the Greek gods looked. Long beards and sinewy arms rising from an ocean of stormy clouds. Lightning bolts ignited them up with dangerous luminescence. I hurried back to the door. It was going to rain soon and I didn't want to be anywhere near this place when the torrent came down. I'd rather be caught by that posse.

"With that resolution, I called out to them again and got no answer. I decided to go in and count out my share and go home. I already regretted ever getting involved with this scheme. And I didn't like Horace Goode any more now than when I met him, adventure or not.

"It didn't matter. When I turned the corner to the front of the tomb, I tripped over something soft and when I looked down, there was Horace Goode. I would say he was face down, but his head was gone. I recognized him by the clothes he wore, even though they were ripped, shredded and bloodstained. I was shocked. But there were three more gory surprises for me—Billy Hardy, Jack Vance and Cliff Lee. Their bodies were strewn about. All without heads. Seeing all that, I decided it might be a good survival strategy to keep quiet.

"Daylight wasn't far away and I would be pretty visible to who or what killed my friends. I crouched a bit and walked over across the entrance, intending to go around back, just in case someone was there. My service revolver was drawn and cocked. Whatever it was killed four men, and I wasn't itching to be number five.

"As I glanced inside the tomb, I saw him, sitting on the stone sarcophagus. He looked harmless enough, at least he didn't have any weapons that I could see. He wore a terribly old fashioned loose-fitting justacorps with breeches, buckled boots and a gray tricorn hat. He was maybe a bit younger than me, but not much, and I was thirty at the time. He seemed a bit small too, no more than five feet tall, I would guess. He had alabaster skin and pitch-black hair oiled down straight back in a two-foot tail and was clean shaven.

"Two things stood out about him. The first being those eyes. They were brown, but glowed red. A hypnotic glow that just fascinated me and I just stood there, staring at him. The second thing was his mouth. It was covered in dried blood. Blood from my friends. I should have ran. I should have shot. I should have done anything but stare into those eyes. But that's what I did."

The session was over. His eyes were heavy and he needed a nap, so I let myself out and went to the café. There wasn't much to do there, but the big news was that the travelling Christian Music Tour was starting next week at the Baptist church. Four travelling shows with Christian musicians toured the towns for miles around. They played here every Friday, taking turns so that they would all be heard. These Friday songfests lasted eight weeks, so that every band could play twice before they moved on to another section of the state. There would be food, drinks and fun for everyone, and all the church folk looked forward to going and singing praises and socializing. Also, it takes place at the Methodist church across the Atchafalaya River.

It sounded like the fair, but without the 'fair' part. I was looking forward to it. However, since those nights were expected to bring in extra business, we girls were going to take turns waitressing with Lila at the café Fridays until ten o'clock. Seemed reasonable enough.

What little we served for lunches was mainly sandwiches and fries. I got to nibble on some red beans and rice for lunch and we just waited for the day to end. I could hardly wait to go home and look up 'justacorps' in the dictionary. It was a very old-fashioned waist coat men wore back in the 17th century, before they were replaced by the more recognizable frock coat that was still quite old-fashioned, but easier to spell.

The evening went well. I listened to my sisters tell their tales of woe about school. The chief complaint being that they were still ostracized because of me. I tried to appear innocent and sympathetic when they talked about that. I wished it was different, but there was nothing I could do about it.

Ozma of Oz was a relief after reading *Dracula* and listening to Mr. Benson's reminiscing. I read four chapters that night while the others listened politely and engaged in their various activities. Mom made tea with milk for me, but sweet cream was a thing of the past.

The next day, I went straight to Mr. Benson's house. He was out on the porch waiting for me to arrive and gave me a hug when he heard me.

Inside, he demonstrated how to make a full pot of coffee. Two cups were waiting nearby, along with bowls of sugar and cream. While we waited for it to percolate, I read a few more chapters of *Dracula*.

"It's done," he said when the pot stopped making dripping noises.

We each had a cup, after I promised not to let anyone know I was drinking this forbidden liquid. After a few sips, we settled back so he could complete his story about the graveyard.

"That man was pure evil, I knew it. But I was under some strange fascination. I wanted to run as far and fast as I could, but I stood there. Helpless.

"'I am your friend,' he told me, though the words were more in my mind than in my ears. His lips weren't moving.

'I am protecting you. These others, they were going to cheat you. They came in early to steal your fair share of the money. So now it's all yours.'

"He stood up and motioned for me to go inside the mausoleum, 'Come in and get your money. I kept it all here for you.'

"'No, thanks,' I managed to croak out. 'We shouldn't have bothered you in the first place.'

"He smiled, 'No bother. It's what friends do for each other, especially after an adventure.'

"There were shadowy figures near him with red eyes glowing with hatred in the dark. The storm behind me was building. Flashes of lightning lit up his chamber, illuminating god-forsaken monsters. They looked a bit like gorillas, but not quite. Maybe unusually large bears, but not really. Something else. Something evil and dangerous. Something wicked.

"Even though I didn't want to, I was inching towards the door of the tomb, towards these things, towards the money I no longer wanted. The storm was gathering force behind me. Lightning illuminated his lair. Those things weren't like anything on earth. They were reptilian, with green scales all over their bodies. Monstrous tails twitched with vicious looking barbs at the ends. Their front arms were very short and ended in claws longer than my hands.

"But that wasn't the worst of it. They were wearing the heads of my friends. They were attached to those monstrous bodies like they belonged there. They looked at me, amused and knowing. There was another in the back. Its head was a grotesque skull of something not exactly human. Something not exactly dead. Something that didn't belong on this earth.

"'Come inside,' the man said, backing up a bit to make

room, 'You belong here. The money belongs to you, doesn't it?'

"'I don't want it,' I whispered. It was so hard to do anything but stare at those eyes and continue to walk forward. 'It will destroy me.'

"'The things we want most always destroy us,' he replied. 'In life, I was Josiah Pickford, the brother of David Pickford who led this colony. He was a good and decent man. We had six families. We came out here to form paradise, using the Bible as our guide and prayer as our guardian. There were problems of course. Nothing my brother couldn't resolve. Then one day she came.'

"'An Indian woman with her daughter on the run from her tribe for some crime against their pagan gods. She was beautiful, and so was the child. I resolved to have the child for my own and took her. David was angry with me and said I must now marry her, but I refused. I would marry a white woman. I drew out my cutlass and struck her dead. Now I can't marry her, I told him.

"'The mother threw some dust in my face and I screamed in pain and fell. I woke up at my funeral. I felt my body brought here but I couldn't move, not until nightfall. Then I went out and hunted. One by one, I fed on my former friends and neighbors until they ran away and left me behind. Demons keep me company now. Demons like me. Soon they will be as one with their new heads, and we can talk together. But I have need for one more.'

"An earthshaking thunderclap sounded just then and I turned to look behind me. The spell was broken. The rain was falling, cold, sweet, and fresh. I turned back to the vault, keeping my eyes down so as not to be hypnotized again. I was near the door. The tomb was empty.

"'Come in. The money is here for you,' I heard in my

head, but I ran for the horses and rode south all the way home. And the rain and lightning guided me here. I never left Louisiana again."

I am going to have nightmares.

On the way back to the café, I stopped at the library to visit Mrs. De Montfort. She seemed very interested in how I liked Mr. Benson and how our reading sessions were going. So, I told her about his escape from the graveyard.

"Why am I reading *Dracula* to him when he's had adventures like that?" I asked.

She shot me a curious look, as if thinking of the right way to answer. Then she nodded to herself before answering. "All this happened in Missouri, right, when the war ended?"

I nodded.

"Right after his infantry division all went home?"

Again, I nodded.

"Interesting. Did you know that Mr. Benson wasn't ever in the infantry?"

"No, ma'am," I answered, knowing I had just been hoodwinked again.

"That's true," she said. "He was a cook, stationed in Shreveport. He never left the state. He did write a story just like that, though. I believe it was his first published work. It was called *The Demon in the Mausoleum*. It seems he's confusing his past with his stories."

"You mean he can't tell the difference between reality and fantasy? Between life and his books?"

"That can happen when people get extremely old, sweetheart."

I was surprised at being called 'sweetheart' by her. She always seemed so formal and almost hostile to me before.

"In his case, he's evading reality by escaping into his books."

"Oh," I replied thoughtfully, "too bad he didn't write love stories."

She laughed. "A most wonderful observation."

Now that I knew Mr. Benson had issues comprehending reality, I listened to his fascinating stories for the rest of the week without getting nervous. Not all of them were spooky. One, called *Till Death Do Us Part*, was about a soldier who came home to the family farm to find his wife was notified of his death in battle and remarried his brother. They reconciled for their mother's sake, and when she died, the veteran inherited the farm and the married couple received a considerable sum of money that their mother saved up over the years. The night before they were to leave, the soldier came into their room and shot them. The last words he said to his wife were, "Till death do us part." Then he walled up that bedroom with the bodies inside and papered over it. He regretted killing them because he was now all alone with no one to talk to. How sad.

I glanced at the plastered-up door in his living room suspiciously but didn't say anything.

Every day, I read to him and he would tell me his stories, always in the first person, always sad, lonely, or nerve-tingling scary. I listened with wide eyes (even though he couldn't see them, he knew I was listening with rapt attention). By the end of the week, *Dracula* seemed kind of mundane.

So, my first week of having a job and not being tormented in school went well. Mrs. De Montfort was pleased with me. Apparently, she had been worried about Mr. Benson being all alone in his house every day. She said she noticed that he seemed more energetic and happy since my visits started. And Mr. Benson was as nice to me as possible. We talked all about the war and Reconstruction and every other subject under the sun. And we drank coffee together, just like I did with Papa in New York. But he kept tea in the house in case Mrs. De Montfort showed up.

When I helped out at the café, things went nice and smooth. Cici still made red beans and rice and put aside the gassy beans. Nowadays though, she kept the ingredients she needed handy for anything other than sandwiches and stopped making daily specials in advance. Breakfast was what kept us up and running. Coffee kept us open for the day. Dinners were few, but enough to keep us open into the early evening. There was really very little work for me there. Most of the day, I read *Florence Nightingale.*

My first week was a raging success, in no small part because of my efforts and positivity. Sadly, the weekend was a disaster, solely because of my spite and negativity.

CHAPTER 29

CRIME AND PUNISHMENT

The day started like most; except I missed my violin lesson with the countess because she had company. That was understandable. I went to read to Mr. Benson for a while. He didn't have much to say, other than that being an old man was uncomfortable. I commiserated as much as I could, but my ability to empathize was limited.

We were just over halfway finished with *Dracula* when I left to go to the café. Business there was not bad. Some farmers stopped in for coffee and biscuits before heading to Baton Rouge to sell their wares. Some of the mill workers were eating breakfast. A few people were just sitting, drinking coffee. Fresh bread was baking in the back and the aroma made the whole place smell wonderful.

Cici called me into the kitchen to help. We were expecting a large crowd later that afternoon. Quentin Davis, a state senator who lived in one of the antebellum mansions north of the countess, had family visiting from out of state. Normally, his servants would do the cooking but their oven was broken beyond repair, so they decided to eat out.

It was quite an honor, she explained. There were other choices. Two restaurants swallowed up most of the local diners, but they were on the other side of the Atchafalaya River and this party had too many people for the drive to be comfortable. They would be in at about one and we were making gumbo, red beans and rice, and French bread. Cici was making the gumbo and I was in charge of the red beans and rice.

Michelle and Anna Marie were called in to help set up the dining room and clean the tables as soon as our other customers left, while Annette was with Guy, and Holly stayed home to help with the housework.

The tables were pulled together. The cloths changed expertly. Plates, glasses and silver found their places with expert precision. Cici was satisfied with our efforts and left to restock the kitchen to prepare for other customers. Gramma Morris was behind the register, socializing with the customers as they paid and left.

Laura Sauveterre was the first one to enter. She was wearing a fluffy taffeta dress and black buckle shoes and appeared very prim and proper. Gramma Morris pointed to the tables that were set up and Laura nodded, curtsied, and left. Within minutes, fifteen people came inside, all dressed like they were going to church. I recognized Quentin Davis immediately. He had the bearing of a patriarch who would tolerate no bad behavior. My guess was that it would take ropes and pullies to get that mouth into a smile.

While I was smashing the beans into pulp, a wonderful idea hit me. I went over to the rejected beans and put them in a pot to reheat. A little gas would be good for the soul. After all:

Beans, beans the magical fruit
The more you eat, the more you toot
The more you toot, the better you feel

Let's have beans for every meal.

When the gassy beans were warm enough, I smashed them as well and mixed them all together.

"Special delivery from hell, Laura," I whispered.

The meal went well although I was told to stay in the kitchen to avoid any kind of disturbance. I complied and washed up the dishes and made everything spotless. I even went to the back and cleaned the restrooms, even though Thrushy did that. I would cause no disturbance that day, at least not for a while. I was very satisfied.

Cici came back just as Lila stepped into the kitchen.

"They loved everything," she told us. "The red beans and rice were the best they ever had. Senator Davis was very impressed. He told me to not be surprised if we get some business out of the capital."

"Oh, Land," Cici called out to me, "I knew I'd turn you into the best cook ever. You make me so proud."

Suddenly, I wasn't feeling very satisfied. But I smiled at them and said that I was happy to help out. Gramma Morris came to the kitchen with some nickels and Michelle, Anna Marie, and I went to the movie show.

The two girls were oh, so happy. Now the restaurant might start doing business again and things would get better.

"It's been a long time since anyone in the family got to go to the movies," Anna Marie told me. "We all worked so well together."

I smiled weakly, "Yes, I think we did."

We sat in the back as Michelle didn't like being in the front rows where everyone could see her. Somehow, I couldn't blame her. I didn't want to be seen either.

The afternoon was pleasant enough until Laura came in with three of her cousins. I recognized them from lunch and my heart sank. Two of the girls were older, very pretty and about Michelle's age, and one was younger, maybe Holly's age. Those four girls sat right in the front row, visible to all. They obviously figured it was their divine right to be seen by everyone. I was being entirely too harsh and I knew it. But knowing it just didn't stop me.

The little one sat down first, and a noise as loud as a thunderclap exploded beneath her. She jumped up indignantly and exclaimed to the top of her little lungs, "Did you see what someone put there for me to sit on?"

The other three girls were absolutely mortified, especially when the whole theater started laughing. They sat down and scrunched low to sit through their humiliation. After a while, they were all squirming around in their seats. The people directly behind them got up and moved towards the back, making a big deal of holding their noses as they escaped what was now the smelliest section of town.

Sherman Richards and Beauregard Porter came in with Frank Wilson and stopped for a second and did a double take at Laura's guests and made a beeline over to talk to them, their faces changing from bored teenagers into smiling blobs of lust. They spoke for a few minutes to the girls and we watched their smiles fade away quickly. They finished up their short-lived conversations and the boys quickly moved back towards us. They were giggling as Sherman waved his hand in front of his nose. The other two were just shaking their heads.

"Leave it to the French to make a perfume called *Eau de Outhouse*," Beauregard whispered loud enough for us to hear but hopefully not my victims.

After all, Laura's cousins did nothing to hurt me. I really took no enjoyment as I watched the squirming and leaning sideways in their seats. The movie hadn't even started yet when they got up and left. We could hear the high-pitched whine of escaping gas that sounded like air seeping noisily through a stretched balloon break from at least one of the poor things. Even worse, the crowd started applauding as they exited.

"Three cheers for fresh air," somebody yelled and the theater erupted in laughter.

I was actually quite ashamed of what I did and ashamed of laughing about it. It was one thing to do that to Laura, but I didn't even know these other girls' names. I felt as low as possible, even while I was giggling. I felt eyes boring into me and turned. Anna Marie had stopped laughing and was looking at me with knowing eyes.

"What?" I asked with all the fake innocence I could find.

"I know what you did. You gave them the wrong beans."

"What's this?" Michelle asked.

"Nothing we want to talk about here," I replied.

"Good idea. Hush up about it, Anna Marie," Michelle warned.

The movies in those days had a newsreel, a couple of cartoons, an action-packed adventure serial, attractions, and the main feature. All in all, it lasted two and a half hours. After the movie, we all used the ladies' room. When I rejoined them, Michelle was looking at the posters for coming attractions while Anna Marie was talking to the Davenport sisters, no doubt trying to be friends again. Michelle saw me and we went over to collect Anna Marie. Maureen and Martha slunk away when they saw me and we headed back to the café.

"Now that I'm out of school, are you all friends again?" I asked.

"I'm hoping," Anna Marie replied. "It depends on their mom."

I nodded and we walked into the restaurant in silence.

"Amy," Cici called from the kitchen, "can I see you in the kitchen for a minute?"

"Coming," I called out and skipped through the door.

Her big hand grabbed my neck and I was dragged over to the counter in front of the empty bowl where the gassy beans should have been. I was caught red handed.

"What did you do?" she practically screamed at me, her hand getting very uncomfortable around my neck. "That girl was totally mean and vicious to you, so you messed with her food. Not just her food, either. Everybody in the family. Do you even have any idea the shame you brought me in my own kitchen? You don't ever mess with someone's food."

She was almost choking me and I was struggling to get out of her hands.

"Cici," Gramma Morris's voice almost sounded like a gunshot. She released me, reluctantly. I ran over behind my defender, as far away from her as I could get and still hear the conversation.

"What were you going to do?" Gramma Morris said softly, but firmly.

"That was all," she replied sullenly. "She deliberately put the bad beans in those customer's food. She made this place look like a bunch of ignorant half-wits were running the kitchen."

"I know," Gramma Morris said grimly. "And Cici, I would never try to choke one of your sons. I know there's no telling how much business we lost. And somehow, it's all over town. Catherine Sauveterre came in ranting and raving like she lost her mind. I had to tell her she wasn't poisoned, after all."

"No, she wasn't poisoned," Cici responded angrily, "but my reputation was. Those beans came out of my kitchen. I don't ever want to see that child's face again, not in this here restaurant. Not today, not tomorrow, not ever."

That hurt worse than her attempted strangulation. I wanted to say something to make her forgive me, but then I remembered Fredrick. She hadn't spoken to her own nephew in years over some stolen cookies. What chance did I have?

"I'm sorry," I said softly, tears flowing down my face, even though I didn't want them to.

"Not sorry enough. Just go on out the front door and don't let me catch you around here again," she ordered.

"That is not how it works, Cici," Gramma Morris said coldly. "The kitchen is your kingdom, but it is our restaurant. It's a family business and she's family. She can still come in here and work the tables and clean up. When the Friday night concerts start, she'll do all the waitressing so none of her sisters will have to miss any of them. But she won't ever step foot in the kitchen again without your permission."

"She'll never get that."

"Then she'll never step into your kitchen again."

There was a bit of a stare-down, then Gramma Morris said crisply, "Amy." She cocked her head towards the dining room, indicating for me to leave.

"If we shut down because people are afraid to come here, it'll be all that child's fault," Cici declared.

"If she puts us out of business, the Lord will provide," Gramma Morris had the final word.

I ran out of the kitchen and cried as quietly as possible on the front porch. This was the lowest point in my life. I had no friends and my family pretty much hated me. I enjoyed learning to cook and now was thrown out of the kitchen. What will happen when Mom and Dad find out? Maybe soon I'd be disowned completely.

That red Oldsmobile drove past me and turned right on River Street. An arm waved to me, but I didn't wave back. I didn't know the man and, right now, I didn't want anything to do with him.

What I would find out later was that Anna Marie was having a conversation with Gramma Morris similar to mine. Everyone in town knew what happened because she told Martha and Maureen. Those two girls could broadcast gossip better than all the radios in the south. My vengeful misdeed was the talk of the town because of them.

Porky came with the wagon and we quietly rode home for our execution. Michelle rode up front between Porky and Gramma Morris. Whatever they said was lost to me. I was in my own world, thinking about how the day would have gone if I had been more forgiving.

Mom immediately confined us to our room the moment we stepped inside. Her anger was palpable. She had a few choice phrases like 'ungrateful brats' and 'business destroying monsters.' Dad was going to handle the punishment when he got home. Just being in the room with Anna Marie should have been punishment enough, I thought. I picked up my *Florence Nightingale* book and made a show of reading it, but I was so upset I couldn't comprehend a word.

Anna Marie dropped onto the bed and stared at the ceiling. After a while she broke the silence, since it was obvious to her that I wasn't about to speak to her.

"Why'd you even have to come here?"

"I had no choice. Do you think I'd share a house, a

room and a bed with you by choice? I have good reasons to dislike you. You hated me for no reason. You never even gave me a chance."

"Who would? You're too smart. The way you multiply in your head and read books like that. It's not right," she responded defensively.

"You mean if we were to become friends, I'd have to be dumb like you? No thanks."

"Hey," she said jumping out of bed and glaring down at me.

I inched away to the other side in case she decided to pounce and start a tussle. Although Papa taught me how to fight pretty well, it always ended up bad for me, especially when I won.

"Why did you snitch on me like some kind of rat?" I stayed calm and got off the bed to face her, keeping it between us. "Did you want Maureen and Martha to start calling you Ratta Marie? Why are you even friends with them? What do you do with them? Sit around and make snarky remarks about everyone else? Only now they don't want you with them anymore."

That struck a nerve. Her hands were balled up into fists and I thought she might attack so I backed away.

"Food for thought," I finished.

"Anna Marie. Amy," Dad's voice carried up the stairs, his tone exuding cold anger. "Get down here. Now."

Anna Marie looked at me for a second. "Doom," she said and ran out of the room and down the stairs.

I followed as fast as I could.

There he stood, behind the kitchen table, angry and fearsome. He held a homemade paddle in his hand which he tapped on his thigh, listening to it slap his pants leg.

"Well, you two really are quite the pair," he spit the

words out, one by one to enhance the dramatic scene.

"Mrs. De Montfort gave me some words from the wise men of this world for you two to ponder while we get to the 'seat' of our problem here."

Oh, this was not going to be good.

"Amy, for you, from Confucius. 'Before you embark on a journey of revenge, dig two graves, one for yourself.' Do you know what that means?"

I nodded miserably. "It means if I just forgave and went on with my life, all this never would have happened. I already felt bad when I saw those two girls who I never met go through it all at the theater."

"Didn't stop you from laughing," Michelle said, obviously now a witness for the prosecution.

"It was still funny," I retorted. "Just because I laughed didn't mean I didn't feel bad."

"You have an answer for everything," Gramma Morris said, rolling her eyes.

"Anna Marie, your quote comes from the Bible, Proverbs 11:13. 'A gossip betrays a confidence, but a trustworthy person keeps a secret.' Why would you even think to tell those girls anything that happens in our family or our business?"

"I don't know."

The paddle came down hard on the kitchen table.

"WHY?"

"I thought if I shared a secret, we'd be friends again."

He shot her an absolutely withering look and it looked like she lost two inches of height.

"They'll never be your friends again, no matter how hard you try, and you'll keep getting hurt if you don't stop trying. Now we four, your mom, me and you two, will go behind the outhouse so we can emphasize that point for you. And Amy's point too. Revenge is a waste of time and just causes hurt to a whole lot of people. People you aren't even trying to hurt."

We silently marched behind the outhouse. The sun was down and there was nothing but privacy as the belt hit our bared behinds. Mom then confined us to our room with no dinner or books. We were to talk and resolve our issues. Her issues, to be truthful. But they festered in Anna Marie's soul. She flopped on the bed with her back to me, obviously rejecting any hope of conversation.

The spanking itself hurt quite a bit. The humiliation was worse. My backside being exposed to my uncle or Dad, or whatever he was to me, was awful. And there was the sense of guilt over what I had done. Everyone in town knew I knowingly served a whole family food that was not good.

Did we put the restaurant out of business? I didn't want to find out. And I didn't want to have to face any of them as we all slowly starved to death in the streets of Faucette because Anna Marie and I destroyed our only source of income.

CHAPTER 30

A PLAN

Holly came in after dinner, looking sad and grim.

"We don't know what's going to happen," she said. "But Gramma Morris thinks things will be just fine. Mama's afraid we might lose the restaurant, but Papa doesn't care. We won't lose the house or anything because of the chickens, eggs and fish. No matter what happens, I love you both and forgive you for what you did," indicating me, "and you for telling your friends about it," to Anna Marie.

Anna Marie immediately got up and hugged her, and I was next.

"You won't lose everything," I told her. "You'll always have my Sunday dress. That will never be lost, and the way you're growing, we'll be sharing it soon. I'll take good care of it for you, so you'll have it to remember me by."

"Remember you by?" Anna Marie harumphed. "Why would we want to remember you? I don't like remembering you and there's nothing to remember you for anyway, except bad things. I used to have friends. I'd go over to their homes and we'd eat together and play games and talk about life and our futures. They hardly even talk to me anymore because of you."

"Me? How do you figure?"

"They don't like you. Their mothers won't let them near you or me now since you live with us."

"How is that my fault and not their mothers?"

"Well, you must be some kind of bad for them to hate you so."

"She's not bad," Holly defended me. "They're like you. They never gave her a chance. If you got to know her, you'd love her just like I do."

"No, I wouldn't," she said, folding her arms.

"No, she wouldn't," I agreed.

Yes, I must really get away.

"So," I asked Anna Marie, "if Mom sends me away, they'll be your friends again? And they're the friends you want to have?"

"Yes, we've always been friends."

"Well, they're the kind of friends you'll always have, I suppose. I can mention to Mom that everyone will be better off if they send me back to New York. Would that make you happy if I try?"

"No," Holly cried out, "that's a terrible idea."

"It would be better if instead of trying, you succeed."

"I'll succeed."

Maybe the Polanski family in St. Louis will take me in. They were very nice. I would never think of doing something so rash and bold (and stupid), but it was nice to daydream about it. But still, it was a plan.

I had to use the outhouse and quietly creeped down the stairs to avoid being seen and questioned about why I was out of our room.

"…your ideas just aren't working," Gramma Morris was saying to Mom.

"I know," Mom replied. "It's a shame she came to us

now. I really think…"

I left. I didn't want to be there. I used the toilet, cried for a bit, washed up, and went back inside. They were still talking, but I didn't want to hear anymore.

"So, if I am never in the café and find somewhere else to be, then this whole thing will blow over?" I double-checked with Anna Marie, while a very unhappy Holly listened in.

"Of course, it will. You're the cause of all our problems. But they want you there every Friday night until the concert season is over. They won't send you away."

"No," Holly said. "We all love you here. You can't go back. You belong here."

"Yes, she can," said Anna Marie spitefully.

"Yes, I can," I agreed. "Besides, Mom just said it was a shame I came here. I heard her."

To prove my ability to predict the future was nonexistent, I added, "It's just a matter of time."

"But Mom and Dad will never send you away, will they, Anna Marie?"

"No, they will never send her away," she said sadly.

But I might send me away.

CHAPTER 31

SARAH

Sunday was pleasant enough. I read a little more about *Florence Nightingale,* which helped me avoid conversation with Anna Marie. We went to church together as a family. My last time going to church with this family, I thought to myself. I played my violin for probably the last time. I read to them and followed our family routine as much as possible.

I woke up early on Monday. I could smell bacon frying in the iron skillet. The adults were on the back porch, talking and drinking coffee. .I could hear their voices, but not the words. I quietly disengaged Holly's arm from around my collar and got out of bed. The pinafore and my light coat were all I needed for traveling. There wasn't much to pack, just what I brought down from New York and the extra dress. My Sunday dress I left out on the dresser with a quick note to Holly.

Dear little sister Holly, when you wear this, think of me. I will always remember you fondly.

I left by the front door while the adults talked softly in the back. No doubt they were talking about me. No doubt they weren't saying anything good. As it was explained to me later, these assumptions weren't very accurate. The conversation was actually about getting Anna Marie to be more accepting of me. But I didn't know that as I left.

While the others were eating, cooking, talking, and sleeping, I quietly used the outhouse and washed up as best as I could. It would be a long walk because I didn't want to go into Faucette. People would see me and I'd be stopped and sent back home, where things would get worse. That meant walking all the way to State Route 43 and over to Baton Rouge. It was only thirty-two miles. I figured I would be there by nightfall. My plan sounded optimistic, but I had strong determination.

I walked briskly down LaSalle Road, putting as much distance between me and the house as I could. Even though I figured I had at least another hour before the other children woke up, I knew Uncle Vincent's car could cover a whole lot of distance, and the brambles and thorn bushes on the side of the road indicated that they would make hiding very uncomfortable.

It was very warm for a February morning, which I figured was typical for winter in the south. I took off my coat, stuffed it in my bag and trudged on. I stopped for a moment at the train crossing. I would save a lot of time and miles if I just followed the tracks over the river but decided against it. If a train rolled through, the collision would kill me. If I plunged into the river, it would be fatal. Even worse, it would ruin my clothes. So, I crossed over the tracks and continued north.

By the time the dark of night was giving way to the purples and violet of dawn, I was in unfamiliar territory. I was unable to see anything other than the road. The land was overrun with giant pine trees. Their refreshing scent filled my nostrils. The soft wind made their tops whoosh a bit and it sounded like they were whispering to me, encouraging my adventure.

A coyote ran in the road a few yards ahead of me and stopped. It sat on its haunches for a few seconds and looked me in the eye. It was an unusual animal with brown hair that was so well groomed I thought someone had brushed its thick coat. I took a step forward and he turned and ran into the meadow.

What an odd animal, I thought to myself. He didn't seem afraid of me or nervous at all. He acted like someone's pet. I continued to walk while thinking of that coyote, oblivious to how the road curved leftwards.

The road looked different to me while walking. The air was still, with the swampy, rich odor of decaying leaves and new life growing from remains. The forest started thinning out. Big trees on one side were contrasted with the saplings on the other. A lush green meadow was on the other side surrounded by crooked and sagging fence posts with fallen strings of rusty barbed wire barely visible in the dirt, almost hidden by the grass. The meadow was dotted with small, stagnant ponds, most of them dressed in green algae. I always thought algae looked pretty from a distance. It wasn't until I got close to it that I realized it was slimy, unwholesome and unclean. Still the ponds were no bigger than large puddles. I only knew they were there because the algae were a different shade of green than the grass surrounding them. By and large, the meadow seemed like a perfect place for a picnic. Too bad there weren't any tables set up.

As I continued down the curve, I saw a light on my right. After a few more steps, I saw a clapboard building and several trucks in the parking lot. A high-pitched buzzing noise wailed out to me, muffled a bit, but loud. After a few more steps, I read an old plywood sign on top of a nearly rotted away post: The Landacre Sawmill and Timber Co.

Wherever I was wasn't where I wanted to be.

It was interesting that I never had an issue with any of the Landacres at school, but my family all think of them as devils, especially Hugo Landacre, Devil-in-Chief.

I hurried past the mill to avoid being seen. The best way to not have issues with the Landacres would be to not meet any of them. The road only went a little bit beyond the mill, where I could hear the saw buzzing through some unfortunate tree. It ended at the banks of the Malmort River where another washed out bridge stopped my progress.

The river gushed and surged by me. The fluids were in a hurry to end their journey and I didn't blame them. The river smelled bad. Maybe the sulfur particles were stirred up from the current, but the rotten egg smell was too strong for me to stay close.

I quickly retreated back down the road and saw two more trucks pulling into the mill's parking lot. With the family feud being what it was, I figured I would wait until the men entered the building before moving back down the road. Twilight was gone and the long shadows of early morning had arrived. I wanted to get back to the main road without being seen, especially by the Landacre family or their employees. Why ask for trouble?

I decided that there was enough light to cut across the meadow and reach the road without having to go past the mill. It seemed like a good idea since another pair of trucks were heading into the parking lot and the mill was showing a great deal more activity.

On my side of the road, the nearest fence post was tilted at a 45-degree angle and propped up a faded *Keep Out* sign, so I walked down a few posts and stepped over a collapsed barbed wire strand. I figured I wasn't breaking any rules by entering over here since I wasn't directly in front of the sign.

Although the meadow appeared lush and welcoming from the road, once I crossed into it, its beauty quickly faded. It seemed like my shoes and socks were attacked by dozens of thorny vines that lay hidden underneath the welcoming grass. The morning dew glistened on the buckles and dampened my calves. I took no more than five steps when the ground became too spongy to hold me up. The mud oozed up the sides of my shoes and I stepped back.

Glancing around, I decided to change course and head for higher ground, but it turned out to be taller grass and I was still sinking with each step. I tried to head back to the road, but the mud was even more active. I didn't want to get to Baton Rouge looking too dirty, so I had to think quickly. I decided the ground near the trees by the river sloped upwards and would be high enough to get me back to the road, so I headed towards the river. I figured that from there the road would be easy to get to.

Unfortunately, the ground sloped downwards before it climbed upwards. The grass was high and I stopped for a second to check my options. I had none.

A slight breeze swooshed through the verdant grass and the highlights danced across the field while my foot sank down to my ankle. It made a hungry, sucking sound as I wrenched free, only to feel my other foot slowly sink all the way to my hem.

"That's the wrong way."

I turned around and saw a cute little girl of maybe six. She looked at me with curious brown eyes.

"That's river land. It's just a few feet of dirt and dust covering the water. You go any farther, you'll sink down and drown."

"River land?" I asked, while lifting my feet one at a time to keep from sinking any farther.

She nodded. "Used to be river, but the water evaporated and dirt and things build up, and then the water comes back and pushes it to the top. Grass grows on it and it looks like ground but it's only a little ground, then it's water."

"Like quicksand?"

"Could be, but I don't think there's any sand in there."

"Oh."

She stepped closer, took my hand and led me a bit farther away from the road where the ground was firm.

"People used to come here to get blackberries in springtime. They're everywhere. But someone always gets caught in the river land. They don't always get out."

That made me nervous.

"Oh," I said forcing myself to be calm. "How do we get out of here?"

"This way." She led me deeper into the meadow. Mud, slime, and nasty water were all around us, but we stayed on firm land.

"There used to be Indians that lived nearby. They piled up loads of dirt by the riverside to mark the unsafe parts of the river valley, but years of rain and flooding wore them down to almost nothing. But I know where they are."

We walked up an incline and then away from the road and veered slightly left, away from the road again.

"So, how did you come to be way out here?" I asked.

"It's not 'way' out here. I live over there, in that big house," she explained, pointed deep into the woods beyond the meadow. "We call it Forest Manor. My name is Sarah

Forest. And I'm out here because my parents are fighting so I went out to get away from it."

I turned in the direction she pointed but saw nothing.

"Oh," I said sympathetically. "Well, hi, Sarah. My name in Amy Collins. I live in Faucette."

"I know," she said assuredly.

She made me a little nervous.

"I'm not sure I see a house over there," I said politely, determined to hide my unease.

"It's behind the trees."

"Oh. That must be a long way away. Don't you worry about the river land or wild animals? I saw a coyote earlier today."

"I know. You were watching it when the road forked and you went the wrong way."

That would explain how I got here. But how did she know that? If she was watching me for that long, surely I would have seen her.

"And no, Amy Collins, I won't get lost. The land knows me and won't let anything bad happen to me."

At last, something I could relate to.

"You know, when I listen to the river swishing and swashing, I feel the same way."

"Then you're connected to the land, at least the water. But here, not so much. You could have died over there. Gotten stuck and never found, at least until spring."

Maybe not such a bad idea. Everyone would be happy then. Or at least feel bad they weren't nice to me. The problem with that is I'd be dead.

"You mustn't leave until it's time for you to go, Amy Collins. Don't run away again, you are more blessed than you think."

"I guess," I replied.

Did she mean 'leave' as in run away or 'leave' as in die? Strange little girl. She certainly seemed to know a lot about me.

The trail she led me down ended back at the road, almost exactly where I left. The river whooshed to my left; the sawmill buzzed to my right.

"You can wash the mud off your shoes at the river. I have to go now. My father is calling. Always stay on the road, Amy Collins."

"I will, Sarah Forest, and thank you for helping me and being my friend."

"My father is calling," she repeated.

I didn't hear anyone calling, but I bent down and hugged her tightly and I turned to go on the road while she walked down the unseen path. I turned back to give her a quick wave, but she gone. There was no trace of her.

I turned back to the putrid selling river and rinsed out my shoes and wrung as much muddy water from my socks as I could. Then I wrung out the mud from my hem. After rinsing my hands and wrists, I headed back to Faucette. Like it or not, it was home. That is, if my family would take me back in.

CHAPTER 32

HUGH LANDACRE

I had just passed the mill and was headed back to LaSalle Road when I heard a truck sputtering behind me. I moved over as far to the right as I could for it to pass, but it slowed down in front of me and stopped.

Margaret Landacre opened the passenger door, leaned out and called to me like I was a long-lost friend or something, "Hey, Amy, Amy Collins."

My heart sank. I had just been spotted by the enemy. The most hated people on the planet. My family would have been happier if I drowned than be seen talking to a Landacre. Well, maybe that was a bit of an exaggeration. Or not. They were all pretty upset with me.

An older man stepped out of the driver's side of the car. Like Uncle Angus, he could have been any age between forty to sixty. His face was lined with care, although his smile lines were quite dominant. It was obvious that he and Margaret were family.

"I thought I saw you walk past the mill," Margaret continued. "Couldn't understand how you got there or why."

"The whole town is looking for you little girl," the man said, not unkindly. "You got everybody worried sick. What did you do? Swim down the river? You're covered in mud."

"I washed most of it off," I said indignantly.

"You missed the smell. The Malmort stinks bad. And you must have been in a mudslide," he drawled back with a chuckle. "Now, how did you wind up here if you didn't swim?"

"I took the wrong turn and wound up at the river. I did *not* swim in the river. I turned around and I took a shortcut through the meadow."

They looked at each other in surprise.

"That's no meadow," the man said. "That's pure swamp. Just river land and quicksand. Snakes and poisonous spiders. You're lucky you got out alive."

"Oh, I didn't see any snakes or spiders, but the ground was pretty muddy. But I had help. A little girl named Sarah."

"Sarah Forest?" he said, all amusement gone now. He looked at Margaret.

"Mm hmm," I replied affirmatively. "She lives out there. Her parents were fighting and she went out to get away from the noise."

"Sarah Forest?" he repeated, more to himself.

"Yes sir, that's what she said. She's a very sweet girl. She stopped me from stepping in the quicksand and got me back to the road when I didn't know what to do."

"Papa, is Sarah the Marsh-girl?" Margaret asked.

"Marsh-girl?" I said derisively. "Another ghost story designed to frighten children into staying away from something?"

"Margaret, yes. Amy, no," he replied thoughtfully. "Back just after the war, The War of Northern Aggression, that is, the Forest family moved in over there in the high ground, beyond the trees. He was a peculiar young man,

Nathaniel Forest. He moved here with his widowed sister and her children. He said they were old French nobility and were on the run. Just like the countess's family, only not believable. Nobody in France cared about the nobility exiles by those days. Certainly not here.

"And his sister was most peculiar. Why they said that, I don't know. Tobias Faucette was the mayor back then and tried to get a little friendly with her, but she somehow frightened him. He quickly decided to have nothing more to do with her. And Nathaniel Forest was just too 'land-smart' to be nobility. He was wicked with a knife and knew how to coax every crab and crawfish into his traps. No fancy-dancy gentleman could do that. Built a small lean-to and turned it into a two-story home. Went to church and did the sermons for a while when the parson was away. He'd help those who couldn't read or write with their legal papers and contracts. He even married a local girl from the Morris line. His sister married and moved away to Houston after that. He and his wife had three children, but then one day, the house caught on fire and they all died. His youngest daughter got out, but drowned in the river land. Found her body three days later. Her name was Sarah."

"I fell for the echo-by-the-river story, but I won't fall for that one," I said politely, but firmly. I did not want to be laughed at again.

He ignored me. "They say whoever meets her in that swamp has someone they know die within a month. Maybe not family or friend, but someone."

"Well, we'll know for sure in a month then," I said politely, though my skepticism must have been obvious.

"Just because it sounds fantastic, doesn't mean it isn't true," he responded calmly.

"We'll find out," I said agreeably, then remembered my

precarious position in my family. "If I'm still here."

"Don't even think you're running away again, young lady," his voice turned very serious. "If the swamp don't get you, I will. And then you'll wish the swamp got you, little girl. Understand?"

I nodded.

"I just thought everybody would be happy I left."

"Nobody who matters wants you to leave. The ones who do matter want you back. Especially your mother."

That was confusing.

"They definitively don't want me back in New York."

"I mean your aunt, who you call 'Mom,' which by the way confuses the hell out of everyone in Faucette."

"I'm sorry about that. I'm sorry about a lot of things. But I was going back to the café. I just wasn't sure they'd want me back. You don't know what happened. What I did."

"Everybody knows what happened. The number one source of entertainment in this town is picking up the phone and listening to other people's conversations."

"That's how everybody knows what goes on in our house.!"

"Everybody's house. Stick to visiting in person if you want secrets. Makes for a better life if you want privacy."

My curiosity got the better of me. "Excuse me, sir. Who are you?" I asked.

"Oh, Amy," said Margaret, "this is Hugh Landacre, owner of the mill, my father."

The devil.

"I thought your father was Hugo Landacre."

"He's my brother," she replied with an eye roll.

"He's my son. You've probably seen him about town He's a fine young man."

"Oh."

He laughed a little. "Now your mother disagrees with that, I'm sure. I'm sure you thought I was red with horns and a tail and carry a pitchfork."

Pretty accurate guess, actually.

"She doesn't talk about you that much except to stay away."

"Well, people make mistakes. Some are long term and some short term."

I nodded, not understanding what he was trying to say.

"And given the circumstances, our issues might take a while to resolve."

"What are the issues?" I asked.

"They're to be discussed with your…with Cassandra Villians. She wouldn't want me to talk about it if you were around to hear it."

I sighed with disappointment.

"And since you were going back anyway, hop in and we'll take you to the café. I understand Cassandra's there at the phone while every able-bodied man and woman in town is out looking for you."

"I'm so glad we found you," Margaret said. "None of us had much chance to talk to you or get to know you because of all the bad blood."

"I'm glad, too," I replied.

She seemed really nice. And I got the idea that when I was her age, I would look just like her. And her father was so pleasant and warm. I guess it must have been Hugo Landacre who was the devil.

"By the way," Hugh Landacre said, "I know you've had problems at school, but never my doing, or Hugo's. In fact, it was my idea to send Quentin down to your café. A peace offering if you will. Laura was supposed to apologize to you, but she said she didn't see you."

"I was in the kitchen. I saw her."

"Obviously," he replied dryly, "you know Laura got the same punishment for putting gum in your hair that you got for putting the wrong beans on their plates. Maybe you two can be friends now."

"Maybe," I said pulling on my hair self-consciencely.

"Regardless, you should have no more problems with any of the Landacres. I have made that pretty clear. Right, Margaret?"

"Oh yes, anyone who does you harm is putting their life in danger," she smiled sweetly.

"If you do have any more issues, come see me. And remember, when you're a Landacre, your problems disappear because you face them and work through them. They'll never go away by you running away. You have to take charge and when you get to fixing them, you'll see how small those problems really are. Then like any other Landacre, you'll resolve them."

"But I'm not a Landacre," I reminded him.

"Well…that's fair enough, you're a Collins. But you go back far enough, we're family, even better. We're friends. And I can fix almost any problem you may have."

We pulled up to the café and he smiled at me.

"I can't fix any problems you have in there, though."

CHAPTER 33

THE RETURN

"Amy, thank God." Mom scurried over to me and hugged me. "We looked all over for you. Mr. Kaker called ahead on the lines to see if there was a stowaway on the train. Betsy and the countess are worried sick. Vincent is scouring the roads for you. Paul is just beside himself and Gramma Morris is at home calling police stations everywhere. What were you thinking?"

"I was thinking that since I destroyed your business and made everybody hate me, you'd all be happier if I was gone. You did call me an ungrateful brat and a monster. And this morning you said it's a shame I came to you."

She stopped in her tracks for a moment. Then she must have remembered the conversation.

"*At this time.* You missed the last part of the sentence. It's a shame you came here *at this time.* I wish we had you years ago."

She hugged me close again.

"And we may have exaggerated a bit about the business failing. It certainly didn't help it any though. And about the name calling, everybody says things they regret. I regret that. But I'm so happy you got back, unhurt."

Lila came in through the kitchen door. She was excited

to see me and hugged me right away.

"Oh, I'm so happy you didn't get hit by a car or fall in the river and get lost in the swamp," she sniffed a bit, "Or did you get lost in the swamp?"

I told them about what happened; my meeting Sarah and how the Landacres told me about her story.

Lila said, "That story has been around a long, long time. After you live here awhile, you'll hear lots of legends and myths, all based on something true. I don't sneer at the thought of you meeting Sarah, so don't sneer at other people's stories."

"In the meantime, we have to get you cleaned up. River water might get the mud off, but it puts a smell on. Especially the Malmort," Mom said.

We could hear the back door opening and the pots tapping on the stove.

"Cici was out getting some kitchen supplies," Lila told me. "Cici, Amy's back."

"I know. Ruins good food, gets mad she gets punished, runs away, and comes back to a hero's welcome. No welcome from me. She should have kept on going and got herself out of the mess she was in."

Deadly silence followed.

"I was in quicksand," I said.

"Her dress might be ruined beyond repair." Lila added.

"Okay. I was wrong," she called out without bothering to come into the dining room to see me. "I'm glad you're out of quicksand, but if you used that head of yours, you'd never gotten into quicksand in the first place."

I rolled my eyes at Mom and Lila. "Is it too late to catch a train?"

I was sent to the ladies' room to wash up. Lila retrieved some clean towels and washcloths for me. I washed off all the river water while Lila rinsed out my dress and socks. While everything was drying, Cici gave Lila an old tablecloth that was frayed, stained and unworthy of dressing a table. Arm and head holes were cut, and I was dressed and non-smelly. Mom remembered she had a pair of boots in the back and I was presentable to the public.

Mom also called Betsy to see if she could rush out the last outfit she made for me. The blouse and skirt would be ready by tomorrow.

I was immediately told to go to Mr. Benson's house for his reading hour. Mrs. De Montfort met me there for inspection and shook her head at my makeshift dress. We stayed with the old man and read and talked afterwards while drinking tea with sweet cream.

"So, you wandered off into the swamp," he said pleasantly.

"Word gets around fast," I replied.

"No word. I knew. I could see you in my mind."

"Oh," I said, looking at Mrs. De Montfort, who shrugged and pointed to his phone.

The party line, I thought to myself. He listened in to Mom's conversation with Betsy.

"You know," he continued, "I wrote a lot of stories in my day. All of them were fiction, except for ones that were true."

"They were all fiction," Mrs. De Montfort corrected gently.

"They were all based on stories I heard. Stories from honest men who had no reason to lie. Odd things happen in the swamp. Weird things move around just out of sight. And there are monsters. Real ones. They're called humans.

"You know, when I got married, my parents had this house built for us. It wasn't so nice at first. It was one room.

Just this living room. When our daughter was born, she slept just opposite us. By the time I was twenty-five, we had three children. Two boys and a girl. I was nothing more than an over-educated farmer. My Mama taught we how to read and write and do basic math, you know.

"I got the lumber together and built a private bedroom for me and Eva, my wife. Girls, of course, need more privacy than boys, so we added on a room for my daughter. Then we decided the boys shouldn't be sleeping in here when their sister has her own room, so we built one for them."

He took a sip of coffee and went on.

"Then the war came. My friend Blackjack Morris and I were drafted. Become soldiers or become executed. Easy choice to make, we thought. We fought until the war ended, more or less."

He paused and directed his eyes at me as though he could see me.

"Well, after Vicksburg, I was stationed under Kirby Smith, over in Shreveport. Couldn't get home to visit. Telegraphs were down. Another Terrance Benson was killed out east and the army sent my wife notice that I died. When I came home, I found out she married my little brother and a had a son. It was awkward, of course, but I stayed to make my mother happy. When she passed on, they moved to Texas so she could be by her family down near Houston. They got the money and my children, and I got the land and house. Never saw any of them again.

"After they left, I walled off our bedroom. The memories were too painful. My brother sent all the children to boarding school in Memphis. I never saw them again."

He shrugged as if he didn't care, but it was obvious he did.

"You walled off one of the bedrooms? And kept it sealed all this time?"

He smiled slyly. "I wasn't using it. I'm still not using it. Everything in there has memories that break my heart. Now here I am old and alone.

"I remarried but she died of the fever back in the summer of '89. We weren't blessed with children. I had two loves in my life that gave me two stories to tell. Don't you like love stories?"

"No," I swallowed, "I mean, yes, just ones with happier endings."

He laughed, "As long as people get old, there are no happy endings."

After we left, I told Mrs. De Montfort that I didn't want to read to him anymore, but she just laughed.

"I think the bodies of his wife and brother are in that walled off room, just like in that story he wrote, *Till Death Do Us Part.*"

"He writes stories designed to scare children," she said. "Of course, he wants to scare you in person as well. And from a practical point of view, the house would stink to high heaven if two bodies were allowed to decompose in one of the rooms. We would know."

She patted my hand.

Mom, Dad and Gramma Morris all agreed with her. The Democratic process dictated that I continue reading. Of course, if the other children's votes counted, then the Democratic process would be thrown out and parental dictatorship would rule. There are some things that all families have in common.

The next day, I wore my old traveling dress while my new pinafore soaked in vinegar and water. My schedule was set. Mr. Benson was expecting me, and so was Mrs. De

Montfort. Betsy was bringing my new outfit over later in the day and she planned to have lunch with us at the café. It would have been a better day if things had stuck to the plan.

Uncle Vincent had a business meeting, so I left with Gramma Morris early that morning. Cici and her sons were already there. She was buttering toast to put in the warmer while the coffee percolated in the pot.

I wiped down the counter and filled the snack baskets by the register with bags of peanuts and other snacks. Thrushy swept the front porch while Finchy cleaned the windows.

We finished with time to spare and Cici's grandsons and I went out on the front porch. Mr. Dupris was opening his garage And Thrushy asked Cici for permission to visit and got it. I asked Gramma Morris, but she was a bit less enthusiastic.

"Young boys don't always want a girl with them you know. Cici might not want you around them."

"If my boys don't have sense enough to keep better company, then I don't care anymore," Cici responded with the malice I had become accustomed to.

Thrushy rolled his eyes and said, "Come on, Amy." And we were off.

A slightly faded red sedan was in the parking lot, a middle-aged blonde woman daintily exiting from the passenger side. She wore very stylish clothes, a tight-fitting green dress with pearl necklace and matching earrings. The chauffeur wore a gray uniform and billed hat.

"That's a 1924 Cadillac V-63," Thrushy told us. "If 'elegant' means better than good, this is as elegant as they get."

Thrushy made an appreciative wolf whistle at the

machine and received angry stares for his efforts.

"That's a fine automobile," he said, oblivious to the hostility.

"I guess," said the chauffeur indifferently.

Remembering how bad that last conversation went when the subject was cars, I went in and paid my respects to Mr. Dupris.

"Good morning, Mr. Dupris," I said politely.

He smiled.

"Good morning, Little Amy. Are you still wondering about all those horses under the hood?"

He didn't seem particularly mean when he said it, but I still didn't like it.

"I met your royal cousin the other day. He seemed very nice," I said.

"Royal cousin," he snorted. "Descendant of slaves."

"1/1024th seems kind of a small percentage to fuel all that disrespect," I said, surprised at all the hostility over such a small percentage of such a small thing.

"You know what a 1/1024th slave is?" he asked, but I knew what the answer was going to be.

"A slave."

"I saw her portrait. She didn't look Choctaw or black. She just looked…blonde. They never found any mixed blood in her at all. Couldn't you two be friends? You are related."

"Friends?" he stroked his unshaven cheeks. "No, I don't think so. If we were friends, then we'd have to talk to each other."

Thrushy and Finchy came back in to talk about the car. I didn't want to showcase my automotive ignorance, especially in front of strangers, so I retreated to the café and used the restroom. After washing up, I returned to the garage to find Thrushy getting a severe dressing down by Pierre Dupris in front of the woman in the car.

This must be serious. He doesn't have a tobacco chew in his mouth.

A blue Buick was parked nearby with the chauffeur now in that driver's seat. A man in an old-fashioned butler's suit was following the conversation standing slightly behind the woman.

She had a pinched, indignant appearance with brown, birdlike eyes and sneering, cold lips. She was obviously enjoying Thrushy's discomfort.

As I approached, I could overhear them talking to each other.

"No more whistling at cars," Mr. Dupris practically yelled at Thrushy. "Understand?"

"Yes, sir."

"No being here when you see that woman," he continued.

"No, sir. I'm sorry, sir," Thrushy was flustered, shaking his head on 'no' and nodding on 'yes.'

"I know he was whistling at me and not the car," the woman hissed at them both. "And I am shocked that he is allowed to be so disrespectful. In my day, that would simply not be tolerated."

"Now Mrs. Thomas," Mr. Dupris tried to sound soothing, but it came off as condescending, "he always whistles at the finest cars. That's why I let him help me here. He appreciates the automobile. I've known Thrushy all his life. There's not a disrespectful bone in his body."

"Is my car ready?" she huffed.

"Yes, ma'am."

Her servant instantly opened the back door for her and she started to get inside. She paused for a moment and glared back at Thrushy first, then Mr. Dupris.

"My brother-in-law will hear about this."

With that, the door was closed behind her. The driver hopped in the front and both cars and their odious occupants pulled away.

"Who was that?" I asked.

"That, little girl, was Mrs. Giselle Thomas. Richest woman in the whole Parrish. And she was sitting in the car when Thrushy here decided to whistle at her car like it was a pretty woman. She thought he was whistling at her like she was a pretty woman. I don't know why she would think that. Did you get a good look at her? Her days of getting whistles are long gone. Well, the more we tried to convince her he wasn't whistling at her, the more she thought we were insulting her. Saying the car is pretty but she ain't. Not that it wouldn't be true, but why say it? Her husband is Chester Thomas, the Superior Court Judge in Baton Rouge. Her brother-in-law is Jared Thomas, the lawyer. You've seen Jared's house, just north of the countess's place. She's in town visiting Gabriella, her little sister. Gabby just had a baby girl so Giselle's in town stirring up trouble, like she always does."

"What trouble? Nothing happened."

He gave me a withering look.

"Are you sure you live on the same planet with the rest of us?" he asked me impatiently. "She's going to make trouble. Some people go to movies, some people have parties, some people listen to the radio, some people read books. That woman makes trouble. And *you*," he pointed to Thrushy, "best not be around here for a couple of weeks until we see what she's going to do. Got it?"

Thrushy nodded, "Yes, sir,"

We went back to the café.

"We had a sweet deal," Thrushy said. "I could help him with the cars and I'd learn to work on them myself. I was going to have a trade."

"I think this'll blow over," I told him, once again demonstrating my complete inability to predict the future.

CHAPTER 34

ESCAPE

I was sent to read to Mr. Benson, who seemed agitated a bit.

"Are you going to be late every day?" he groused at me.

"Well, no sir. I got a little sidetracked at the café, but I came here as fast as I could."

"Well, that's not very fast."

"Did you want me to read *Dracula* for you?" I asked firmly. He may have been an old man, but he scared me and I wanted to get out of his house.

"No, not today," he said softer, as if he could read my thoughts. "I want you to read me my own stories."

He directed me to a cabinet shelf full of yellowed magazines from the last century. Most of them were called *American Tales*, though some were entitled *Bizarre Tales* and *Criminal Tales*.

A Perfect Teacher was the first story. It took place right before the Civil War in a small town in Louisiana. The teacher was a young man who decided he wanted to live in a perfect town with perfect people. First, he would have to create the perfect school with perfect students. He needed a perfect wife to help him. He called on one of his older students "a pretty young thing of 16 years." He announced his intent was to marry her but was rebuffed by her parents immediately.

'But I am a perfect teacher and she will be a perfect wife."

'A teacher can never support a family. You need a real vocation, not some spinster woman's job,' was the heartless reply.

'But I must be a teacher for life,' he said. 'It is my calling to form perfect students to build perfect lives and make a perfect world.'

'People are not perfect and you will fail.'

Before the week was out, the parents died in their sleep and the teacher married their daughter. The doctor who suspected poison mysteriously fell down a stairway and died. The perfect teacher created a perfect classroom. All his most imperfect students always seemed to have fatal accidents. His perfect wife gave him an imperfect baby who had to be fed in the middle of the night. Both the baby and newly discovered imperfect wife soon died of fever. Sadly, for the perfect teacher, he lived in a town that tolerated deficiency better than he did. He might have succeeded in creating the perfect town he wanted. But sadly, he had to move away in a hurry because people grew suspicious and angry. Ordinary people just don't like perfect people.

"Is this about you?" I asked after I shivered.

"No," he laughed sinisterly, "but after I read it out loud to my class, I had very few discipline problems."

"I can imagine."

I escaped from Mr. Benson's house unharmed, but psychologically scarred. I skipped and ran back towards the café where I would be safe. The gas station was crowded with maybe two dozen hostile men. They were listening to a blond man yelling about how they weren't going to stand for it anymore while the crowd yelled louder and louder.

There were no customers in the café when I got there. Cici and her boys were in the kitchen looking miserable and Gramma Morris was reading the newspaper.

"We'd do better business in the morgue," she said casually when I came in.

"Yes, ma'am," I agreed. "People would just be dying to get in."

She snorted, "If nothing else, you can make me laugh."

We did the crossword together for a while then Betsy and Darlene came in with my new outfit.

"Something big is going on by the gas station," Betsy said. "Mr. Morris is talking to a bunch of men. It sounds pretty bad, whatever it is. They're all up in arms about something."

"Something about Thrushy," Darlene added.

"Oh dear," Gramma Morris said and got up to look out the door. "Thrushy whistled at a car and Jared Thomas' sister-in-law thought that he was being disrespectful to her and threw a fit. I guess they're not going to let it go."

We could hear the stomping of boots getting closer, so I peeked out the door. A crowd of twenty men were making their way down the street towards us. The blond man who must have been Mr. Thomas wasn't with them. He apparently let the ignorant and uneducated do his work for him.

Gramma Morris fretted for a bit then looked resolved, "Cici," she called out quietly, "I need you to hide the boys in the storeroom. Amy, go with them."

I retreated to the kitchen but stayed by the pass so I could see what was going on. The crowd hovered near the front door but stayed in the street. Pastor Seth Josephson saw the mob and trotted over to see what was going on. A few men broke off and scurried down the sides of the building. I walked to the back door and stepped out. There they were, watching me.

"Send them out," one of them called to me. He held up a rope tied in a hangman's noose. I jerked back inside and locked the door.

Shouting and angry talking created chaos up front. I could hear Pastor Josephson and Gramma Morris trying to reason with the men, but they were being shouted down and the language those men used was shameful. The back door was being pounded on. Cici started to weep helplessly while Betsy tried to comfort her. They were both oblivious to me as I hurried over to the storeroom. Thrushy and Finchy were in the corner, petrified with fear.

"Quick," I hissed at them, while shoving the boxes of goods off the trapdoor to the wine. We opened it up and they lowered themselves down.

"I'm going to open the backdoor now. Let's hope they all come in searching for you. Look to the back. If it's safe, I'll step off the porch and you can see my feet. Get going as fast as you can and head to the general store and crawl under to the back and then run to the creek to the railroad bridge and catch a train." Then I remembered one of Papa Collins's rules, "Don't look back. If they don't see you, then you'll get away. If they do, looking back only slows you down."

They nodded like they understood and lowered themselves down and started crawling away. We could only pray now as I opened the back door.

"Amy, don't," Betsy said, but it was too late.

There were four of them. Big, unshaven and mean looking. Three of them had that wolfish Kaker look. The other one was definitely from the Foyt family. They piled in all at once and started searching through everything for Thrushy and Finchy. I casually looked out the door towards the general store. Nobody else was there, so I stepped down and headed towards the corner. They had to see my feet from any angle down there.

I hurried back inside and looked out the back window. There they were, behind the store, soon to be out of sight and swallowed by the embankment. They were safe. No one was searching for them over there. Soon they'd be waiting for the next train west to Baton Rouge. A movement caught my eye. Also watching was that man in the gray fedora. He nodded approvingly and turned to me with a knowing smile, placing his index finger on his lips. Then he casually strolled back to the front and turned into the hardware store.

I could hear a train pulling out. I could tell from the way the engine faded it wasn't going to Baton Rouge. It was heading east to Covington. I knew nothing about the towns east of here, just that my friends would be safer there than they could ever be here.

Those men left the door to the back room open when they headed towards the dining room. They never moved the empty boxes and never saw the trapdoor. There was still arguing up front. Cici was still crying. Betsy and Darlene were comforting her as best as they could, but the chaos was frightening. No one knew what just happened, but they knew they failed to get their prey. Since the four men were done in the back, Gramma Morris told them they all needed to go away.

"Thrushy and Finchy aren't here and they never were. All this fuss was for nothing."

We went to the front door and stared out at the mob. The men looked embarrassed; it showed clearly.

"Cici's sons must have caught an earlier train when they realized just how much trouble they were in," said the obvious leader, a buck-toothed little man named Elias Karp. He sadly told his followers, "We'll get them when they come back."

He gave me a hostile glare. "And we will get them. Mark my words. And if I find out they had help, she'll live to regret it."

I shrank back from those hateful eyes.

"Did anyone check the sheds out back?" someone called out.

"I hope so," he responded but he marched through the kitchen and out the back door like he owned the place

The men were so disappointed that they sent two more men to search through the café another time. After a couple of minutes, they agreed that Thrushy and Finchy somehow got away.

Elias Karp went around back to check the sheds personally but found nothing.

"Where are the lookouts we sent back here?" he called out.

"We were searching the kitchen while you guys were all jawboning up front," one of the Kakers called back defensively. "The girl let us in, so we looked around."

"Amy," Gramma Morris snapped at me, appearing quite angry.

"Let's just get on home, boys," Karp called out.

It wasn't quite like he gave up yet. His 'boys' were dispersing because Depjim arrived with Angus Nye and they both had rifles.

CHAPTER 35

ADJUSTMENTS

"If you're going to have that many unpaying customers in here you ought to hold a town hall meeting," Depjim joked to Gramma Morris.

"If I knew there would be so many criminals in here, I'd have volunteered the back shed to be used as an extra jail cell," she replied tartly.

"But where are my boys?" Cici whimpered from the kitchen.

"They're safe," I said. "They're headed on a train to Covington."

I explained what happened and my role in their escape. The anger I saw in Gramma Morris's eyes was replaced with nothing short of respect as she squeezed me close.

"You are most definitely a Faucette," she told me, as though a greater compliment was not possible.

Betsy and Darlene both hugged me really close afterwards. But the real bearhug came from Cici.

"You're the man of the hour," Angus said, while Cici was smothering me in gratitude. "Well, woman of the hour, anyway." He paused for a second, "Well, maybe child of the hour. That works."

We all laughed at this lame humor, mainly just in relief

that the ordeal was over.

"Child, you will never know how grateful I am to you for getting my boys out of harm's way."

I blushed. "You know, I really didn't do all that much. I only got them hid and gave them the all's clear signal."

"That was plenty. If I can ever repay you, I'd be so happy."

"Well, there is something you can do to make me happy," I said, thinking of my visits with the countess.

"Anything, child. You just name it."

"Would you talk to Fredrick, your nephew, and reconcile? He would be happy. He's all alone since his wife and family died."

Her eyes filled with tears and she nodded, too choked up to speak.

"I didn't know," she said barely keeping her composure.

"Didn't know they died?"

"Didn't know he ever married."

She hurried out the back to have a good cry while the rest of us still celebrated our victory. I got the honor of walking over to the countess's house to ask if Frederick could visit his aunt after work.

It was quite the visit. Her grandson and two great-granddaughters several years younger than me were there. A violin was placed in my hands and I played for them. The countess had a grin from ear to ear because I had a good sound that day and both great-grandchildren asked for lessons after I finished. The countess was back in business as a music teacher.

Frederick drove me back to the café. We didn't really talk, as I was inside looking out and he was on top driving. But when we stopped, he got down and bowed to me, so very old-fashioned. Cici was waiting on the corner and he drove off with her to her home in Amenville, where they had their own family reunion, and many others afterwards.

The rest of the week was spent making adjustments. Thrushy and Finchy were gone now, so their work was left undone and someone would have to take up the slack. I was to be that someone. So, when I was done reading to Mr. Benson, I was back at the café, signing for deliveries, keeping the sidewalks clean, and removing trash. Since my reputation for tampering with food had not abated, I still was not allowed in the kitchen.

My Friday nights were still going to be spent at the café working the night shift with Lila, since the town needed to see that I was being taught a lesson. Lila made it known she loved the idea of having me help her and my new routine was set.

The rest of the week went well enough. 'Signing for deliveries' also meant unloading the wagons, putting the food where it belonged, cleaning and prepping the produce, and doing everything nobody else wanted to do. I also poured and brewed coffee, worked the register, waited and cleaned tables, swept and mopped the floors, cleaned and polished the silverware, scoured and scrubbed the restrooms, and wished I was back in school which didn't seem so bad now.

Business seemed to pick up a bit. Mr. Dupris now stopped in every morning for coffee and toast.

"Well now, Amy," he said one day, "You are one impressive young lady when it comes to work. Most girls are afraid of it, but you seem to be doing everything around here these days."

"Oh, it's not so much," I giggled back. "I'm just happy to help and I'm learning the business."

"Oh really?" he replied, perking up a bit. "You know, I

could use you at the garage. Someone who works is quite the commodity."

"Commodity?"

"Item of value. In this case, valuable employee. If you really want to learn a business, the automobile is the business of the future. The horse is obsolete. The car is going to do all the work. And they always need maintenance and repairs. And I can get you in on the ground floor."

I wasn't really happy with the 'item of value' part, but I listened politely as I refilled his cup.

"I can give you the same deal I gave Thrushy," he went on. "I'll teach you the trade, instill some car knowledge in that pretty little head of yours. The sky's the limit. Besides, it'll be quite the attraction, *Dupris Auto Shop, Where the Prettiest Mechanic in the State Works*. We'll make millions."

I heard a loud harumph behind me and turned to see Gramma Morris glaring at him.

"Any man who'll take his car to be worked on solely because a pretty ten-year-old girl works there is not a man I would *want* her to meet."

"Well, we wouldn't advertise her now, she has to learn to do the work," he replied. "Give her eight or nine years, and wow. Everybody will want to meet the woman mechanic. There'll be newsreels. Newspaper reporters. She'll be famous."

"You'll be famous." Gramma Morris looked like she was going to pour the coffee on him instead of in his cup. "She'll be a laughingstock."

"Nonsense. Think about it. She's getting a chance of a lifetime. An apprenticeship to be a mechanic is not something to scoff at. I'll give her the same deal I gave Thrushy."

"Some deal," Gramma Morris snorted. "She does the

work, you get the money."

"What's the deal she's getting here?"

The other patrons cheered. My guess was that this was the first time Gramma Morris lost an argument, at least a public one. Of course, I was never going to work for Mr. Dupris. He was nice enough, but he somehow made me nervous. Also, I didn't like being around a man who chewed and spit out tobacco. I found it to be a disgusting habit.

Oddly enough, some of the men from the mob started coming in for coffee or breakfast as well. Gramma Morris thought they were coming in because they felt bad about how they behaved that day. Lila, being less inclined to see the good in people, told me they wanted to see how we fooled them when Thrushy and Finchy got away. Either way was good. There was enough business to keep us going.

At home, we finished *Ozma of Oz,* and started the next book in the series, *Dorothy and the Wizard of Oz.* I was ready to move on to something else, but I lost the vote 8-1 because Guy was visiting Annette.

I was playing less folk music on my violin and more classical pieces and church hymns. *Nearer My God to Thee* was the countess's favorite, so it was the one I played the most. Cleaning her house should have been easier, but as I cleaned each room, she found another one that hadn't seen a dust cloth in years.

I asked her once if she knew Mr. Benson, since they seemed to have so much in common.

"He is a vile old man who writes awful stories about monsters and murder, and he always tries to make people believe he's writing about himself, and it wouldn't surprise me if he was. He was an irregular, you know. Rode with

William Quantrill up in Missouri and Kansas. Bushwhackers and robbers, all of them."

"Mrs. De Montfort says he was a cook in Shreveport."

"The irregulars were criminals and they were being hunted down one by one and killed. Then, for some unknow reason, they were offered a pardon," she went on as if I didn't say anything. "No one down here thought for a minute Terry Benson rode with such a villain. And when he rode back from the war and told everyone he was General Kirby Smith's private cook, no one thought otherwise until they figured out he couldn't fry an egg if the hen was on his shoulders giving him directions."

"Sounds like my New York mother," I said.

"Well, he wasn't exactly *that* bad," she corrected. "Maybe if he ever got married like he was supposed to, he wouldn't be so…awful."

"He never married?"

"Land, no," she chuckled. "He had a common law wife before the war. Always kept to himself after she left. You know, I heard his father was pure mean and loved hurting him and the other children. His father died in a card playing accident before I arrived in Faucette."

"Card playing accident?" I asked.

"Yes, dear. An ace of hearts fell out of his sleeve by accident and his 'friends' shot him dead. So, it was just the four of them after that. Terrance, Reginald, Cathy, and their mother, I forget her name, but it doesn't matter, it was so long ago. When their mother died, Reg and Cathy moved on to Texas and Terrance stayed here."

"Why did he wall off the bedroom?"

She shrugged. "Rumor had it he walled it off because his father's ghost haunted the house, so they made an arrangement to divide it up between them. His father gets his old room. Terrance gets the rest."

"Oh, I didn't know ghosts make deals."

"That's all right, dear," she said while patting my hand. "I didn't even know they existed."

Between reading children's books to my family and horror stories to Mr. Benson, I found time to continue reading my biography of *Florence Nightingale.* Quite a variety in my reading material. And I was beginning to understand why Mrs. De Montfort had decided to become a nurse. It seemed like a wonderful and fulfilling profession.

Over the course of the week, I noticed things were changing a little bit in our town. We found out that Thrushy and Finchy were in Biloxi. They stayed on that train until the conductor noticed them and asked them to get off, which they did without incident. The brothers wandered around lost and bewildered until the preacher from a local black church found them and gave them shelter. They were soon working in a garage for actual salaries.

The Sunday sermon was about love. The Bible is all about love. Jesus is all about love. The church is all about love though that last part did not seem to pertain to me. Outside of my family and our few friends, I felt nothing but coldness and hostility. My sisters were grudgingly accepted back by their friends in Sunday school, though Anna Marie had nothing more to do with the Davenport sisters.

CHAPTER 36

A NEW JOB

On Monday, Mom had an appointment with Doc Gannon and wanted me to go with her to see how pregnancies worked. Uncle Vincent took us in his truck. We had to stop at the crossing as the train roared by with their commuters.

"It's too bad Mr. Kaker runs the train station," I mused.

"Why is that, sweetie?" Mom asked.

"Well, there are stops back and forth all day, but only a couple of them stop long enough for people to walk to the café and back. We could set up a booth of some kind and sell the packaged goods, like peanuts and soft drinks. The passengers could get off the train long enough to get a snack and back on without missing a beat. But Mr. Kaker won't allow it, I'm sure. He doesn't seem to like us. Me in particular."

Vincent and Mom looked at each other and smiled.

"You might say Durrell Kaker is in training these days," Uncle Vincent said dryly. "His cousin Wendell is working the station for a while. He won't give you any trouble at all."

And a new job was born. I walked to the train station carrying a tray loaded with drinks on one side and moon pies and peanuts on the other. I worked the nine o'clock stop and walked up and down to platform. I only sold two sodas, but it was ten cents more than we would have had if I stayed at the café.

The ten o'clock stop was a complete zero. I spent more time talking to the new Mr. Kaker, who seemed the most pleasant of his family. Eleven o'clock was the lunch stop while the freight was unloaded, so I didn't bother. The other stops were all a total waste of time. I told Cici and Gramma Morris that maybe it wasn't a good idea after all. But they said to give it a week.

The next day was better. The commuters got out when the train stopped and I sold all the soda and quite a few bags of peanuts. The moon pies seemed to be too childish and messy for them, so I carried more soda and peanuts for the next run, along with some chips, which sold out pretty quickly.

Although I was tired by the end of the day, I was more than content. My efforts increased our revenue by a decent amount. I had discovered an unknown market and we cashed in on it as best we could. Some of the passengers asked me my name and promised to be regulars. I was on friendlier terms with folks from Hammond, Covington, and Baton Rouge than my hometown.

CHAPTER 37

AN OLD FRIEND AND A NEW FRIEND

Thursday was a great coincidence to me. I was on the station when I heard a New York accent from a familiar voice. I watched a group of important men in dark suits talking about setting something up at the station. They were all pleased with themselves. All the stations in the state would be an absolute goldmine.

"Excuse me," I hesitantly interrupted the one man I knew from my childhood.

They all glared at me with dark and unsmiling faces. Not quite hostile, but certainly not friendly.

"Aren't you Mr. Frank Costello from Manhattan?"

There were some slight head shakes and a couple of nervous laughs, but I didn't understand why the question would have any kind of reaction from total strangers. Mr. Costello seemed not just surprised but stunned. The man he was talking to seemed amused, but not quite happy. I must have interrupted an important conversation.

"Who wants to know?" he responded gruffly.

"I'm Amy Collins. Michael Collins was my father. You remember him?" I lowered my voice to imitate a man, "'Not *that* Michael Collins.' You gave me a teddy bear for my seventh birthday."

He smiled. "Yeah, I remember. He was a good man. That was something like three years ago. You haven't grown any. Too much spicy food, huh? What are you doing down here anyway?"

Well, I didn't want to say my Mama didn't want me anymore and my step-father was creepy, so I just said, "I live here now. My aunt has a restaurant a block away and I come here to sell things." I nodded with my head to the nearly empty tray.

"Looks like you do very well, young lady," the man next to him said quietly.

Young lady. That always meant something bad was coming next.

"So, tell me, why isn't your aunt selling here and sending you someplace like," his eyes zeroed in on me like headlights on a car, "someplace like…school."

Oh no, and this man seemed quite serious and even worse, important.

"Amy," Frank interceded, "do you know who this is?"

He certainly looked familiar, but I couldn't place a name on him.

"I'm sorry, sir," I said to the man, "should I?"

The whole crowd laughed loudly, even the mysterious, important man.

"Get this. She knows the bootlegger from New York but doesn't recognize the governor," said a younger, more friendly man.

"Mr. Huey P. Long," I said.

He looked different than the picture in my classroom.

"My family says you should be president. You really care about the little man."

"They're very kind," he smiled. "And you are right. Huey Long, at your service. Now, tell me why you're not at school. We make it free for everyone to go."

Uh oh.

"Well sir, I just took the final tests for fourth grade and they said I passed so I could stay home until next school year."

"Why is that?"

"Why is what?"

"Why did you test through fourth grade for one and why didn't they put you in fifth grade?"

"Well, the teacher's sister-in-law and her husband hate my family for some reason and the teacher is mean and the students hit me and push me into swings because I can multiply without using paper which they think is dumb and one put gum in my hair so I had to get it cut and there was a fight and the lady who runs the school board gave me the final test and said to stay away."

"Oh, your aunt owns a restaurant near here?" he said politely, obviously wanting more details but too polite to demand them

"Yes, sir, the Faucette Café. It's down the road a bit."

"Well boys, I don't know about you, but I'm suddenly hungry and I want to meet this little girl's aunt."

"Oh, she's not there, sir, she's in privacy."

"Oh, how nice. Another little citizen waiting to be born."

"My Gramma Morris is there though. She really owns it. My mom, Aunt Cassie, she wants me to call her Mom, she runs it though not right now, but she does the paperwork and things."

"Lead the way," he said impatiently.

As we briskly walked to the café, I heard a couple of the men grumble a bit about how time is money and we're wasting time.

"You're never wasting time talking to the people," the

governor snapped back. "I am their leader. I have to know where they want to be led."

As we passed by the drug store, I saw the man in the fedora leaving with a small package. He smiled at me, then his face betrayed his amazement when he recognized that the governor was with me. He casually walked up to his Oldsmobile and got in, shaking his head in wonder.

When we walked into the café, I called out to Gramma Morris, "We have customers."

She seemed like she was about to faint when she saw the governor.

"Cici, how much iced tea do we have? Put on everything. Amy brought in a crowd."

Cici looked out the window to see what was going on and gaped at the governor for a couple of seconds, then started running around the kitchen getting her thoughts together.

"Amy, pull some tables together. We have the most important people in the state here," Gramma Morris was getting breathless with excitement.

The governor had an easy laugh. It was obvious he met many star-struck citizens during his career.

"Well now, ma'am, we'll only be a while here. Just coffee or tea is fine," he started.

"Amy, go get Lila. The Governor is here," Gramma Morris was completely flustered.

"I know. I brought him," I said trying not to let her excitement get me flustered as well.

"Well, pour some coffee."

One of the men helped me put two tables next to a third and they all sat down. Gramma Morris calmed down enough to bring water glasses and a pitcher.

I smiled and went back to the kitchen.

"I already told Lila we need her," Cici said as I entered.

"Thank you," I replied, taking deep breathes to stay calm. This was, after all, a big day for us all. "What's today's special?"

"Shrimp gumbo," Cici replied.

"That sounds good. Have I ever had any?"

"No," she growled. "And you won't be getting any of this batch either. I've been making smaller and smaller batches of everything because business is falling off. Besides, you have customers to tend to. Get out there and tend."

"Gramma Morris," I called from the pass, "don't forget about today's shrimp gumbo special."

"Did I hear shrimp gumbo?" Governor Long called out.

"Yes, sir," I called back. "Let me get you a bowl."

"On the house," Gramma Morris added, obviously forgetting about our finances.

"No, not on the house," Governor Long called back. "*We* all have jobs and money. And with this crash, not everybody does and that doesn't make any sense. City folk want to eat. Country folk want to sell food. Trains and trucks want to transport goods, and nothing's happening. Just doesn't make sense."

"You are so right," Gramma Morris replied. "We've been watching business just dry up. The railroad discontinued a few runs, which hurt our business. Rumor has it they may not be stopping here anymore, and the children have to catch it to school in the mornings now that the bridge is out—"

"What bridge?"

"The one over Faucette Creek there."

"Rob?"

"It's been down awhile, lost in a tornado about a year

now. Funds aren't there to rebuild it," a small rabbit of a man replied.

"Get them."

"Sorry, Huey?"

"Find the funds. New Orleans gets tax money for public projects and they don't even vote for me. These fine folks pay taxes too. What are they paying them for? Bridges. Roads. The things that make life work. That's what we're in business for. To make things work."

"Well, the budget is pretty well set—," Rob said, looking a bit nervous.

"Then take it out of your salary or resign and I'll find someone who can get the job done. I don't pay people to tell me what I *can't* do," the governor said with an iron smile. He is very serious.

"Yes, sir, Huey," Rob said with fake enthusiasm.

A breathless Darlene ran in the café.

"I heard you had the Governor in here today,'" she panted out. "Was he as nice as he sounds on the—" she stopped when she saw the table, headed by Governor Huey P. Long. "Oh my."

"I like to think I'm nice," he said with a smile.

"Where did you hear that at?" Gramma Morris asked.

"Everybody says he's nice."

"No, I mean that he's here?"

Governor Long and Frank Costello were suppressing smiles while the rest of the table was staring impassively. Trying to keep from laughing, I thought.

"Where's Lila?" Gramma Morris was back to her usual take-charge self. "We have a restaurant to feed. Amy, run upstairs and get her down here."

"I'm here," we heard her call out from the kitchen. "I'm putting on my apron."

"Wendell Kaker called up his wife and told her he saw the governor and he was headed here."

"But how did you hear about it?"

"The whole town heard about it. It's the magic of telephones."

At least the magic of eavesdropping on other people's calls.

Betsy, Mayor Rich Norman, Doc Gannon, Pastor Seth Josephson, Scott Tanner, and almost the whole town were there by now, waiting their turns to talk to our famous guest. The booths and diner counter were full and people were swarming in and out, shaking the governor's hand and fawning over him.

Some just came and went, but most ordered food or coffee and listened to the conversation. The café was the busiest I ever saw it. People were packed as close together as possible and more people are pulling up outside. The gumbo was served to the governor's table only. Everyone else who wanted to eat ordered sandwiches. Even so, Cici was worried we might run out of food, but we didn't. We *did* have to restock everything in the kitchen the next day, though.

"Yes, it's really him," Gramma Morris was saying to someone over the phone. "If you want to meet him, I'd advise you to get over here right away. Their food's already been served."

I had the honor of waiting on their table while Lila handled the rest of the crowd. It was surprisingly quiet, considering how many people were there. They were all listening to Huey P. Long speak.

"You folks have it backwards. I'm here to meet you. Without you, there's no me."

He stopped to listen to a question from a man named Willard Moss, who I saw in church but never spoke to. I didn't hear the question, but the answer drew a large cheer from everyone.

"The train will continue to run through Faucette until it's not needed. And the bridge over River Road will be fixed.

"Rob here," he waved to poor Rob, who obviously wasn't a man who liked being the center of attention, "will see to it. And it will provide jobs to people who need work. We will weather this storm together."

Another cheer.

I had to worm my way through the crowd to get a pitcher of sweet tea for my table. Cici wiped down the pitcher and filled it with ice while I stirred an ungodly amount of sugar into the unsuspecting tea. I shook my head. Papa Collins had told me many times, 'If you have to put anything in your tea, you need to be buying better tea.'

"That Mr. Long seems like such a nice man," Cici said to me. "I would sure like to go out and meet him, but I'd be afraid he'd think I'm some uppity black woman."

"I don't think that's true," I said, as I walked out with a full pitcher of fresh brewed tea ruined with what seemed like a pound of sugar.

"Our cook says she hopes you enjoyed lunch today," I said. "She would like to meet you, but she's afraid you may not like negros."

He looked at me for a second with a mixture of disdain and amusement.

"I like everybody who works hard and takes pride in what they do," he replied curtly. "Everyone," he shouted to the crowd. "Louisiana has the best chefs in the country, and I may have just eaten the food from the best of the best."

He turned and looked at the pass where Cici ducked back.

"Send out the cook," he called out while the other diners applauded.

Cici rather sheepishly went out to their table and the governor stood up and hugged her close. The clapping stopped as the audience gasped in amazement. But it started again when he released her and sat down. She went back to the kitchen and the room quieted down.

By now everyone who wanted to speak to him had their say. The event was winding down. I don't know how many people took advantage of the chaos and ordered tea or coffee and boldly walked out without paying. Scott Tanner was still at the counter, sipping on a third cup of coffee, under Gramma Morris's watchful eye. Mayer Rich Norman was sitting with Doc Gannon and Pastor Josephson at one of the tables. Betsy was chatting with Darlene on the other side while I was cleaning and wiping down tables.

"I almost forgot why we came here," he said to Gramma Morris. "Why is Amy selling soda at the train station instead of going to school?"

She gave him a nicely condensed version of my treatment at the hands of Mrs. Porter.

"A smart young girl like this needs to be educated. Where's the next nearest school?"

"Nueville."

"That's too far away. What's the next?"

"Baton Rouge."

He shook his head in dismay.

"I saw a Catholic church at the station. Do they have a school?"

"Yes, but we're not Catholic and they charge for classes. And she's already passed fourth grade."

"Call them," he commanded.

Gramma Morris meekly complied. Pastor Josephson was not happy about this development.

I heard Gramma Morris say quietly, "No, I'm serious, Father Cassidy. I am with Governor Long right now and he says to get down here pronto."

"I am worried about her immortal soul," Pastor Josephson was saying to the governor, "and putting her in that papist institution could damage her chances for salvation."

"You know, Pastor Josephson, my mother was Baptist. My father was Catholic. Every Sunday, I hitched the horses to the wagon at six a.m. for mass for my dad's parents, and again at ten a.m. for church for my mom's folks. I think all four of them are in heaven playing bridge together."

Pastor Josephson wisely accepted defeat.

I had seen Father Cassidy a few times while walking through town, though I never actually spoke to him. He was a big, bald man with a ridiculous combover, serious dark eyes, and the beginnings of age lines.

The governor called him to the table as though they were long lost friends.

"Over here, Father Cassidy. Grab a chair and sit right here next to me."

The priest faked a smile and did what he was told.

"You know," Huey Long started, "we were talking about community outreach and how important it is. The whole northern part of the state is Baptist, the southern part is Catholic. And you know what? They don't understand each other. That's why I think it's good to reach out to each other. Help each other out. Take each other in."

He glared at the confused priest with piercing eyes.

"I can't really say I disagree with anything you say, but

I can't really say I understand what you're saying," Father Cassidy replied, obviously being cautious.

"Community outreach. Amy, get over here," he commanded.

Frank Costello watched the whole scene with great interest. Rob looked miserable and the others were obviously bored.

I scurried over to the table and stood between them.

"Father Cassidy, meet your new community outreach project, Miss Amy Collins."

I curtsied politely and banged my side on the table when I came back up, sloshing coffee from several cups onto the tablecloths.

"I heard all about you and your allergy towards poise," he said dryly. "Perhaps if you didn't bend your knees so far down, things like that wouldn't happen."

"That's why she needs you," the governor explained. "She needs a little help in learning the graceful arts. But she has already passed fourth grade ahead of the other students and is wasting her whole life selling sodas on a lonely and dangerous train platform."

I really wasn't lonely and couldn't see how the train platform was hazardous.

"I fail to see how she is in any danger at the train station," Father Cassidy was unimpressed with Governor Long's logic as well.

"She could fall off. I mean, she can't even perform a curtsy without bumping into something. We can't let her risk her life selling moon pies, you know. And that's where you come in. You grant her a scholarship to finish fifth grade at your school and you do a good deed."

Father Cassidy made a face. "Why would we give her a scholarship when she's not even Catholic? When we have parishioners who can't afford to send their own children there? Especially when she might accidentally die from her own clumsiness? As you yourself already said, she's a danger to herself and anyone who comes near her."

"Let me do the exaggerating. You want her in your school because community outreach makes me happy," Governor Long responded. His eyes turned to steel. "You know, not everybody has had it so good all their lives like you. Some folks, like this young lady, kind of had a rough time of it. A little help from the rich and powerful like yourself would be most Christian."

"What do you mean 'like me'? I'll have you know we were so poor that I walked around barefoot until I was eight years old."

"So? I have it on good authority that this little girl was *born* barefoot."

Everyone laughed at that, even Father Cassidy, though he obviously didn't want to.

Seeing that charm wasn't working, Governor Long changed tactics. He tilted his head down a bit and gave the priest an evil grin.

"You know, I hear stories of convents and monasteries where they found dozens of bodies of poor abandoned orphans buried and forgotten, sometimes for hundreds of years."

"That never happened at St. Linus," Father Cassidy said defensively, getting up with his fists clenched.

Four of Governor Long's men stood up with him. Two of them pulled back their suit jackets to show off a pair of holstered pistols. Father Cassidy sat back down.

Wise man.

"So, you're saying that if we think there might be dead bodies under the buildings and dug through the foundation, leaving nothing but rubble and ruins behind, no church, no school, no Catholic presence at all until it can be rebuilt in a time where there is no money to rebuild, it would all just be a government mistake?"

The priest gave the governor a withering look and answered him by talking to me.

"Amy, be there at eight o'clock tomorrow morning. You will have a full scholarship until the end of the school year. No fees. I will meet you at the gate. After all this elaborate arm twisting, I presume you already have a uniform."

"She'll have it by tomorrow," I heard Betsy's voice behind me. "I've made a few so I have the pattern and the material at the shop. And it's not like Amy needs a lot of material. And she hasn't grown any since our last sitting."

By now I was wishing I was six feet tall.

"Leave a little early and you can pick it up before school."

"It doesn't matter how early I leave; I still have to take the train across the creek."

"Oh. Well, do the best you can do, I'll have it."

Father Cassidy sighed, "I'll wait for you until quarter after. If you can't have one by tomorrow, we'll make an exception. I have to go now. I have a school to run."

"She'll have it," Betsy called out to him as he left.

With that, Betsy caught the attention of Governor Long.

"That is so kind of you Miss…"

"Deveraux, Betsy." She laughed nervously, "I'm your biggest supporter, Governor." She curtsied perfectly.

He caught her left hand and squeezed it before letting her go.

"Can you tell me why you're not married, as pretty and

kind as you are?" he asked, looking at her bare third finger.

"Never been asked," she responded breathily.

"That's not right. I was never happy until I married my wife." He jerked his head to his assistant, "Rob."

"Yes, Governor?"

"Escort this lady to her shop and have her show you the town."

"Um, Governor, she might not want a total stranger to—"

"Hush," the governor commanded imperiously.

"Miss Deveraux, Rob is a vital man in my administration. He's kind, single, employed, unattached, and efficient, as well as not married," he continued smoothly. "He also puts his big fat foot in his mouth every time he's around a pretty woman. That's why he's single. Give him a chance. I vouch for his character, but not his social skills."

He pulled Rob aside and whispered, unaware I could hear them, "Just get her number and call her this weekend. Take the train out here and get to know her. From what I can see, she's pretty, intelligent enough to have her own shop, and kindhearted enough to give up her evening to put together a uniform dress for a little girl. Don't blow it. She could be quite the catch."

Rob and Betsy left a little before the rest of them did. Rob seemed awkward and confused, Betsy looked annoyed.

Within minutes, the others were screeching their chairs back to leave. The governor gave Gramma Morris two hundred-dollar bills at the register and hugged her as their party left. Mr. Costello hugged me good-bye and told me he was happy to see me again. Mayor Norman walked with them back to the train station.

"That must have been something," Mayor Norman said to Huey P. Long, "Having to hitch up the wagons twice each Sunday for each set of grandparents."

The governor snorted, "Don't let yourself get fooled too easily, Rich. We didn't even *have* a horse."

The remaining residents finished up and left as well. Soon it was just us and the mess.

"Whatever did we do in this town for excitement before you arrived?" an older woman said to me as she left, not unkindly, but not friendly either.

"Who was that?" I asked Lila after the door closed behind her.

"That was Vicky Degas, Jared Thomas' sister. Her brother-in-law is Hugo Landacre's cousin."

"Oh."

Gramma Morris was not so happy during clean-up.

"How did we ever get to the point where the family is so split up that one child goes to a completely different school than the others? How are we going to pay for the tuition next year? What did you get us into?"

"Well, I'm sorry. I thought I did good."

I ran out the back far enough to hear the creek talk to me in its soothing, incomprehensible language.

She was behind me when I turned around to go back. She put her arm around me and whispered an apology. We listened to the trees talk to the wind and walked back in together. Lila and Cici had finished up the cleaning and went to stock up on supplies. We talked about how exciting it was to meet the governor and have so much business in just one day. How excited I must be to start another brand-new school. And most importantly, how bad she felt that she ruined my successful day.

"When you decide to make big mistakes," she advised,

"don't make the ones where you worry about the future so much that you ruin the present."

We went home and had a great big celebration without spending any of the money we earned that day. Mom used it to pay bills. We were solvent again.

I would be attending a different school, as Gramma Morris reminded me. I was going to have less things in common with my sisters than ever. Although I was even more out of place, I was as happy as I could be.

CHAPTER 38

THE NEW SCHOOL

Uncle Vincent drove me to the café with Gramma Morris the next morning. I had a plate of biscuits and gravy and went to Betsy's shop to get my new uniform. It was a little tight, but she said it would only take a minute to let it out. I told her it could wait until tomorrow.

"No, it can't," she replied playfully. "When people see how tight it is, that will be a reflection on me. If you don't look good, I don't look competent. Then they'll go to Baton Rouge to Penny's and buy off the rack. Then I'll lose my business which is also my home and I'll wander down the streets begging for pennies so I can buy moldy day-old bread until I starve to death underneath a railroad bridge. All because this dress is too tight."

It was obvious I missed the point. She giggled a bit when she saw the expression on my face.

"Humor, sweetie. Ha-Ha."

"Oh," then I changed the subject, "How did your date go with Rob?"

"That was *not* a date. All he did was walk with me back here. Didn't say a word the whole way. When we got here, he asked me if he could have my number and give me a call.

"'Why?' I asked, 'Are you going to have a friend call me?'

She imitated his voice, "'No,' he says, 'I want to call you. Me. It's just that I usually don't like talking to people.'

"'Oh, you prefer to talk to, say, tables?'

"'Well, no, they only listen. Tables just don't add much to a conversation.'"

We both laughed at that.

"You've heard the term 'painfully shy?' That poor man must be in constant agony. It would be easier for him to cut down a pine tree with his teeth than to call on a girl."

"I don't know," I replied. "The governor told him he thinks you'd be quite the catch."

"Wonderful. You know what happens to the 'catch,' don't you? They cut off its head and tail, scrape all the scales off, disembowel it, cut out the bones, and deep fry what's left. I'll be healthier left in the sea."

I concluded that Betsy was not an optimist.

The pessimist in me decided that if I didn't leave right away, I would be late. Dressed in my now perfect uniform, I hurried off to my new school.

True to his word, Father Cassidy was waiting for me at the door and I was properly introduced to Sister Barbara, my new teacher. She reminded me of a bull without the horns. She was big and strong with a face wrinkled by smiles and eyes that betrayed warmth and love for everyone. Her black habit failed at making her look severe. She put her hands on my shoulders and guided me to my desk in the front row. There were seven students including me.

"This isn't public school," she said gently. "Each grade has its own room. So, the class size is a little smaller than you're used to."

"I think I'll like that very much," I said.

"We have a paddle in the back if you don't," she replied while the other students tittered. "Now everyone, time for morning prayer."

They recited their prayers by memory while I listened.

"Good morning, class," Sister Barbara said when prayers were over.

"Good morning," we all replied.

"I have the distinct honor of introducing our newest student today. This is Amy Collins."

They all looked at me silently.

"Some of you may have heard of her. She seems to have made quite an impression about town the last few weeks with her adventures. Now, as you know, I love adventures and I think all of you should go out and have as many adventures as possible."

Then she leaned over my desk.

"Only…not…in…school."

She leaned into me closer with each word while I shrank back.

"We met her before," said a girl on the far side of the room. She did look familiar, but I couldn't quite place her. The extremely pretty girl next to her must have been the other member of 'we.' She was familiar also.

"Oh, did you Meredith?"

"She did," I replied, delighted to see her again and I remembered her friend's name now. "Merry, at the five and dime store, and your friend there is Lizzy. I forgot your last names."

"You'll learn them," Sister Barbara told us. "Because I want you to take roll. Helps you put faces to names."

At least there were only six this time. Meredith Baxter, Carmen Birnardo, Elizabeth Farrell, Ron Faucette,

Jonathon Prejean, and David Terrell. We were destined to be lifelong friends.

The boys were polite but mischievous. They were always in some kind of trouble. Nothing serious, but they seemed to spend more time in Father Cassidy's office than the classroom.

As it was Friday, end of the week quizzes were passed out. I did abysmally. Sister Barbara laughed at them and told me I'd do better after I adjusted. Skipping a grade and missing a week can really damage a test score. The girls took me in like a long-lost sister and promised to help me get back up to speed. When the girls compared grades, it was all A's (not counting my less than excellent scores) while the boys struggled to get C's.

"That's because boys do different chores when they get home," Sister Barbara defended them. "They work fields, chop weeds, bundle hay, and when they play, it's baseball, football, and things like that. Girls do inside chores, so they finish faster and have time for studies. In five years, you'll still finish your chores faster but spend your time gossiping, socializing and doing silly stuff. Then they'll have the better grades."

We'll see about that.

The day went well and I actually enjoyed it. I did miss my job on the train platform though.

"Well, of course you miss the freedom of being excused from school," Mom told me. "I can understand that. Your classmates were all kind of mean."

Kind of?

"And the way you described the job at the train makes it sound really nice. And I know it's a radical break in your routine. I understand all that. But just think: You've officially skipped a grade. And here I wouldn't have thought that school would've even wanted you."

"They didn't. They just thought it was better to accept me than to have the school and church torn to the ground."

"*Another* smart decision. So much easier to teach children in a building than on top of a pile of rocks."

Is she serious?

I really wanted to keep my job at the station. Maybe I would have some luck with Mrs. De Montfort.

Chapter 39

The Robbery

I told Mrs. De Montfort, "I liked what I was doing before. I was helping the family."

She said, "You still are. Being on the Governor's good side is much better than selling stale peanuts on a dangerous train platform."

It's not dangerous. I wish people would stop being absurd.

"It's not fun to have to change your routine, especially the way you do. Therefore, I have some good news for you. Mr. Benson still wants you to read to him after school."

Oh joy.

The next story I read to him involved a young man who was treated viciously by his father, always goaded into fights and brutally beaten. He ran away and joined the army. When the soldier returned from the war, he started a fight with his father and after he won, he walled the older man in his bedroom, never letting him leave.

I shuddered when I looked at the plastered over doorway. As usual, I was glad to leave the house. Even work at the café was better than reading to Mr. Benson. I felt safer there than being alone with the old blind man.

I had to get ready to wait on the tables at the café while everybody else got dressed up for the concert at the

Methodist church on the other side of the Atchafalaya River.

"Why can't she come with us?" Holly wailed while we were eating dinner.

"You know why and she knows why," Gramma Morris harumphed. "The child needs a good long lesson in forgiveness. She needs to learn that forgiving is better than avenging."

"And you don't?"

"We're not avenging. We're teaching."

"It's okay," I said. "After all, I've never been to one of these things, so I don't know what I'm missing. So why would I feel bad?"

"You're just saying that," Michelle said. "It was really good last year. They have a generator that connects to a public address system with a microphone and speakers. There's Kettle corn and hot dogs, though we don't get any. It still smells so good."

"And there's games and a cake walk and a sand lot and everything," Holly enthused. "It's just not fair you can't join us."

"She is family," Annette added tentatively.

"We'll see how it goes tonight." Gramma Morris showed signs of relenting. "We may not even need to be open late on Fridays. Or maybe we should stay open until midnight, depending on business."

"I doubt there'll be much business," Annette opined. "Everyone who has money to buy food will buy it at the show."

"We'll check the receipts and see," Mom said. "I think it's nice of you to stick up for your sister though."

It was just Lila and me for the first hour or so. I only had one pot of coffee on and wiped down the counter hundreds of times while we chatted back and forth with each other.

"I'll have to bring another book next week," I told her. "The way business is, I could probably read *War and Peace* all the way through without interruption."

The front door opened at that moment, its bottom scraping on the tile floor to announce my first customer. It was that man in the gray fedora. He took the hat off, hung it up on the rack and sat down at the counter.

"I'll just have a coffee, Amy," he said softly with a smile.

"Right away," I replied and hurried to the pot, wondering how he knew my name. Was it from the fight at the school? Rescuing Thrushy and Finchy? Running away?

He added some sugar and cream and sipped it a little.

"You know, sir, it was nice of you to let me help Thrushy and Finchy get away like that. I was worried," I told him.

"You think I'd give them up? To Jared Thomas?" he shook his head. "Jared Thomas may run the town, but not all the people in it."

"I've seen you around town before though," I said after a couple of silent moments.

"That would make sense," he replied softly. "I've seen you around town as well." He smiled. "I was shocked to see you leading the governor over here with that New York bootlegger."

"Well, he's my friend," I said, although I knew that the word 'friend' was not entirely accurate.

"The governor?"

"The bootlegger. That was the first time I ever met the governor."

"How many governors have you met?"

"Including him?"

He nodded.

"One."

He looked at me for a second.

"You remind me of Cassie."

"You know my aunt?"

"It's a small town. The only people I don't know are the ones I haven't met." He smiled.

"That makes sense," I replied politely. "I suppose I could say that too."

"I suppose so," he said. He tossed a quarter on the counter, even though the coffee was only five cents.

"I'll get your change."

"No, it's yours. It was good to talk to you, Amy Collins."

"And you, sir."

He was out the door when I realized I didn't ask him his name.

"That was Hugo Landacre," Lila told me. "I should have known we'd see him sooner or later."

"That was Hugo Landacre? He didn't look like a devil at all."

She laughed. "That's because he's not one. He's just a foolish young man who hurt a lot of people, mostly himself."

"How so?"

"Talk to Cassie about that. It's *your* family's secret."

"She won't tell me."

"That's because it's a secret."

She expertly changed the subject to my life in New York. I told her about the subway, tall buildings, the noise, and people.

"I wouldn't want to live there," she said. "Not if they don't have tall pines and green grass. Not healthy."

"I haven't been here that long, but I would have to agree. I would be miserable if I had to go back there again."

"That's good, because you won't ever have to," came a familiar voice in rhythm with the scraping door.

"Mrs. De Montfort," exclaimed Lila, with all the fake happiness she could muster, "it's been ages since we've seen you in here."

"That's because it's been ages since I've been in here," she replied tartly. "Although it's grand to see you again, Lila, I really wanted to talk to Amy. You can make me a cup of tea. I'm partial to Earl Grey."

"We have Lipton. But I am so very thrilled I can make you a cup."

Lila had a gift for sarcasm. It was why she never married, or so Gramma Morris told me. She stepped back into the kitchen before Mrs. De Montfort could reply.

"How that woman stays employed is beyond me," she whispered to me.

"She doesn't have issues with any of the other customers as far as I know," I replied, unhappy with myself for not defending her more aggressively.

"Certainly not the *men* customers, anyway," she concluded. "But that's not what I wanted to talk to you about. How did you like your first day in Catholic school?"

"It went well. The other students were all nice to me. And the teacher seemed fair enough. Strict, but fair. She certainly didn't seem like a mortal enemy."

"I would hope not. I would have hoped for at least that much at public school."

I was unsure of how to respond, so I changed the subject.

"Are you sure we're not related? I could understand if your name was Smith and my mother's maiden name was

Smith. But De Montfort just isn't that common."

"Not many names are as common as Smith. We might be more related than you think; it just depends on how many generations you want to go back."

If not getting answers was a profession, I would be rich.

"I've spoken to Father Cassidy many times over the years. He is a good man. He didn't take kindly to the governor's threat to tear down the school if you weren't admitted, which I can't say I blame him, but everything is fine until the end of the year, when your scholarship ends. Then it depends on if you can pay the entrance fees and tuition if you can continue.

"Now I want you to know things are changing around here. The school is going to expand. There will be a separate high school in two years. The land's been donated by Mr. Benson.

"Mrs. Porter will finish the year and then leave our district. The way she treated you was completely unacceptable. Her brother-in-law is Hugo Landacre, you know. She thought she was doing right by her family."

"I think someone told me that already. He was just here. You missed him."

"I wouldn't have if I had my revolver. Anyway, the board agrees the whole riot never would have happened if she handled the class differently. Which brings me to my point. I want you back in public school. It's an absolute embarrassment to me that you are going to a private school."

"Because you're the head of the school board."

"There's a whole lot more to it than that, dear," she said quietly. "But it's not something we want to get into at the moment."

Lila came back with the tea and we sipped on it for a while.

"But if you want to stay in Catholic school, even if you aren't Catholic, I would be willing to pay the tuition myself, provided you produce the grades, of course."

I was speechless.

"Think about it, dear," she said and left, just as a few more diners came in.

It was a decent amount of business that night, but everyone was gone by nine o'clock. I started to use the restroom by going through the kitchen, but Lila stopped me. She was under strict orders to keep me out, so I went out the front door and around to the toilet. I saw Depjim making a patrol around town. We waved to each other. I slipped on some spilled cabbage leaves on my way there and resolved to pick them up on my way back. After all, Finchy and Thrushy were no longer there to take care of that sort of thing.

Sure enough, I slipped in the slimy cabbage mess again on my way back. The leaves must have been there a while. Before I could get started, I heard the pinging sound of an unhealthy car as it stopped on the street. Four men got out: Scott and Doug Tanner, Harvey Kaker and that fourth man they were with before. I followed them inside to fetch them some menus.

They all sat at a booth and ordered Hamburger steak sandwiches, chips and soda. They clowned around and tried to flirt with me which made me nervous.

They've been drinking. I can smell it on their breath.

I went behind the counter and cleaned, even though everything was spotless.

"You mean you know her?" the stranger asked incredulously.

"She's like a distant cousin of some kind," Scott Tanner said.

"You can't be serious," he said in a disbelieving voice, like they were stupid or something. No doubt it was a tone of voice they heard often.

"Why not?" Doug Tanner asked.

"You can never go home again."

"Don't want to," came the succinct reply.

"Me too," said Scott.

"How about you Harvey?"

Kaker shrugged, "Nothing here but family. Gotta be better somewhere else."

Another shrug.

"Hey there, Little Miss Waitress, time to go," the fourth man called out to me.

I went over with the bill and they laughed.

"No, dear. You give us the money from the register," said Harvey.

"No, I'm not. You're going to pay, like everyone else."

The fourth man pulled out a revolver bigger than the pistol Depjim carried. I just stared at it.

Just when I'm being tolerated by my family again, now this. They'll never forgive me.

"NO," I yelled at them.

Lila ran out to see what was going on. She pulled me away from the table and told me to go to the kitchen, but I stayed in front of the counter.

"Oh my God," Lila exclaimed. "Doug and Scott Tanner? Harvey Kaker? Are you crazy? You won't get away with this."

"Just get the money and let us worry about that little detail," said the fourth man, enjoying the moment. "You know, the two hundred dollars the governor gave you."

"NEVER," I yelled back at them. "Besides, it's spent. Mom paid off bills with it."

Lila grabbed me by the neck with a speed I never would have guessed she had and dragged me to the kitchen door and roughly pushed me through it.

"What are you thinking? This isn't worth your life," she almost screamed at me. "Now get in there and stay there where it's safe."

If I had thought about it, I would have concluded that she was right. But I didn't think about it. I was thinking more of how disappointed everyone would be with me if I didn't at least try to stop them. Gramma Morris already told me I might have put them out of business with my stupid little prank. What would a robbery do? I ran out the back door and found Depjim down the block, just past the gas station.

"Depjim, Depjim," I called out to him, "they're robbing the café."

"Stay here," he called to me and ran back, but I followed him.

We hurried back down the street and just as we passed by the corner of the café, they came out.

"There they are. They're robbing us," I called out.

All four of them stopped and looked at me and Depjim who had his service revolver pulled out.

The fourth man reacted first. He turned and shot. Just as I realized the danger I was in, I slipped in the cabbage leaves and hit my head hard when I landed. There was no pain as I faded into a warm white light.

CHAPTER 40

RECOVERY

I missed the most exciting night in Faucette history. Six bullets were fired. Depjim was shot in the thigh, but the bullet went through which was a good thing for him. I was grazed in the upper arm. It was slipping in the cabbage leaves and landing on my head so hard that knocked me out. Lila was pistol whipped. Harvey Kaker was killed outright after firing wildly at Depjim. The other three robbers got away uninjured.

Pastor Seth Josephson called my family to the front of the Christian concert to pray with them for my survival in front of most of the town. I was lifted into Dad's wagon and slowly drawn home and laid down in bed, while Anna Marie and Holly were relegated to the couch downstairs.

The New Orleans Times-Picayune ran a headline that stated: *Heroic Little Girl Thwarts Robbery*. The events of that evening were told and retold all over the country. It hit a nerve with many people when they came to the last line: Amy Collins at last update is in a coma.

My family was inundated with letters and post cards. Many contained nickels and an occasional dime for me to go to the pictures when I woke up. Governor Long called, assuring the Taylor-Tanner Gang, as they were now dubbed by the press, would soon be caught. He was wrong.

I missed all of it. I was in another world where it was white and warm, and I felt as loved as anyone could ever be loved. I was unaware of what was going on in my life. There was music and soothing voices talking to me, though I didn't understand the words. I was floating, flying, spinning, falling. I was happy, content, joyful, and laughing.

And then it was time to go back. All of that magical world disappeared. Little puzzle like pieces of darkness replaced the warm whiteness, covering the light until the whole picture was complete and the light and warmth were gone. But I knew I was loved and everything would be all right.

The oil lamp was flickering softly on the table. I was in bed and covered in soft blankets. The air was cold, but I was warm. A chair was pulled next to the bed and Mom was asleep, her head at a very uncomfortable angle. I still felt lighter than air and started to get up.

The pain attacked my whole head and took my breath away for a moment, then I gasped to breathe. I was no longer lighter than air.

Mom was up and next to me in an instant. Her clothes stretched over her belly tightly. The baby was still little, but too big to hide behind loose dresses.

"Shh, shh," she soothed. "You're all right."

"They made me come back," I said, disappointed to have left my white space, but happy to be back home.

Mom paused for a moment, unsure of what to say, then said simply, "I'm glad."

That was as good an answer as I could hope for.

My bladder ached. I had to go. The chamber pot materialized on the bed and the blankets were pulled down.

I was in a strange nightgown. I reached to pull it up and there it was.

"A diaper?" I said, disappointed and humiliated. "Again?"

"Yes," she replied a little impatiently. "You've been asleep for over three days now. You don't think you needed one?"

"Three days?" I said while using the vessel, embarrassed about going in front of her, but it would have been worse for me to use a diaper at my age. And as I became more aware, my right arm was bandaged and taped to my torso. Being independent just wasn't going to work for me right now.

"Three days," she responded. "Once again, you had us all worried sick. You even made headline news. Now it's not just us. The whole country is worried about you this time. What were you thinking?"

"Thinking?"

"Why didn't you just give them the money?" she asked, exasperated.

"Money?" It took a second to remember it all. "Oh, I thought you'd all hate me even more if I lost all our money."

"Hate? Hate? You come in here and Anna Marie's grades go through the roof. Holly adores you. Paul lives to have you read to him. Michelle and Annette love having you around. And Gramma Morris."

"Yes, she hates me the most."

"NO, I love you the most," Grama Morris said from the door, more than a little agitated. "You just don't understand how I am. When you have a house full of children, you have to be strict and no nonsense. There has to be order. That's what I give. Order. I had six children myself. They all grew up to become very successful. I had two sons who became sailors and work on cargo ships, a son who drives a streetcar in New Orleans, two daughters who married hard working men, one lives in Bogalusa and one in Natchez. And my oldest daughter became a nurse and married a man who retired from the army as an officer. She's a widow now but she's still a very important woman. All because I taught them discipline. And I teach you discipline, not from hate but from love. If I didn't love my children and grandchildren and great grandchildren, then I'd let you run around town until you accidentally kill yourselves. Or in your case, until you destroyed the whole town."

I looked at her sideways.

"Well, you have to admit that everything is different these days," she added defensively.

"Never mind that," Mom said firmly. "Now, Cici made you chicken soup for every day until you get better. I'm going to heat it up now. It'll be a whole lot easier getting it down you now that you're awake."

"How did I drink it if I was asleep?"

"We put a teaspoon under your tongue while we sat you up," Gramma Morris said. "And you are quite heavy for such a light little girl."

"She's right," Mom said with a smile. "I don't know how you could be any heavier even if you were heavier."

They both laughed. I wasn't amused. My head and arm hurt too much.

"Okay, now let's get you up and walking," Mom said.

They each took a side and lifted me to my feet. My head really started to hurt but my arm hurt more.

"The next time you decide to take a tumble, try not to hit your head," Gramma Morris told me as we walked into the hallway. "You might get a headache."

"I already have a headache."

"See what I mean? You should listen to me," came her triumphal response.

"Your arm is fine, but the bullet definitely got a part of you," Mom said. "We'll take the bandage off for now. Doc Gannon wanted it on while you were unconscious so you wouldn't aggravate the wound."

We got a robe on me and headed downstairs to the kitchen to enjoy some tea and sweet cream. Apparently, Dad engineered another trade. Eggs for cream. About an hour later, he came in, picked me up like I weighed nothing and gave me a bear hug.

"You know, standing up to four full grown men and not backing down is something Michael Collins would do. Not very smart. But standing up to four men with guns? Even Michael Collins wasn't *that* dumb. Cassie's going to have to work with you on common sense. You need to know what's important."

"Well, I thought keeping from getting robbed was part of my job. You wouldn't want me to just give them the money."

"You didn't stop them from taking the money," he said. "They got it anyway. All the night's receipts. Depjim's all laid up and the parish sent over a nice young man to replace him for a couple of weeks. But I'm sure we can break him in around here. Things were nice and peaceful for the last three days. But now that you're awake, I'm sure that'll change."

Jason squealed from the corner and jumped in my lap, then scurried over to the stairs and started shouting to the other girls to wake up and come see.

"Amy's awake."

"Jason," I tried to sound calming, "leave them be. Today's a school day."

"They need their sleep," Dad explained to him, but first came the stomping noises from upstairs and then came the girls.

The blankets from the couch were flung in the air as the other girls rushed to greet me. All smiles, laughs, cuddles, and hugs. Even Anna Marie.

As usual, Doc Gannon was called and he came over with his little black bag. He did the usual poking and prodding, tapping and pressing. He spent a bit longer examining my eyes this time before he announced that I had another concussion and would miss some more school. I was to be kept quiet and put on a bland diet. How any restaurant could stay in business with him as the town doctor was beyond me.

"What's the point of having taste buds if you can't use them?" I pouted.

"Because you use your skull more often than you're supposed to, and you use it for the wrong things," he replied dryly. "Remember, no excitement."

"Her?" Gramma Morris scoffed. "How do you expect that to happen?"

"Tie her to a chair if necessary."

The girls went to school and Jason went with Aunt Sharon. They all had strict instructions to not tell anyone I woke up. With my stomach's reputation for acting up and the doctor's strict instructions to have no fun, Mom didn't want a lot of visitors.

That night when the other girls came in, they brought my schoolbooks and a note signed by Sister Barbara and all my classmates. It was just homework, reading assignments and get-well wishes. I felt happy, but sad, as well. I got more mail from my teacher and classmates in one day than I did from my family in New York in six weeks.

The week went by in a pleasant lackadaisical way. I spent most of the time sleeping or reading. I could go on the back porch and enjoy the fresh air. Although Mom thought it was too cool, she accepted that my northern blood made me more immune to the winter chill. I was not allowed to go to the river, or even outside, as Mom thought I was acting kind of off balance and she didn't want me to fall. At least I wouldn't have to curtsy to anyone for a while.

I had dizzy spells, but I didn't mention them to her because I didn't want to worry her or the little life inside her. Besides, although I really enjoyed my quiet time, I wanted to go back to my new school.

Mom conducted farm business in the mornings. Suppliers, vendors, customers, and salesmen visited every day. She sat with them at the table while I read quietly in the living room. None of them were allowed to speak to me except to say 'hi.' They weren't visiting me anyway.

Some of them were looking for chickens or eggs, others were bill collectors looking for money. Everybody bought something or got paid. Nobody stayed for long. Mom made a point of telling them all that I didn't need any more excitement and she wanted to keep me quiet.

On Wednesday, Mom called Aunt Mary to tell her I was all right while I was dozing off. The conversation didn't seem to go well. It seemed that the Giraffe wanted me sent back to New York. Mom bluntly told her 'no.' The conversation became quite heated, and then I heard Mom say, "No, I'm keeping her quiet for now. She doesn't need a whole lot of activity."

She hung up the phone and sat next to me and squeezed my shoulder, resting my head on her collar.

"You belong here," she said.

Later, she would tell people I responded by saying, "I know. The pine trees told me." I don't remember saying that, but then again, I was asleep soon after.

I slept off and on the rest of the day and the day after. My sisters all told me that they never wanted me to leave, which was nice. I really was feeling kind of silly for thinking everybody hated me, but I was too busy dreaming to give it much thought. Doc Gannon came by and said I was getting better, though I may not be showing it yet, and told Mom to just leave me be and let me sleep.

I was lucid again by Friday. This would be my last day of recuperation. The girls all went to school but every one of them hugged me good-bye. Holly asked me if I was going to read to them tonight.

"I have to work," I replied. "Besides, you're all going to the music show."

"Wrong on both counts," Mom said firmly. "We're having family night tonight, so you can read to us."

"Yay," Holly yipped and danced around the room.

Annette was less enthused. "Wait a minute. Guy and I were going to drive home together after it was over. Amy, I love you more than you'll ever know…"

"But…" I continued for her.

"I'm really getting bored listening to those stupid Oz books," she completed.

"Me too," said Anna Marie and Michelle simultaneously.

I didn't want to hurt Holly's feelings.

"How about I start to read those stupid *Anne of Green Gables* books after we're done with this Oz book and I can read to Holly on Sundays." I looked at her. "Just you and me?"

She liked the arrangement, though I detected a lack of enthusiasm among the others and they were all soon sent out the door. The older girls were tired of listening to me read and I didn't blame them. Especially books that were designed for much younger readers.

"What about my plans with Guy?" Annette asked, the beginning of a sulk showing.

"Invite him over," said Mom. "He likes chocolate-strawberry cake, right? I'll ask Cici to bake us one in his honor."

She seemed happy with that.

About an hour after they left, Mrs. De Montfort galloped to the door on a tan and black horse. It was a surprising sight to see her on horseback. I would have thought she'd drive up in a Cadillac with a chauffeur and footman to open the door for her.

Her mode of transportation didn't seem to surprise Mom in the least though. They whispered to each other while I read on the porch. I knew that whatever they were talking about must have been important because although they weren't angry, they were quite animated.

After a bit, they called me over and had me sit at the table. A cup of hot tea with sweet cream was put in front of me, so I was content. They made small talk for a while asking me about New York, Aunt Mary, Julia and Patrick, the Giraffe, and his family. They obviously were avoiding talking about something, but I listened politely, even though I wanted to scream, 'Get to the point.'

CHAPTER 41

AN ANNOUNCEMENT,
A SECRET, A PARTY

"Your Aunt Mary and Uncle Gio still want you to come back to New York," Mrs. De Montfort told me at long last.

"But I like it here," I cried out, looking to them both for support. "I belong here."

"You do," Mrs. De Montfort said. "I believe it, Cassie here believes it. From what I hear, even the pine trees believe it." She smiled a bit at that attempt at humor. "And you will stay here. But they may try to get all legal on us. Your birth certificate does say that Mary's your mother, you know."

Why wouldn't it?

"That gives their lawyers a lot of ammunition. But we will fight and win. I've done research on this Giovanni Corelli. Odious man. But who knows? It's never a matter of right or wrong. The lawyers only want to win. They don't care if they destroy lives in the process. So, you may be hearing some things in connection to that, if it gets to court. We are an old and proud family, but like all families of stature, we have a few secrets that don't need to be known."

"You said 'we,'" I replied, "So you *are* a relative of some kind. I *knew* it."

"That's right, Amy," she confirmed, then she took a sip of tea and looked straight at me with those piercing blue eyes. "I am your grandmother. Cassie and your Aunt Mary are my daughters. Your Gramma Morris is my mother."

I don't think I was surprised by the news. What surprised me was finally being told something.

"Why do they call you Mrs. De Montfort, then? Why not Mom or Mama?"

"Because eleven years ago I got mad. Remember, your grandfather was a major in the army and I was a nurse in the great war. When the troops were sent back home, my husband, Major James De Montfort was stationed in Europe and I stayed with him. We were gone, serving our country for three years by then. Your Gramma did her best with the girls, but it didn't really turn out well and we blamed her for things we shouldn't have. They both made bad mistakes which reflected on us. When Mary eloped with Michael Collins, Jimmy's career was over. The general staff decided that if a man can't manage his family, how can he handle his soldiers? He would never get his promotion to Colonel and he retired in 1921. He disowned Mary and never spoke to her again. The same was true with Cassie, but for another reason, of course. I wish to this day I could have seen how petty and stupid it all was. Now he's gone and he never got another chance to tell either daughter he loved them. And he really did."

"Not as much as his military career," Mom said under her breath.

"Cassie, please. There's enough blame for everyone. Regardless, we're speaking now. I regret ever disowning you over such a thing."

"What thing was that?" I asked.

"Well, I'm not going to say. It's just too petty. We'll just say it's one of our family's secrets. Talk to Cassie yourself about it."

"When you're older," Mom said firmly.

"Come on," I pleaded. "It's a family secret and I'm family."

"And it's a secret. It wouldn't be a secret if I told you about it, now would it?"

"Well, if it's a family secret and I'm family, shouldn't I know it?"

"It's not that kind of secret. It's a secret *from* family. And you're family."

I exhaled sharply. This was going nowhere.

"That's just the one secret," Mrs. De Montfort told me. "There are so many secrets we will be telling you; I doubt you'll believe what characters are in your bloodline. The *big* family secret is one that will really shock you. But it's not time to tell you that one either."

"Well, here's a not-so-secret," Mom said, obviously changing the subject. "That Rob fellow the governor forced to walk Betsy home asked her for her number and called her. They went to the picture show and ate at the café. They're seeing each other again this weekend."

At that moment, the phone rang.

"I hope you can forgive a foolish old woman like me for acting so petty," Mrs. De Montfort said.

I went over and hugged her, more by obligation than by love.

"What do I call you now?" I asked.

"Gramma De Montfort will do," she smiled.

"How did you know she's awake?" I heard Mom ask, exasperation dripping from her tone. "What do mean everybody knows?…They just do? Okay, well that'll be great, thank you."

"That was Mrs. Gannon. Doc Gannon is stopping by. He says the whole town knows you woke up."

The phone rang again.

"Hi Betsy, yes, oh do. How did you find out?...Who's that?...Oh....Yes, she'd love to see you."

Interesting conversation.

"Betsy's dropping by," Mom called out to us. "Jasper Groves told her you woke up."

"Who?" we both asked.

"He's the man inspecting the bridge to see what kind of preparations need to be done before they start to replace it."

"How would he know?"

Horses' hooves clomped in the driveway as the countess arrived. She was being helped down by Killy while Fredrick stood by with a picnic basket.

Mom answered the phone yet again.

"Well, okay, I guess. Aunt Sharon is on her way over with food and some cream for us to sweeten up. She'll be right over. She just loves talking to the countess. And Jason will enjoy being at home for a while."

Mom seemed confused but was resigned to having a party.

Then the phone rang again. Depjim stopped in to get my statement while Mom was talking to whoever was on the other end. I wasn't very helpful to him. My memory of that night was vague. But he told me that was rather common when something like that happens.

"It was a big night for us." He winked.

He walked with a cane but seemed unhurt. He was back on duty and said he enjoyed having a helper. But soon things would be back to normal. At least the new normal.

At that moment, a reporter called. Mom made short work of him.

"She's awake. Happy ending." And then she hung up.

Mayor Norman pulled up in a beat-up Chevrolet. He had a vase full of flowers.

"From my garden," he said proudly as he gave them to me. "There's wisteria, azalea, rhododendron, along the sides because it's still out of season for them. But you know what's in the middle?"

"Roses," I said sniffing them as was required to prove I appreciated them, which I did.

I missed who the next caller was because Pastor Josephson and his wife showed up with a jug of freshly made eggnog. Gramma De Montfort quickly confiscated it since I was on a bland diet.

Doc Gannon arrived just in time to see that villainous deed and nodded his approval. He took me to the back and examined me, again concentrating on my eyes. He smiled at the results.

"She'll be fine," he pronounced. "But I have to say, I'm disappointed in how you're keeping her quiet. I've gone to graduation ceremonies that had less people than this. Bland diet until the end of the week. Oatmeal will do her a world of good."

He was such an annoying man.

Mom and Gramma De Montfort were talking on the front porch and the others were chatting with each other about me. I always had someone near me who wanted to hear my story. But I did hear Mom say she loved calling her Mama again.

I went out to the main room and mingled while Doc Gannon went back to his office. After his car was safely gone, I fixed a breakfast plate for myself. I had a piece of cornbread and butter, one little pork chop, some grits with sauteed onion and pepper, and for dessert, a ginger cookie that actually had sugar in it. It was wonderful. Bland meals could be quite tasty when I fixed them myself.

Father Cassidy stopped by with a gift of rosary beads and a brand-new Bible. He and Pastor Josephson found each other and struck up a friendly conversation.

The phone rang and this time it wasn't *about* me, it was *for* me. Sister Barbara put on all my classmates one at a time so they could tell me how glad they were I was all right. Although Jonathon Prejean phrased it as, "I'm glad you're not dead."

"So am I," I replied dryly.

Dianna Wilson, the night operator, stopped by and wished me well. She didn't stay long as she didn't like crowds. Mom very profusely thanked her for coming, then answered the phone again.

"Phyllis," Mom cried out happily, and Gramma De Montfort hurried over and the two of them spoke to the mysterious Phyllis for a short time.

"She's your aunt," Gramma De Montfort told me. "My oldest daughter."

The countess insisted that I get out my violin and play a couple of pieces for everybody. I was shy about performing in front of so many people, but their applause left me very little choice. When I was done, I was properly fussed over and complimented. Some of the folks began leaving, which I welcomed because I was starting to get tired. But others were arriving. Most of them were friendly neighbors who I hadn't met yet.

Betsy arrived and caught the tail end of my playing. She made a point of complimenting me by congratulating the countess on her teaching ability. The countess smiled indulgently and gave me a tight hug and told me she was tired and wanted a little nap. She mentioned that it was nice to be old because she could take a nap any time she wanted, while young people have to stay awake, no matter how tired they may be. When her carriage rolled away, that seemed to be the queue for most everyone else to leave.

Betsy and I talked together in the front room while Gramma De Montfort, Aunt Sharon and Mom talked in the kitchen.

"So how did your date go with Mr. Rob?" I asked Betsy, even though I already knew it went well.

She laughed, a musical sort of sound. "You know, it went well enough. As I told you before, he's not just quiet and shy, he's *painfully* shy. I was in pain watching him try to start a conversation. But I invited him in anyway…the studio, that is, not the house, of course, and, well, the cat somehow got in the studio."

"You have a cat? I never saw it."

"The studio is my business. Can't have an animal walking around. Some people are allergic to them, you know. Well anyway, he sat down in the wing chair and had tea. I thought he must be slow or something, he hardly said a word. But he wouldn't be working for the governor if he really was that slow. But when he got up to go, he brushed off some cat hair and said, 'You know, I hope I didn't get any threads on your poor cat.' That broke the ice.

"I loved that line and we started to talk. He's really quite the charmer."

Gramma De Montfort called over to her, "Don't fall for him yet. Just because he charms today doesn't mean he won't run around tomorrow."

The phone rang and, after the first ring, I knew it was for us so since I was closest, I answered it. It was Rob, almost as if he knew we were talking about him.

"It's Mr. Rob," I called out to everyone.

"Yes, sir," I answered his question. "I'm up and doing fine."

There was a long pause.

Painfully shy was right. This was downright awkward.

"Well, I'm glad you're feeling better. I'll tell Governor Long. He'll be happy to hear it. Let me know if there's something I can do for you."

"You know, there actually is something you can do for me," I said, having been struck by a wonderful idea. I smiled at Betsy.

"What's that?" he asked innocently.

Betsy was waving both hands at me in a stop-this-now gesture.

"You can say hi to Betsy."

She took the call while giving me a dagger's look and said hi to him and started laughing right away, in a flirty sort of way with a big smile on her face, while patting her hair in place, as if he could see her over the phone.

I just loved being the center of attention. And then...I was told I woke up maybe two hours later. Everyone else was gone. Only Mom and Aunt Sharon were left. They sat drinking coffee. I walked over, put my hand on Mom's stomach and looked at her with blank eyes.

"It's a boy," I told her with absolute certainty.

I then put my hand on Aunt Sharon's stomach. She flinched and was obviously uncomfortable.

"You'll have a girl."

"I'm not pregnant," she responded, somewhat angrily, I was told.

I didn't hear her. I don't remember any of this conversation, but they both assured me I did touch them and made those predictions. While they stared out after me, I went out to the back porch and went to sleep until everyone else came home. It wasn't until the next day that Mom scolded me for saying such a thing.

Aunt Sharon couldn't have children.

CHAPTER 42

THE TREASURE MAP

Saturday was a day of rest and recovery. I had a week's worth of schoolwork to make up and turn in on Monday. No argument was good enough to have me stay home any longer. If there was a possibility Huey P Long was still scrutinizing my progress, then he would be monitoring my school attendance and no one in town wanted anyone to be on his bad side, at least not until the bridge was rebuilt. I finished right before dinner time and helped set the table. Mom figured that since I was strong enough to stay awake all day and do schoolwork, I was strong enough to eat regular food. That was good because I was really developing a hatred for oatmeal.

Mom and I rode with Uncle Vincent and Aunt Sharon to church the following day. Uncle Vincent was his usual cheerful self, wondering why we always called it 'Sunday' when more often than not it was cloudy. And there is no 'Cloud-day' in the week. I wished I had thought of that one.

Aunt Sharon was very distant and stared out the window, totally ignoring me. I apologized to her, but she simply nodded and got out of the vehicle. Uncle Vincent caught my eye and rolled his eyes with a I-don't-know sort of look.

I went to my Sunday School class to face the abuse of the other children. Only it wasn't so bad. Getting shot and being injured by marauding desperados earned me quite a bit of respect. Even Robbie was proving to be friendly.

"Where's the bullet hole?" he asked.

I pointed to the bandage, which was much smaller now.

"It's not a bullet hole. I was grazed. It was the fall that really hurt me," I replied patiently. "I hit my head again, just like at school."

"All that fuss over a little flesh wound? You can sure turn a nothing into pure melodrama," said Laura. "You should write movies."

"Laura," Mrs. Gardner said firmly, "would Jesus approve of that remark?"

"No, ma'am, but he would agree with me," she replied defiantly.

"Would you like to sit with your parents today and see if they agree?"

"No, ma'am," Laura said contritely, but that look of resentment she shot at me told me she was nowhere near contrite.

I told them all about the robbery, trying not to exaggerate more than necessary to make it a good story.

"That was brave," Martha said. "I think I would have given them the money."

"No guarantee they wouldn't have shot me anyway."

"I guess," she said, more to herself. "When are you coming back to school?"

"Well, I have to go to Catholic school, at least for the year. I'll be going back tomorrow."

On Monday, I was back in school. Even though I was only in class for one day before my injury, all the girls made a point of hugging me and telling how much they missed me.

"When I said I want you to have adventures," Sister Barbara said with an impish smile, "I was thinking maybe a trip to New Orleans. But at least you didn't disrupt the school with this one."

The whole class erupted in laughter. I smiled, but I can't say I thought it was a funny remark. Probably because I was still tired and weak. Even so, I resolved to make it through the day.

Things got better by recess. The school had an inside bathroom and when I came out, Merry was waiting for me.

"Come on," she insisted. "We're having a meeting and need you."

I was confused but followed obediently, curious, but happy to be included. David Terrell had an old paper in his hands he was showing off to the others.

"It's a treasure map," Merry told me excitedly.

David quickly showed his prize to me. It had line shadings, land features and crudely drawn trees. Almost in the center was a big X, with little shovels drawn to each side. *Smith's Gold* was written underneath it.

There was no doubt who the Smith was. General Kirby Smith, the only Confederate general who never lost a battle, who oversaw the western half of the old Confederacy after the Yankees captured Vicksburg. Famous in Louisiana, unknown everywhere else.

"You're coming with us," Merry half told, half asked me. "It'll be so much fun with you there."

"Well, when will you be going?" I asked tentatively. "I'm still a little weak from my…adventure."

"You'll be fine," Elizabeth assured me. "It won't be until Saturday and today's only Monday. Besides, we're the inseparable seven. You have to go."

"Yeah, inseparable," agreed Carmen.

She held her hand out, palm down. Merry and Elizabeth immediately put theirs on top, followed by the three boys. I put mine on the very top and they all started a chant of whoa, getting louder and louder, and we all threw our arms up high as we finished in a whoop.

Sister Barbara observed us and sauntered over.

"You children planning an adventure?" she asked with a smile. David folded his paper and slipped it into his pocket.

"We are indeed, Sister," he said with a smile. "An adventurously adventurous adventure. For fifth graders only. You remember what you said on the first day of class?"

I didn't. I wasn't there.

"You said there's something magical about the number five. We're going to prove it."

She laughed. "David, don't you ever lose that spirit. Just make sure you have fun. And Amy," she said looking at me with smiling eyes and a warm gaze, "I'm putting you in charge of making sure it's an adventure no one will ever forget."

"Yes, ma'am," I said, wondering if I had just been insulted.

She strolled back to the classroom humming *Ave Maria*.

"What about snakes or gators?" I asked.

"It's too early for them. They don't come out until spring," Jonathon said, as if he were a great herpetologist.

"What about seriously dangerous things like zombies?" Elizabeth asked.

"Zombies?" I repeated, wide eyed.

"There aren't any zombies this far north," David said,

rolling his eyes. "They only live in New Orleans."

"If they're zombies, do they live?" Carmen asked. "Aren't they dead? Just moving around a bit?"

"They don't bother anybody," Jonathon opined. "They just do zombie things. Why would they bother us?"

"They could be guarding the treasure," Elizabeth said.

"They don't guard anything," Jonathon said a bit louder with frustration. "They don't exist."

"What doesn't exist?" Father Cassidy said from behind us.

We turned to see him smiling down at us.

"Zombies," Elizabeth said quietly. "I hear about them all the time."

"But you don't see them," David pointed out.

"I see our new student fills your heads with…novel ideas," he said looking at me as his smile faded.

I waited for one of the others to come to my defense, but they were all quiet.

"Now listen, there are strange things in this world, but if you follow Church doctrine, you'll know see they are never even mentioned. And if the doctrine doesn't say something exists, it doesn't exist."

"Just ask Galileo," David said with great false sincerity.

"Come to my office, David, and we'll continue the conversation while you others go to class."

As sincere as Father Cassidy's arguments were, we remained unconvinced, but Elizabeth told us she would come prepared. We agreed that she would be in charge of protecting us from zombies as we went back to class.

Mr. Benson had a new short story for me to read after school.

"It's a dark comedy," he explained. "It was never published. Too much dark. Not enough comedy."

I might have found some humor in it if I had a magnifying glass *and* it was under a microscope.

It was called *How to Become Alone.* It was about a farm boy named Tom. He lived with his mother, brother and younger sister. Their father was mean and drunk and downright evil, always encouraging or demanding that his children do criminal deeds, usually just cattle rustling or petty thievery. Tom loved to get away from his family and go out hunting with his friends on the weekends, especially his best friend, Mike. Life went on and they all got married and had families of their own, which made the hunting all the more important to put meat on the table. Tom's father had died by then and the family settled in to a quiet life where they tried to become respectable in the community.

One day, while out deer hunting, there was an accident and Mike was hit by a ricochet 'just above the inseam,' which made his family complete. His wife was sad that there would be no more children and Mike and Tom worked out an arrangement. Mike's wife would 'borrow' Tom every summer and every spring have another child. Although people knew Mike had been wounded, they just assumed it was a miracle that he was able to fully recover.

When the war came, they both marched off, but only Tom came back. During the war, Tom's wife found out what had happened and ran off with a discharged soldier from Texas, taking their children with her. Tom struck it rich in the war. He deserted with some friends and followed Sherman to the sea. These scallywags comforted the widows and orphans who had their houses burned down and gained their trust. Once they found out where what little gold or jewels they had were hidden, they robbed them. Tom came back a wealthy man, intending to marry Mike's widow and the mother of some of his children, but she already remarried and moved to Little Rock.

His younger sister was a grown woman and going to have his little brother's baby. They got married in Baton Rouge after giving assumed names. After the war, no one cared about anything. When their mother died, they moved to Texas to keep their secret. Tom was all alone.

"I can see the dark in that story, but I can't say I found any comedy in it."

"That's common in comedy," he replied. "Some people love Ted Healy and The Three Stooges. Some do not. I don't have an opinion on it. I never saw them."

I looked into his unseeing eyes and wondered if he was trying to be funny, but I left not knowing one way or the other. The wagon rolled up and I heard Dad call out to me. I quickly said good-bye to Mr. Benson, happy to get away from him, as always.

I got in the wagon and Dad urged the horses on. We passed by Thomas Street instead of turning.

"We're going to the café?" I asked. "I thought we were going home."

"Eventually."

When we turned down Faucette Avenue, I saw close to a dozen cars parked on both sides of the road. All the people who were friendly to me were there and cheering as we pulled up.

"Hurry up, Amy," Jason called out excitedly. "We have a nice flour cake with chocolate frosting on it for your surprise party."

"Surprise party?"

"It's a little gathering for you and Annette," Dad said with a smile. "To celebrate your recovery and her birthday. Remember, some of us got to meet the governor because of you. He's rebuilding the bridge and he's going to talk to the railroad people. The whole town is thrilled you're here."

"And we want you to know it," Holly called out. She and the other girls all ran over and hugged me and led me into the building. Well-wishers were everywhere, some were people I had seen before while running errands but never actually met. Sister Barbara was there, along with some of the other nuns.

"Still planning on that adventure, Amy?" she asked me, eyes twinkling.

"Adventure?" Gramma Morris asked, eyes rolling. "Just going to school is an adventure for this one."

"This is different," I explained. "We're all going to look for buried treasure."

"Who all?"

"My friends at the church school."

"I don't know," she mused.

"I do," Mom came up behind us. "She needs friends and these are good people, even if they are of the wrong religion."

I winced, but she was totally oblivious.

She continued, "If they want her included, I say she goes."

I glanced at Sister Barbara who was busy suppressing a smile. No damage done.

"Thank you, Mom, for letting me go."

Gramma Morris made one of her harumph sounds. I hugged her, too.

"Thank you for caring."

I leaned over to Sister Barbara. "Thank you for not being angry."

"I've heard much worse," she responded with a smile.

Hugh Landacre was just pulling up in his Oldsmobile. When he got out, he said loudly, "Well, Amy, I am so glad to see you after your…incident. Remember what I said, just because it's fantastic doesn't mean it's not true."

The crowd fell silent. Hugh Landacre was not very popular here.

"What does *that* mean?" I heard Holly ask Annette, who pleaded ignorance with a shrug.

"Thank you for saying so, Mr. Landacre," I said warmly.

My family may not have liked him, but this was obviously my party and I was going to be a gracious hostess.

"Everybody," I said loudly enough, "Mr. Landacre was kind enough to give me a ride home after I was lost in the swamp by the mill."

I paused, remembering that day. Remembering Sarah. Someone dies when she appears. For a brief moment, I saw Harvey Kaker.

"He told me that just because something's fantastic, doesn't mean it's not true."

Mom thanked him for coming with such sincerity a stranger never would have guessed how much she hated him and his family. She even offered him a piece of cake, which he accepted.

"You know," he said, looking at me but his voice booming so that everyone would hear him, "years ago, we ate here quite a bit. I always remembered how good the food was. Especially the cake." He pointed to his plate with his fork. "Then we had to stop coming because…well things happened."

"What things?" I asked him.

"THINGS," he said, in a bogeyman voice. "Things you should ask your mother…" He seemed flustered for a moment, "Or aunt, that is."

"Things we don't talk about," Mom responded dryly.

"Of course," I said, resolved.

"But I understand that little Amy is a whirlwind in her academics," he changed subjects, "which is understandable, given who her father is."

"My father?"

Mom interceded coldly, "Michael Collins was very smart, just not given the opportunity or education he needed."

"That's the way it is with most people," Mr. Landacre said smoothly. "And I've seen enough of little Amy to know there's too much potential to let wither on the vine. So, I want to pledge, right here and now, to pay for her tuition at St. Linus until she graduates."

"That is so kind of you, Mr. Landacre," Mom said, her sincerity being replaced by triumph. "But we'll have to decline. My mother already made that offer.

"Good," he replied with false joviality. "Saves me money."

Everyone laughed and the party went on, though Mr. Landacre left soon after. Somehow, I thought he had lost something and Mom gained something, but I didn't know what.

I thought about it on the way home, but quickly put it aside. Anna Marie and I were in the same grade now and she asked me to help her with her grammar. We went over the sentence structure and the rules. I could answer her question on how a sentence is built. I could not tell her why it was so important.

"It just is," I said, shrugging.

"Gee, Miss Du Lin can do that good."

We giggled a bit at that. It was the first time the two of us just laughed together.

"School's so different now," she said wistfully. "I don't have near the friends I used to."

"I don't think you ever did."

"No, not really," she sighed. "But I want real friends, not sometimes friends like the Davenports."

We had a small dinner that night since everyone ate at the party. It was nice to just snack for a while then do my nightly reading. After everyone scattered to get ready for bed and Mom was doing something with Jason, I found myself alone with Dad.

We hadn't spoken to each other very much after the spanking, but then our conversations were always short and to the point. Most of what I knew about him I learned from other people.

"It was nice for you to pick me up today," I said shyly.

"Well, I guess I can do that from now on, for a while. It's good to spend time with family."

"Yes, now that he has his days back," Mom said, just coming into the room.

"Oh?"

"Yes, it seems your Dad had a tiff with Durrell Kaker a month ago. Banged him up a bit. So, Durrell calls Depjim about it. Didn't like the response and filed a criminal complaint. Paul got thirty days in jail, but not the nights, seeing as how he's got a family and all. Durrell doesn't like that one little bit and kicks up a fuss about it So the judge gives him the same sentence for contempt of court. Same cell. They got to talk about old times together."

"Hmm," Dad said thoughtfully. "Well, like it was with Angus. Maybe Edgewater was too big a town, too big a job. Maybe they didn't stand a chance. Maybe it was a bunch of youngsters listening to out-of-touch old timers who didn't get the word that the world changed. Kinda like The Great War and The War between the States. The old men lead the young men to their death. Maybe it's time to move on."

He stared off into space.

"Durrell and I should never have had such a fight. Thirteen years we should have been friends. What a waste. We figured it was time to go back to being friends."

"So, I can start inviting the Nyes over again like we talked about? They are family to most the children, you know."

"Of course, you can, just not when I'm here. He always plays the part of the big tough macho hero. Then when he's around that woman, all his bones melt and he turns into oatmeal with clothes on. No sense in talking to him. Just talk to Brigitte."

She sighed.

The next day was Tuesday. It was quite warm. Almost like a summer day in New York. Mosquitos were starting to fly around, hunting for victims to steal blood from or infect with horrible diseases. In school, the energy was low. It was hard to concentrate on Sister Barbara's lessons when there was a treasure map right there in the classroom. Safely hidden, of course. Sister Barbara would not compete with anything for our attention.

After a never-ending morning, recess finally arrived and we all gathered together to plan our journey. Jonathon's father had a large flatboat that could hold nine people.

"It's seven feet long, three feet wide with three benches and four paddles," he told us. "We'll have space for all of us and the treasure chests."

I was feeling much better by now, as Elizabeth predicted.

"When do we go?" I asked, forgetting I had already asked that question.

"Saturday," Merry said.

"Oh, no. I have my violin lesson."

"Well, cancel it," an exasperated Elizabeth said.

"I can't. She doesn't have a phone."

"Who?" Carmen asked. "Who's your violin teacher?"

"The countess," I replied.

"That is so nifty," Merry exclaimed. "Does she let you ride in her carriage?"

I nodded.

"Let's stick to the subject," David commanded. "Can you walk over to cancel it?"

I shook my head. "It's too far to walk."

"There must be some way you can get a message over to her," he said.

"Wait a minute," I exclaimed. "I know. Her driver is Cici's nephew. I'll see if I can change the date to Thursday."

Catastrophe averted.

Cici was glad to send the message. But Thursday would be tough. I would have school, Mr. Benson, violin lesson, and the café. Then strike it rich two days later. I can't say I was expecting to find real gold and silver, but just being around my new friends would be treasure enough.

On Wednesday, the thermometer touched eighty degrees. We got together and decided what kind of supplies we needed. Jonathon was providing the boat, of course. Mom and Cici were making sandwiches for us all. Elizabeth, a thermos of lemonade. Merry insisted on lots of water and peanuts. David was going to bring cookies. Carmen was bringing biscuits. Ron, being of a practical nature, said he would bring toilet paper.

"After all, what goes in, must come out," he misquoted Newton.

The boys guffawed. We girls looked at the ground, studying the grass for a minute or so to hide our embarrassment. Ron offered to bring something else, but we girls, also being of a practical nature, agreed that toilet paper might not be bad. We appreciated the Scott brothers' invention; we just didn't want to discuss it.

I was happy and excited about our upcoming adventure but today I had little time to think about it. My violin lesson with the countess went well but my reading day was even stranger than usual. Mr. Benson had me go out to his backyard where he had a storm cellar where he aged moonshine. I checked the iron trapdoor to make sure it was locked. No one was welcome to his moonshine. Then he had me read another short story he wrote called *The Curious Children*.

It had the common theme of a young veteran from the Civil War who returned home from the carnage, haunted by a demonic presence that was trapped in an old bottle that glowed red and purple in the night. The demon guaranteed to him satisfaction in life. Charm, charisma, attractiveness, love, money, and above all, youth. A body that never aged. The young man became a teacher. When his students left school and started their married lives, he continued to teach them (the women, anyway) the art of love. After all, a man who has charm, charisma, attractiveness, love, and money gets everything he wants.

To maintain this hedonistic lifestyle, all he had to do was feed the monster. Sadly, the creature's diet was children.

He dug a large pit in his backyard and turned it into a storm cellar, with an iron trapdoor that opened from the ground. A staircase led down to the bottle, which sat on the floor and shimmered slightly red in the dark. The whole door would glow warm in his backyard.

He rode trains to nearby cities and entranced orphans and other neglected children with stories of how he had a magical friend who could make their dreams come true. *Just come with me and see. What have you got to lose? You must be curious.* If they showed just the slightest bit of interest, they were his. The demon's actually.

Some came at the first invitation. Some were still cautious. He would smile at them. *Aren't you even the least bit curious?* Of course, they were. Of course, they left with the charming older man. Of course, they never came back. Of course, the bodies were never found. Of course, no one missed them.

Then one day in the December of his life, he realized that he made a deal with the devil and forfeited his soul to the fires of hell. How could he redeem himself from such a fate?

It was easy enough. First, he prepared a mixture of cyanide, arsenic and chocolate. Then he charmed his last child into the dark and rancid basement.

"Drink this potion at the bottom of the stairs," the evil man said. "It will ensure that all goes well. You know how it is with magic. A little precaution is always a good thing."

The bewitched child nodded, even though he didn't know what he was agreeing with. The poor dear drank the potion and opened the demon's bottle. His body was vaporized and sucked into the flask; the stopper snapping shut behind. The man closed the door and started to walk towards his house when he heard the bottle explode and a horrific scream of agony and rage. Then nothing. The warm glow of evil was forever gone. The man was no longer a young man. Fifty years of corruption caught up with him. His body was withered and fading. But he redeemed his soul. He thought.

Of course, I had nightmares that night.

Mr. Benson made sure I knew he had a storm cellar just

like the one in the book. I wondered what awful things were in there.

"Did you see it?" Gramma Morris asked with a heavy sigh.

Annette rolled her eyes in agreement, while Michelle stared ahead impassively. Anna Marie and Holly were doing homework in the kitchen.

"Yes," I replied. "It's right there in his backyard. He had me check the lock before I started reading to him."

"He lives too close to the river to dig a deep hole like that. It would flood and collapse."

"I think he gets more fun out of scaring you than he does listening to you read," Lila added. "Why do you let it bother you?"

"But what if it's real? Not the demon and vampire parts. He already said the only monsters are people. What if he's one of them? An old, retired monster who likes to reminisce about his olden days of murder and mayhem."

"Amy, please," Gramma Morris exclaimed. "Murder and mayhem? Where do you get these things?"

As she walked away, shaking her head, Lila leaned over to me, "Next time, try saying this."

My sisters giggled at the idea.

As I nodded in agreement with her plan, Dad pulled up in the wagon. Time to go home.

Aunt Sharon stopped by after dinner, deep in thought. She gave me a funny look and spoke privately with Mom and Gramma Morris. There were squeals of joy. They all came back out to make a family announcement.

"Your Aunt Sharon is pregnant," Mom practically gushed out at us. "We all thought it couldn't happen, but it did. According to Amy, it's going to be a girl."

They all glared at me strangely.

"In fact, Amy knew about it before Aunt Sharon did."

"Certainly surprised me," Aunt Sharon drawled.

Luckily, the joy of a new life entering the world overshadowed my one and only moment of clairvoyance. Aunt Sharon was fussed over and hugged and treated like a queen. Everyone was happy.

Mom took me aside and looked at me sternly.

"Amy, how did you know Aunt Sharon is going to have a baby? She didn't know it herself."

I shrugged, "I don't know. I really don't remember saying anything about it. But isn't it grand? I bet she really will have a girl."

"I have no doubt," she said, looking at me curiously.

We were having an unusually early spring that year. People were fishing in the creek at both the Malmort and Atchafalaya rivers. Birds were singing about how happy they were. The animals were getting restless. Flies buzzed and landed on everyone's face, especially mine. I'd shoo one away, but it only came back a second later. I could not get rid of it. They all joked about my pet fly.

It was over eighty degrees every day that week and the air smelled different. The indoors everywhere smelled musty, even with the windows open. The outside alternated between pine, salt and stale swamp water. School was sultry and boring. We sat through our classes politely, but nobody learned anything. Tomorrow held so much excitement. Education couldn't compete with anticipation. Daydreams were the item of the day until we were set free. Well, *they* were set free anyway. I had to go to Mr. Benson and read.

"I have an idea," I said as he let me in. "How about you and me write a story together?"

"Oh?" he asked with a raised eyebrow. "A collaboration? I'll think about it. Did you have an idea in mind?"

"I do. It's a about a Civil War veteran who comes home from the war. He somehow got some money when he came back and when his mother died, he bought the land from his siblings. His father was a mean old man who died years before. Like it so far?"

"Sounds like one of mine already. Why did his siblings leave?"

"Because they were afraid of their brother. He was mean, just like his father."

"Oh," he said thoughtfully.

"So, this man came back with money somehow. However, how he got it was bad. But in those days, it was good enough just for him to have it."

"Ill-gotten gain."

"Exactly. Now because his father was mean, this man was mean, although he didn't realize it. He was acting the way he thought he was supposed to act. But even with the money, no one wanted to marry him. And he was lonely. And he hurt people very badly. And everyone was afraid of him and stayed away. And he was even more alone."

"There are consequences for being your father when you know your father was evil," he said thoughtfully.

"Well, the man became the town's teacher because no one else wanted the job. All the students were afraid of him because he was such a strict disciplinarian, and he enjoyed using the paddle to keep order. But it didn't stop him from being lonely. Then one day, he decided that he could be kind. He tried to be caring. Soon, people were kind and caring to him, and he liked that.

"He became a wonderful man and a great teacher, but whatever mean things he did in the past haunted him. So, he wrote stories mixed in with supernatural things, to give people a hint of all the things he regretted. Fearsome stories of demons and monsters.

"No one could understand how such a nice man could write such things. After a while, the man accepted the fact that he was a good man who had done bad things, which made him no different than anyone else. And the more he accepted himself, the more the town loved him. And he grew to be very old. Soon, one of his students had a ten-year-old granddaughter who started to read to him. She thought he was wonderful, in spite of whatever happened in the past. And he lived happily ever after."

"Happily ever after?" he snorted angrily. "No. He created a hell on earth for himself by being unforgiving and mean-spirited. And by the way, I was married once. And we had children together. And I loved all three of them. But I lost my whole family after the war because of my infinite stupidity. I completely broke ties with my father, but I thought we could reconcile and be a family. But that was a mistake. And I never forgave myself for that mistake."

His anger abated.

"You and I," he continued, "we each have a family secret. And it's the exact same thing, only we're at different ends of it. I think you're old enough to know it. Your friend, Mrs. De Montfort, didn't think you were ready to learn it, but I think you are."

"She's more than my friend," I replied. "She's my grandmother."

"I know. She told you that, did she?"

"She did. She didn't want to be mad anymore."

"Well, that's a good thing. Does she let Cassie call her Mama nowadays?"

"She does."

"Good. Abigail's blowhard husband thought he was top brass material. Got himself all huffed and puffed like one of those Macy parade balloons. But one little pin prick and he was all blown away. He blamed his daughters for him not making colonel. If he really wanted to know why he didn't make colonel, he should have looked in the mirror. He blamed Mary for that, and Abigail went along with it."

He sipped some coffee before switching subjects.

"My father was a brute. He wanted me to be a brute, his right-hand man. He trained me to be mean. And he tried the same with my idiot brother, but he was too simple. He didn't have to be as useless as he turned out, mind you. My father found a weakness and turned it into a disaster. He was as evil as a man could be. Hurt me and my siblings every day, mentally and physically."

"I'm sorry," was all I could say.

"Well, I grew up and married a woman from Nueville and went to live there. She was wonderful. Her name was Eva Woodcock. Together we worked on a plantation. I got room and board and a little spending money while she helped out in the house for not much more. She taught me about my good side. Made me a kinder man. Less prone to anger. Taught me to read better than anyone in my family. Inspired me to learn.

"Then my father promised me the northern half of the family farm and a house if we'd come back to live. It was to the north of us. Burned down in '87. This house was his house. The home that held so many horrible memories.

"'It's better to have your farm than work for someone else,'" he lowered his voice into a low, menacing growl. "'I didn't want anything to do with him. But Eva said we need to forgive. 'We throw away our future by dwelling on the past.' Those were the words she said."

I said, "Very wise sounding. She must have been special."

"She was more than special. By the summer of '59, we had three children of our own. I stayed as far away from his part of the property as I could and things seemed to work out. My father was dreadful to live with but wasn't a bad neighbor. And he had his drinking buddies, so I didn't see him all that much. Things were going good and I was making something of myself.

"But then the war came. The military gave me two options: go and fight Yankees or get shot. Not the best choice in the world, you know. So, I enlisted, along with my friend Blackjack Morris. We called him Blackjack because he loved losing at card games. He tried to stay home with his wife and three children. He thought he had a good excuse. About three years earlier, he was in a hunting accident. Got what made him a man shot clean off."

I blushed but kept quiet.

"I picked him up and got him to a doctor and we saved him. He had marriage problems after that, of course. Cindy Lou, his wife wanted more children…so to speak. Not to mention he was the joke of Nueville after that. Nobody wants to be laughed at. Especially over something like that."

"Well, we got them to sell their farm and move down here. They bought a small farm on the other side of the Atchafalaya River. Only we four knew what happened next. Blackjack, Cindy Lou, Eva, and me. I visited them regularly and Cindy Lou had a few more babies. Nobody down here knew about Blackjack's…problem or what happened to him. Everything was good. Eva didn't like it much, but she tolerated my adultery so the Morris family could grow and thrive. A good farmer has children to help him work the land.

"The army doctor was discreet about Blackjack's…issue, but he was just too healthy to stay home. So, we went to war together. Fought together at Shiloh. Then we were stationed at Vicksburg during the siege. We slipped out right before it fell.

"We went to Shreveport and wound up in the kitchen for a while. Cleaning pots and peeling potatoes. General Kirby Smith really didn't do a whole lot after Vicksburg. Just defended what land he had left. It was tedious and boring.

"Well, we deserted after that. It was obvious the war was over. The old men in Richmond just prolonged it for some stupid reason. We went north for a while because we knew we had to hide out or be shot as deserters if they caught us.

"It was all easy enough. We found a couple of dead soldiers on a battlefield after a skirmish and took their tags and left ours on their bodies. Everyone thought we were dead. I thought we were being clever, but that was the worst mistake I ever made.

"We joined up with Quantrill's raiders, but that was a dead end. They didn't even fight soldiers. Just killed and plundered farmers and unarmed country folk. Folks like us. There'd be no mercy for him and what was left of his men when the war was over. It wasn't long before we decided it was time to find something else to do.

"We joined a crew of like-minded friends and patiently followed Sherman's army. Those troops were monsters.

Pure evil. They broke into raiding parties and pillaged, raped, and murdered anyone who got in their way. When they got drunk and passed out, we crept into their campsites and robbed them blind.

"Every so often they weren't drunk enough to stay passed out, so it became a skirmish. But, since our guns were in our hands and they had to find theirs, we always won quickly. We found an old, abandoned mausoleum to store our loot in so the horses weren't overloaded. By spring of 1865, there were a lot of us. And a lot of bluebellies doing the same thing. We decided to quit and go home. We had enough gold and jewels to satisfy us and Georgia was picked clean. We went to our treasure, divided it up and went our separate ways. By the way, no vampire was in the tomb waiting for us."

"I figured as much," I deadpanned.

"Deserters were everywhere. No one knew or cared about me or Blackjack so it was safe to come home. I dropped old Blackjack at his house and went home. When I rode in, everything was wrong. The place was an abandoned, overgrown mess. I came here to see where my family was at.

"My God, what I found here. It was worse than any Greek tragedy. All the years of mental cruelty and beatings destroyed my sister and he took advantage of her. Right in front of my mother. She tried to stop it and he hit her so hard she lost her awareness. My brother spent the days passed out on laudanum. Useless as always.

"Then they got word I died in battle and that hell spread over to my family. My father convinced Eva to bring the children to his house. Took advantage of her grief and helplessness. Got her pregnant, all while my sister was expecting. Then afterwards, he sent my children to Baton

Rouge to live in an orphanage. Said they might not be mine and he didn't want them. She was going to leave with them, but he locked her in the bedroom until he came back from the station. That all happened right here in this house. In that room. The one I walled shut."

He pointed to the wall behind us.

"I trounced my brother into the ground for letting it happen. Don't think he felt any of my punches or kicks. Didn't make a noise, anyway. All doped up on laudanum. I couldn't do anything like that to the others. They were women.

"'How could you let this happen?' I screamed in my sister's face. 'How could you let your own father do this to you?'

"Well, she was crying too, all upset. Then she let me have it with her own little family secret.

"'He's not my father.'

"'What? Sure he is. He's been your father all your life. Just because you did unnatural things with him don't change that.'

"'No,' she said, 'He's your father. He's my step-father.'

"I looked at my mother, just sitting there in that ruined body, and she nodded.

"'Who was your father?' I had to ask; the anger gone for a moment.

"'Bartholomew De Pilord.'"

I was stunned. "Your family was bound to the De Pilord family? The countess?"

"That's right. Her husband's uncle was my sister's real father. He was not the cream of the crop for that family. But what do you expect from a group of people who pretend to be royalty when they're just a bunch of crooks and foundlings? It seems that Bartholomew was a professional gambler and drunk. Then one day an ace fell out of his sleeve and the other players filled him with lead."

"I thought that was what happened to your father."

"Don't believe everything you hear. Nobody ever gets these stories right except me. The rest of them always add or remove details to make their family line look better than what they are.

"Anyway, I waited for my drunk miscreant father to come home and I shot him down. Told my brother to take him to the storm cellar and bury him deep, because if I had to do it, there'd be two graves.

"Nobody missed him. His drinking buddies never asked about him. Neither did anyone else. The whole town figured he got drunk and fell in the river and drowned. Someone thought we should organize a search party, but that idea didn't pan out for lack of interest.

"When my mother died a couple of weeks later, I gave them all her money and sent them all off, including Eva. Don't know or care where they went. I searched high and low for my own children. No orphanage ever said they received them. They were lost forever. The people who let it happen just needed to get out of my life, especially Eva."

"But Eva was your wife," I said.

"She cheated on me. She was having another man's baby. I couldn't be with her after that. It wasn't right."

The sheer unfairness of it was breathtaking.

"But Cindy Lou had *three* of your babies. You cheated on Eva. And besides she was forced into it."

"That was different. What's acceptable for a man isn't acceptable for a woman. We live by different rules. Besides, she agreed with my…understanding with the Morris family. Blackjack understood why I did what I did. Cindy Lou was like you. Thought it was unfair. That ended my visits over there, in fact. I was completely alone in my own home."

"You didn't have to be," I said softly.

"Try to understand. It wasn't just another man's baby. It was my *father's* baby. My nephew. I could never get over something like that.

"Then one day I got a little drunk and went to the storm cellar to piss on my father's grave. And there they were. Three little graves. I found them. Next to the demon who killed them. That chapter of my life was over.

"Oddly enough, that gave me closure. All my anger and bitterness just went away. I even remarried. But she died of the fever soon after. We didn't have any children. I just decided to be alone and write my stories.

"Since I was the only educated man left in town without responsibilities, they asked me to be the teacher for a year until they could find a permanent one. I was a bit of a disciplinarian at first. I wanted to be a perfect teacher and mold together perfect students, but that doesn't work. Ask Mrs. Porter. After a while, those students became replacements for the children I lost. I loved them all, though they may not have known it. It didn't bother me that it took them over forty years to find another teacher."

"That's such a sad story," I said softly. I reached over and held his hand, even though I was somewhat angry at him for throwing away his wife.

He squeezed my hand.

"That's my family secret, not your family secret," he said, shaking the hurt off. "It's what happened before. Remember what I said about Cindy Lou Morris and me? We had three children together, with Blackjack's blessing. One of them was Nathaniel Morris."

I waited for an explanation.

"Nathaniel Morris married Louisa Faucette. I think she

had six children. One has a name you might be familiar with: Abigail Morris De Montfort."

"Gramma De Montfort?"

"My granddaughter. That makes you my great-great-granddaughter. That's why you've been reading to me. So, you can get to know your family roots."

Dracula would always be anticlimactic to me after that day.

I was almost in a state of shock when I got back to the café. Lila was stunned when she heard his story.

"That's so much worse than I thought," she said. "That man is harmless now, but in his day, he was hell on earth. A lot of the old people, the ones in their seventies today, have nothing to do with him. Didn't want to send their kids to school either but had no choice. I knew there was something to it. And all those stories he wrote…"

She shook her head.

Almost immediately after we quieted our conversation, I saw the familiar fedora silhouette move across the window to the door. Hugo Landacre walked in and stepped up to the counter.

"Hello, Amy," he said pleasantly. "May I have a glass of iced tea?"

"Of course, Mr. Landacre."

I zoomed over to the pitcher and poured him a tall glass. I thought he might want to speak to me so I made a point of wiping down the counter near enough to where he could see me, but he just sipped and stared straight ahead. Then he snapped his head down and looked at his watch.

"I have to go now," he said and gave me a dollar. He walked out without worrying about his change.

"What's he doing here?" Lila asked. "He never used to come here. If Paul saw him in here, one of them would have to be carried out."

I shrugged. "But it's nice to get a dollar for a five-cent glass of tea. Too bad he doesn't come in every night."

"Your mother would throw that tip in his face and Paul would pound it up his behind."

"Ouch. That is one serious feud."

"You come from a serious family."

And I had one serious adventure the next morning. I was up before five. I had to move over Holly which sadly woke her up. I told her to go back to sleep, but she was more awake than I was, so we got up together. She chatted a mile a minute about our adventure down the creek. She reminded me to use good adventure etiquette.

"Be careful, find treasure, avoid quicksand, beware of zombies. We do live close to New Orleans, you know. Don't let any of the boys kiss you and if they try, hit them. Be kind. Say please. Be sure to say thank you. And remember, I just love pearls."

"That's all very good advice," I replied, suppressing a smile. "Except for the hitting people part. I learned my lesson good about that sort of thing."

I had my knapsack and pronounced myself ready when Merry came to walk with me over to Jonathan's place so I wouldn't get lost. Mom and Gramma Morris let her in and asked her all kinds of questions about her family and the plans of the day. They were soon satisfied that we would have a fun and harmless day boating down the creek.

"It's really close. It's just off the main road. Where your place backs up to the Malmort, their place ends at the creek. We have plenty of room in the canoe for all the treasure we find. We have two empty seats in the boat, you know."

"Two empty seats." Holly's eyes lit up. "Can I go too? I'm small enough."

"You're almost as big as me and Jonathon didn't invite you."

"Not because he doesn't want me. Because he doesn't know me."

I turned to Merry for help, but she just shrugged.

"She can walk with us to the boat, I suppose, and let the others decide, but I won't say they'll let her. The walk is close enough, she can get back home if they say no."

Thanks, Merry.

"Well, in that case," Mom decided, "she can walk with you and see the boat. If they let her come, then she's good. If not, she will…" and she looked right at Holly with those eyes that could be so intimidating, "say thank you and come back home without sulking. She can do things here or go visit her own friends that are her age."

No help there.

"And be back for dinner."

"We will," I said, as if I had any idea how long we would be.

I was happy I woke Holly up instead of Anna Marie. I thought Holly would explode from the excitement.

Our first adventure without a single adult near us was going to be fun. We said our good-byes and headed out. The walk was less than a mile down an unmarked road in the opposite direction of the school.

They were all there, ready to go. Jonathon had the wooden boat loaded on a wagon already. It was long and wide with smooth sides and was obviously well cared for. A perfect vessel for the little creek. But a horse was hitched to the wagon and Jonathon's older brother, Ricky, was holding the reins.

They eyed Holly with suspicion but relented when she asked politely if she could come with us.

"You can come, I suppose," Jonathon sighed. "But if we find as much gold as I think we'll find, somebody will have to stay behind until we get a second trip going."

"I'll stay," I said, feeling guilty that I brought her when she really wasn't invited.

"I'll keep you company," Elizabeth offered with a laugh. "It'll be fun. We can protect each other from the swamp creatures. I brought a wood cross to keep the zombies away."

It was a little over a foot long with rounded edges and lots of swirls. The beige paint sparkled in the morning sunlight. It was beautiful.

David said, "I'll stay with them. They'll need a man to keep them protected." He tried to appear brave and fearless but looked rather small and ineffective instead.

"Thank you, Sir Knight," Elizabeth curtsied perfectly.

I wished I could curtsy like that.

"Anything for you, my fair damsel."

Oh please.

He bowed and went to help the boys load the wagon.

"I wish I kept my mouth shut," Elizabeth sighed, obviously not happy with this new development. "He just doesn't get sarcasm."

"I'm not going with you," Ricky said. "I have chores to do, but Pa doesn't want you ruining the bottom of the boat pushing it to the Malmort, so I'm just taking you there. I don't have time for this kind of foolishness."

"Oh?" Jonathon asked innocently, "What kind of foolishness do you have time for?"

We all giggled at that come back.

When she was surprised, Merry always spoke in questions. "Wait a minute? We're going on the Malmort? I thought we were going on the creek?" she asked.

"Well, yeah, Carmen and Ron's parents won't let them go on the Malmort. We had to say it's Faucette Creek. What's the difference? They both head in the same direction."

He pointed to the X on the map. "Besides, the treasure's on the Malmort."

"That makes sense," I said cautiously. I thought it was very daring to ride down the river their parents specifically forbade them to go on.

The others nodded and we hopped on the wagon and headed towards adventure.

Once the boat was laid on the ground, we loaded it with supplies while Ricky rode away. Jonathon sat in the back, between Merry and me. Holly, Elizabeth and Ron were in front of us. Carmen and David sat in the very front and looked at the map to get our bearings. It was pretty straightforward. About two miles of river then it bends east towards Faucette Creek and there we'd find a long sand bar on the other side of the river. Behind the sandbar was a house where the treasure was buried.

"Okay, everyone," David clapped his hands like we just finished an important meeting. "Comfort breaks. Guys to the right, girls to the left. I don't think you want to get out in the swamp to pee."

We all did as we were told, since it was an excellent idea. The boys were waiting for us when we returned.

"Yeah," Jonathon was saying, "we could just go over the side, but the girls would have to hang out. Might capsize the boat."

"It's the price they pay," Ron said knowingly. "When guys pee, it's piss. When girls pee, it's perfume."

"Did he just say that?" Elizabeth whispered to Merry through clenched teeth.

I think he was expecting a shocked laugh from us, but all he got was a stunned silence.

"Now I know why your sisters smell so much different than the other girls," Jonathon said dryly.

That got the expected laughter.

"Well, I suppose this is better than last year," Carmen said to me.

"Yeah," Lizzy added, "they had a private club at Ron's house with a big sign that said, 'No Girls Allowed.' Sheesh."

"Well, this does sound like a step forward," I replied.

"I think they took the sign down too soon," Carmen called back with a laugh.

It was time to push the boat off into the river. Merry and I got that job since we were in the back seat. Jonathon couldn't help because he was carrying the map. A weak excuse, we thought, but we wanted to go, not argue. The current swished us along at a good clip. We hardly used the paddles. Jonathon used his the most because it became the rudder that steered the boat.

We were soon searching for landmarks as we glided down the brown waters of the River of Bad Death. It had a sickly yellow cast to it and smelled like a cross between a hint of death and rotten eggs. Holly made a face and held her nose in distaste.

"That's okay," I told her. "The river flows through the sulfur rock of Devil's Basin in the Sulfur Hills on its way here. Aren't you glad we don't live near Devil's Basin?"

She nodded and all the others agreed.

"Hey Elizabeth," David called out from the front of the boat, "you know what's more dangerous than a zombie?"

"What?" she asked innocently.

"This." He leaned forward in a squat and passed out the

noisiest fart I ever heard. Worse than anything from the theater.

Holly looked at me with eyes wide in surprise and disgust.

"Boys are different," I said.

The air almost changed color from the noxious fumes he released. The only thing to do now was hold our breath. Poor little Holly had to close her eyes as well. After we all recovered, Ron sent him a withering look.

"Did you eat raw skunk butts for breakfast?" he deadpanned.

Much as we didn't want to, we all laughed, even Holly.

"You must have had some of Amy's beans," Carmen said.

I was mortified.

"How did you even know about that?" I asked defensively.

"She didn't mean anything by it," Merry told me. "And everybody in town heard about it. My father thought it was low class. I think my mother did too, but it's hard to tell because she was laughing so much."

Jonathon said, "My dad knows those people and laughed the whole night away."

"My dad wanted to buy you dinner for doing that, but my mom put the kibosh on that idea," Carmen called back.

"Oh yeah, we all know that story. And you can hit like a mule too," Elizabeth said.

Ron told us, "It was great when David Nye yelled out, 'Three cheers for fresh air.' I about fell off the chair."

"Mess around with Amy Collins at your own risk," Jonathon added. "But we don't care. We don't mess around with anyone. Either you're our friend or we leave you be."

"Well, be my friends then," I said cheerfully. "I don't

give a hill of beans for what anyone says."

There were a few appreciative groans and we drifted on.

"Let's just keep the mustard gas bottled up," Ron told David. "We might need it if we run into zombies."

David called out, "About two miles down, the river bends and that's where we'll find the sand bar. We'll paddle around the bar to the bank. There are some old posts where there used to be a pier. We'll tie up there and find a path that takes us to the ruins of the old house. There's a big live oak in the back and the outhouse. The treasure is buried right between them. X marks the spot."

Jonathon pushed the map at Merry and me and pointed to the small X near the center.

"Where are we at?" Merry asked him.

"Here. At the top."

"That's only two miles? Looks a lot longer," she said doubtfully.

"It's the scale of the map."

"Oh."

We were having so much fun.

We had paddles for the boat, shovels and a pick for digging, and lunch for eating. Elizabeth pulled out her cross and held it in her lap to ward off zombies since there might be some on guard to prevent marauders like us from stealing the loot. We had lots of space for carrying back treasure. We were true adventurers, soon to be *rich*.

Holly was fidgeting with excitement. I told her to calm down, but she didn't.

"How did you get the map?" I asked.

"I found it."

"That was a helpful answer," Merry said dryly.

"Where?" Carmen added

"In the library. It was folded up in a book, *The Life and*

Adventures of Jean Lafitte. It's got to be his very own map."

Merry and I looked at it. It was on old ledger paper with ruled lines that didn't seem right. Merry figured it out.

"David, this paper is from an old catalogue, one of those blank order forms in the front. The left side would be torn when it was pulled out of the book. This is just a piece of old paper."

"Well, yeah, it was copied from his map," he said defensively.

"How do you know?" she persisted.

"Because it was in the book. Whoever copied it must have had the original and had to return it somewhere before they caught him."

"Before who caught him?"

"Other treasure hunters," he said with obvious annoyance. "So he copied the original map and hid it in the book. Then something happened and he never came back for it. Now we have it. and all that gold and doubloons and pieces of eight and jewels and who knows what else.

"Let's go, me buckos," he yelled out. "Fortune waits for no one."

CHAPTER 43

BAD PLANNING MADE OBVIOUS

"Look, there's a snake," Carmen called out from the front after a moment.

Holly and I saw the brown head effortlessly swimming in the opposite direction of us, followed by its undulating body.

"Naw, it's a twig," Jonathon dismissed the claim without looking.

"Going upstream?" Carmen asked.

He shrugged, "Strange things happen on the Malmort."

Another one swam alongside us for a bit, glancing at the boat before changing its course towards land.

"Was that a twig?" Holly looked back at me.

"No, that was a cottonmouth," David replied calmly.

"I thought you said they don't come out yet," Merry said to Jonathon.

"They don't come out till spring," he replied.

"It *is* spring," Elizabeth said, annoyed.

"No, it's not," Jonathon said in his best scholarly voice, "Spring doesn't start until March 21st and today is only the 20th."

"Did he just say that?" Elizabeth asked us all in disbelief.

"Snakes go by the weather, not calendars," David called back.

"Yeah, they can't even read one," Ron agreed.

"Billy Kaker can read one," Holly said to me.

"Two legged snakes don't count," I replied.

"There's another one," Carmen called out.

"Is there any water in this river or is it all snakes?" Merry whispered sharply to Jonathon.

"Okay, okay, I miscalculated. So, keep your hands in the boat."

"Miscalculated?" Merry said in disbelief. "Elizabeth, does that cross work on snakes and swamp creatures?"

"Let's hope we don't have to find out," she called back, waving it over the water for divine protection.

"Hey, look. There's a log heading our way. Right there," David called out. "To the left there. Don't hit it."

"That's no log. That's an alligator," Carmen corrected.

"Wow, that has to be seven feet long."

"Okay," Jonathon said, at last sounding a little worried, "*really* keep your hands in."

Holly started crying. She made like she was going to try to get in the back seat next to me, which could have seriously negative consequences.

"No, don't do that. We're having an adventure. It's not an adventure if we don't get a little scared," I reassured her.

"That's right," Elizabeth agreed, squeezing Holly's trembling shoulder. "The boys know what they're doing."

"Of course, they do," I told her with all the fake confidence I could muster.

"Hey, Jon?" said Elizabeth. "Is it much further?"

"Maybe a mile. The river turns and we'll see the sandbar."

From the corner of my eye, I saw an enormous alligator,

over twice as long as the boat, splash into the water from the far shore. Merry and I looked at each other. I knew her heart skipped a beat, just like mine. Holly tugged at Elizabeth's sleeve and pointed.

"It's a dinosaur."

"No, sweetie," Elizabeth soothed. "It's just an alligator. A big, slimy, disgusting alligator. But not a dinosaur."

"Where are all the paddles?" Merry hissed to the others. "Let's help the current get us out of here."

"It's alright," Jonathon said, continuing on his course of being wrong every time he spoke. "They're just as scared of us as we are of them."

I hope.

"I don't know, Jonathon," said Merry. "I'm pretty scared of it."

"And it doesn't look particularly scared at all," Elizabeth observed.

It seemed to changed course and go upstream and we all breathed a sigh of relief.

"I want to go home," said Holly.

"Yeah, so do I," said Merry, while Elizabeth and Carmen furiously nodded their heads in agreement. "I mean, look at the sky. It's getting cloudy all of a sudden. I don't want to go on in the rain with all these creepy crawlies around us. Especially if they're hungry."

Dark clouds *were* filling the northern sky, transforming the morning blue into steely gray. These were not the fluffy white clouds of a pleasant spring day. These gray clouds promised rain for weeks. The greenery was getting darker as the sun was slowly being blocked. A cool wind blew at us from the north.

"It's warm now, but it'll be cold after the rain falls," David said casually.

Merry reasoned, "Maybe we should go back and try again in the fall."

"No," Jonathon said through clenched teeth, "we're here now. We just barely left."

"We can be here in November too," I suggested softly.

"That's not a good idea," he replied reasonably enough. "Someone else might get there first. Besides, the current is moving too fast. If we turn around and paddle back, we'll just stay stationary until we get tired and then we'll follow the current anyway."

I thought about that while looking at Merry.

"Hey, Jon, if we can't paddle against the current, how were you planning on getting back?" I asked, already knowing the answer but hoping for something better than reality.

There was a long pause while everyone listened for the response.

"Well, we'll have treasure."

That was the answer I expected.

"How will we get the treasure back home?"

"We'll figure it out. I didn't plan that far ahead."

"Good question, Amy," Merry whispered to me. "Why didn't you ask it *before* we all got in the boat?"

Elizabeth giggled nervously, but I could tell she was not amused.

Jonathon was getting exasperated. "Will you stop worrying? You act like a bunch of girls."

David chimed in, "You know, if the girls are scared, maybe we should pull over and think this through a bit more."

A bit?

"Good idea," Elizabeth said. "I'm sure we can figure out a way back."

"Yeah," I agreed, "we're smart. We can get back. I just know it."

I hope.

"Let's just follow the map," Jonathon said. "Why turn around now with nothing? Just a little further and we'll be there. And we'll be rich. Then we can figure out how to get home. No sense in giving up before we get there. 'God helps him who helps himself.' And I just know great things are about to happen."

CHAPTER 44

ATTACK

A tremendous *whump* sounded right behind me, followed by splintering wood and the boat went spinning wildly in a circle. Everybody screamed and looked to where the smashing roar originated. There it was. That monster-alligator had swum behind us and hit the boat with its scaley head. The sneak attack knocked us all off balance.

I was pushed back into Jonathon and reached around him to grab Merry to prevent her from falling overboard. The side was splintered a bit from the attack, but we were still afloat.

Holly was too shaken up to cry but I could tell she was terrified. Elizabeth had an arm around her and was whispering in her ear. Carmen was helping the boys paddle the boat to shore. The rest of us could only watch as the reptile swam up and hit us again. This time the boat completely capsized. Everyone was thrashing through the muddy cold water trying to get back to land. The boat floated downstream while it slowly submerged to its final resting spot.

"We lost the sandwiches," Ron yelled out, both angry and disappointed.

"The hell with the sandwiches," Jonathon answered. "My father's boat!"

"Where's that gator?" Carmen yelled out.

"Where's Holly?" I yelled.

That horrible beast was underwater and lurking out of sight, waiting for one of us to make a mistake. I could have made it to shore easily, but I stopped to look for Holly. I expected her to be next to me since we were so close together on the boat, but somehow, she got separated and I didn't see her at all.

"Holly," I called out.

We were all yelling for her as we swam for shore.

I heard her a second later. She was about ten yards downstream from me, swimming against the current and staying in the same spot in the middle of the river. I focused on getting her to safety. It was an easy swim to reach her since the current was helping me. I swam up behind her and pushed her rear end, propelling her towards the land while kicking as fast as I could. We were in wading territory now, maybe six feet from shore and I was shoving Holly as fast as I could. Merry was already safe but splashed back in and grabbed her. An oar from the ruined boat was floating nearby and I grabbed it, just in case that monster-gator came back.

I reasoned that if I had a weapon and whapped that unholy thing, it would swim back into the river and leave us alone. Holly and Merry were on shore with the others and I hurried towards them.

"Watch out, Amy," Elizabeth and David were yelling out to me. "Hurry, it's behind you."

And it attacked.

The monster's teeth sank into my lower leg and I was dragged to the middle of the river while it shook me like a soggy rag doll. The current carried us downstream at a rapid pace. I saw my friends, safe on the bank watching me in shock and disbelief and then it pulled me underwater.

It dragged me deeper towards the muddy bottom while I tried flailing at it with the oar to no use. I had no leverage and the water made my blows to the head useless. The evil reptilian eyes stared balefully at me as we sank lower. It realized its triumph.

When my knee sank into the river mud, he released me and swam over me. He tried to crush me, but I rolled out of his reach and pushed up towards the surface. That horrible mouth found me again and we repeated the process. It tried to crush me and again I rolled free. Instead of swimming to the surface, I turned and faced downwards.

Alligators attack by squatting down on their tails and using them as a giant spring to push upwards and attack with great speed and momentum. It rushed towards me with an impossible speed. Although it was dark under the water, I saw enough of its wide-open mouth to make my own assault. I aimed the oar handle at his mouth and rammed it as far down as possible, at least three feet. He jerked away and tried shaking his ugly head to dislodge the paddle as I swam up and away as fast as I could.

The whole ordeal couldn't have been longer than three minutes, but my lungs ached for fresh air when I hit the surface. I shook my head to get my bearings. Nobody was there. The boat was gone. I was near the far bank of the river and the sand bar we were searching for reached out into the river just like David's map said it would. It was an easy swim and I climbed on it and collapsed, breathing in as much smelly river air as I could. It was so much better than swallowing the putrid tasting river water.

Unfortunately, the river water was happier in the river

and I went through another bout of digestive rejection. No water closet for privacy, no chamber pot, no comforting words, no nothing. Just make my mess and try to clean up as best I could. I stripped down to nothing and shook my clothes to get the sand and mud off between the bouts of vomiting and diarrhea. I knew I was going to be on another bland diet when they found me but that was the least of my problems.

The cool air was now cold. I got dressed but the wet garments offered me no protection from the weather. A blast of wind attacked my drenched clothes as the rain started falling. Clean water from God was welcomed. I could not believe that I used to go to this foul river just to watch it flow. I wanted to get as far away from it as possible and never see it again.

The rain was falling hard and the temperature dropped precipitously. I shielded my eyes so I could look around and get my bearings. River. Swamp. Trees. There were cypress growing in the shallow part of the river and big, tall pines bending down before the attacking winds.

Although I still felt awful and my leg ached, I knew I had to move on or lie down to sleep. And I knew if I went to sleep, I would never wake up. So, I wrung all the water and sand I could out of my hem and walked down the sandbar to the riverbank.

Water rushed by me in a hurry, carrying branches and stumps. Obviously, this was not the time to swim back across to go home. Especially with those loathsome things lurking below the surface. The rain fell so hard it felt like needles hitting my head. I walked through the wet, slurping sand to the edge of the bar. To my right were a couple of posts that were once a part of a pier.

Was this our destination? If so, there would be a path

leading to the old house. Shelter. Of course, there was about five feet of flowing river between the end of the bar and the first post. That meant going back in the water to get there. I didn't see anything that looked reptilian and since my shoes were sinking in the sand, I realized I had two bad choices. Continue to sink in the sand while waiting for help or wade over to the pier and see if there really was a path that led to refuge from this storm. My feet were sunk into the sand down to my ankles, so I curled my toes and pulled them up one at a time. Decision made.

I squished through the sand to the end of the bar and waded through the soft slimy river bottom to the post. The unclean water made my wounded leg ache worse, but the rain washed off the mud relatively quickly when I stepped back on land. Squishy land, but land. I pushed through a couple of clusters of reeds and made a muddy step up.

I wandered around in a large circle until I found a small, rutted trail a horse-drawn cart used frequently. And more importantly, it was used recently. A ribbon of green grass blew flat from the wind, surrounded by muddy wagon ruts. The wind was getting stronger and colder.

I hurriedly followed the trail. It twisted in a northerly direction, rising as it went. The rain attacked me and the grass around me was flattened into submission by its aggressive thrust. I stayed on the grass between the ruts as I staggered against its fury, knowing the muddy grooves would make me slip and slide. I was completely lost. Although I knew the trail would always get me back to where I started from, the question was: Where did I start from? And with all the deadly animals out there, did I want to go back?

But two things were happening that gave me hope. Seashells were filling in the furrows, meaning at least this much of the trail was important enough to try to keep wagons from sinking in the hungry mud. And the rain was letting up. It was just a sprinkle, but the angry black clouds were as thick as ever.

I continued walking. A barbed wire fence blocked the path with a homemade "keep out" sign, but I was too tired to worry about it. I tore my dress while squeezing through the vicious strands of restraint.

Twilight was falling and I knew it would be dark soon. Continuing down the trail, I followed a long, winding curve that seemed to go on forever. It led me to a clearing.

CHAPTER 45

THE OLD HOUSE

There it stood. It was an old cabin, small and run down. I stepped up on the sagging porch and out of the rain. The door was locked. I checked the frame for a key, but only found dust, the only dry thing I had seen in hours.

An old wooden rocking chair stood lonely and inviting in front of a boarded-up window next to a firewood box that blocked the wind from the east. I found shelter from the storm. Not very warm shelter, but anything was better than being out in the open waiting for the next deluge.

As if on cue, the deluge came harder than before. I couldn't even see two feet off the porch. The weather showed no mercy. Standing water puddles were growing at the edge of the little shack. I sat shivering. The firewood box may have blocked the wind, but a moist draft struck me from all directions. At least I could rock in the chair, using my good leg while sitting on my wounded one. I stared out into the rain and after a while, the cold didn't bother me anymore. I was too tired and sick to feel anything but exhaustion. Even my leg's throbbing didn't bother me.

The rain pounded the roof melodically and I relaxed as the sound faded from a loud cacophony into a soothing melodic rhythm. I closed my eyes while the chair slowed down to a stop.

"Amy, dear."

Her voice was gentle but insistent. At first, I thought it was just an illusion. The barrage of falling rainwater must have melded with my feverish dreaming. But no, I heard it again. It was not rain tones and wishful thinking. It was a real voice. Human and concerned.

I awoke, shivering and wet. The rain had faded into an insistent drizzle, but at least the wind stopped. It was dark. A very old woman stood next to me, leaning on a broom and holding a hurricane lamp to illuminate our faces. She smiled at me with gentle blue eyes.

"You're sick, sweetheart. You need to go in the house," she told me kindly.

She wore extremely old-fashioned clothes; a blue print dress with a white lapel and sleeves that ended with lacey frills. Her hem ended just above her scuffed black shoes. Although her mouth had no trace of a smile, her eyes grinned at me. It's what I noticed first and remembered the most.

"The key is beside that last log, just barely out of sight. You can slide it out with your foot. Go ahead and open it for me while I finish up with the sweeping."

She put the lamp down just below the boarded-up window and swooshed the errant water off the porch while I searched for the key and easily found its hiding place. It was an old-fashioned brass barrel key, so its coloring blended into the wood. I unlocked and opened the door and waited for her to finish.

A cool draft drifted out of the house after a I opened the door. It wasn't as strong as the wind that pummeled me earlier, but the last thing I wanted was more cold air blowing on me.

"We have to keep the water off the wood or it will warp. Get the lamp for me dear, would you please?"

"Yes, ma'am," I replied.

I went back onto the porch and grasped the lantern and quickly returned into the little shack. It was only one room with a table, two chairs, an antique wood burning stove, and a water pump set off in the far corner. A rickety bed was in the next corner, near a stone fireplace with an old railroad tie used as a mantle. A worn-out sofa sprawled out in front of it. The old woman was already at the stove with a cover removed.

"My arthritis always aches me when it rains, but we got a full load of dry wood waiting for us to make soup. Right now, let's get you warmed up a bit. The matches are right here. Get that jar of kerosene off the mantle there, dear. The one with dark fluid."

"Yes, ma'am," I replied.

The only other things on the shelf were old dolls with creepy eyes and a couple of Mardi Gras masks. There were also a few old programs for music festivals dating back to the late 1890's. She stepped over and told me how to pour the kerosene evenly over the kindling at the bottom of the fireplace and had me pull a rusty, blackened screen in front of the flames. After a moment of enjoying the warmth, I lit the stove for her.

"That was quite an adventure, dear. Not many full-grown men could have gotten away from that alligator. None that I know of, anyway.

"How did you know about that?" I asked.

"You smell like river, your clothes stink to high heaven and you have nasty bite marks on your leg. And judging from the teeth marks, it had to be a big one."

She smiled, this time showing her painted wooden teeth.

"And speaking of smelling like river and stinking clothes…"

She showed me where a large pot was hiding behind the stove and I filled it with water to boil. While we were waiting, she had me get a couple of basins out from under the stove and I filled one almost to the top. The other only a quarter of the way. She had me strip down and gave me a washcloth and towel along with a bar of lye soap. I washed the mud river residue off my skin and dried off. When the water was hot, I filled the other basin and washed my clothes, then rinsed out my underwear and shift and set them near the fire to dry while I wrapped up in another dry towel. I pumped water on my head and soaped down my hair at her suggestion. I was rather happy my hair was so short today. It was a lot less work.

The house was warm and I was comfortably wrapped in the towel. She produced a can of Campbell's soup and I made dinner for us. More precise: I ate dinner from a chipped bowl while she watched me.

The heat felt wonderful. We sat together on the couch watching the fire's flames flicker. I was wrapped up in a dry blanket and soon was laying down with my head on her lap while the fire fascinated me with its flames.

The fever was making me weak again and I was getting sleepy, only this time I was content.

"Do you live here?" I asked her.

"For longer than you could imagine," she replied. "I love it here. No matter where you go or what adventures you may have, home is always where you are happiest. But you know that, don't you? You knew from the moment you got off the train that you found home. Your real home."

"I know. And I want to go home now. Can you tell me how to get there?"

"Certainly, Amy, but not now. Right now, you need to rest and rebuild your strength. You had a regular little trauma out there today. And I can tell your fever is coming back."

"How do you know my name?"

"We know all about you, dear. You're family."

"Oh. Well, pardon me please, but who are you?"

"Constanza Faucette," she replied, as though that was the most normal name in the world.

"Constanza Faucette? So you were named after Pierre Faucette's second wife? A lot of my classmates were named after her daughter Catherine."

"You could say that. But right now, I want to tell you a story. It's a simple and sad tale of a young woman who loved the wrong young boy. They said they were going to be married and they spent all their time together. They went to dances and had picnics by the creek. They drank wine together. I think the wine was the villain of the story."

"Alcohol. It gets into a lot of stories for adults. Too bad they can't be like children and just leave it alone."

"Too bad, indeed."

She hummed for a bit.

"The boy genuinely loved the girl. But he truly loved another one too. There came the day he had to choose which one to marry. One girl was happy. One girl was disappointed. If only she made better decisions. If only she didn't drink that wine."

"Alcohol," I repeated sleepily. "My father, my real father from New York, died because of it."

"Your father from New York was your real father?" she asked with a smile.

"He loved me more than my mother ever did. And I never had to call him uncle."

"Then Michael Collins was a wonderful father. He knew how to love his family. That is the mark of a good soul. No matter what things you find out about him, always remember he was good to you."

"You're not going to say something bad about him like everyone else?"

"Would it do any good? All that matters is he loved you very much."

"He did," I agreed. I didn't even wonder how she knew his name.

She told me many things about my family history and the town. Her words were soothing and musical and I felt myself nodding.

The story played in my head while I slept a feverish sleep with hallucinations and visions. I was in the white place again. Michael Collins was there, saying 'I'm sorry. I hope you know I love you.'

"I do. I love you too. You'll always be my Papa. My first Papa."

Mrs. Carnahan was there and smiled at me. I tried to apologize for her violin getting smashed, but she didn't care about that. She cared about me.

There were other faces, other voices, but none I would remember. But I recalled old conversations that had meanings I didn't understand at the time.

"Call me Aunt Mary from now on. I'm too young to be your mother."

"Call me Mama. Every little girl needs her mama."

"Is she your daughter or niece? You make it hard to keep track."

"Fertile Myrtle."

"You'll come work for me."

"Remember, when you're a Landacre, your problems disappear."

Soon there was nothing but white. No more memories. No more stories. No more dreams. I was drifting away, unable to remember anything. Not wanting to remember. I was content.

And then I saw Harvey Kaker. He wasn't sinister anymore. He seemed pleasant. He even spoke to me.

"It's not your time."

CHAPTER 46

OLD FRIENDS AND A NEW JOURNEY

"Oh my God. Is that her?" I heard.

"Is she…" another voice.

"No, but she's in bad shape."

"Amy?"

I woke up and saw Constanza.

"Aunt Mary really was my aunt, wasn't she? My real Mama is Aunt Cassie. That's why she wants me to call her 'Mom.'"

But her face melted away into Helen Farley, who answered, "Of course, Cassie's your Mom. Would your real Mom ever send an angel like you away?"

I was still on the couch. The fire was gone, replaced by ashes. Reba Farley was arranging more wood in the hearth. The rain had stopped and the sun was shining through the open door.

"Then Michael Collins wasn't my real father."

"No, I don't think so," she said, eyeing me shrewdly. "But then, I think you know who your real father is."

I nodded. "I'm a Landacre. Only I don't have that name. Michael Collins may have done some bad things. But he was still a good man. And he gave me his name. And Collins is a good name."

Reba Farley came up to me. "Sure it is. It suits you well. Would any other family raise you to just barge into someone's house, throw her clothes around and use our clean towels without rinsing them off? Who else would raise their child to get mud everywhere, open food that doesn't belong to her and leave the can and bowl on the table for someone else to clean up, and then just go to sleep?"

"Shush, Reba," Helen said crossly. "The child is hurt and feverish."

"I'm sorry. Constanza said I could. She helped me with the fire and blanket."

"Who?" they both said at once, looking at each other.

"Constanza Faucette. The nice old woman who lives here," I replied weakly.

Reba put an ice-cold hand on my forehead.

"She's burning up.,"

I drifted back to sleep. Whatever I dreamed after that, I don't remember.

I do remember being forced to sit up so they could get me into my dry clothes. They helped me walk back down the trail to the river. When I was too tired to go on, they half carried, half dragged me through the moist, almost cold forest.

"Did she see the still?" Reba hissed at Helen.

"It doesn't matter. She won't remember it."

"I didn't see it," I said. "That was the treasure between the tree and the outhouse? Just a still?"

Reba snorted.

"Just a still? It's treasure enough for some folks. Treasure enough to keep us in business, even though those government people want to destroy it and those mobsters want to take it for their own."

"It's *our* treasure," Helen said kindly. "It's not pirate ship gold and anything so imaginative. But it is hidden because some people want to steal it. Other people want to smash it. But that still keeps us in this boat. It's better than pirate treasure, you know? After all, you can't drink gold."

"Makes you sick if you tried," Reba agreed.

"And it would be hard to swallow," Helen added helpfully.

"Can't be worse than Malmort water," I muttered.

"No," she agreed with a nod, "not if it tastes like it smells. You're the expert on that subject."

The houseboat was moored to one of the pilings and Reba grabbed a rope from its side and pulled it close to us and climbed on to lower the gangplank. I was guided on board to the main cabin where I was laid down on a cot.

"Give her a shot of the shine," Reba said.

"What? She's ten."

"Water it down some then. It'll do her good. Here. Put this cloth on her forehead. I just wet it down and it's nice and cool. That will help with the fever."

They sat me up. That moonshine was liquid fire. I could only gasp at the burning sensation as I thought about the blackened cinders of what used to be my stomach. It took a while for the burning pain to go away.

But then something felt wrong. I had forgotten something important. But what? Another dream? Another conversation about who I was? What could be important under these circumstances? It was something vital, I was sure. But what? I was physically uncomfortable with not remembering.

And then I realized what it was.

Breathing.

I forgot how to breathe.

I gasped down air and panted in and out until I was back to normal.

"That was helpful?" I tried to say but my voice came out as a breathy squeak. "I'd rather drink the gold."

"It didn't hurt," Reba replied briskly.

"Not you."

"And you're not getting gold to drink. Waste of good money."

I would never recommend giving moonshine to a child, but it helped. They later told me that my dull, yellow, uncomprehending eyes brightened up afterwards.

The cloth on my head was like ice, but it felt good. I was so hot from the fever on the outside and the moonshine on the inside. I may have been sick, but I was content.

Reba was starting the boat's engine. Helen left me for a moment to remove the mooring cables and the houseboat slowly exited the piling. She sat me up so she could sit next to me and leaned my head on her shoulder.

"Poor dear," she soothed. "We'll get you home."

I nodded. I was too awake to go back to sleep but too delirious to stay in reality.

"Do you know who Constanza Faucette even was?"

"She lived in that house," I replied with a phlegmy cough.

"She was Pierre Faucette's second wife."

"I know. She told me."

The cloth was slipping from my hand. She caught it and waved it in the air before putting it back.

"What else did she tell you?" she humored me.

"It was a misunderstanding. The first family had a father to teach them skills and trades and they inherited some cash and all the property east of the Atchafalaya. The second family could only watch him waste away, so they got all the land west of it. The second family came out ahead, but they considered it a fair division. Good or bad, that was their decision. None of their children complained. Besides, all the descendants have so intermarried that most everybody in town is descended from both lines. To hate one line means to hate yourself."

"The Bible says something like that. To hate someone different than you is like hating God," she said.

"A lot of people hereabouts hate God then," Reba called back.

Helen rolled her eyes and squeezed me close while we watched the shoreline slowly crawl along beside us as we chugged upstream. Then Reba made a sharp turn. The bottom of the boat groaned a bit as we dragged on the slimy bottom.

Helen wince at the noise.

"Are you sure the water's high enough?"

"No choice," Reba called back gruffly. "Unless you want to get out and carry her."

"We're on Faucette Creek now, Amy," she told me as if I didn't hear their little exchange.

"That's nice," I replied.

The bite on my leg was really starting to hurt. Otherwise, I think I would have fallen asleep again.

"Hey, you," Reba yelled to someone on land.

His silhouette was in the shadows so I couldn't see who she was talking to, but the body shape said it was one of the Foyts, riding alone on horseback.

"Ride on to Doc Gannon's and have him meet us at the café. We have Amy Collins. And she's alive."

She settled back next to me and said, "Your poor Mom's been weeping all this time like her heart was broken."

"Half the town went calling just to say they were so sorry for how they treated you and her," Reba called back. "Your Gramma Morris is planning a memorial service for you at the Baptist church on Friday, and the Catholic church is letting out so your friends there can attend. You've been gone since Saturday, you know."

"What is today?" I asked.

The fresh cool air was doing me good. I was still weak and feverish, but I was at least awake.

"Wednesday," Helen answered. "And everybody's been so worried about you. Every boat, canoe, raft, or anything that floats is on the river looking for you. Everyone thinks you died."

"Why are they looking for me then?"

"To give you a good Christian burial of course. Who wants their remains inside an alligator's stomach slowly getting turned into alligator…stuff."

I glanced at my injured leg. Angry red streaks were moving up from the teeth punctures.

"Did they get the alligator?"

"No, but everybody's looking for it," Reba called out.

"And I mean everybody," Helen emphasized. "Every alligator that could be found was killed cold dead. Got some big ones too. But nothing like the one that attacked your boat. Judging from the damage it caused, they figured it had to be over seventeen feet long. The biggest one they got was only about twelve feet. They were happy there was no trace of you inside it's stomach, but with each day, hope grew smaller. Even so, the past three days were rough in alligator-land. At least two dozen of the critters were executed. Nobody cares if they were the guilty one or not. No such thing as an innocent alligator, you know."

"And poor Cici's been making alligator soup, stew,

steak, and alligator popcorn all day every day," Reba called back as the boat bottomed out again.

"Alligator popcorn?"

"Yep, cut into popcorn sized pieces and deep fried. They've been giving it away to the search parties. People are coming all the way from Baton Rouge to be here," Reba said.

"For alligator popcorn?"

"No, silly. For you," Helen chuckled. "But they need something to eat, you know. And then there are all these alligator corpses just lying there, so they got turned into food. And Ely Foyt took the rest and skinned them and started sending the hides to New Orleans for shoes and purses and things."

Reba continued, "And there are still lots of live ones out there, just swimming around and causing problems. Just waiting to be executed until we find that killer."

"The crowds are astounding," Helen said. "The café can barely keep up with the orders. The hardware store had to send a car to Baton Rouge twice for ammo. People are staying overnight at the hotels and boarding houses, and the butcher and bakery have non-stop customers. One man brought his fiancée here after one night and she ordered her wedding dress at Betsy's and five bridesmaids' gowns as well.

"And you know, you've been gone for three days and nights. Depjim told us to come back to our camp to pick up some shine and wine to keep everybody warm, so we're getting a couple of dollars profit as well as having the privilege of bringing you home."

"Your death has been the best thing to happen to this town since the governor visited," Reba added some practicality to the conversation.

"Oh. How nice."

The alligator bite on my leg was beginning to throb.

"The governor called by the way," Reba added. "He's mighty unhappy this happened. Says to Depjim and the Mayor, what kind of town you got down there? You can't keep one little girl safe for even one week? So, he sent in the state police. Betsy's new beau, Rob? He's been here all week. Sleeping in her shop, though people wonder if he's sneaking into the house at night."

"I'm sure he's not."

"Don't be too sure. Betsy's a fine-looking woman."

"Prettiest one I ever saw," I agreed. "But isn't he kind of…shy?"

"No man's that shy. And she's not getting any younger, you know. And here he is, single, handsome, sort of, employed with the government, vouched for by the governor himself, and riding the train all the way out here just to see her. Either something's going on or they're going to get married. You just mark my words."

"Nothing's going on," Helen said definitively. "He's out all day on a boat searching the shoreline for the body."

"What body?"

"Your body, Amy," Reba replied, exasperated. "Everyone thinks you're dead. Remember? Why do you think there's all this activity going on? You don't know how lucky you are you found our cabin. You'd have died of exposure out there. We had frost every night. How come you didn't run out of wood? We never bring in more than a day's worth."

"Constanza Faucette chopped some for me."

"Constanza Faucette again? Child, she's been dead for centuries."

"But it was her," I protested weakly. "She told me where

the key was to get in. She had me light the fire and cook the soup, showed me where the towels and blankets were kept. She helped me wash my clothes and talked to me."

I paused for a second.

"Actually, on second thought, I think I did everything. She just told me where the things I needed were stored."

"If you say so, dear," Helen said.

Well, that certainly stopped the conversation. Just as well. The houseboat slowly brought Faucette closer, although it seemed to slide on the bottom of the creek more often than glide across its surface. The tall pines were swaying in a cool breeze, whispering secrets that only trees could understand. Some crows flew overhead, cawing out a greeting in bird talk. The scenery changed slightly with each second but stayed the same. It was peaceful, quiet and serene, with life and death chases and battles always just out of sight and sound. I understood why the Farley sisters lived in the houseboat.

The last curve gave way to the bakery. I saw the Baptist church in the distance. The fish market and butcher shops were ahead and I could see my final destination—the Faucette Café.

CHAPTER 47

ARRIVAL AND RECUPERATION

There was a large crowd waiting for us. They were cheering and throwing hats in the air. Mom and Dad were the closest. Holly was jumping and dancing around in glee. Cici was at the back door waving to us with an ear-to-ear grin. Behind her was the countess. Betsy and Rob were there, along with Darlene. I could see Brigitte and Angus Nye near the dock.

Standing at the mooring post was the man in the fedora. Hugo Landacre. My father. He stood almost next to Dad. He was about a foot shorter and at least one hundred pounds lighter. I understood now what Doc Gannon meant when he said I came from smallish stock.

Reba tossed the line to Hugo and he securely tied it. Helen lowered the gang plank. Dad started to come forward, but his wooden leg prevented him from limping up such a narrow and rickety bridge. Hugo stepped over and whispered to him. Dad nodded sadly.

With that, Hugo stepped up the plank, picked me up and carried me off the little houseboat. I was then handed off to Dad, where I really belonged. There was more cheering as Mom ran up to hug me. Gramma Morris was right behind her stroking my hair.

"Instead of being the human tornado, do you think maybe you might consider just being a severe thunderstorm?" she whispered to me.

We laughed a bit. My sisters were all there. Holly couldn't hug me while I was in Dad's arms, but she squeezed my hand while crying with joy. The others all touched my head somewhere and said things like, "Thank God you're back."

Doc Gannon was already examining my bites.

"Get her in the car," he whispered to Mr. Dupris.

Mom and I were soon in his office where he tortured my wounds with iodine and alcohol. He bounded my leg in tight bandages, gave me some pills for the infection and sent us home. No walking, no exertions, no excitement, no fun, and a bland diet, as always.

While I was being treated, Hugo announced to the crowd what I already knew. He *was* my biological father. He admitted that he knew when Cassie De Montfort told him she was pregnant that he was the father but adamantly insisted it could have been someone else. But he always knew he was the father.

"Hell, Hugo," said Mr. Dupris, "everyone in town already knew that."

Everyone but me.

"So, you know," Mom said to me sadly. "I was going to tell you, but I was waiting for the right time."

"Now's a good time," I said, even though Doc Gannon's pain pills made me pleasantly sleepy.

We were waiting for Dad to pick us up in the wagon after he dropped the other children off home so I could lie down on the trip.

She sighed.

"When Hugh Landacre found out that I was pregnant,

he was furious. He was a captain in the army during the Spanish-American War and was recalled to duty during the great war. He left the army as a full Colonel. He fought alongside heroes and patriots. Men he respected.

"His oldest son, David, was a man he could be proud of. He ran the sawmill and managed over one hundred workers. He eventually left the family business to become the head of a large timber company in Georgia where he became rich and powerful. All Landacres are supposed to be rich and powerful.

"Hugo was the second son and he did not meet his father's standards. He had a winsome charm and a jaunty style, but I was to find out, he had something lacking. It's called a backbone. He could never stand up to Hugh, and Hugh hated him for it. He wanted his son to be a real man like his brother.

"Hugh was extremely disappointed when Hugo told him that I was pregnant. Hugh had better ideas for Hugo's wife than the daughter of a career army officer who couldn't make rank. I was also just some waitress with a family name that I tarnished and nothing else mattered to him.

"Hugh had a low opinion of our branch of the family. Gramma Morris can't read at all. Even though my mother rose up to become an army nurse, even though we were from the same family tree, even though we were a respected family, we weren't good enough to be in the Landacre family. Especially after Mary ran off with Michael.

"So, when Hugo told Hugh that Estelle Beaufort was also going to have his child, Hugh made the decision that Estelle, being the daughter of a lawyer and niece to a judge, would be his daughter-in-law. Those were the only factors Hugh considered.

"Hugo just said, 'Yes, sir.' And Estelle and Chuckie got the Landacre name and all the love and respect. We got nothing but hatred and contempt."

"To justify it to themselves, Hugo said that anyone could be your father. His younger brother passed on the idea that it could be almost every man in town. I was a shamed woman.

"I went to New York to have you. Hugh and my mother each gave Mary and Michael five dollars a month for your expenses, but I don't think you saw much of it."

"You mean Papa only pretended to love me? It was only for money?" Now my soul was hurt as well as my leg.

"No," she replied firmly. "He loved you. He took the arrangement seriously, the way a real man would. He taught you how to fight, though I wish he hadn't. He had you drink coffee with him, though I wish he hadn't. He taught you to tell puns, though I wish he hadn't. He wouldn't have taken the time to teach you anything if he didn't love you.

"Your Aunt Mary wanted the money, but not the child. Still, she raised you for ten years, and did a good job."

At least Mrs. Carnahan did.

She stroked my hair for a minute, then continued.

"Hugh later told me that he did not want Hugo to handle the situation that way. He wanted everything to be quiet, but it was too late.

"'Maybe you should have given him some guidance,' I said back to Hugh. 'He only does what he thinks you want. Obviously, you gave him reason to believe that.'

"I never spoke to any of them again. Estelle will always hate me and wants everyone around her to hate me. Even Betsy didn't talk to me for years. Betsy and Estelle are first cousins, you know."

"I thought she was a little hostile when we first met."

"So did I. You melted her heart in five seconds."

"Well, if there was any hope for my grandfather's career in the army to be restored, it was destroyed. There were a couple of previous scandals of some kind that hurt him. Then the theory was that a man can't command a battalion of men when he can't keep order in his own house. And the war was over. He was very embittered at both Mary and me and never spoke to us again.

"He died in 1925 with his obituary stating he was survived by his two sons and one daughter, our older sister Phyllis. We weren't even mentioned. My mother stayed angry at us for years. We weren't even allowed to call her anything but 'Mrs. De Montfort.' so Gramma Morris called her that too to show her how petty and mean-spirited that sounded. But that didn't work.

"I moved back to town when Gramma Morris asked for help at the restaurant. My own café was doing okay in Baton Rouge but nothing great. I got what I could out of it and moved back. Since I can read and write, I handled the books and paid the bills while Cici did the cooking and Gramma Morris did everything else.

"I married Dad against Gramma Morris's advice, but we're happy enough. The one-legged bank-robbing jailbird and the fallen woman make a perfect pair of social outcasts. You could not have asked for a better stepfather than Paul. He gave you a home and love, and a wonderful family of brothers and sisters."

I nodded.

"I know he's kind of quiet around you, but he loves having you around. He just didn't want to make you nervous by trying to get too close. He was brokenhearted when we thought you were gone. All of us were. You were the only good thing to come out of him inviting Michael

Collins to town."

"I thought they were friends."

"Not quite," she smiled. "Your father converted to Christianity during the war. God gave him a lot of peace after Edgewater and losing his leg. He tried to get Michael to become a churchman as well. It didn't work though."

"Oh, so they weren't friends."

"I'm sorry, babe," she said. "No one could be friends with Michael Collins. Too much anger."

Never towards me.

A knock on the door interrupted us. Gramma De Montfort was there with Mr. Benson.

"You know," Gramma De Montfort said after hugs went around, "if not for you, Amy, I would still not be talking to my daughters. You will never know how grateful I will always be for that."

She still looked stern, but she was smiling now.

"Speaking of family secrets," she began, "we have one for your mother."

The convoluted story of our family relationship was told to Mom. She was shocked and stared at her former teacher with her mouth open. I couldn't tell if she was thrilled or appalled. But before we left, she gave him a big hug.

"Thank you for telling me that, Grampa Terrance," she said.

"Why is he Grampa Terrance and not Grampa Benson?" I asked.

"Because he's a man. The grandfathers are called by their first names. The grandmothers by their last name."

"Why is that?"

She shrugged.

"Because they're men and we're women."

"I already knew that much."

The adults all laughed and Mom and I settled down together. The wagon pulled up to the door and it was time to go. Dad loaded the back of the wagon with pillows to make the journey pleasant and Mom sat in the back with me, her baby protesting from within about the loss of space. After a few more good-byes, the horse started moving towards home.

"Why wouldn't you tell me all these things before?" I asked Mom as the wagon bumped and rolled. "Everyone hated me because of something I couldn't help and I never knew why."

"I was embarrassed."

"Oh. Well, let's not be embarrassed. Let's just go home, Mama."

The End

Epilogue

I remember drinking hot chocolate with my Gramma Amy after those reminiscences were done.

"Wow, that's quite a story. But why do you want us to call you Gramma Amy instead of Gramma Webb?"

"Because I'm a woman."

"I already knew that much," I said unknowingly copying her words.

"Well, Jenny, sometimes when the rules are so ancient that people don't even remember why they exist, maybe it's time to change them."

"Oh," I said, disappointed in the answer.

But I could change the subject.

"I bet Sister Barbara never advised anyone to have an adventure after that."

"You would lose," she replied absently. "She always said that a life without adventure is only an existence."

"I guess," I said, after giving it some thought. "But you had more adventures in your first year in Louisiana than I did in my first ten years of life."

She smiled and looked out the window.

"Jenny, that was just the first eight weeks."